MW00614857

SHORT TIMER

by

Billy Devlin

Copyright ©2022

All rights reserved. No part of this publication may be reproduced, distributed or transmitted in any form or by any other means without prior written consent.

Publisher's Note: This is a work of fiction. Names, characters, places and incidents are a product of the author's imagination. Locales and public names are sometimes used for atmospheric purposes. Any resemblance to actual people, living dead, or to businesses, companies, agencies, events or institutions is completely coincidental.

Copyright ©2022
All rights reserved
IBSN: 978-0-578-38431-3

PROFITING OFF THE MISFORTUNE OF OTHERS, A PROFESSION
ALMOST AS OLD AS THE FIRST ONE.

Chapter One

Death Begets Life

A dog bite. The medical examiner's official ruling would probably be listed as an infection. Something like sepsis or staph. Still, the proximate cause of death, should it go that way, would be indisputable even if it wasn't officially recognized: The upper and lower canine teeth of an eight pound part Bijon Frise, the rest a mutt-mix, had penetrated the skin just above his ankle, opening a floodgate for whatever loitering bacteria had been using the dog's mouth as a bus stop waiting room to enter and wreak havoc upon an already compromised immune system.

It was the day before Easter, for those who celebrated. The dying man was thirty-one and lying limp on a bed which had its sheets changed an hour and a half ago and looked due again now. He was sometimes in, but mostly out of consciousness. The IV affixed to his slight, still sun bronzed, motionless arm probably caused the hematoma that colonized his entire inner elbow area. An oxygen tube ran from the wall behind the bed to the lower part of his nasal septum with plenty of slack but not convincingly attached. His mouth was limp and disengaged, hanging open just enough so that had it been a car window, any spring rains that tended to flare up without warning would drench the seat.

Rain.

Shit.

From his place standing against the wall by the door, Alan Copeland quietly slid sideways toward the hospital room window without lifting his feet. Looking across the crown tops of the palm trees he saw a gathering of clouds over the ocean, dark bottomed and with bad intentions. A quick survey across the landscape from one end to the other. No luck. The strip mall was on the other side of the building. And with that, the possibility of a slightly open car window was replaced by the anxiety that comes with wondering if he'd been ticketed or by now even towed. A glance down at the stainless steel Tag Heuer, he thought how he might discreetly excuse himself to run down and move the car to the hospital parking lot, willing now to pay in twenty minute-increments whatever it cost for the right to do so. Hell, he'd even valet it. Or maybe he'd simply leave and check in later.

Copeland was forty-seven. He had every tell tale sign of having been overweight as a child. Now as an adult he felt a need to carry himself a different kind of bigger, leading with his chest pushed forward when walking, ordaining it the center of his being. However, despite what he might have seen in the mirror and any designed efforts to be so, he wasn't formidable in any way. He just appeared big the way something inflatable does. There was nothing that could be mistaken for athleticism, stealth or physical prowess in his bigness, save for his voice, which was forceful and baritone. And where his head was large, his hands were small and connected to cartoon fingers. He never wore shorts, as anything other than loose fitting pants gave away that his toneless legs turned inward at the knees then back outward toward the ankles before settling his body weight into feet with hopelessly fallen arches.

From the hospital window, Copeland looked back at the dying man then over at his hay-smoked pie crust father, mother and sister who'd arrived the previous morning and Yanni standing close enough to suggest there had been a mutually forged acceptance of sorts between them despite their having met each other for the first time. The four were presently distracted from their vigil by the television overhead broadcasting coverage of the morning's raid. A team of gloved and goggled INS Border Tactical Unit commandos stormed into a private residence less than five miles from the very hospital they were all now in. The mission was to forcibly extract Elian Gonzolez, a six-and-a-half year old Cuban refugee boy whose name had recently become a household one, from the assumed custodianship of local relatives after the boy's mother perished at sea. Footage of the terrified child in his uncle's arms recoiling from the barrel of an automatic rifle appearing to be pointed at them played on a loop while news anchors fielded statements from experts of different opinions. The dying man's mother held a palm to her breast, breathless and invoked the name of the Lord in a murmur. The sandy-haired and for the moment cried-out sister shook her head in defeated disbelief and his father, wire-rimmed glasses recessed into the jowly cheeks, he the sort of Iowa every-man

4

whose business card featured a thumbnail portrait of his smiling face, was mumbling something disparaging about communism and the current presidential administration. Copeland's interest in the Elian Gonzolez saga was zero now and only less than fleeting when the story of the raid broke hours earlier.

He again slowly slid sideways, this time toward the door, waiting for Yanni to look over so he might catch his eye. He'd decided that he'd motion to him that he was going to step out for a quick moment. When Yanni did turn around, Copeland didn't need to ask him to come over. He was already on his way. He looked up at Copeland and in just above a whisper spoke while ever so slightly gesturing with his head toward the hallway. "Can I have a word with you?" He had an accent. Greek, that he probably pretended was Latin. Despite being hushed, the request was delivered with every annunciated syllable ensured an opportunity to equally participate in the sentence.

Copeland, too, spoke quietly. "Yeah, sure. Of course. Of course. Yeah-" His delivery was brusque, even with the doubled-up efforts at not only suppression, but projecting concern. It was the kind of Long Island inflection that doesn't fade over time after leaving the region but curiously becomes Brooklyn flavored, more goombah-gruff, less whiny. The two men soft-stepped out of the hospital room, the dying man's family not showing any signs of noticing but undoubtedly did and were probably grateful to have some time alone as a family without the presence of outsiders.

In the hallway, a few deep breaths, sighs and aversions to direct eye contact came from the two men even after the door shut behind them. It was a dance, of sorts. Yanni went first. A delicate clearing of the throat. "I'm not sure of the relationship between you two. What it is, exactly."

The inquiry was understandable, Copeland figured. He didn't seem, at least not on the surface, to be the type who would share any kind of friendship or even social acquaintance with the dying man, let alone one significant enough to include a request, no...actually it had been a plea, to visit him on what was likely his deathbed. And with that, Copeland looked back toward the hospital room door. "Yeah, I gotta tell you...I was completely caught off guard when he called. It was the last thing I expected to hear. I was just...I felt like someone punched me in the stomach. I cancelled the rest of my day and got right over here as soon as I could."

"Do you know why he called you?"

"No idea. I'm gonna guess-"

Yanni cut him off. "I do. I dialed the phone for him." The reply came across as if he was catching Copeland in a little white lie before it could even be told.

Copeland pretended not to hear what Yanni had just said. He shook his head and motioned back toward the room again. "His family? Them bein' able to get down here-?" He let the thought peeter out since he had nothing to cap it off with and segued into something safer. "...Just please God, let him pull through, y'know? Think good thoughts."

Yanni looked at him with eyes that were cross-examining his sincerity. Copeland decided at that point not to make any more attempts at engaging in platitudinous jibba-jabba. There was no reason to, he figured, so he simply chose to stop talking.

Dicé nienté, as the old wise guys would say.

Dicé nienté.

He inhaled deep, expanding his chest then crossed his stout arms in front of him and lowered his head in an effort to remind Yanni of how much smaller he was than him. In doing so, his neck contracted but widened and the appearance of several chins materialized. He let his eyeballs slowly drift up to the lid tops, then laid them down upon Yanni.

"You had a business dealing with him?," Yanni asked.

"He's a friend of mine." With his patience being tested, Copeland decided to turn the tables, even though there was no real reason to. It was simply something he did by nature. "Funny, I never heard him mention your name."

As intended, Yanni was put on the defensive. "We'd recently found our way back into one other's lives."

Copeland nodded, not quite sure. "He did mention a few guys, but I think I wouldda remembered a Yanni. Greek for John, right?"

"That's right." Yanni was intent to stay on topic. "But you had business? With Grant? You and Grant had some sort of business arrangement?"

Copeland shrugged, deeming the fact an afterthought. "I got friends, not just Grant, that I do business with." Then he decided he'd had enough. "Where you goin' with this, Yanni?" Before the last word was delivered from his mouth, Copeland turned almost reflexively and without discretion to look at a passing young Latina nurse, who despite the hair tied behind her head and loose fitting green scrubs, was fetching.

Yanni was disgusted. "Grant asked you to come so he could speak to you. Unfortunately...obviously...he's not in any condition to do so right now."

Copeland turned back but said nothing. He simply waited for Yanni to finish. Yanni suddenly seemed less confident, his frustration level reflecting that. He began to get emotional, closing his eyes and clenching his lips while looking away. Copeland watched, without throwing him any kind of towline. Yanni went on. "I won't go into details, but they're in trouble, they're enduring a terrible, terrible hardship. Grant's family. They're about to lose their house."

Copeland waited a moment before responding, letting the statement hang in the air between them, which made Yanni more uneasy. "I'm sorry to hear that, Yanni." Another head shake with pursed lips. "And now this." Copeland tried to come across as caring and genuine as he possibly could and actually wasn't far this time from being only one or two blocks away from convincing.

Yanni took a deep breath. "He was hoping...Grant was hoping...that in case he didn't make it...that you might be able to do something for them."

Copeland feigned being confused. "Well, they'll certainly be in my thoughts and prayers. What a horrible time for them." Then he turned his tone of voice to a consoling one. "But I think we should try to stay positive, Yanni. Think good thoughts. Grant's gonna come through this. Okay? He's gonna come through this. Let's not be negative."

Yanni genuinely hated every fiber of this man, from the soles of his Italian loafers to the thinnest, soon to be destined for a shower drain strand of hair on his head.

Copeland again looked behind him to hide his being annoyed, then back. "Listen, I need to run down to the car for a second. Can we pick up on this when I get back?" His turning toward the elevator underscored that it wasn't a question but a statement.

On the elevator down Copeland was for the moment alone. He considered what Yanni was asking of him and resented him for it. He even resented the dying man, Grant, for proposing the idea. He looked at the stainless steel button panel next to the door. On it was a tapestry of visible finger smudges. Copeland wondered when it was last cleaned and how many different hands touched it since, leaving the accumulation of anonymous, greasy, glandular secretions mixed with grime, dirt and probably microscopic bits of body dander. He was glad he'd depressed the lobby button with the knuckle of his forefinger. No wonder they say hospitals are the last place a sick person should be. Then he returned to thinking about the dying man and Yanni. How emotional Yanni got while playing proxy for Grant. And with that, he no longer resented him. Instead, Copeland realized that he'd just been given a bit of very important information. Yanni didn't think Grant was going to make it. He believed he was going to die and felt terrible pangs of not only grief, but guilt. Probably for their having been estranged. Copeland knew Grant was not unfamiliar with estrangement. He hadn't been in contact with his conservative, God-fearing midwestern family in years and had very few close friends left. That, he'd heard from Grant's own mouth.

The elevator cab slowed and settled. A chime-bell hybrid rang soft, the doors parted open. A young doctor in scrubs with a perfect head of hair stepped on without looking up from the screen of his mobile phone. The ever so slight grin on his face gave away that whatever business he was tending to was not medical. Copeland admired not only the full head of thick black hair, but the young doctor's still developing slow-motion swagger and felt a tinge of envy. He couldn't be out of medical school five years, probably lived in a killer high rise down on Collins with a trustworthy doorman, the kind that saw everything and still saw nothing, and drove a BMW that'll be upgraded to a Porsche as soon as his lease is up. The same way he'd probably already upgraded to a string of young, South Beach model girlfriends from the better looking nurses at the hospital. Like the Latina one in the hallway outside Grant's room.

Copeland got off the elevator in the lobby. As he walked out of the hospital into the smothering south Florida steaminess, he went back to thinking about Yanni and Grant and the very strong possibility of his own life changing by way of good fortune, something he never would have imagined earlier that morning when he'd gotten out of bed with his quick morning shot of feeling sorry for himself before the first cup of coffee. The brokerage license revocation could well be soon designated to a mere footnote status. Down the block then around the corner where he saw what he decided now would be a harbinger of things to come. His thirty months into a thirty-six month leased Jaguar hadn't been towed. He got closer and saw that the windows were fully closed and there wasn't a ticket tucked beneath the wiper blade. Yes, something good was definitely happening. He opened the door and started unconsciously humming one of the lesser known songs from Billy Joel's *"The Stranger"* album. He turned the ignition over and thought about upgrading off this lease to a Porsche, himself. He drove to the hospital parking lot and got out at the valet stand where he was greeted by a thin Hispanic man, exchanging a claim ticket stub for his keys. Moved by an overwhelming sense of generosity, Copeland handed him one of the two twenties that along with a ten was in his pocket as a pre-tip and went back into the hospital.

He stepped off the elevator on the floor where Grant's room was located, planning on retreating to the opposite side of the hallway to a lounge area, avoiding any possible interaction with Yanni. He noticed the activity by the hospital room door, personnel moving in and out. Copeland's heart rate ticked up. Another look up and down the hallway. He saw the Latina nurse walking in his direction, a chart in hand. Another look back at Grant's room where a doctor whom he hadn't seen earlier just stepped out of. Back at the approaching Latina nurse. Copeland watched as she got closer. She really did have a perfect face, he thought.

"Excuse me-"

She stopped and looked at him, not quite rude but giving every indication she was capable of it. Her posturing was all business, a 'what can I do for you and please make it quick as I have lives to save' self-awareness.

"My friend is in 1021. Grant Millar. I just stepped out to move my car, maybe twenty, twenty-five minutes ago and..." He looked at the door and made a gesture suggesting hesitancy. "Is everything...okay? I don't want to make an entrance at the wrong time."

She turned, looked down the hall and with it, her demeanor changed. She barely mouthed to herself the room number as she turned back to Copeland. "Oh...oh, I'm sorry." She was physical evidence that these things never get easier. "It's my understanding that the patient has...expired. I'm so sorry."

Copeland's breath was visibly taken away with hearing the news but not for the reason the Latina nurse assumed. He'd felt the weight of his entire body giving way like an ignited controlled demolition, his knocked-knees the only thing keeping him standing and thankfully they answered the call. Now his heart rate was well into the red zone. While Copeland might have felt it unfortunate that Grant passed away, he undoubtedly reminded himself that his demise was inevitable and expected, even overdue, albeit not from a dog bite. He then thought about the process. He would need an official certified copy of the death certificate and assumed that once it was presented to the insurance company, they would be bound by the terms of the policy to settle the claim immediately, which meant anywhere from a few weeks to two months. He then experienced the euphoric feeling of pure catharsis that comes knowing two hundred and fifty thousand dollars, unburdened by taxes, will soon be his.

The Latina nurse was still looking at him without any idea that in the privacy of his thoughts a brass band was playing under a sky of fireworks. Copeland hung his head and nodded, appreciative and tried to look solemn. In the moment just before she could turn to go on her way, Copeland asked, "What's your name?"

"Lorena."

"Nice to meet you, Lorena. Alan." He extended his hand as he typically did, smiling with extra confidence to make up for his small hands.

Chapter Two

The House Down By The Swamp Road Turn

It was visible from the road and would be until the sun curtsied behind the line of persimmons directly west of it. The pickup, a '71 Chevy somewhere closer to the beginning of a restoration than to the middle of it, was parked front end up to the threshold of the open door of the garage that doubled as a mechanic's workspace. Its rear window was still intact, spared from the bullet but splattered on the inside with blood, brain matter and skull fragments. The mess was not fully dry but well into the process of curing and a second shift of flies took turns trying to get through the narrow sliver on the driver's side window hoping to get drunk on it all. The humidity was less oppressive than it had been earlier in the day but not by much. Still, the distinct and odious smell of death doubled and then doubled-down again. He was on the top end of middle-aged, just east or west of sixty. His face looked fabricated, made of wax. Deep bruises under both eyes, the balls of which were rolled back as far as their housing would allow. Small rivulets of blood from his nostrils had cut paths through the salt and pepper stubble above his lip. From his ear on the side that tilted downward ran another that was more voluminous and still looked wet to the touch. It formed a pool on the shoulder of his threadbare black tee shirt. His limp arm hung to the side, an unnatural landing, with the gun in hand cantilevered over the seat above the floorboard. In his other hand was a small, wood handled wire-bristle brush used for cleaning things like rust off of metal.

The house on his property could be hit from the garage with a solid stone's throw. One of the nuts from beneath the nearby Pecan tree would have never made it. It was in many ways similar to the other residences that were visible, the ones not set so far back off the road that led down to the swamp road turn. Small, one story. Dull white with faded vinyl black faux-shutters. Between it and the garage was a half-court sized concrete slab, cracks on it with weeds pushing up from the ground beneath. A rusted black post with a backboard and basketball hoop affixed to it stood sad and alone, like an old forgotten spinster still hoping to be asked for her hand.

The property had an orderliness about it probably due more to unconscious habit than pretension, as pretension didn't exist in these parts much beyond modifying the suspensions of four wheel drive trucks. Where other front yards saw the landscape include furniture intended for indoor use planted outdoors and lawnmowers left where they crapped out, here there were vestiges of simple pride. While no stars and stripes currently hung from atop the flagpole, it was still maintained for that intention, not repurposed to harness a tether to an excitable pit bull like the one three houses away and across the street.

It was rural impoverished America down by the swamp road turn. Forgotten or just neglected.

It wasn't long until the dead man would be noticed, not by one but two neighbors and within moments of one another. Directly across the street, a young housewife wearing an extra large tee shirt that might or might not have belonged to her husband had tiptoed down her own driveway to the post-mounted mailbox. She was barefoot and had regretted being so almost immediately but not enough to turn back to fetch slippers. She stopped by the roadside and looked around as she typically did when retrieving mail, then reached inside to get whatever was waiting for her but stopped and did a quick double-take back in the direction of the pick up truck up by the garage across the street. She squinted, unsure of exactly what she was looking at. At the same time, from around the bend leading off the swamp road turn, another neighbor appeared in a mobile auto glass replacement van. He was done with his day's work. Having looked over at the house, something too caught his eye. He did a double-take and stopped. He got out of the van and looked at the young housewife whom he knew. He was older, maybe sixty and wore suspenders. In his hand was a bulky cellular phone. No words were exchanged between them despite sharing common foreboding thoughts. She stayed in her place and he made his way toward the pick up truck with no attempts made to mute his trepidation. He stopped twenty feet from it, needing to go no further. He turned and walked back toward the street, looking at the young housewife. His face ashen, telling her all she needed to know.

"Sweet Jesus," she said, and brought a hand to her mouth.

He closed his eyes and nodded, lips pressed together. He turned and looked over at the house, then down to the bulky cell phone in hand and hit the buttons. He gave the details to the operator and stood by waiting not far from his van. The young housewife walked toward him.

"Did you hear anything?," he asked her.

She shook her head, unsure. "I dunno. I mean, maybe...but you know-"

Of course, he understood. The sound of a gunshot in these parts was never cause for alarm.

"Is it...is it Marty or-?," she asked.

"Marty."

The young housewife gasped and then gasped again. "Oh, sweet Jesus." She looked away and nervously moved her hand to different points on her upper body, chin and forehead in intervals, motions that could be interpreted as an out of sequence sign of the cross. Then tears began to well in her eyes.

Soon another neighbor wandered onto the scene, a reed-thin young man wearing cargo shorts with knee high pull-on chore boots and a foul tee shirt with an even more foul message printed on it.

"What's goin' on?"

He wasn't answered, so he looked at the place that seemed to have their focus. "*Hol-eee* shit. *Hol-eee* fuckin' shit. That what I think it is?-"

Again, his question was ignored. With his eyes fixed on the pick-up truck, his face puckered, sucking on the wad of long grain dip tucked in his mouth's lower gum line then turned away and discharged a stream of tobacco infused saliva that slapped down on the asphalt.

The young housewife took a step closer to the neighbor with the auto glass repair van, lowered her voice ever so slightly and asked, "is he...for sure?

She was answered with a nod of confirmation.

"Sweet Jesus."

The third wheel chimed in again. "What happened? One of the Rehage's kill his self?"

Again, he was ignored.

Another neighbor approached. He was older than the housewife but younger than the auto glass repair man and looked clean cut, with glasses. Middle management material.

"What happened?" he asked, directing the question to the elder. Unlike the reed-thin young man, he was answered.

"Marty."

"Oh, my God." Then the newcomer had a thought. "Where's Kenny Wayne?"

The reed-thin young man interjected. "His car's right there. He gotta be home." He was pointing to a small, dark blue economy car without hubcaps parked near another Chevy pickup in front of the house. "Someone should try an' call him."

The first radio car to arrive pulled up, a young deputy familiar to them all got out of the car. He looked at those gathered and acknowledged them, then proceeded to walk up the driveway with the same consternation the neighbor who repaired auto glass did. He got to the pick up truck window and crouched forward with hands on knees for a better perspective. He then looked at the door handle and might have thought about opening it but instead looked into the cab of the truck again and seeing the gun in the dead man's hand felt comfortable enough to surmise that what had happened was as had been reported. Standing upright, he snorted out the putridity that had just made its way up and into his nostrils. Or maybe he was just now noticing it. He waited a moment, either in contemplation or out of reverence, then turned back down the driveway. As he got out to the street, the others looked at him as if expecting to have some new light to shed upon what had happened.

"Anyone home?," the deputy asked, directing his question to the auto glass repairman.

The reed-thin young man answered for him. "Kenny Wayne's car's there. He gotta be inside." His input was no more welcome by the deputy than it was by the others before. Naturally, the lights of the deputy's patrol car had begun to attract moths of its own, and soon three more neighbors had wandered over. When Mrs. Johnson appeared, she did so without anyone noticing. She was in her late-sixties, a retired school nurse who emanated an undeniable self-reliance. Her manner of dress alone was testimony to the fact that she was the kind who never lost faith. As usual, Darlene was with her. Darlene was her adult daughter and disabled, cognitively. She was the only one who seemed to be unaware of the present circumstances and with that, unaffected by it.

"I'm tellin' you, he's home," said the reed-thin young man again, and again his statement was disregarded.

The neighbor with the mobile auto glass repair business gave a look to the deputy, an ever-so-slight motion of the head, then turned to take a few steps away from the others. The deputy got the message and walked over to join him in a sidebar.

"For what it's worth, Stacy-" Then, the auto glass repairman stopped, like he might be having second thoughts on sharing information.

"What's that, Tom?," the deputy asked.

"I mean, I don't want to be talkin' out of school here, but...it's my understandin' that Marty mighta been under some kinda...investigation-"

The deputy looked less confused than he did skeptical. "By the law?"

He was answered affirmatively with a nod.

"Oh, I don't know about that now, Tom."

"I'm just sayin'. It was my understandin' that could be the case."

"Naa, I would know 'bout that, Tom." The deputy couldn't be more confident in his assertion.

"I'm just sayin'."

"Well, where'd you get that from?"

Again, a hesitation. "He kinda...in a beatin' 'round the bush way...hinted at it. Marty. He kind of hinted that he was in some kind of trouble with the law."

"Naa. I would know about that."

The moment teetered on awkwardness and the deputy changed directions. "So where's Kenny Wayne? He inside, y'think?"

The auto glass repairman considered the question, looking at what was pointed out as his car parked by the house.

"Looks like he may be."

"Please God, he ain't in there all high," the deputy said.

When they both turned back to look at the house again, Mrs. Johnson could be seen at the front door, knocking with Darlene at her side. The deputy called over to her. "Mrs. Johnson, maybe it's best you not-"

She ignored his half-hearted directive, put her hand on the doorknob and gently turned. Pushing it open, she stuck her head in and announced herself. "Kenny Wayne, honey? You home?"

"Mrs. Johnson," the deputy called again. "I think you should hold on there a second-" His words may as well have fallen onto old tree stumps. Mrs. Johnson went in, Darlene behind her.

The interior was underlit, cooler than outside. It was clean. The smallness of the double hung windows saw personal effects relegated to the shadows. A roll arm couch that had surrendered any form it might have once had was positioned against one wall. There was a small coffee table by it. On top, a few magazines mostly related to cars and hunting and a nearly empty bottle of Mountain Dew, recapped. The television set, a recent model, stood like a centerpiece, disproportionately larger than everything else in the room. It faced a club-type chair that had next to it a wooden one positioned like it was playing the role of motorcycle sidecar. There was a faint, lingering hint of the smell of cigarettes in the air that was probably perpetual, an undertone suggesting someone in the house might have been a smoker but always did so outside. The kitchen abutted the living room, its floor tiled in worn linoleum. Through the window was a view of the backyard. Enormous trees that over the years had made their way up from the swamp, riddled with Spanish moss that in an early morning fog could be mistaken for an army of long bearded ghosts. The kitchen table had a plastic cloth covering that seemed to have no functioning purpose beyond being a veil. Most meals were likely eaten over the sink or in the living room by the TV. Beyond the refrigerator was a hallway, along it a bathroom and at the end two bedrooms across from one another. One door was open, the other closed. Despite the house being soundless, a stimuli hung in every molecule of air suggesting someone's presence. Mrs. Johnson suddenly looked nervous.

Outside by the street, another Sheriff's department car arrived with an ambulance behind it, momentarily taking the attention off of Mrs. Johnson's having entered the house. More neighbors showed up and with it, the murmurs and whispers began.

...Marty Rehage.

...Killed himself.

...Shot himself in the head.

...Where's Kenny Wayne?

...Right up in his driveway.

...Behind the wheel of the pickup he was restorin'.

...Where's Kenny Wayne?

...Shot himself in the head with a .38.

...Someone said he was under investigation.

...Where's Kenny Wayne?

...Shot himself in the head.

...Sweet Jesus.

Inside the house, Mrs. Johnson walked from the living room, Darlene on her flank. She called out again, slowly walking through the kitchen.

"Kenny Wayne? You home, honey?"

Mrs. Johnson tentatively made her way toward the bedroom door that was partially open, again calling for Kenny Wayne. At the door she stopped, visibly uneasy. After a pronounced pause, she looked inside. At a desk facing a wall sat Kenny Wayne Rehage in a chair with his back to her. In his hands was an *XBox* controller. He was navigating through advanced levels of *Grand Theft Auto: San Andreas.* His fingers and thumbs were on autopilot, moving from button to button unrushed and with supple fluidity. Earphones on his head ensured the world outside stayed there. No more than twenty years old, he was gangly thin with tightly-cropped light brown hair. He had a little patch of blonde peach fuzz on his chin and barely enough over his thin, upper lip to dust a cookie. On the inside of his right forearm just above the wrist was a pronounced scar, jagged, raised red and looking like a lighting bolt. He wore a tee shirt that was too big, probably on purpose and loose sweatpants. White tube socks on his feet, slides-sandals over them. A small pile of clean, folded laundry was on his narrow bed and a still damp bathroom towel on the floor near two pairs of identical basketball sneakers, one older than the other. Mrs. Johnson watched him for a moment, then knocked on the open door of the bedroom so as to get his attention. He didn't respond, so she knocked again louder. He turned to see her standing in the doorway with Darlene just behind in the hall. He wasn't startled, not even surprised to see her.

"Kenny Wayne, sweetie-?" She stepped inside.

He lowered the game control and began to shake his head, preemptively refuting what she was going to tell him.

"Sweetie, you know where your father is?"

He looked back at the video game, trying his best at ignoring her. She moved in closer, then sat on the edge of his bed so she was next to him.

"Sweetie, what I'm gonna tell you is gonna hurt."

Kenny Wayne again turned and shook his head but this time he couldn't find refuge in the video game.

"It's gonna hurt real bad, Sweetie. But you gotta know. There's been an accident and I think you're daddy's not good. Your daddy's not good."

Kenny spoke. "Nothin's wrong, Mrs. Johnson. Nothin's wrong." He had a childlike innocence about him.

"The deputy's here and they're tending to what's gotta be tended to. Let's go out into the living room and sit down, okay?"

With the shelter of denial no longer available to him, Kenny Wayne began to shake. His face morphed into the contour that precipitates weeping, then the levee of his emotions gave way. He fell into Mrs. Johnson's arms and cried uncontrollably.

Behind them in the doorway, the deputy and the neighbor with the auto glass repair van stood watching as Mrs. Johnson held the distraught Kenny Wayne with her daughter Darlene now putting her arms around both of them, so they looked like a single, interwoven mass of grief.

Kenny Rehage shook off the distant memory of the traumatic experience. It felt longer in the past than it had been, probably because of the life he lived in between the present and that time. By all indicators, he'd landed on his feet, now in a far better place than he'd started. Physically, he had filled out slightly but still was gangly, only less so. While his facial features lacked the criteria for being considered handsome, he was attractive. His skin had cleared up, his hair was styled with conventional modesty in mind. He wore a pressed soft pastel collared shirt buttoned at the wrists, dress slacks and shoes. His current home, a modern Fort Lauderdale rented one bedroom condominium with floor to ceiling windows and a balcony overlooking the Atlantic, was on the opposite side of the Floridian spectrum from the swamps of the panhandle he grew up in. The apartment was sparse. Bright, with an emphasis on whites. It was clean, sterile to the point of it easily being mistaken for a model unit and without any touches of femininity. He was still looking out the window down at the sidewalk along Ocean Boulevard at an aging woman who looked nothing like his old Okaloosa County neighbor Mrs. Johnson, the retired school nurse, but the adult disabled child walking a half-step behind her brought him back to that place. He steadied himself and stepped away from the window and proceeded to look for his car keys.

They were in his hand.

He hesitated then made his way to the front door. He stopped at the mirror to give himself a once over look before leaving. He still had plenty of time and realized no matter how long he stalled, Alan would still be later than him. Kenny wanted to keep him waiting, something he'd never done before. He wanted to get there after Alan arrived. Not a lot, just enough to annoy him as a parting gift. Or maybe he was having second thoughts.

Chapter Three

Paesan Balls

Alan Copeland loved AIDS. The very hearing of the word triggered a hormonal blast in his nervous system that bordered on orgasmic. He'd once told Karen he wanted to get a pet and name it after the disease to ensure his affection for the animal never waned. She, of course, was appalled and admonished him to not dare repeat what he'd just said to another living soul. He probably rolled his eyes at her, as he had a habit of doing, then unnecessarily reminded her of the tens upon tens of thousands of dollars he donated to AIDS related charities each year. Copeland liked to shock and play for a reaction, especially when times were good. And good they were, all because of his entrepreneurial foresight at recognizing the value of buying life insurance policies from men afflicted with the AIDS virus. It was nothing less than ingenious and obvious at the same time, he'd tell anyone who'd listen. The pool of prospects was deep from Palm Beach all the way down to the Keys, gay men, childless and unmarried with a high percentage estranged from families of origin. Many of them needed the money, some just wanted it. The cash offered by Copeland for the right to be listed as the sole beneficiary on the policies, sometimes for as little as five cents on the dollar, could be used immediately instead of being earmarked to benefit someone after their death who might not be in their good graces or in their lives at all. Copeland rationalized that these viatical life settlement arrangements were not only mutually beneficial but he was also providing a well-needed helping hand, pointing to the volume of clients he'd accumulated as evidence. The product, he would say over and again, sold itself.

The traffic signal overhead turned to green. A high pitched car horn blasted from a modified-low riding Honda behind him. Copeland hated that sound as much as the revving of its engine. He snapped back into the present, a quick peek into his rear view mirror to give the *maloccia* to the driver behind him who not only would never see it, but was also justified in beeping. One more look back at the old and tattered billboard on the side of the road that had commanded his attention and the satisfied grin was back on his face. Faded red, white and blue with a barely legible message written upon it *en español*, something about keeping Elian Gonzolez on American soil. After all the years, the events surrounding the young Cuban refugee were forgotten by most, but not for him. He would always associate Elian Gonzolez's name with the death of the first person afflicted with AIDS from whom he'd bought a life insurance policy. In the first three years following Grant Millar's passing, Copeland purchased over four hundred more of them, with a mortality rate topping eighty-five percent within twelve months of acquisition, averaging death benefit payouts of slightly over three hundred thousand dollars per, bringing a gross return on his investments to more than one hundred million dollars.

He opened and closed his hands, getting a fresh coolness back on his palms from the wooden steering wheel of his Rolls Royce Phantom and hit the gas. Soundless. The twelve cylinder, twelve-mile-to-the-gallon cloud was of a design putting it at the pinnacle of automotive luxury, of which the most valuable characteristic to Copeland was its filtering out nearly all of the noise from outside, especially in places like the one he was driving though now, where the people loved to beep their horns.

The phone rang, Copeland connected off the first ring with the push of a button. "Hey, what are you doin'?"

"It's me."

"I know it's you. What are you doin'?" It was the same as saying, 'hey, how you doing?' Not a question, but a statement made by people originally from New York acknowledging whomever was being addressed had their attention.

In the sing-songy manner she typically spoke in, a hybrid that was equal parts nursery school teacher and frustrated shopper at the customer service window, Karen brought him up to speed on her day. *"Well, what's very annoyyying is that Chance just informed us that he needs to take time off-"*

Copeland interrupted, "who?"

"Chance."

"Who's Chance?"

Her pause was weighed down by annoyance. *"The President of the Miami-Dade Boys and Girls Club, is who."*

"How am I supposed to know that?"

She responded with another audible sigh right into the phone receiver, punctuating her frustration that he should be aware not only of all the charitable organization boards she sat on, but the individuals charged with running them.

He quickly deviated ever so slightly off topic. "What's he make? This guy, Chase? Like three hundred grand a year, right? Non-profit, charitable organization, my ass. Three hundred grand for-"

She cut him off, hard. *"Chance. His name is Chance. Not Chase. And what's annoyyying Alan, is that Chance,-"* she emphasized his name again for effect, *"...hasn't learned how to navigate through his personal issues in a way that doesn't compromise his responsibilities to the children."*

"Three hundred grand a year for baby-sittin' a bunch a-" he stopped himself. "...What a fucking scam these guys got." His statement was served up without the least bit of self-awareness or irony.

"He's not motivated by money, Alan. Believe me. He's needed. And well worth his board approved compensation, might I add. His not being there will have a negative effect on the program. I'm telling you, this is a big deal. A veryyy big deal-"

Alan half-smiled. "Then send someone over there, bring him up to the rooftop and hang him by his feet off the side of the building and tell him, 'you sure you need that time off, asshole?'"

She wasn't amused. *"I don't know what's with this slipping back into talking like you're in the Maaafia, Alan. You talk like that tonight at the Yost's, you're going to make them and everyone else uneasy."*

His demeanor instantly changed, gravity overtaking his smile. "I'm not talking like I'm in the Mafia, Karen. That's a stupid fucking thing to say. No one is 'in' the Mafia. You sound ignorant when you talk like that."

Her tone of voice suggested retreat. *"Just...the filter. Please. And it comes through practice. Okayyy? The fil-ter? It needs...practice. Constant practice."*

"You know, just for the record, I could talk any way I want to the Yosts or to anyone else who's gonna be there. What are they gonna do? Not take my check? I could show up with my dick out."

An uncomfortable silence from the other end, then- *"you know what I mean, Alan. And I'm not saying this for me."*

Copeland had a thought. *"You know, I might just do that. Show up with my dick out. Dick in one hand, checkbook in the other."*

"Alan. Stop being a child. Just stop. I'm not saying this for me. It's for you. You understand that?"

It was his mother from beyond the grave. Another short silence and he nodded in as much agreement as he was capable of, even though she had no idea of his having done so.

"What else?", he asked

"Nothing," she said. *I just called to see what you were doing."*

"Well, I just left a lunch meeting, I'm drivin' through-," he looked out the window despite probably not needing to. "...Little Havana headin' back. I gotta take care of this other...thing, then stop by the office, and headin' home after. I think." His delivery of the word 'thing' gave cause for questioning.

"What 'thing' is that, that you're heading to now?"

It seemed of little consequence, like he might have even forgotten himself what he had to do. "This...thing I gotta take care of." He could hear her little laugh on the other end. She may as well have said it, 'there you go again, talking like you're in the *Maaafia*.' "A meeting with the kid from the office that works for me. Kenny. About nothing you'd be interested in. Absolutely nothing. *Okaaay?*" The inflection in his voice gave her what she was looking for: His words were spoken with a natural fluidity and to completion. Still very much Five Towns, Long Island, but without effect.

"Alright then," she told him. *"...I'll talk to you later."*

"I'll talk to you later."

"Love yoooou."

"Love you."

Both sign-offs fell short of being convincing, his slightly less than hers.

They were married now going on four years after a brief and unexpected courtship. It was the second go-round for Copeland, the hat trick for Karen, who was three years older than him. Neither gave the impression they were ever physically attracted to the other, underscoring the importance gin must have played in the relationship for her and light switches did for him. Still, the union seemed to make sense. He checked the box of being wildly successful in business, projected an alpha type-manliness she liked and was funny in a way that bombasticity can be entertaining. She had her own money and the significance of her societal pedigree couldn't be discounted. The relationship seemed to be maintenance free, without the complications that often come wagon-hitched to previous marriages. He was estranged from his only son, now in his late-twenties and his first wife, who he still referred to without emotion as 'that cunt,' was fully paid off. Karen's last husband, Howard, whom they sometimes saw out socially and got along with, was thought of by Copeland privately as a little bit of a *vonce*. She had two grown daughters, one from each marriage, who of course didn't care for Copeland. Nor did he, them. They saw the personification of vulgarity and he saw warthogs, one rougher on the eyes than the other. Good news for all involved was that Karen's girls were already on their own when she and Alan moved into the first new house before the one they were in now. Getting married again was a surprising choice for Copeland at the time, especially since he'd not only just regained his footing financially but by all indicators was in the process of touching all the bases off the home run he'd just hit. It was probably as good a time as any to be a bachelor. A mitigating factor in the decision to wed was that he never planned to let his vows to Karen get in the way of old habits. And Karen was the kind who could pretend not to notice if ever she did. One play Copeland knew he would never make after making real money again was falling into the trap of setting up house with a trophy. That, he long believed, was the epitome of impracticality and short-sightedness. He also believed the real trophy for him was Karen's stepfather, the characteristically silent, politically wired developer with a vapor-like mysterious quality, often referred to only by his last name. Haberman enjoyed rich but discreet relationships in both the State capital and up in the Beltway, regularly sought after for his political fundraising influence as well as his counsel during times of crisis, usually in the political arena as well. It wasn't lost on Copeland the standing of the well-heeled and monied that went out of their way to shake his hand. Still, Haberman was a trophy Copeland had yet needed to show off. In fact, his own wealth was growing at a pace that he was probably about to be considered the trophy by Haberman, if he wasn't already. It didn't matter. Copeland and Karen got along well. So he went through the *pro forma* motions of making her feel attractive, in return she not only promoted him within the circle of elites, but gave him space. When she did occasionally grieve him, as all wives are wont to do, it wasn't terrible. His just finished phone call with her was probably as extreme as it ever got, short lived and half charged. And that was with her brushing up against the one subject to him that was a raw nerve. His fascination with the *paesans*. Wiseguys. Italian gangsters of the New York City, five-family variety. 'I don't know why you're so enamored with them,' she'd say. It would get his back up every time, the kind of defensiveness that comes with a tinge of embarrassment baked in, like someone being reminded they'd once wore their shirt collars popped up or put man make-up over a facial blemish. 'I'm not enamored with them, Karen.' He would admit to respecting them though, something she would be unable to understand, the perspective of a middle-class kid that seemingly was surrounded by them on all sides growing up. They lived in Atlantic, Lido or Long Beach, some were still in Brooklyn and Queens, others out in Massapequa or even Oyster Bay. He knew what families they were affiliated with, their ranks within, the places they hung out at and the legitimate businesses they purported to be in. When trying to pinpoint the exact element of this attraction it came down to being more than their sacred sense of loyalty to one another, the codes of conduct and honor they lived by. It was the respect they commanded. The palpable confidence they had, especially in confrontation, the way they reacted in any situation.

It was balls.

Copeland thought he had balls and to a point might have, but not *paesan* balls. No way. Those were balls of a different variety. Balls of the highest order, top shelf balls. He would consider the times in his life, the once or twice he'd been mistaken for being Italian. He didn't offer a correction, not even a half-hearted one. It was almost like an unearned compliment he would take and hold onto and cherish for as long as he could.

But Karen had a point.

He was a king, now.

A giant.

Above it. Anything he wanted to have, anywhere he wanted to go could be actualized through monetary transactions. There was no room in this life for gangsters. No room at all for any *paesans* or their balls.

Karen was right.

But still he couldn't help admiring them, even from the gilded place above he now sat perched. He knew he had to keep quiet about it, so he'd packed the sentiment in an old hope chest stored away up in the attic of his heart, like an old toy or piece of clothing he couldn't bring himself to throw out. And every once in a while, when no one was around, he might in the privacy of his thoughts go up to visit it.

The congestion on Flagler Street snuck up on him. The sudden traffic buildup was a result of either a bad accident or two-lane road work. No way it was a fender bender or a pothole. Too heavy, too quickly. It was going to be a crawl. He thought about his meeting with the kid from his office unsure of what he wanted to see him about.

The kid.

He's no kid. He has to be at least twenty-five. No, maybe twenty-four. Regardless, he's still not a kid. Then he thought about blowing it off but wouldn't let himself. He respected him. No, he wasn't going to leave the kid hanging. Then, some head pivoting and lane cutting to get as far right as possible to find a side street to turn down. He'd head south, way south, then do the zig-zag side street shuffle over to I-95 and go up and around through downtown. The first car he cut in front of let him, maybe to just admire the Rolls or maybe in the hope Copeland might pull over and reward the gesture with a hundred dollar bill. The next car he cut in front of rolled down his window and launched a string of expletives, as if Copeland was responsible for a lifetime of personal hardships.

The landscape began to change the closer he got to Coral Gables off the busy thoroughfare he'd turned off of. Very little traffic, it was a wonder that no other cars were opting to pursue a detour. The roadsides and sidewalks were clean, litter free. The houses, uniform with just enough variance in thoughtful detail to suggest individual personality. In front of them were narrow driveways crowded with polished luxury car lease obligations. One street after another, staggered with stop signs and speed bumps and still no other cars before him or behind. One intersection after another and the repetition began to grate on Copeland.

Stop.

Go.

Slow down.

Speed up.

Slow down.

Stop.

Go.

He was now inexplicably irritated, far more than he should have been, considering he'd just gotten out of bumper to bumper traffic and was wondering now why he was suddenly so determined to not only get to his destination, but on time. At the next stop sign he made a left for no reason. There were still no other cars coming or going in either of the four possible directions. Down one more block, then another right turn.

Then the sudden slamming of his foot down on the brake pedal. The vehicle responded, corralling the forward thrusting energy of fifty-seven hundred pounds of metal and dispersing it throughout the braking system while Copeland's two hands choked the steering wheel. He was paralyzed, eyes now locked on the eyes of the man who appeared like an apparition before him that he'd nearly plowed into. Male and black, he could have been thirty-something, he could have been fifty-something. He was of dark complexion, not quite with the deepness of Haitian skin but more melanin rich than the typical African American. His face was an expressionless rock, devoid of any emotion. Slits for eyes, the area around them appearing to be swollen, but matching. Like he'd had an allergic reaction or maybe just finished crying. His arms exposed beneath the short sleeves of his tee shirt stayed at his side. They were narrow, sinewy, suggesting a strength about him that came from genetic predisposition as opposed to a workout regiment. His faded jeans appeared to sag, indicating he was probably beltless, but not by design. He could have been in those clothes for several days, but didn't come across as homeless. He stared at Copeland and Copeland stared back at him, terrified now of what might have been. Not a word left the man's mouth. He simply stayed in place, looking at Copeland as if he was studying the deepest corners of his soul. Copeland dared to peek in his rear view, as if for an explanation of where this man could have possibly come from. He couldn't have lived in the area. Coral Way was far enough ahead of him and Route 41 was even further behind, Flagler not even visible. It was as if he'd been dropped out of the sky. The man then turned away, offering only an ever-so-slight shaking of his head that could have been taken as a rebuke and carried on. Copeland continued to watch him, still terrified. He watched him walk down the side street without once looking back.

A car horn sounded from a late model Lexus behind him. Copeland jolted back into the present, a quick peek into his mirror but this time didn't give a nasty look to the driver behind him. He thought about turning left to follow the man, but the man was now out of sight. For how long, he didn't know. The car behind him beeped again. Copeland took his foot off the brake and gently pressed down on the accelerator, choosing to go straight. He continued for another block but was unable to contain his restlessness. He pulled over to the side of the street, turned the car off. He made sure his doors were locked and sat back, closing his eyes and waiting for his heart to stop racing.

Chapter Four

Occam's Razor

Kenny Rehage stood in line at the *ventanita* of Marielena's and didn't care that it was moving slowly any more than he cared he drove out of his way and into the *barrio* to get there. He wanted his pull. It was Rosie's fault for getting him hooked. She introduced him to *cafe cubano* and now had the moxie to guilt him whenever he said he wanted one, her and the sugar-shaming-anti-caffeine kick of the past four months. And with that, he smiled, then wished he hadn't.

The other waiting patrons he stood among were mostly Spanish speaking blue collars. Sun darkened skin, calloused hands, boots dirty and caked with crusted thin-set mortar waiting to order late lunches or like him, get their jolt. For many, a *pastelito* to go with it. The abounding conversation was loud and affable, exchanges in machine gun rapid-fire bursts punctuated by bellows of laughter. It was part social event, part ritual that included the *gordas* behind the counter, supporting players in the revelry. While being a regular on this line, Kenny's presence was somewhere between ornamental and that of a party crasher, as no one paid him any attention other than the staff when taking his order, which they always did politely but with reservation. Aside from the obvious ethnological differences, they assumed he wasn't 'of' them but born to privilege, and understandably so-

...Mira a la ropa-

...El reloj-

...El carro de lujo.

The Cadillac with the blacked out windows that they'd seen him drive up and then away in, each time he showed up. Kenny looked at the eldest of the *gordas*, the namesake of the cafe. Marielena. She was probably in her late fifties, but with women like her one never knew. He felt a commonality with her that on its face many would never be privy to knowing about, herself included. Like him, she was far from the place she started economically, now reaping spoils that come with hard work, or like in Kenny's case, luck in the discovery of an aptitude coupled with the discipline to put it to use and having a wealthy, insecure boss. He looked at her, fixed upon a stool by the cash register with worn out numbers on its keys, able to operate it blindfolded and in the dark by now. Singles, fives, tens and twenties. Six days a week, ten hours per-

...Tap tap tap, ching ching ching.

Where the other customers never thought about it twice, he knew the money flowed in like double-greased goose shit through the proverbial tin horn. Ol' Marielena was probably clearing for herself two-hundred thousand a year by his rough calculus, giving her far more in common with the people in his current world than any of the *jamoneros* in line playing grabass while waiting for their order. The obvious difference between them was that she still held onto her old *guajira* identity, wearing it like a sash, where he upgraded. He had to. There was no room in the place he lived in now for even the smallest of swamper relics, not even the occasional wearing of a camo-patterned Mossy Oak trucker's cap. -

"Hola." The *gorda* in her mid-thirties, probably Marielena's daughter, was looking at him now from the other side of the counter.

He smiled at her. "How you doin' today?" Hints of twang were still in his delivery, but certainly polished up now. He could have easily passed as from Tallahassee. She got right to business, all with a smile that wasn't entirely insincere.

"What can I get for you?"

"A *cor-ta-dito* please, thanks."

She scratched out a ticket and handed it to Marielena at the register who announced the fare by stating only the numbers. *"Un-veinticinco."*

Marielena made change from the twenty he gave her. As she did, she frowned. Annoyed. Not like he'd passed the bill to her scrunched up into a ball, but close. She was the sort who found any reason to be dour, clearing two hundred grand a year, two million or just two rubbed together nickels, it didn't matter. He stepped aside for the next customer and waited for his order to be filled and thought about his good fortune and Alan Copeland being instrumental to it...then wondered if he should feel guilty and decided he didn't. It was too late to entertain those kinds of thoughts. Instead, he wondered if he'd be done with everything in time to make his pick-up game that night. The endorphin blast he would get from ninety minutes of fast-paced pickup basketball was even better than the pull he'd come to Marielena's for.

Immediately after his father juiced the back of his head across the interior of that '71 Chevy pickup he was restoring, Kenny Wayne saw his own life proceed upon a path that might not have been surprising. Bouts of pensive sadness and guilt brought on by questions impossible to answer haunted him when he was most vulnerable. The visits and check-ins from concerned family members and neighbors living by the swamp road turn faded and his lack of direction continued without resolve. Only Mrs. Johnson stayed on him and he purposely avoided her. He began sleeping in more regularly and after rising, his bed was seldom made. Plates and glasses piled up in the sink, pizza boxes got extended stays on the living room coffee table by the TV and there was no longer a reason to hide the bong. Where it was once only weekend nights wasted away with friends, now it was midweek and days as well, since he didn't go back to work for Bobby Flavor. Kenny Wayne figured he'd get something else when he was ready. In the meantime the old routine resumed. Beers, blunts, chew, video games and reminiscences of high school hand jobs. The same old stories told over and again that he and his buddies took turns covering, versions varying depending on who was narrating. Benji was from out past County Road by the Newhall who worked at the Dollar Store where he thought he had it *pretty-sorta good* and Boss Hogg, Kenny Wayne's power forward teammate from twenty-five pounds ago was still weighing his options. Pete trimmed trees for Bobby Flavor and Calvin Milsap, who dropped out two weeks before graduation, had

Apalachee blood and got some sort of a regular government check. They saw themselves as a band of brothers, swampers for life.

Proud and loud-

'Swamper Fi, 'till I die!'

...And inevitably someone around the fire with a relative in the Marine Corps would take offense and there'd be a fight.

That fidelity between Kenny Wayne and his fellow swampers in arms was tested soon thereafter. It involved a once in a lifetime opportunity to own four pounds of marijuana at a quarter of its market price. Benji had a connection, a deckhand on a sponge boat from Tarpon Springs who'd fished a bale out of the Gulf that had assumedly been jettisoned by its previous owner for one reason or another. Calvin had arranged to sell two pounds off the top to a guy he knew way up by Laurel Hill, paying back the initial investment staked mostly by Kenny Wayne with money he'd gotten after his father's affairs were settled. Pete committed to taking a half pound for his girlfriend Alison to bake into cookies and brownies since *'edibles is, like...the future, no joke'* and Boss Hogg was confident he could *'sell the rest, local...you know, to friends...but just this one time. Unless, y'know...of course-'* He was not one to shut the door on future opportunities. A traffic stop that was unlikely as routine as it advertised itself to be, saw to the inevitable arrests and buck-pass-finger-pointing which did nothing to lighten any of their individual responsibilities as far as the law was concerned, succeeding only in decimating friendships.

Swamper Fi, 'till I die-

...Or get busted for weed with intent to distribute.

For his involvement, Kenny Wayne was given a suspended sentence of one year to be followed by another of supervised probation which might have been considered lenient, but after his initial meeting with the person charged with supervising that probation, he wondered if he'd rather do hard time instead. Okaloosa County Probation Officer Lee Chaulker was only a year older than Kenny but had a swagger fitting a veteran halfway through a celebrated career...or a first year bureaucrat with high up departmental family relations, which was his reality. His office was small, looking like a snow globe of basketball memorabilia. The worthless kind. He got the departmental mission statement out of the way in less than a breath, rattled off the protocols of the applicable court supervision then covered his own personal expectations in relation to them. He spent the rest of the intake briefing talking about what was once a frayed wire of a topic for Kenny Wayne but now seldom thought about. And with it, the young probation officer took on the demeanor of friend, confidante, investigator or maybe even confessor, discussing Kenny Wayne's high school basketball career and what happened, or more specifically didn't happen in relation to it. Unbeknownst to Kenny Wayne, Lee Chaulker had gone to Niceville High where, as a member of their basketball team, he could technically claim to have played against Kenny Wayne despite never having been on the hardwood floor at the same time as him, aside from during warm-ups. Kenny Wayne had no recollection of ever having set eyes upon him. He sat in silence and endured listening to reminders of his accomplishments and the nicknames bestowed upon him back then: *Silky Milk, Swamp Kobe, Killa Vanilla* and a few he'd been unaware of, like *White Trash-Nash*. Where

Kenny Wayne himself couldn't recall how many points he poured in against Niceville during the fourth quarter of the County Semis his junior year, Lee Chaulker most certainly did, along with a tally of his assists, all recounted with fan-boy intensity. So naturally, along with the mandated random drug tests and proof of steady employment, Kenny Wayne was encouraged to start playing basketball again in a way that a pentecostal minister might direct a wayward parishioner back to the Lord.

Kenny Wayne chose to remain agnostic.

He and hoops were irreconcilably divorced.

He took a job at The Waffle House on Route 189 not far from Elgin and settled into a new routine. The recent upheaval of his social life, coupled with the conditions of his being on papers left him clear minded yet with little else to focus on, making the commitment to the job one by default. Soon, he was promoted to night manager, putting an even greater distance between himself and the world he once knew. Eighteen months into his Waffle House tenure, Kenny Wayne was paid an unannounced but not unexpected visit from his probation officer. It was toward the end of his shift, the beginning of Chaulker's. *Here we are a'gin, two ships a-crossin' in the night, lit'rally.* Kenny Wayne didn't tell him they weren't literally two 'ships' crossing in the night as nothing would have been gained from that. During their exchange in which Chaulker did most of the talking, he shared job performance feedback he'd received not only from the Waffle House General Manager, but the regional supervisor as well. Kenny Wayne Rehage was in their estimation, *exact-ly* the sort of associate Misters Joe Rogers, Senior and Tom Forkner had in mind when they founded the Waffle House back in 1955 and that Kenny Wayne's future with the company was unlimited. Their biggest concern was losing him to a Cracker Barrel poacher. Now, if pressed to find one thing, Chaulker told him, one *itsy-bitsy-lil'* thing they'd like to see changed *but honest to goodness, no pressure*, it would be to see the boy smile more. Kenny Wayne took news of the report without visible reaction, prompting the young probation officer to ask him if a long term career at the Waffle House was something he could see himself pursuing. Chaulker was surprised when Kenny Wayne answered in no uncertain terms that it wasn't. He had no plans on staying after his probation ended, offering nothing else regarding his future or aspirations. Interpreting that, and not incorrectly, as a desire for a fresh start in somewhere other than Okaloosa County, Chaulker made a suggestion and with it an offer that blurred the lines of professionalism, his last ditch effort to satisfy the very thing he'd secretly been after since their initial intake meeting.

Lee Chaulker had a cousin in Fort Lauderdale, a third party administrator for insurance companies that settled claims on their behalf. He was willing to reach out to him on Kenny Wayne's behalf if that line of work seemed like something he'd be interested in. Steady, well-paying and by all indicators, fitting Kenny Wayne's behavioral strengths and personality type, it should. There was, of course, the obvious obstacle in that those with criminal records were precluded from being granted adjuster licenses in the State of Florida, but Chaulker assured Kenny Wayne he would feel comfortable making a recommendation to the State Insurance Superintendent's office to relax any disqualification period that might hinder the issuance of one, quickly pointing out in disclaimer fashion that he would do this for any case similar to his, *given y'know...the nature of the particulars, facts and what not.* While the suggestion and offer was met with a reaction that neither showed enthusiasm nor disinterest, it was obvious Kenny Wayne was open to it, if not plain interested-

...Then came the caveat. Aside from the administrative hitch, which Chaulker assured Kenny Wayne could be smoothed out as *standard operatin' pro-cedure,* there was another component which most definitely lay outside the parameters of their court appointed relationship: reaching out to his cousin in Fort Lauderdale and recommending he hire Kenny Wayne as an adjuster. That would be considered a personal favor...*somein' one ol' high school baller would do for another.* However with this, a *quid pro quo* was involved and still be contingent upon an outcome: Probation Officer and former Niceville basketball bench warmer Lee Chaulker would make the call on behalf of Waffle House night manager and former panhandle basketball legend gone bust Kenny Wayne Rehage, provided he played him in a one-on-one game to twenty-one-

...And beat him.

From the moment his docket had been assigned to him, Lee Chaulker's curiosity as to where he might now stack up against Kenny Wayne on the basketball court was irrepressible.

They met in a Crestview park on a Monday during Chaulker's lunch hour, Kenny Wayne's day off. Both the tennis and basketball courts were empty. On the far side of the park the County jail could be seen and Kenny Wayne wondered who of his old friends might be inside. Some small talk efforts by Chaulker, one word answers, shrugs and acknowledgements from Kenny Wayne. Chaulker then began to stretch out. Kenny Wayne just wanted to be done with it. When the time came to get it on, Chaulker tossed the ball to Kenny Wayne to shoot for possession.

Hit or miss.

Kenny Wayne checked the ball back, ceding the honors to him. From the foul line, Chaulker quickly bounced it once and in a single fluid motion, shot and stuck it-

...His ball.

The probation officer went on to score seven straight before Kenny Wayne took advantage of a missed swipe attempt and walked in for a rudimentary lay up. With his ensuing possession he launched a twenty-five footer that bounced hard off the inside of the mounting plate of the rim and half the distance back toward him. He put his hands out to grab it but Chaulker, in a nearly invisible flash, intercepted the ball and went on to sink three more. Kenny Wayne managed to put up only two more points, unimpressive close range jumpers. One off the backboard, the other dropping in after pinballing the rim for far longer than it should have. He had been closed out with only having scored three points to Chaulker's twenty-one. The post-game commentary from Lee Chaulker was part euphoric gloating, part rationalizing in an attempt to honor the player he remembered Kenny Wayne as. *Your genius back then was seein' the whole floor...makin' plays happen outta nothin'. East-west-north-south. I'm a pure shooter, more up and down, y'know? So a-course I'm gon' be better one-on-one, where you need the other four on the floor, y'know?*

On hearing that, Kenny Wayne looked away, probably to roll his eyes. He then continued to endure listening to the ecstatic

49

Chaulker's self-patronization, recounting his never having given up despite not starting a single game at Niceville, even on Senior Night but a love of basketball saw him continuing to play. Intramurals at Community College and now in the Men's Leagues he played three nights a week. He went on with his testimonial until he was checked by a sudden sense of decorum and sportsmanship, considering Kenny Wayne might be somewhat humiliated. He told him he was still going to reach out to his cousin in Fort Lauderdale and recommend he hire and train him as a claims adjuster. He had planned on doing that all along, regardless of the game's outcome-

...Exactly as Kenny Wayne figured.

It was the least Chaulker could do, he swore. Especially considering how rough Kenny Wayne had it, what with getting caught up in the wrong crowd and his dad's untimely death while being under investigation by the Feds. For Kenny Wayne, the hearing of those words struck a nerve, yet he didn't react. And when Chaulker extended a hand to shake Kenny Wayne took it, as he did the ball just used to beat him when Chaulker offered it as a gift, encouraging him to use it. Another handshake and the assurance of his being in touch soon, Lee Chaulker had to get back to the office. Kenny Wayne stood on the basketball court watching his probation officer float on air to his car and drive off, undoubtedly feeling as good as he had in years then looked down at the ball in his hands. He thought Lee Chaulker wasn't that bad of a guy, despite bringing up what he did about his father. He then looked up at the hoop thirty-five feet away. He frowned, set his feet and released the ball toward the hoop-

...Swish.

...Nothing but net.

Less than a year later, Kenny Wayne Rehage was in Fort Lauderdale working as an automotive insurance claim adjuster. The process of adjusting the claims he was charged with was mastered in a short period of time and soon he was handling more than was expected of him. He'd also taken heed to Lee Chaulker's advice to start playing hoops again. Mostly at playgrounds. Kenny Wayne soon began to feel more alive than he had in years.

There was no reason the claim on the red Mercedes coupe with the damaged rear end should have taken any longer than fifteen minutes to wrap up. Lauren was in her early twenties and had moments earlier greeted Kenny Wayne in a manner suggesting he himself was responsible for the damage to the car instead of the one there to make it whole again. While he went through the motions and took the requisite photos, she maintained a condescending impatience while periodically grabbing her upper lip with her teeth and holding it there. Subtle head shakes and hands planted on hips with arms akimbo. Soon thereafter Kenny Wayne was double-teamed when Alan Copeland reluctantly marched down to get involved. He introduced himself to Kenny Wayne by warning him that the insurance company better not fuck around and limit the auto body shop to using aftermarket replacement parts. Kenny Wayne politely informed him that wouldn't be an issue, his stepdaughter's policy was written on a full replacement cost value. Alan wasn't placated, still impatient and annoyed. Kenny Wayne took no offense to the hostility or curtness, instead surmising correctly that the stepies didn't like one another and Alan's being there wasn't of his own free will.

Then, an unexpected eruption from a home across the street. A stout, middle-aged Bahamian housekeeper had stormed from the door, angry. The lady of the house, her presumed employer, followed seconds later. In her late fifties, she was dressed in a hot pink designer velour tracksuit but shoeless, hair pulled back tightly, unnaturally feline eyes on a face free of makeup that stretched on all sides to the back of her head giving it the appearance of an alabaster candle. Calling after the housekeeper, she made half-efforts at getting her to stop with a hybrid of commands and explanations. All three sets of eyes standing beside the red Mercedes coupe looked over and watched the housekeeper turn back and respond to her employer, her thick accent making whatever she'd said unclear but unmistakably had all the hallmarks of one walking off a job. Lauren and her soon to be stepfather Alan Copeland had simultaneous reactions that couldn't have been more diametrically different-

...Oh my God. She is being such a bitch to that poor woman!

...That was me, it'd be don't let the door hit you in the ass. Who makes a scene like that in front of the whole neighborhood?

Alan and Lauren exchange half-second glances of unmitigated contempt for one another.

The homeowner across the street's command/explanations soon morphed into apologies and the commentary continued.

I should get my mother to hire that poor woman.

Fuck the two of them for makin' a scene.

Kenny Wayne was silent, not watching but observing. The exchange between the feuding parties simmered ever so slightly down to what appeared to be a dialogue and in that, hints of a plea came from the woman who owned the house. Kenny Wayne offered for the first time his own commentary but not directed to Alan nor the girl. It was said more for himself.

She's not goin' anywhere.

He was surprised not that he'd vocalized his thoughts but that Alan and Lauren were looking at him waiting to hear a reasoning for the forecast that sounded so certain. Pressed, Kenny Wayne repeated it and Lauren was disgusted, insisting the housekeeper should leave in a display of underdog, perpetually oppressed, working-class-heroine female empowerment. Alan didn't editorialize, instead wanting an explanation for Kenny Wayne's opinion.

Hold on. What makes you so sure? Are you Nostradomus?

Kenny Wayne had shrugged, then opined that if the housekeeper was really committed to quitting, she wouldn't have stopped to argue. She'd have just clean-walked away. He then referenced what had to be her old, humble car parked in the driveway, pointing to it as evidence of a financial pinch, which caused Lauren to again gasp. Then wanting to get back to the business of the claim he'd been dispatched to close, he politely shrugged and tied up his rationale with a quick flurry of points including the difficulties getting a job that weighs heavily on previous employer references-

...Gasp!

...Yeah, life's a bitch.

And, Kenny Wayne added, having to learn the needs, routines and peculiarities of whatever family she next went to work for with no guarantee it will be much better there-

...Gasp!

...You never know.

Focusing on the bright side, Kenny Wayne then pointed out that for at least the next two weeks the housekeeper would probably have it easy, with her she-devil boss on angel cake behavior. Maybe even fattening the envelope on payday. Lauren wasn't relieved, again suggesting that she should have her mother hire the woman, where Alan was intrigued by what he was hearing. Kenny Wayne suspected the slighted housekeeper was probably not long for that job, but her exit would be on more practical terms, less emotional. *If I'd a guess...she's gonna be kinda...secret squirrel 'bout it.* She would quietly line up another job, give the customary two week notice and move on without fight or fanfare. Hearing this, Lauren now looked like she'd won something. Then as if on cue, by all appearances the homeowner across the street had committed to contrite pleading, almost genuflecting before the Bahamian housekeeper who listened, slowly let her guard down and nodded in agreement to something. After a brief pause, the housekeeper followed her employer back into the house.

Kenny Wayne took no visible pleasure in his by all indicators accurate prediction. When asked to explain how he called it, he said that it was simply the most obvious result, given what he saw playing out. Alan was fascinated, asking what the word was for that kind of thinking. Kenny Wayne didn't know. Alan suggested/half asked if it was something like *'where there's smoke, there's fire'* but Kenny Wayne couldn't concur. He was back to completing the claim adjustment and Lauren reluctantly let loose the words *'Occam's Razor,'* regretting doing so immediately after the words left her lips. And in a single motion that suggested they were a confederacy, Alan and Kenny Wayne looked at her as if there was a bird's nest on her head. She rolled her eyes and took a few steps away, muttering something condescending about both of them.

Alan looked back at Kenny Wayne with a frown thinking to himself that he didn't know exactly how just yet, but this country bumpkin, redneck yokel could make him money.

"What's your name?"

"My name's Kenny Wayne, sir. Kenny Wayne Rehage."

"How much they paying you on this job, Kenny?"

Kenny stood off to the side of the *ventanilla,* the small coffee cup in his hand now empty. After finishing he liked to savor the sweetness in his mouth. When he was ready, he took a deep breath, moved over to the counter and placed the cup in the designated bus tray. He looked over at the *gorda* who took his order and nodded to her, which she returned. He didn't bother trying to make eye contact with Marielena.

As he walked down to the street, he wondered if Alan might try to kill him after all this was done. Or rather have him killed. He had mentioned on several occasions of having connections back in New York. *Maa-fee-ah* connections. Other times he used the words *whacked-out*, snapping his fingers when he said it. The recollection of Alan doing so made Kenny snicker.

Approaching the car, he held up his keys, hit the button and with a chirp the lock released and said laughingly to himself, 'boom.' He opened the driver side door, got in and started the engine. He checked his teeth in the mirror then gave them a quick tongue swabbing, getting one last vestige of flavor.

Mmmmm.

Rosie really had to lighten up off this kick. Then he promised himself not to think about it anymore.

Or her.

With that, he drove off.

Chapter Five

Little Fires

Copeland got back on his way after the adrenaline spike ran its course. He had a terrible thirst that had come on suddenly and wondered if it was related. Or maybe it was something like, spin the wheel…diabetes, even though he knew very little about it. His lifelong habit of interpreting any physical sensation that wasn't ordinary as symptomatic of a malady still reared its head from time to time. He blind-reached onto the floor of the back seat for an unopened sixteen ounce Diet Pepsi, not once considering the possibility of waiting to get down to the main road and stop at one of the ubiquitous fast marts to pick up a bottle of water. When he turned off of the residential side street, he saw in the near distance a medical complex. On one of the buildings that might or might not have just been remodeled, workers were installing signage high above the ground using a crane and scaffolding. Lettering, on the exterior of the parapet. He knew exactly what they were doing but not yet the name being spelled out in recognition of a donation made.

Hmmm. Who sprung for this one-?

As far as philanthropic communities go, Southeast Florida's was considerable. Still, its class of donors able and willing to pony up enough to have a hospital tower renamed for them was a short list. He was certain he knew whoever it was.

...Hmmm. Why didn't I hear about it-?

Not that he was looking to drop a whopper like that at the present time, he still felt a tinge of envy. Naturally, the clinic in the Design District was a part of his next thought.

His clinic.

And with it came a sigh of relief, as his name wasn't on it.

...Thank God-

...Thank fucking God for that.

What a great call it had been going with the 'Design District Free Men's Health Clinic and Support Center' instead of the 'Alan J. Copeland Free Clinic' that he actually considered for less than a second when he opened it. No, if his name was going on anything, it was going to be something like the one he was passing. A medical center building. Not a 1,500 square foot shit box with tired Keith Haring knockoff graffiti murals painted on the sides.

Again, he admired the tower.

An intersection, hmmmm-

...Good placement, good vizz-

He was still vexed by whom the building was being renamed for and noted the amount of spaces and letters already up.

...Well, it's definitely not Ira Zell-

Then, Copeland reconsidered. Maybe it was Ira Zell and he was adding his wife Margie to the marquee. A quick calculation. Since the four letters already up weren't placed in sequential order, installed like lugnuts on a car tire are tightened, it made the guessing a challenge.

...One 'U.' Two 'H's.' One 'D'-

...*Definitely not Ira Zell-*

He spent the next two traffic signals trying to solve the puzzle before surrendering in frustration.

...*What am I doing? Playing Wheel of fucking Fortune?*

The clinic.

And again, thank God his name wasn't on it.

Copeland's founding the Design District Free Men's Health Clinic and Support Center was a stroke of genius in his estimation, yet one he never publicly boasted about since the purpose of launching it was strictly to access more leads for viatical insurance policies to purchase from men afflicted with AIDS. They came in clusters, as opposed to his having to go out to look for them individually, as was the practice when first getting into the life settlement game. With the clinic, the fishing was done with long nets instead of pointed sticks, eventually taking on the role of hatchery. The added bonus was the testing services being free to the patient didn't mean Medicaid was extended the same courtesy, making the clinic a surprisingly unexpected source of revenue as well. Where Copeland originally planned to have little day to day involvement in the operation of the facility, he did have a clear vision of what should greet the patients after Karen cut the red ribbon on the doors the day it opened. He wanted it to have the feel of an *Abercrombie & Fitch* retail store, casual and hip with an administrative staff of attractive young men in tight fitting tee shirts and on the medical staff, no white lab coats worn. The waiting room was comfortable, walls adorned with imagery of subtle reminders that whoever was there was not alone in their fight and that recovery was possible even though the science and statistics of the time begged to differ. He insisted that the staff never use the phrase 'stay positive' or 'think positive', but find other ways to get the point across. If the doctors and nurses rolled their eyes at him, they did so behind closed lids. Copeland also wanted music by Edith Paif and Billie Holiday piped into the waiting room, believing it was subconsciously reassuring in a maternal way, confirmation that he had no idea how depressing not only the lives but the lyrics of both singers and their songs actually were. At the back of the waiting room taking up nearly the entire wall was a retro photograph featuring a tanned and thin college-aged Alan Copeland with his arm around another smiling and particularly handsome young man with perfect white teeth. All appearances suggested the two were the best of friends-

...Full of life-

...Carefree-

...Wallowing in the privileges of youth.

And below it, a small placard read:

'In Loving Memory of Jordy Stein, Always Room In His Heart For A New Friend.'

What was incongruous between the photograph and the tribute was that the young man pictured with Copeland was not, as unspokenly implied, a casualty of the AIDS epidemic. Nor was he homosexual or a part of any other high-risk catagories. Jordan Stein of Englewood

Cliffs, New Jersey, died in a car accident during his senior year at Syracuse University. What earned him a place on the wall of the Design District Free Men's Health Clinic was nothing more than his having been a childhood summer camp acquaintance of Copeland that happened to be in a photograph which Copeland thought he himself looked great in. When he shared this little secret with Karen, she was slack jawed-

Hold on now, Karen, there's no law saying you have to die from AIDS to have a memorial put up on a wall-

...But her reaction to his audacity wasn't followed without that impossible to hide *oh-my-gawd* chortle. It was things like this that had attracted her to him, his simultaneous balancing act of being obnoxious, outrageous and entertaining. That, and his underlying insecurity that only she, as if no one else in the world was equipped with the lenses to do so, had recognized in him.

The purpose of the Design District Free Men's Health Clinic and Support Center had since run its course, its obsolescence brought on by medical advances which made living with and managing the HIV virus a reality. For Copeland, continuing in his business of acquiring life insurance policies would have to include an expansion of his horizons beyond those with AIDS. But unlike a dairy cow no longer milkable, the clinic did maintain enough functionality to save it from the slaughterhouse. So, it still stood but now with a soot-covered patina, alone and ignored in the shadows of an I-95 on-ramp with signage truncated to read 'Design District Clinic,' with nothing outwardly visible to tie Copeland to it-

Thank God-

Thank fucking God for that.

...Aside, of course, from what was listed on his tax returns.

At the next traffic light, Copeland's thoughts were off philanthropy and onto the young girl's tits in the white Jeep next to him. Not that she was aware he was looking at her. He'd sooner give her the keys to his car that grabbed her attention than the satisfaction of knowing he'd responded to what was obviously an audition, a trawling for a pass which she might grab hold of, or for the sake of feeling momentarily empowered, shoot down. Her posturing was painfully obvious, the quick look-check in the rear view and open handed pitch-forking her golden mop of wind tousled hair, the tightened lips like her temperature was being taken the old school way, bare-bronzed shoulders swaying to the reggae music that could have as easily been the traffic report. To Copeland, the charade was more predictable than the landslide bowel blast following a coffee enema. No, he wasn't going to buy in and let her see him look over.

Nope-

...Not for you, toots.

Not today.

And then a quick glance in his side view after the high-pitched banshee wail of an idling Japanese racing bike sliced through the air in sets of three. He smirked for himself, thinking of the girl in the Jeep alongside him-

...But the dickhead on the Yamaha might bite.

...There's a mating call for you, toots.

...He might even be almost done with the payments on that fucking noise maker.

No, Copeland preferred the bullshit ritual-free exchanges when it came to sexual transactions. Every single time. When both parties involved didn't pretend to be anything other than what they were. He actually saw those girls as honest, even finding room in his heart for a compassionate thought when he imagined their waiting at the hotel elevator, post-tryst and flush-up fifteen hundred smackers but still wondering how it turned out like this for them.

Vroom-

Vroom-

Vroom-

Weeeeeeeeee-

The motorcycle that may or may not have been paid off raced around him then in and out of lanes, rocketing ahead of traffic only to come to a stop at the next signal that was timed to red for that exact reason.

Fucking jerk off.

A look at a McDonalds drive thru and Copeland thought about getting something to eat despite his just having eaten an early lunch and having had breakfast late. He decided against it and wondered what the Yosts would be serving for dinner. He wondered who would be there to put a softly placed hand on his arm for money. Karen had probably told him but it went in one ear and out the other without stopping long enough to take a breath. It was inevitable, the very reason for the invitation. Much like his preferred sort of prostitute, the Yosts didn't pretend their dinners were anything different than what they were but without the harrowing examinations of conscience by hotel hallway elevator banks afterwards. Copeland was glad to give his support to whomever the Yosts asked. At least he claimed to. They had, after all, at the behest of his step-father-in-law Haberman, spearheaded the campaign of the new State Attorney General whose incumbent opponent, Nate Newman, had become a pebble in Copeland's shoe two and a half years earlier.

Pfft. What an asshole.

There wasn't any animus in Copeland's head-shake and sigh, suggesting the whole ordeal was considered now more unfortunate than anything else.

Pathetic.

The former State Attorney General would have been better served treating Copeland like a friend instead of mounting his high, white horse of righteousness and putting crosshairs on his back. Copeland was sure it was rooted in Newman hating his own people while at the same time wanting to be perceived as their champion. Instead of concentrating on rapists and murderers and carjackers running buck wild and seemingly unchecked, Newman decided to take up the mantle of the disenfranchised investors claiming money lost with Copeland and his company was stolen. It never surprised him that the same people who would trip over themselves to send the firm checks anticipating high rates of return were the same ones who pretended to be unaware of any risk involved.

Well look at him now, right?

May as well go prosecute Halakah violations, schmuck-o.

Copeland wondered again who was going to be at the Yosts. A handful of fat wallets. Probably not Haberman, but the usual band of gypsies and smell-feasts. The political hacks and their lickspittles, lobbyists and mid-level bundlers. And of course, the lawyers. The lawyers who loved them all.

Fucking lawyers. Fucking law-yers.

And he grinned. He couldn't help but admire their racket. Copeland made a practice of exclusively retaining attorneys who honed their craft in the halls and chambers of the public sector before setting out to work for themselves armed with a surfeit of insider knowledge and relationships. They were his conduit into the provenance of ultimate leverage, where new legislation could be written and established statutes amended, grease for the rails of profit, manufactured hindrances for aggressive regulators. And in cases of unbending and suspicious idealists like former Attorney General Nate Newman, turn their resources to finding and supporting a candidate better suited to playing with others in the sandbox.

Look at you now, putz.

Could have had a future.

Just another little fire for the ol' Alan-ator to put out.

Little fires.

Little fires.

Little fires.

He had no idea what Nate Newman was even doing now.

When Copeland established the firm he called it the *Mutual Fidelity, Benefits & Trust Company.* As soon as the words formed in his mind they were blurted out as if traveling on the back of a spasm and into ink, no consideration given to options. It may have as well been a pizza topping. Copeland was a staunch believer in using generic names for corporate mast heads, simple little red houses in the middle of the block. They should have no connection to anything sentimental or personal, like immigrant grandparents or a beloved childhood dog for no other reason than having one less thing to feel shitty about when dissolving them, which until that point in Copeland's business life had been the rule rather than the exception.

The first clients of *Mutual Fidelity, Benefits & Trust*, or 'MF' as Copeland liked to call it, were furnished by way of reference from people he knew. His pitch to them was worked and reworked, honed into as close to a perfect script as possible. Critical was that the tone embodied discretion and respect which meant soft sell. The art of subtle persuasion ran against every fibre in his being, every instinct he'd ever had for as far back as he could remember. The focus and discipline he dedicated to it was enough to impress a Shaolin monk. Word choices steered clear of mawkishness, low on syrup, focusing on a reserved practicality. While the presentation couldn't be completely without compassion, the empathy served up was delivered in deliberately measured micro-doses, small physical gestures. An understanding nod of the head, slight pursing of the lips or blinking of the eyes that held ever so slightly longer than usual.

Then, the clinic-

Then, the donations-

And the support of every HIV/AIDS related charity in the state.

Through a fast moving word of mouth, he was being approached by terminally ill policy owners throughout Broward and Dade Counties looking to sell their life insurance policies as opposed to him doing the approaching and with that he had far more opportunities available to him than funds to pay for. The answer to his three pound truffle problem lied in one of his previous lives-

...Investors discreetly mined from a boiler room stock brokerage house. With this opportunity before him, Copeland refused to allow the lifetime ban from trading in securities to count as a snag, less than the smallest of potholes in the road worthy of slowing down for. He structured 'MF' listing himself as a consultant, with strawman partners as official company fronts.

Little fires.

Little fires.

Little fires.

He knew immediately that former colleague Scooter Wrobel, who was back in New York doing his act at one or another of the Wall Street chop shops would be perfect to bring on, figuring he could just as easily be addicted to pornography in flip-flops year round as he was up in Gotham. A little more thought had him convinced he should add Aléjandro Perez. He was a local that sold non-depository mortgages at his company that always seemed to have a new name and address. Copeland figured the sand had to be running out of that hourglass and the offer of a change would probably be welcomed. Rounding out the trio would be Howie Yglesias, a non-practicing lawyer who raised equity for the acquisitions of multi-families in Overtown and the liquor stores, laundromats and check cashing locations strategically positioned nearby. Between them with himself calling shots, Copeland was confident raising capital would never be a problem.

Ever.

Where tact and delicacy of approach was crucial in acquiring policies from the dying in need of money, soliciting investors hoping to profit off of their misery was another story. The phone bank sales pitch was cut and dried business, where efforts of contrived thoughtfulness would never be questioned. Consistent fifteen to eighteen percent annual yields made any concern for the plight of an unknown life insurance policy holder nothing more than a footnote. The sales pitches were straight forward, maybe even something of a hard sell in that a point was made at the onset of the call giving the perception the time of the salesman was of a slightly higher value than that of the potential client.

...So now that you understand what we're talking about, these 'Life Settlements' are the only investment which can truly be said to provide-

...ABSOLUTE. RETURNS.

Absolute.

They're a-

...MARKET. NEUTRAL. INVESTMENT OPPORTUNITY.

That means they're not tied or locked into any traded stock, bond, currency or commodity markets. They're unaffected by any political or economic turbulence. Once you're invested, the only variable is time. That's it. The bottom line is this: When the insured person dies, the return on the investment is actualized. When the insured person-

...DIES.

The investment.

PAYS-

...OFF.

Then, the psychological jiu-jitsu-

*...Now, maybe it's not for you. Not everyone is comfortable, this being
people's lives we're talking about. But the truth is-*

...WE. ALL. DIE.

*You know that. I know that. And so do the people we're buying the
policies from.*

THEY. KNOW. THAT.

And they're happy they have the policies to sell.

THEY. ARE. HAPPY. TO. SELL. THEM. TO. US.

The percentage of cold-called potential investors that remained
on the line to listen further did so at a rate far exceeding any other tele-
solicitation of stocks, mortgages or aluminum siding than Copeland or
any of his associates had ever witnessed by margins that were nothing
less than astounding.

The physical call lists for the solicitation leads came from the
same place the boiler rooms got theirs. Some were purchased from
vendors that specialize in this provision, selling rolls upon rolls of
names and phone numbers divided into a variety of categories and
subcategories. Credit card holders, professional guild members,
homeowners with second mortgages, subscribers to financial
periodicals and magazines. But the blue chip leads were landed
through an underground blackmarket. Names and phone numbers of
unknowing investors were directly transcribed from microfiche records
onto index cards by sneaky backroom file clerks at the major
investment banking houses, harvested and sold to chop shop managers.
Where the *Mutual Fidelity Benefits and Trust Company* sales pitch was
meticulously scripted by Copeland, so were the answers to the expected

frequently asked questions, always at the cold calling salesman's fingertips.

...Absolutely! Tracking agents do provide information to investors regarding the whereabouts and mortality status of each insured. That is correct and I'm glad you asked that-

...We actually use independent escrow services, even in states where it's not required. That's standard, across the board operations for us at Mutual Fidelity Benefits and Trust-

The choosing of which specific cold call lists targeting the ideal potential investor also reflected Copeland's special brand of genius.

...That's a great question, Doctor. I wish more investors would ask that. Yes. We have an in-house team of compliance experts that actively work with state regulators.

When it came time to open the clinic, Copeland hired the nearly unhirable Elliot Lopinsky, M.D. The young physician was older than he looked, bearing a striking resemblance to the comedian Jon Lovitz and while he spoke very quickly, had difficulty looking anyone in the eye. Copeland referred to his in-house medical advisor as *Dr. Gropinsky*, a nod to alleged incidents with his hands and the women he felt compelled to put them on. When they came up in conversation, Copeland dismissed the allegations as innocent miscommunications, misread social cues by an obviously socially awkward man-child. The purported indiscretions with his prescription pad weren't as easily written off to naivete. While many of Elliot Lopinsky's personal habits and predilections remained private, they weren't aggressively discouraged by Copeland, simply redirected and managed for Copeland's own benefit. Understandably, the doctor did whatever was asked of him. Had he not, his prospects would be limited to working as a physician on an offshore oil rig. So when a candidate for a life insurance policy that might otherwise be disqualified due a preexisting condition for something like-

...Already having AIDS-

...Lopinsky would dutifully facilitate a clean-sheeting of the application, overlooking the pesky fact in the bloodwork report. And his medical authority was utilized when the signing off on official projected viatical policy maturity dates was needed, making up unrealistic life expectations on insured subjects not dying quite fast enough. Lopinsky was valuable, if not indispensable. If it meant intervening when a neighbor would call the police complaining that he was leering too long at their underage daughter or one of the girls in the office objected to his using the ladies rest room, Copeland found a way to smooth it over.

Little Fires.

Little Fires.

Little Fires.

The girl in the white Jeep pulled up alongside him at the next light, this time on his right instead of left. Again, she got nothing from him. As if confronting his conscience face to face and telling Satan to get behind him, he grabbed the phone and scrolled for Karen. She picked up on the last note of the first ring.

"Hey."

"The hospital in...uh, Coral Gables. There's a tower, a building...on the corner...it looks like it's been remodeled and it's getting someone's name on it. Do you know anything about it?

A short pause. Karen was thinking. *"The new Infectious Diseases Center?"* she asked.

"I dunno. You tell me. There's a name going up on it."

"It's the new Infectious Diseases Center. What about it?"

"Who paid for it?"

"The building?"

"Yeah. Who's name is going on it?"

Through the phone he could hear the database of her mind humming. Then, *"Coral Gables Memorial...Infectious Diseases Center...Henry Mulholland, I think."*

"What? Who the fuck is Henry Mulholland?! Sounds like the name of a horse thief from a western." On the surface, his reaction to not knowing who the benefactor for the new Infectious Diseases Center was seemed to upset him more than if he had known him. The truth is, Copeland's response was going to be a one-size-fits-both indignation, regardless. "How much did he drop on it?"

"I think twenty-five. I'm not sure."

Copeland shook his head, miffed. "Who is this guy?"

"I don't know, Alan. I think he's like...an investment banker from up in Palm Beach or something. Why? What does it matter?"

"No reason. I just passed it and was wondering. Twenty-five million, huh?"

"That's my understanding. So, what're you doing?"

"What am I doing? The same as when I talked to you ten minutes ago. Still in the car." He felt bad for sounding snippy. "What about you?"

"Same as when I talked to you ten minutes ago. Still dealing with this Chase thing." She might as well have said, *'I know you are but what am I?'*

He changed gears. "So, who's gonna be at the Yosts?"

"God. I don't know." Then a thought. *"You know, Gracie didn't say."*

Copeland knew it really didn't matter but refrained from sharing the sentiment. He looked over to see if the girl in the white Jeep was still driving alongside him. She was ahead of him by a car length. "You gotta see this young blonde with big tits in a Jeep driving alongside me, Karen. Trying to get me to look at her."

"I'm sure."

"They're so obvious."

"Only because they don't not need to be, Alan."

"What's that supposed to mean?"

"She probably looked over and figured she knows the type."

He took to defense upon hearing the last part. "Was that a shot? Did you just say that as some kind of shot at me?"

Karen protested. *"No! I meant she saw the Rolls Royce, the wealthy middle-aged man driving it, you know how girls are-"*

"It sounded like you took a shot."

"I didn't take a shot."

He didn't want to engage in a battle, especially not one over semantics. "So who's gonna be at the Yosts?"

"I just told you, Gracie didn't say. Or maybe she did and I just forgot."

"Oh, yeah."

73

He seemed perplexed then by a possibility that he didn't want to entertain. "You know, Karen...I'm not an idiot. I know people kiss my ass because I got money, because I'm rich."

Her response was bordering on derisory. *"And you're only figuring this out now."*

"No. No, of course not. You know what I mean. It's just-" he stopped. "If I was a bus driver you wouldn't have given me the time of day," he told her.

"Oh my God, here we go. We're going to go through this again?" She deliberately decelerated her delivery, proceeding to talk to him not quite like he was a child, maybe an adolescent. *"No, ho-ney. Unfortunately and no secret to anyone, I have a history of being attracted to painfully obnoxious assholes. Not counting husband number two, the doormat. Howard was a reactionary thing, bad advice from a therapist. So if you were a bus dri-ver and we came into one another's lives and you even just held the door open for me once? Chances are we would be having this con-ver-sation with you not behind the wheel of a two hundred thousand dollar Rolls Royce, but driving a Metro bus crossing town."* A pause. *"What do you want me to say, Alan?"*

Silence.

"Alan?"

"Yeah, I'm here."

Karen continued, unprompted. *"And since we're on that subject, if we knew each other when Stacy Bernstein invited everyone to her Sweet Sixteen except little Alan Copeland, I wouldn't have gone to the party. I would have hung out with you instead, you schmuck."*

Alan managed a half-smile. "You ever wonder how fat that bitch is now?"

74

"No, Alan. Never once. I never met the girl let alone seen a picture of her. Maybe you should just try to think good thoughts for her. Y'know? Hopefully she's matured into a compassionate person and is enjoying a fulfilling, healthy life."

Silence.

He didn't deserve Karen. She was so much better than him. He held his breath and stayed silent.

"Alan? Did you hang up?"

"No, I'm here."

"Are you okay?"

"Yeah, I'm fine."

A long pause. *"Okay. I'll see you at home, then."*

"Yeah. I'll see you at home."

"Love you."

"Love you." Then, a thought. "You do know that the car was more like three hundred grand," he told her.

"Lovvvee yooooou."

He disconnected. He looked up and to his right, the girl in the white Jeep was no longer anywhere to be seen.

Stacy Bernstein's Sweet Sixteen. Amazing how some of those things from the past still haunted him, when now they wouldn't even qualify as the smallest of little fires that they in actuality were, smaller than he'd known in years.

Little fires.

Little fires.

Little fires.

Chapter Six

Agents Got No Game

Kenny drove back toward the route he'd diverted from.

Calm.

Not thinking about Copeland, at least not obsessively so.
Periodic thoughts back to Rosie, a look at the Cadillac's dashboard
clock and imagining her at work, what she might be doing at that exact
moment in time. Probably helping someone, politely projecting
interest or concern for what they came into the store for, all while for
her own amusement a running commentary played out in her head that
was usually the cause for the incandescent and seemingly spontaneous
smile that so often took over her face and nothing to do with what was
being conveyed by the client or their personal home decorator. As he
ran that possible scenario in his head, the surrounding backdrop it was
set against became opaque, not standing a chance competing with the
imagery of her likeness. Her perfectly tempered, never contrived
expressive face that always gave away how quickly her mind worked. It
humbled him. The way she walked, able to paradoxically remain fluid

yet goofy, something only she could do. And when she'd reach over to wipe a non-existent spec of food from his face, he knew what she was doing and secretly appreciated it. For a moment, a brief and fleeting moment, he believed that everything between them would be fine. Then a piercing streak of sunlight reflecting off the car in front of him kicked his propensity toward tempered expectations out of its catnap, letting it short circuit any happy future Rosie thoughts.

A deep sigh.

He hard squinted and moved to the next lane, then came fast upon a road turtle that had every prerogative to be in the right hand lane but for the love of God not the left, and certainly not riding the line on both. The slow moving car was a tan Buick, something like a LeSabre over fifteen years old. The rear end looked like it was doing its best to keep its ass off the pavement, worn out coil springs resulting in it sitting lower to the ground than the front. The interior was clutter-packed with unidentifiable stuff, a cache of belongings and odds and ends, gear and...things, useless chattels, blankets, bags, boxes, the appurtenances of a nomadic hoarder. Kenny moved to the right and accelerated hard to spend as little time in the Buick driver's blind spot as possible and looked over. A squat and heavy mop-headed old man with noticeably oversized ears had both hands gripped on the top of the steering wheel like he was holding himself up to look over it. If Kenny intended on shooting him a rebuking '*holy shit move over, wouldja*' glare, he didn't follow through with it. Instead, he was disappointed with himself for being annoyed and wondered where the poor old guy was coming from, where he was going and what in the hell he planned on doing with the milk crate that was among the things wedged on the ledge of the backseat headrest. Kenny then settled into his preferred lane and looked into the side view mirror at the hoarder's Buick getting smaller and smaller when something caught his eye. Another car had replicated his move in the exact trajectory getting around the old Buick. Kenny's first thought was uncertainty, feeling like he recognized the sedan despite it being generic. The next sensation came with his actually recognizing it.

Wonderment.

Then, he was angry.

What is he-?

Is that...?

-Is that sonva-bitch followin' me?

The sedan made no hard attempts at concealment. Kenny almost expected him to speed up and pull alongside, honk the horn and give him a big ol' wave like they were en route to the same tailgate party. Kenny eased off the gas, slowing down to confirm it was in fact, Walter Reed following him. He then took the right lane to let him gradually catch up, controlling his pace so that their running alongside one another was inevitable but not obviously intended. And when that happened, Kenny maintained a position next to him.

Come on now, look over.

You know I'm here.

Nowhere to run.

You know.

Any longer and you're gonna look stupid.

Of course Reed feigned surprise at seeing Kenny. Then a smile and a finger point, like he'd just dropped two off of a great pass made on the basketball court. He looked like an aging frat boy, wearing a plain suit and white dress shirt with his bland tie loosened and prematurely thinning hair that he didn't try to make the most of, resigned to imminent baldness. Trying to maintain a natural bearing, Reed sped up ever so slightly then decelerated the same way, allowing Kenny to move ahead by a small distance. He then sped up, catching him and slowed down again, the motions passing for a badly choreographed routine, an awkward *cha-cha* playing out between the cars. They ignored one another, Reed trying to play off being natural, Kenny silently stewing. His presence increasingly fretted on Kenny the more he considered it and he felt a sudden urge to confront him. The next time he found their cars drifting parallel to one another, Kenny looked to catch his eye. He motioned for him to follow him. Of course, Reed played confused. Kenny sped up, his eyes set on a corner gas station less than a quarter mile ahead and on the right. He made a play for it, putting his directional on earlier than he ordinarily might as an instruction for Reed to pull over there behind him.

The parking lot offered plenty of room, despite the five four-pump islands and convenience store. Kenny pulled in and stopped in a position that when he pulled out, he would be able to do so moving forward without turning or having to put the car in reverse. He shifted into park but left the car running and got out to the soft chime of the open door alert. Not hurried, not jumpy, but also without lingering. Reed pulled his car in, assuming a place directly behind Kenny's car so they were in a line. Kenny didn't walk over to him. He wanted Reed to get out. When Reed did, Kenny put his hands in his pockets and looked around the parking lot, then at the intersection, contemplative before taking two steps toward Reed's car and stopping.

"Kenny, what's going on, m'man?"

Kenny waited a second, grinned and shrugged. "You tell me."

Reed played dumb. "What do you mean?"

"C'mon, Walt."

Reed took one more crack at the charade, smiling but nervously now. "What? What are you talking about?"

"You're followin' me, man."

Reed's response was pre-fabricated, ginned up the minute he realized Kenny saw him. "No. No way, man. It's not like that, not like you think-"

"How is it then, Walt? 'Cause I gotta tell you, it's really not a good look and all-"

"--"

"...Not exactly in the spirit of...y'know-"

"--"

"...A little bit of a violation of...*uh*...trust. Or goodwill, or whatever we're supposed to be havin' here."

Reed could tell that Kenny was peeved, even holding back some and wanted to stop the damage from worsening. "Look, I'll be straight with you, Kenny-" It was his turn to stop and consider his choice of subsequent words. "We wanted to make sure you got there without any problems."

"We?" Kenny was even more annoyed now.

"Me and Trey."

Kenny looked around as if expecting to see him, then asked, "where is...Trey?" He said his name without affection.

"He's gonna come straight from the dentist. He's got this crazy toothache. Maybe a root canal thing, who knows-"

Kenny processed the irrelevant information while Reed hoped the situation was in the process of defusing. But Kenny wasn't done. "What kind of problems y'mean? Like I might change my mind? Is that what you're afraid of?"

Reed *aw-shucks'd* it, looked away, turned back and held up his hands. While he didn't vocalize it, there was no mistaking his sentiment. "Kenny, I'm sorry, man. It's just that...you know-"

Kenny cut him off. "No, I don't know, Walt. Y'ever think maybe you followin' me...tailin' me like I'm the one you're after...might not be the most productive thing for y'all? Makin' me out like I'm the bad guy?"

"--"

"I don't have to be doin' this. You know that, I know that."

Reed had nothing else, so he went all-in on the apology and rationalization. "This is just such a big thing, man-"

"Yeah, well it sends the wrong message, Walt."

"No, man. It's not like that...seriously."

Not satisfied, Kenny settled into his heels, planted his hands back in his pockets and gave every indication he was in reconsideration mode. It was obvious and now Reed was nervous, thinking three months work was down the shitter. "Kenny, I'm sorry man. I...I'm a friggin' jerk. Okay? It's on me, not Trey. I was afraid you might get cold feet."

Kenny's only response was another shaking of the head not while looking at him, but instead out at the passing traffic, forcing him to wait to see what would in effect determine not only how the rest of his day would play out, but maybe even his career.

Walter Reed was a Special Agent in the Federal Bureau of Investigations with no genealogical tie to the legendary Army Major and Medical Center namesake. Despite his efforts at patronizing Kenny, he had an obvious smugness about him, a complacency that comes with accomplishment whether it was earned or simply assumed. He was a Virginia boy of the catalog beltway variety, those whose fathers profited either directly from the government or because of it. He made Kenny's acquaintance while playing in the same pickup game at the Lee YMCA in Fort Lauderdale, a regular Monday to Friday evening run that Kenny typically made three times a week. Despite the poor ventilation, dodgy air conditioning and otherwise tired facilities, it was a popular game that attracted the better local former college and high school players now in the workforce. Kenny liked the up-tempo but responsible pace and there always seemed to be someone with whom a synergy could materialize with few words exchanged. While he didn't dominate in a man-amongst-boys manner, Kenny was consistently one of the better players. His creativity and pass-before-shoot style made those playing with him look good, if not better than they were. Naturally, it made him popular.

It was more than two, but less than four weeks after a surveillance of his routine established a pattern when Special Agent Walter Reed dusted off his sneakers and Division III skills and began showing up to get in the game.

When first hearing his rural twang, Reed saw dirt-

...Both figuratively and in personification.

He knew the type.

Dirt was the nickname Reed tagged on a quiet classmate that came to his hometown of McLean by way of somewhere in the hills of West Virginia. Reed hadn't thought of him in years. Dirt lived in one of the apartments in the shadows of town where the people who serviced the domestic needs of the wealthy locals came to live and take advantage of being able to go to the public high school, the same one Reed resented he had to go to instead of where he went before his family's financial stumble. Dirt also worked summers with the early morning grounds crew at the country club where Reed's parents were still members. To his consternation at the time, one of the club's oldest and most revered gentleman members had taken kindly to Dirt and assumed the role of mentor. Fewer things infuriated Reed more than seeing the hillbilly interloper invited for periodic rounds of golf with his garage sale clubs and hand down white metal spikes, while he himself was limited by his parents to what he was allowed to sign for at the clubhouse. When seeing Dirt at the school homecoming dance the following fall, awkward in a brass buttoned navy blue blazer slightly big in the shoulders and long in the sleeves, he couldn't help but make sure everyone knew the jacket was a charity loan, then and again years later at school reunions.

He knew the type.

He took his time making first efforts at chatting Kenny up on subjects that extended past hoops. General weather, traffic and polite-personal.

Where you from?

No shit?

I heard they got some great fishing up there.

Ever have Amberjack? That's some good eatin'.

Reed was careful, not too pushy or intrusive. He adopted not a twang but a demeanor of weighted indifference when speaking, like they might not be from the same exact place but somewhere along a shared latitude. He made a conscious over-effort at not projecting any ulterior motives for his friendliness beyond being found and fed the ball to get a clean shot off, which he often was and without ever calling or waving for. Every move Walter Reed made was deliberate, done to service the sole reason for him being at the Lee YMCA evening game on the days when Kenny was: to establish a relationship on the chance there might be a gateway to Alan Copeland found within it.

Two weeks and a day after meeting Alan Copeland while adjusting the damage on his stepdaughter's car, Kenny Wayne Rehage went to work for the *Mutual Fidelity Benefits and Trust Company*. Upon arriving at the office, he discovered that not only wasn't his role defined, Copeland had completely forgotten ever having met him. After the quick realization and insincere apology, Copeland took him by the arm and into his office and immediately chopped his name in half. From there on in he would be Kenny and not Kenny Wayne, as Copeland didn't want to give the impression that any of the people who worked him fucked their first cousins. He pointed for him to sit on a couch then began rolling calls as if he weren't there.

Kenny did as he was told.

He sat.

Quietly.

Waiting.

He spent three days waiting, the last of which saw the work day end, leaving him alone in the office with only the janitor, who asked in broken English how much longer he'd be there. The following day as he was about to ask if there had been some sort of misunderstanding, Copeland motioned for Kenny to follow him-

C'mon. Take a ride.

And in the car he would sit beside Copeland much like he did in the office.

Quietly.

Waiting.

Again, Copeland rolled calls as if Kenny weren't there, speaking freely and without discretion. When he acknowledged his presence, he asked questions about Kenny's past, including pointing out the jagged, raised red scar on his inner forearm and asked how he got it, which Kenny told him resulted from an accident he had as a kid. Copeland let it go, so as not to interrupt the ingress into sharing thoughts and anecdotes from his own past, both real and imagined. And somewhere within one of those interactions, a Tourette's like gear-changing brought with it the subject of compensation, delivered on the back of a single breath. Whatever Kenny was earning weekly as an automotive insurance claims adjuster would be doubled.

For now.

But you better not fuck me.

If I take care of you, you better not fuck me.

There was still no explanation of what he would be required to do in exchange for his pay. Unbeknownst to Kenny, Copeland had been silently weighing the pros and cons of starting him out on the phones, but the idea of putting him in Scooter Wrobel's boiler room so soon might scare him off. To pair him with Aléjandro Perez concentrating on more boots on the ground retail investor solicitations seemed a good fit but ultimately decided on having him trail Howie Ygelsias, who among many other facets of the day to day business, oversaw policy acquisitions. He needed to show him how it worked from the outside in, not the inside out. Copeland had been well aware that Ygelsias would immediately try to stake a proprietary claim on the new blood and mold him in his own vision, as these businesses were all about allegiances. It didn't matter who signed this paycheck so much as who would be signing the next one. If Kenny was to be Copeland's and Copeland's alone, he would have to be kept close to the nest for a bit. Shortly thereafter he was dispatched to the new home Copeland and Karen were building down in Normandy Isles, charged with keeping an eye on things.

Make sure this contractor isn't fucking me.

Make sure no one's hangin' around who shouldn't be.

Make sure nothing's coming in the front, goin' out the back.

The first eight months of Kenny's tenure at the *Mutual Fidelity Benefits and Trust Company* was uneventful, spent in a holding pattern, out of sight and out of mind with only sporadic visits from Copeland that felt like social calls and the afterthought check-ins from faceless secretaries. It changed when on one of his visits Copeland succumbed to a whim.

Come on. Take a ride.

Kenny was ready to be introduced and conscripted to the non-practicing lawyer Howie Yglesias and the world of viatical acquisitions harvesting. Yglesias was born and bred in Homestead but now Miami was home. He became it. He dressed Miami. He thought Miami, dined Miami and partied Miami but was all too often asked if he was from L.A. Kenny experienced when shaking his hand for the first time a sense of something overwhelmingly odious. Nothing tangible like in the texture of his skin or grip pressure at exchange, nor even in his synthetic smile, veneered white teeth flashing like a caution sign, but more like a charged electrical current that made its way from Ygelesia's soul down his arm, through the palm of his hand into Kenny's consciousness, divulging secrets no one would never want made public. Kenny began accompanying him on his rounds, quietly observing as he was shown the procedural component of finalizing the purchasing of policies-

> *...Just a few signatures...here...then right here-*
> *...Annnnd just one more right...here-*
> *...And that should do it.*

Then a check would be handed over, which was always paperclipped to the seller's copy of the contract so the amount was conspicuously visible at all times. And that check, like some sort of panacea to those receiving it, was desperately grabbed and clutched onto, not with their hands...no...never their hands...but with their eyes. It was as if their hands were committed liars, with their measured and hesitant movements, efforts to pretend the payment for their life insurance policies was nothing more than a postscript to the transaction, borne of the guilt felt from selling out. It was the ultimate sell out. They were being paid the literal value, in the eyes of an industry, of their very lives. These appointments, typically in the homes of the clients, were little more than simple contract closings, which led Kenny to wonder if he was supposed to be doing on Copeland's behalf with Yglesias what he had been doing for him at the home building site.

A small, one room, rent controlled apartment in Dania Beach three blocks from the ocean that may as well have been three thousand. Inside, musty and dank. Stagnant, stale air. The apartment's anemic curtains that hadn't been opened in years prevented any natural light from coming through the small windows. And then the sound of a commercial jetliner making its final approach into FLL, a sound she no longer heard, but still made the curtains shiver. On the walls hung several framed prints of Bavarian landscapes, long taken for granted, the glass in front of them covered with an oily film consisting of dust, moisture and residual cigarette exhaust. Another frame. Not hanging on the wall but resting on a shelf next to a small plastic plant. A single, eight-by-ten black and white photo. An Army man, smiling. Sparkling eyes. She'd probably long forgotten it being her favorite one of him. An end table covered by a lace doily with yellowing edges. On it, a small wooden music box and radio that might or might not have worked. An ornamental ceramic beer stein with the Baden-Wurttemberg coat of arms on it filled with pencils and rubber bands, far too many for any one person to make use of. She was gaunt and old but not as old as she looked. Gray skin, pallid. On a narrow unmade daybed that she also slept upon, she sat in the same house dress, white socks and broken down slippers she wore every day. An oxygen cylinder stood nearby on a portable cart, the tubes hanging alongside waiting to be called upon. Yglesias sat at the table looking over the paperwork with Kenny next to him, his eyes still studying every inch of the room, then going from the ashtray on the table to the pack of cigarettes in the woman's hand, not realizing he vocalized the question of why she still smoked and if she ever thought about quitting. And she answered him with a shrug and in an indistinguishable, soft German accent, her words holding little emotion, almost clinical in delivery. *They made her feel good.* The cigarettes. *She didn't have many comforts and this was one of them.* Her killer. The cigarettes, her only comfort. Later, as they walked back to the car and Ygelesias tucked the envelope holding the signed contract they'd just closed into his shirt pocket, the woman would only be party to one more of his thoughts. *What's wrong with you, man? Trying to get her to quit smoking? Do you not get it?* Kenny protested that he was only making small talk with her and was immediately rebuked, reminded that by law she still had seventy-two hours to walk back the agreement. Kenny wondered, *and then do what? Join a health club?* He held that thought as Ygelesias continued his lecture.

You don't want to give her any ideas, guy.

I didn't know that, sorry.

Well, now you do. I won't tell Mr. Copeland. Let's go get something to eat.

When Copeland first explained to him what they did at the *Mutual Fidelity Benefits and Trust Company*, Kenny imagined it was just another one of the many unusual jobs out there, specialty jobs that most people didn't even know existed. He wondered who the first person was that had the idea to turn this practice into a business, much in the way one might wonder who the first person was to set eyes upon an oyster and decide to break it open and eat its slithery, briny innards. Copeland had told him, warned him that he wouldn't be at all surprised if it felt strange at first, interacting with people that knew they would soon be dead and explained that was only because of the way society conditioned us in dealing with death and mortality, following up with his staple, go-to rationalization that they were providing a service to people, which didn't seem untrue based on what Kenny had seen thus far. He could honestly attest to the fact that in that small, dank rent-controlled apartment, the cancer ravaged and chain-smoking woman, of free will and sound mind, signed her life insurance policy over as she waited around to die. There was no sleight-of-hand trickery involved, no double-talking and no fine print hiding in the footers of the contract. Still, to Kenny it felt strange. Sad. Depressing. But unethical-?

...No.

A few weeks later, more than three, but less than five, Kenny had heard the woman from Dania Beach died and hoped she'd spent all the money she got from the policy, though it was unlikely. That afternoon he and Yglesias sat at the kitchen table of a brightly lit townhouse in Fort Lauderdale. It was located in one of the homogenous developments that seemed to permeate the area, uniform structures, white with red roofs, small patches of Zoysia grass in front and neighbors that tended to keep to themselves. The interior was modern and clean. The appliances had been untouched, unlikely a single meal ever prepared upon them. The stainless steel refrigerator had take-out menus held to the door by magnets. What had struck Kenny as odd was the sparseness of the walls. The pictures were generic, afterthoughts purchased for the sake of taking up space. There wasn't a single framed photograph personal in nature, not on the bookless bookshelves, end tables or countertops. No imagery showing evidence of any loved ones or reminders of a place once called home. Not even a beloved pet. The condo was rented by two divorced men in their late seventies. Roommates. Both were about to sell their life insurance policies to the *Mutual Fidelity Benefits and Trust Company*. They sat across from Yglesias and Kenny, relaxed, tanned and dressed in clothing that was casual but incongruous with what men their age might ordinarily be wearing, more likely seen on college students or aging surf gods. The only tell-tale of their ages in relation to their attire was the white sneakers with velcro straps on one of them. The other was fully committed, he wore flip-flops, the kind with a bottle opener on the soles. They had a mirthful, mischievous ambience to them. Eyes darting around to make sure nothing fun was going on that they should miss out on. Neither projected a mean spirited nature. Instead, a *appetit-de-vivre* that leaned toward indecent merriment and recklessness. This meeting, or closing of viatical settlement agreements, was a happy hour. A literal happy hour, designated as such by one of the geriatric party monster clients when he asked if anyone wanted a beer.

Kenny politely declined.

Yglesias accepted.

Three bottles of Heineken were opened with the bottom of a flip-flop like it was a toy never tired of being shown off.

Clink-clink-

Cheers!

They were natives of Pennsylvania, the Main Line suburb outside of Philly. Both had lived slightly better than upper middle class lives. Their respective existences ran parallel in that despite enjoying success, their lives had become unremarkable at a certain point. Into their early sixties things slowed down. Extra-marital affairs were no longer realistically viable diversions and fewer business trips were taken with the discreet massage parlor visits. Boredom set in for both which manifested into acute dissatisfaction and resentment. Their wives had crossed from matronly into the grand matronly, a stark, glove-to-the-mush reminder that their own virility had passed its expiration date, slipped away into the night without so much as a goodbye. They found themselves castaways in the darkness, adrift in a purgatory of stultification. Until they discovered the small, magic, blue pill reset button. The good life that once was had reappeared in the doorway, horned and tailed, pitch fork in hand, grinning and breathing fire-

...Heeeere's Johnny.

From there, the very looking across the bed at their wives became not only more unappealing but outrightly repulsive. A short spell of wildly unacceptable actions nuked both marriages into otherworldly orbits, resulting in the collateral damage of estrangements from children and grandchildren. It didn't matter. These two didn't give a shit. Their children and children's children were all looked upon as ungrateful takers, enjoying the spoils of their hard work. Now, it was time for them to enjoy themselves. To put themselves first. Doing so was set after with both guns blazing, a vigor that suggested the lost years might all be reclaimed in a single afternoon. They were going out with the bangiest of bangs, celebrating their own funeral celebrations preemptively, with all the trimmings of a Viking Chieftain's *sjaund*.

Clink-clink-

Cheers!

One of them interrupted Ygelsias's closing pitch when he realized Kansas State was playing Kansas later and reminded himself to get his bet in, then asked the other what the spread was and who he liked. The discussion took a quick turn to hookers. Yglesias turned and gave a sneaking, impish look to Kenny, catching his eye and grinning. *How great are these two?* Kenny did his best to mask his shock at it all. The discussion was on the merits of each variety of call girls, the opinion of one of the men being Russians beat out Latinas, then Asians. The other claimed it was Asians, Latinas then Russians. Yglesias was turned to for the tie breaker and played politically savvy. Latin for the win, Asians to place and Russians to show. As long as they didn't have a cock. And of course the two men exploded with laughter. Then-

...Just a few signatures...here...then right here-

...Annnnd just one more right...here-

...And that should do it.

One of the men reached into his pocket, producing a small vial. *Who wants to do a rail?* And a small mirror materialized. With the ink still wet on the contracts, Yglesias had the professional fortitude to expedite a polite retreat, a swig of the beer and telling the men they had another meeting but would try to call them later to hang out if they got done in time, which roughly translated into 'no fucking way, the sooner we're outta here, the better.'

Cheers!

Clink-clink.

Yglesias and Kenny left, but not without one of them warning Kenny that he should lighten up, as he'll come to see soon enough that life's short. Kenny nodded politely, smiled sheepish and told the man he'd try. On the way to the car, Yglesias chastised Kenny for looking so shocked. *We get all kinds.* Kenny found it odd that they would seek the company out to sell their policies in that it didn't look like they needed money. Another rebuke and head shake. *They don't come to us. What's wrong with you, guy? We find them. Yeah. You gotta go out and find the business. Did your mother ever have Tupperware parties? Well, we host parties to recruit guys like that. We got big screen TV's with the games on, strippers, booze, blow, weed. Whatever it takes.* Kenny still couldn't hide his disbelief. *Big business, guy. Big business. Tons like 'em all over South Florida. Millions in policies. Millions.*

Again, Kenny found it depressing. He didn't feel sorry for those two like he did the lady in Daria Beach. He genuinely disliked them. They were selfish bastards. He thought about it a little more and considered them cowards, too. Unable to do what they were supposed to do by their families, no matter how bad they thought things got for them, no matter what they thought they missed out on. And from what he heard, they never had it that bad at all. In fact, they had it pretty damn good. They had no idea what the definition of hard was. Then he wondered if he was being a little bit of a coward himself.

Throughout the continuing orientation process, Ygelsias talked down to Kenny. He rolled his eyes at him, shook his head and sighed condescendingly. Kenny understood it wasn't personal, just one man's demeanor, the kind of person who saw everyone as a threat.

They found themselves late one morning at a guest house set behind a majestic Indian Creek mansion. The man occupying it was skilled in the art of the freeload. In his late fifties, he was once a giant, now just tall, arthritic and experiencing something that had yet to happen to him: He was being shut down. Cut off. Turned out. And at the worst of times. He was a former football player. His knees were shot, as were his hips. His kidneys were failing with his liver not far behind. The Percodan had done its job, as advertised. And now his long-time bro-host was evicting him. The new wife insisted. He'd give him five grand to get on his feet, but she can't find out. Five thousand dollars. For twenty years of loyal wingmanship. Five thousand dollars. His N.F.L. signing bonus was three hundred thousand. It wasn't supposed to be like this. The All-American offensive lineman, who when he'd had enough of professional football after two seasons and professional football enough of him, set his sights on Hollywood. He believed Stallone didn't have shit on him. The young football fanboy movie executives embraced him with open arms, reinforcing his belief. He laughed at their jokes and they entertained his ambitions. Then, it was over. Where the N.F.L. was a flame out, Hollywood was a slow burn. Left with nothing. No savings. Just a Chicago Bears helmet. Photographs and memories of forgettable films he was inserted into the background of by the football fanboy movie executives, his bro-host the primary enabler. And the copies of unproduced, painfully hackneyed screenplays he'd written as starring vehicles for himself. He had those. And the watercolors he'd painted when he decided he was an artist, too. And the music. He had the music. The simple guitar chords that accompanied fatuous lyrics, sang in a voice that was unremarkable at best. Stallone didn't have shit on him. The only thing he did have that could be considered of value by anyone other than himself-

...The policy.

He had that.

While the viatical settlement agreement was reviewed, Yglesias and Kenny endured his glory stories of yesteryear in a tone of voice that rang less of triumph and more woe-is-me.

...Just a few signatures...here...then right here-

...Annnnd just one more right...here-

...And that should do it.

Whatever he was going on about neither Yglesias nor Kenny heard. They'd turned him off. The only thing they were interested in was what was scribbled above the dotted lines next to the little yellow sticker flags. Kenny thought about the clients they visited until that point. Upon reconsideration, he didn't have pity for any of them. Not even the old German lady in Daria Beach. They all made their own choices, her included. They all made their choices. When they left Indian Creek, Yglesias pointed to where he thought Hulk Hogan lived, then at the basketball coach Rick Pitino's house but had nothing to criticize Kenny over. Still, when Copeland checked in with him later for a report on Kenny's progress, Yglesias shit-talked him.

Of course he did.

Copeland had Kenny spend time eventually in the phone room with Scooter Wrobel but specifically didn't want him rolling calls. The same with Aléjandro Perez but still, he had bigger plans for him. What exactly they would be, he didn't know but sometimes found himself when in Kenny's company involuntarily thinking about his own son Scott, from whom he hadn't heard in years. Way back in the far reaches of his mind, he wondered-

...Maybe-

...Maybe-

...If the kid worked out-

...Maybe...he can-

He always stopped short of finishing the thought.

Come on. Take a ride.

Copeland kept him close while trying still to keep him at arm's length, a juggling act of incongruity. Despite getting periodic cash bonuses in the thousands of dollars and being given a Rolex, Kenny was often kept waiting outside or in the car, summoned only when Copeland needed him. Even when they went by Copeland's house. He had never been properly introduced to his wife. It was Karen who saw Kenny out by the car once-

Who's that?

...And sashayed out to introduce herself, apologizing for her husband being so rude. *New Yorkers.* And she smiled, assuming that would explain everything. Kenny thought Karen had a nice way about her, despite the brash and flash and knowing he would never want to be seated next to her table at a restaurant. The shrill tone and pitch of her voice caused his fingers to stiffen on reflex.

He slowly became numb to the business practice and few things shocked or even surprised him. Any bad taste he originally had became dulled through repetition. When he sat in on a meeting with Copeland and an insurance company executive who was discreetly funneling leads for clients, clients who 'might be getting their affairs in order,' Kenny wasn't shocked or dismayed, as he might have been a year earlier. Even if the sharing of the information the executive was providing seemed to run against the grain of what an insurance agent is supposed to do. Kenny remembered something to that effect when he'd taken the course for his adjuster's license. He let it not bother him, in that the client wasn't going to be affected. They could always decline an overture. It was no different than getting junk mail or a robocall. And maybe they needed the money. Maybe the money would help them. His rationalization carried on when meeting fund managers, to whom better grade bundled lots were sold to. Not the shit ones peddled out of the boiler rooms. There were, as with any investment, varying projected return dates reflected by their value.

One-to-two year.

Two-to-three.

Three-to-five.

But the real cherries were the ones classified as short timers, those with life expectancies of under a year. And from there they were broken down into smaller informal subcategories used by the staff at the *Mutual Fidelity Benefits and Trust Company.*

'*Likely,*' short for likely not to make the end of the year-

'*Getting close,*' which meant under six months-

'*Circling the drain,*' weeks as opposed to months-

...And *'shovel ready,'* more or less meant *pull those fucking contracts up*, always heard to the imaginary tune of a heartrate monitor alarm flat lining.

And sometimes in those rated and bundled policies a few that might not have been as ripe as implied, inadvertently or not so inadvertently slipped in. Copeland shrugged when he explained. *It happens to the best of us.*

Kenny soon thereafter learned what the wet-ink policies and clean-sheeting was. A clean bill of health signed off on by a friendly physician despite the exams not being entirely accurate. Copeland was preemptively defensive in explaining them to Kenny.

It only happens occasionally-

And his justification was passionate. This was a simple leveling of the playing field. It helped people that might otherwise be taken advantage of by these companies.

And it only happens occasionally-

He schooled Kenny in the insurance companies long history of finding loopholes and reasons to cancel policies of their insured. That happened all the time. Far more than any policies being clean-sheeted.

That only happens occasionally-

He told him how insurance companies found convenient ways from fulfilling their responsibilities to the indemnified. He'd seen the simple clerical errors used as reasons to cancel policies or refuse renewals. *They're not the good guys, kid.* They had some very clever, high-paid people whose job it was just to find the smallest of details to cancel an insured's policy if it suited them. *You heard that executive last week bad-mouthing his own company? You heard him say what they do?* Kenny had no recollection of hearing an insurance company executive say anything to that effect. *Besides, it all evens out in the end. It's all priced in.*

Kenny chose to take Copeland's word for it because he liked his job. Strange, as he didn't like anyone he worked with, with the exception of Copeland's secretary Brenda. He didn't like the insurance company executives, the fund managers, Yglesias, Scooter Wrobel, Aléjandro Perez, the creepy doctor at the free clinic or the guys in the boiler room. But strangest of all-

He was starting to like Copeland.

He'd grown on him.

In spite of himself.

He'd grown on him.

Special Agent Walter Reed watched Kenny, able only to guess what was playing out in his mind. "Maybe I'm a little bit out of line asking you to understand-"

Kenny shook his head. "What did you think? I was gonna back out? I gave you my word-"

"Again, I'm sorry. This is never easy, man. Believe me. It's never easy."

Kenny looked at him, hints suggesting he was lightening up. "And you pretendin' to be my buddy-"

"Well, first of all, that's not too hard to do, you're a good guy-"

"Oh, don't kiss my ass, Walt-"

"I'm not! You're a good dude. Everything I've seen. You're a solid guy. A solid dude." He tried to digress. "You know they say you can tell a lot about a guy by the way he plays. And you're as unselfish on the court as anyone I'd ever seen. That wasn't lost on me, man.

Believe you me, that was not lost on me." Kenny didn't bite. "I've gone through this with plenty of assholes and had to put on the old happy face."

"Just listen to yourself. That makes it more of a violation of trust, far's I see it."

Just when Reed thought he'd made a step forward in remedying the problem, he was now knocked two back. He held up his hands, surrendering and Kenny didn't follow up. After a few moments, Reed tried to sum things up. "So, are we good, Kenny?" He then wished he'd waited a few seconds longer to ask.

Kenny didn't answer.

Reed got nervous and made another mistake. "This thing blows up, I'm going to get crushed, man. Trey's going to get crushed, our supervisor and probably even his boss is going to get crushed. I can't even begin to tell you-"

"None of that's my problem, Walt."

"I mean, just getting that car approved, the decoy, the wiretap. That was a full blown op in itself. And to get it done so soon after the warrant? This never happens. I mean, I don't expect you to know these details, but it never happens like this."

Kenny had seen Reed squirm enough and seemed to have a change of heart. "Alright. I get it. We all screw up. And at the end of the day, you don't know me any more than I know you. So maybe you couldn't be a hundred percent sure-"

The breakthrough gift Reed was hoping for came and a theatrical sigh. "Thanks for tryin' to understand, Kenny. Again, I'm really, really sorry. I should have known better. And I meant what I said with you being a solid guy-"

"Alright, let's just...get on with it."

"Oh, I could hug you, man. Thank you."

"I'd rather you not do that."

Kenny let up a little but left the vestige of a scowl on his face to let Reed know he still was annoyed.

Reed took another animated deep breath of relief. "I mean, this scumbag Copeland is just such a big damn fish, Kenny. You know that. He's a whopper. And maybe with a potential homicide in the fold makes it harder for him to buy his way out this time." He didn't immediately see the magnitude of impact his statement had on Kenny. The look in his eyes shifted from being close, to far away. They hardened, showing a different side of Kenny, his previous demeanor established as only one of aggravation, whereas now he was clearly enraged.

"Fuck you, Walt. I'm gonna call the lawyer."

Chapter Seven

Breathe

Copeland picked up US-1 where it met the I-95 down near Vizcaya only to be kneecapped at the top of the onramp by a suddenly manifested cluster, a DOT crawling maintenance crew less than a quarter mile ahead. Two of the northbound lanes were forced to alternately merge into the others.

He wasn't angry.

Not even irritated.

He didn't curse the workers nor any one of the dozen possible things to cast blame upon for slowing him down the three minutes that would have seen him beat it. A simple, controlled breath was his only reaction. It was an unusual transformation in temperament, something taking over his entire mindset that hadn't been there two turns or even five hundred feet previously. With Karen being fresh in his mind it might have been...maybe...finally, a result of her incessantly preaching the benefits of breathing, meditation and being better than the cause of a situation when it was maddening.

Be better than the moment, Alan. Be better than the moment.

Nom-Oh-Namaste-Namah-Nanah-

The yoga and meditation charade. That's where she got it from.

Nam-Oh-Namaste-Namah-

SHAMA-LAMA-DING-DONG! WHOP-BOP-A-LOO-OP! A-WOP-BAM-BOOM-!

Alan, grow up. Show some respect.

...TUTTI-FRUTTI! OH-RUDI-!

And he smiled when she stormed out of the room, again pretending to be angrier than she was. He thought it made sense when the Beatles were doing it. They had records to sell, he'd called out after her. And here he was stuck in traffic, himself and a controlled breath.

Okay. Is this guy gonna let me in?

At least she'd toned it down with the new age shit since the time she'd gotten into it. Maybe that's what it took for him to be open to the general idea of not letting things set him off, things that he couldn't control.

Thanks, buddy. You're a prince-

He fell into the line of other cars and looked out across the north by northwestern skyscape of the city, then across the bay over at the vista of the blinding white high rise towers in Miami Beach, many of which hadn't been there five years earlier. He felt a sense of satisfaction, a proprietary stake in the city itself, as if he were partly responsible for the recent real estate boom and cosmopolitan allure.

Then, what started out as a validating grin incited by a memory from around 1980-

Florida? No one's made money in Florida real estate since there's been a Florida!

His mother's best friend's son shot down the possibility. Any excuse to make Copeland feel inferior or ignorant. Any opinion, any suggestion stomped on, rubbed out and then shit over. He was a couple of years older and considered by Copeland a cousin. The sentiment was returned by considering Copeland less than an acquaintance, not even his mom's best friend's son.

His father works for my father.

And always accompanied by a *don't ask me why* gesture. It was because of him that Copeland still hated Corvettes.

Florida? No one's made money in Florida real estate since there's been a Florida!-

...His father works for my father.

Copeland took another look back over the skyline of Miami Beach.

...His father works for my father.

The validating thought then betrayed him, turning bittersweet. Copeland loved his dad but sadly came to a point in his life where he realized he didn't respect him, something that wasn't nor would ever be divulged to another living soul. He'd figured they were two different classifications of experiences, love and respect. One was an emotion, the other something difficult to put one's finger on, but earned and accrued. Copeland wondered if both feelings had to be reciprocal in order to exist, since he knew his father loved him but never saw any evidence as he grew older that he was respected by him. That was fine, as the feeling was mutual. But he did love his father, as his father was a decent man. He went to the office each day and came home each night to his family, rarely with anything to report. He was good to Copeland's mother, in that he always yielded to her wishes, whims and desires. He seldom said no, always providing the things Copeland and his sister not only needed but wanted, which at times had to have involved personal sacrifice. He never complained, but probably not because of stoicism. The truth was he'd been defeated without ever having been in the contest, a go-through-the-motions functionary not only in his career but in his family life as well. His lifelong propensity to risk aversion and avoiding confrontation turned him into a doormat for everyone from Copeland's mother and sister to his neighbors, his boss and even his boss's son. Through it all, Copeland had never seen his father express frustration or any kind of outward suffering that comes with humiliation, unsure he'd even been aware he was being subjected to it, as it was low decibel and in perpetuity. Yet like many children, during Copeland's early years he lionized his father since all boys need heroes. Strange to him how a perspective could change so dramatically over the course of a little less than a quarter-life. And with it, that very thought awakened the Saturday afternoon Coney Island nursing home visits of his youth. To see his grandfather, his father's father, the immigrant. The imagery played out in choppy, flickering eight millimeter movie clips of his mind.

His grandfather.

His father's father.

The immigrant.

Sitting in a chair trapped within the grips of dementia, looking up at Copeland's father smiling as they entered the room. The young Copeland assumed the smile was one of paternal pride and joy but the old man didn't know if he was sitting poolside at Grossinger's or in the basket of a hot air balloon high above a field of lollipops. The smile was more likely for the store-bought Entenmann's crumb cake his mother was holding. The room, in a twelve-story white brick building directly off the boardwalk, had a revolting sour smell, the sense memory of which still caused Copeland's nostrils to contract. Hints of urine and medicated skin lotion hanging in the air that he remembered as clearly as the crumb cake and the smile on his face.

His grandfather.

His father's father.

The immigrant.

Who he was told would regularly and loudly insist that he not be called a butcher, never a butcher but a meat-cutter. Who wanted nothing more than assimilation and the American dream for the family he would have when he came to this country, so much that trading out the surname Kaplowitz and adopting an Anglicized version was a small price to pay for making the doing so easier for his children. He was the real hero. And that one Saturday when they bid his grandfather goodbye until the next week, walking from the nursing home to the car parked on a side street, seeing the three Puerto Rican boys peering inside, looking to see whether there was anything worth breaking a window for. For years Copeland had thought it was his father that chased them off with an aggressive charge. It wasn't. The choppy, flickering eight millimeter movie clips of his mind had been cut and

spliced so a boy can have a hero. The unedited, *in veritas* version
showed his mother, Mabel, initiating the defense. His father's efforts
only followed her's, a few impotent displays of stammering and
gesticulation and threats to call the police. And looking back, the
reality of how much younger and smaller the Puerto Rican boys now
were, no more than thirteen or fourteen and scattered terrified as if a
pinless grenade landed at their feet when his mother screamed at them.
Copeland pitied his father, the man who was supposed to be his hero.
Watching him cut the lawn on weekends in the summer, the loose gold
chain with the symbol that translated to 'life,' that would work its way
out of the V-neck collar of his undershirt as he pushed the mower, his
thin arms and narrow accountant's shoulders hunched forward. Life.
Some life. The polyester plaid shorts that showed too much pale
skinny leg, tight black socks pulled up his calves and tennis shoes on
his feet.

Alan, you should be doing that for your father!

No, Mabel. I want to do it.

Alan, help your father!

I don't want any help, Mabel. Let him be.

It was one of the only times he stood up to Copeland's mother,
as he was probably enjoying some kind of sanctuary in the chore.
That, or committed to an act of self-flagellation. And he'd stop to
wipe his brow and tuck the chain back inside the shirt only to see it fall
out seconds later. There was something emblematic of his character in
the repetitive motion of doing so over and again-

...Stopping-

...Wiping his brow-

...Tucking the chain back inside his shirt.

...As if he expected a different result this time.

If in his heart Copeland believed his father was genuinely satisfied with his woeful station in life, that he'd desired an existence completely devoid of spirit or passion, of being the windless flag of a man that he was, it would have been okay. But he knew his father secretly yearned to be more. The extended private moment time in the bathroom mirror and the cologne he wore was evidence. And his futile attempts to dress like the men in the Canadian Club whiskey ads of the Penthouse magazines he poorly hid in his bottom dresser drawer. Copeland's father, like every other man, wanted to be noticed. He wanted to be virile but never did anything about it. And when his father's time came not longer after his mother passed, Copeland felt guilty for not being inconsolable as he was laid low. The underlying grief he did feel was not over his father's death, but over his life. The life he chose not to live. Copeland never doubted his father was a decent man. He simply wished he'd done more in his lifetime for himself. Copeland did love his father, but that love was overshadowed by a lack of respect for him.

Dd-Dd-Dd-Dd-Dd-Dd-Dd-Dd-Dd-Dd-Dd-Dd-Dd-Dd-Dd-

...Copeland's Rolls Royce Phantom had drifted ever so slightly out of the lane. He snapped to attention hearing/feeling the staccato stutter steps of the rumble strip on the shoulder and immediately corrected, blinked and gave his head a chastising shake, chasing off the strains of melancholia he allowed in. And after what started as a good thought, no less. A thought of triumph. Only to be followed up by a downer. He thought to call the office and check in with Brenda but something made him think of his stepdaughter Lauren and her having recently gotten engaged to Marcus Mendelsohn or Mendel Marcusson or whatever his name was.

Fuckin' putz.

According to Karen, Lauren wants to get married in Tuscany.

Big surprise, that. A destination wedding, which for Copeland was a word pairing right up there with root canal or ass rape. Fewer things were more painfully drawn out than destination weddings, a succession of overly produced, unoriginal force-coordinated events halfway around the world-

I'd rather be stuck in an elevator halfway around the world.

He considered how he might be able to redirect or negotiate having her get married locally but reality dictated that his voice would be entirely ignored in regard to it. All he heard in his head was Karen's voice-

Oh, Alan, it'll be beautiful. Tuscany!

Copeland's response to her looked like he'd had a gas pain.

You know, you're not happy unless you're miserable, Alan. You know that-?

Not true, Karen.

...It's a condition that plagues you, my dear.

No, I'm not happy unless I'm happy. I just think going all the way to Europe for a week with all those...people, most who we hardly know...for a...wedding that...let's face it, there's no guarantee will-

As if on cue, a nondescript sports utility vehicle drafted up alongside him. The passengers were a man and a woman, late twenties and as ordinarily nondescript as the vehicle they were traveling in. She was behind the wheel, he was in the passenger seat, leaning over the console screaming at her. Hollering. He was nearly frothing at the mouth with anger, his stiff forefinger pointed inches from her face. And as soon as he'd hesitated to take a quick breath to reload, she swung toward him and returned the volley with equal fury.

Whoa, *keep your eyes on the road, toots.*

Copeland then noticed in the backseat of their sports utility vehicle, an empty children's car seat.

And he smiled.

Oh, to somehow freeze the moment. Save that very scene and bring it to Marcus Mendelsohn or Mendel Marcusson or whatever his *putz* name was and have him peek into this little viewfinder of what very well could be the coming attractions of his life...albeit probably not in an ordinary sports utility vehicle. Lauren wouldn't be caught dead in a Nissan.

Where the hell am I goin'? What the fuck?

Copeland interrupted his wishful thinking for a moment and seemed suddenly confused.

Great. This is all I need. Like my grandfather, the meat-cutter. Sitting in my own soiled underwear feeding the seagulls on the boardwalk. Do me a favor and just put two behind my ear.

Then it came back to him. Copeland wasn't sure why Kenny wanted to see him. The kid. He was going to meet him simply because Kenny had asked him to. Copeland loved that about him. He loved that if the kid wanted to talk to him about something that would involve more than a one word answer, he asked for an audience. He'd ask if he could step into his office and shut the door behind them or

111

swing by the house. Or walk out with him to his car. He didn't like to send emails or even talk over the phone and never explained why. It just wasn't his style. There was something so honest about it, something so safe and discreet. Copeland wished they all were like that.

The phone rang.

"Yeah?"

It was Brenda.

"Hey, Alan-"

"What's up? I was just gonna call you to check in."

"Just giving you your calls." He waited for her to continue. *"You have Caleb Flynn from Flushing Capital, return when you can. Tom O'Donnell, same thing. Return. When you can. Nolan Beekes, said nothing urgent and your father-in-law, Mr. Habermann-"*

"What did he want?" Copeland sounded almost excited, and without realizing it.

"Just return when you can." A pause. *"Do you want me to...try him? Mr. Habermann?"*

Pause.

"No. No. Anything else?"

"That's it. That's it for right now. You're aware you have a conference call with the group from Triad Properties at Three-Thirty about the follow up for the Ponce de Leon development?"

"I thought we punted on that?"

"You didn't tell me that. Do you want me to cancel?"

Copeland thought for a second. "No. We'll do it. Fuck it, we'll do the call. I'll be back in the office by then."

Silence.

"Alan?"

"Yeah."

"Oh, you're there. I thought you dropped."

"No, I'm here. That's it?"

Pause.

"That's it."

"Okay. Call me if anything comes up."

"Will do, Alan."

"Oh, Brenda. One more thing. Can you schedule a massage for me at Five?"

She must have had his day's agenda in front of her because she questioned his request. *"You're aware you have dinner tonight with Mrs. Copeland? The Yosts? Six o'clock."*

"Yeah. That's right. Book it for four then, we'll be a little late to dinner."

He disconnected without saying goodbye, as was his habit.

Kenny.

The kid.

I wonder what he wants.

A silent moment of reflection, then an epiphany-like thought-

He's leaving. He's quitting. He's moving on.

Copeland just sensed it. Kenny was taking another job and wanted to tell him face-to-face. Copeland didn't have any indicators, any empirical evidence to point to that. It was just a feeling, a feeling about the way Kenny asked to see him this time that he could sense it was about something significant.

113

A deep sigh.

It shouldn't come as a surprise, Copeland thought. As much as Copeland wanted this for him, this business, the kid never was really cut out for it. Despite his talents. Too nice. Too innocent. And he still wasn't licensed. Copeland couldn't figure out how a kid so smart was able to fail the test both times, figuring him for one of those dyslexics. Or he didn't want it. He had tilted his hand already when he told Copeland that he could see himself someday enrolling in college, getting a degree then teaching high school and coaching basketball. Copeland had spit his coffee out.

You gotta be shittin' me! I gotta give it to you kid, that is the first time I ever heard you say something stupid-

And the ever-so-slightly defensive posture assumed by Kenny, the first and only time he'd looked like he wished he could walk back something just said.

Go to college for four years? Pay money for tuition for what? So you can make less money than you're makin' now? You got any idea how many college graduates would drag their balls over broken glass to get the package you got? Look where you live! Look at the fucking car you drive!

Then Kenny dropped the subject and seemingly let it blow off down the road like a plastic bag in a windswall.

Copeland knew why the prospect of Kenny leaving bothered him so much. He equated him to an investment, something like a biotech stock that's valuation wasn't determined by a conventional bottom line metric, a price-to-earnings ratio, but the possibility of producing a groundbreaking innovation. And when it arrived, its price would skyrocket a hundred fold. Maybe in Kenny's case it wasn't going to be in viaticals, but he was going to make Copeland money in something, and a lot of it. He could feel it in the marrow of his very bones and simply couldn't allow him to leave, dreading few things more than the possibility of letting go of something right before it matured.

Copeland sped past the sports utility vehicle with the fighting couple in it that was pulled off in the shoulder of the road ahead. He didn't notice they'd gotten that far ahead of him. The multitasking had probably become too much for her, or she was throwing him out of the car.

Who knows?, Copeland asked himself.

Maybe he's not going anywhere.

The kid.

Kenny.

A positive thought found its way back into the fold.

Maybe he wants advice on something.

Copeland considered the likelihood of the kid asking his thoughts about getting married to that little girlfriend of his and the possibility triggered a miniscule grin on his face that he didn't know was there. If that was the case, Copeland wouldn't need a little viewfinder for him to peer into portending what the future might hold for him.

No. No way-

This kid had great instincts. He would tell him that.

...Great instincts. Trust them.

Copeland wanted it to be that, Kenny asking him what his thoughts were on his getting married. It would make his day. Not to mention, it would be good. If the kid got married, he'd be dependent on him. Leaving to take another job or go to college wouldn't be so easy. He'd be dependent upon him much like his father was dependent upon his mother's best friend's husband. And then he drove in silence for nearly the entire distance between exits.

He scrolled through his phone list and hit a number.

"Mr. Copeland's office."

"Brenda, it's me."

"Hey, Alan." She said it as if they hadn't spoken five minutes earlier.

"Can you try Habermann?"

"One second." She put him on hold and seemed to be back as quickly as she left. *"He's in a meeting, I left word."*

"Okay."

"Do you want me to try anyone else?"

Silence.

"No. Not now. Thanks."

Again he disconnected and with it he thought of Scott, as it was probably inevitable. He wondered if he was married, then figured he'd have heard. Part of him respected that Scott didn't come sniffing around when Copeland got rich. But part of him wished he had. And the changing of his last name didn't bother him, although he pretended it did at the time. What's one more change over the course of a few generations? But what a choice. From Scott Copeland to Scott Stillwater.

Stillwater.

Copeland still couldn't say it with a straight face-

Stillwater.

He may as well have changed it to ball-sniffer.

Stillwater.

Like he's some kind of American Indian now. Perfect for...he had to think about what his son was doing for a living...an Associate Producer at National Public Radio. Whatever that means. Probably in charge of mailing out the cloth tote bags to the Upper West Side cat ladies that donate twenty-five dollars or more during the fundraising drive.

Stillwater.

And a moment followed, one of complete honesty. He failed as a father. But so did his father, in his own way. And who knows? Maybe the meat-cutter did, too. He wasn't around to see him during his prime time. Copeland then realized he was thirsty. He threw his hand behind the seat for the bottle of Diet Pepsi, having forgotten it was on the passenger seat next to him and when he did grab it, saw it was empty.

The kid's probably gonna tell me he's leavin'.

Then he thought about the possibility of pitching him on doing something in real estate. Maybe have him sit in on that Triad Properties conference call later about the follow up for the *Ponce de Leon* development prospectus. With Schwartz. Maybe there's something worthwhile there. That could be good. Maybe we'll do that. Get into that deal.

Florida real estate. No one's made money in Florida real estate since there's been a Florida!

It then dawned on Copeland that he had been driving in silence the whole time. He asked himself why he wasn't playing any music,

117

forgetting how much he hated silence and for good reason as things he didn't like to think about always had a way of showing up.

Let's play some music. Let's hear Mick and the boys.

He fiddled around with his sound system and *Beggar's Banquet* began to play with the unmistakable intro to *Sympathy For The Devil* leading the way. He turned up the volume and relaxed into it.

SPLAT-

Abstract, mostly white and grey bits of green and yellow goo exploded down and across his windshield. It had to have been a pelican.

Mo-th-er-fuck-er!

He looked up through the windshield like he might be asked later to give a description of the offending bird, but saw nothing.

Breathe.

Nam-Oh-Namaste-Namah-

And he actually managed to laugh.

Chapter Eight

One Small Bundle

Kenny sat in his car in the exact place he'd parked. Reed moved his sedan to a different part of the lot to better blend in or give the impression he wasn't keeping an eye on Kenny, maybe taking the time to address the damage he'd caused and considering how to control it. But all the same, he was watching and waiting. Kenny knew Reed was nervous and wanted to laugh at the obviousness of his efforts to look natural, how childish it all was and wondered what exactly they taught these guys in the Academy. And he sat with the engine running solely for the sake of the air conditioner, giving Reed nothing more to see than a simple shaking of his head, the ever-so-slight, side-to-side movement within that little area between disbelief and disgust, all while keeping the agent in view from the corner of his own eye. There was little doubt Kenny had a much better idea of what was playing out in Reed's head than Reed could guess what was playing out in his, even if he couldn't hear what he was saying.

Reed was on the phone with his partner, Special Agent Trey Stubblefield. It was on speaker mode, resting unseen in his hand next to his leg. His frustration was two-pronged. "...I can hardly understand a word you're saying, man-"

The response was muffled and spoken slower than previously. *"I th-aid whaa-duh-ya-mean doeh-noth-uh?"* It sounded like Stubblefield's tongue was three sizes too big for his mouth.

"He's not doing shit! He's just sitting there-"

Stubblefield could be heard sighing. *"Muh-buh he's jus...coo-uh off-"*

"What?" Reed had no idea what his partner said.

"I..suh...muh-buh he's jus coo-uh-off-" It was as if he could see Reed's facial expression through the phone and was triggered by it. *"Fuh-mah...I juh-wauh ou-a th-fuh-kuh dent-uh off-ah. I caaa feel muh fuh-kuh face-"*

Reed then mumbled to himself, inaudibly so Stubblefield couldn't hear. "Great friggin' day to pick to go to the dentist." He looked over again at Kenny sitting in his car even less discreetly than he thought he'd been before, then looked back down at his phone as if it were the personification of his partner. "You think I should call him?"

"Whuu?"

"Lucic. You think we should call him?" Stubblefield could be heard emitting the kind of grunt one serves up when a terrible idea is presented. Reed went on. "...I mean, he would want to know about this right away. I mean...like...right away."

He paused to allow Stubblefield to respond. He didn't.

"What do you think, Trey? Should we call Looch now or wait a little bit? Again Reed looked at Kenny sitting in his car. "You can just grunt once for yes...twice for no."

"Fuh-yu."

Another look toward Kenny, then he made a command decision. "I'll call him if he drives off. But not 'till then. As long as he's still here, he's in play. Maybe you're right. Maybe he's just cooling off."

Stubblefield's response was unintelligible.

"Maybe I'll give it another minute and knock on his window-"

Another unintelligible statement came from his partner on the other end, this one seemingly emphatic. It sounded like he'd just gotten into his own car.

Reed continued, more speaking aloud for his own benefit than for Stubblefield's. "I'll play it by telling him I'm sorry and to go ahead and call the lawyer. And if he wants to walk, it's entirely within his rights, he shouldn't feel bad. We were the assholes here and I totally understand. Play it that way."

A pause. No response.

"You know what I mean, Trey? I won't guilt trip him. I'll just tell him...my bad and good luck to him, thanks anyway." Another pause. "Maybe see if he calls my bluff."

"Uhhh-Uhhh-" The directive was assertive and delivered with a sense of urgency.

"What?"

"Wheh-ahhhh-you?"

"Where am I? In my car, where do you think?"

"Uhh knuh! Wa-huh? Wa-huh ahhhh-you"

Reed looked out toward the intersection traffic signal. "Oh. North West Forty-Second and Gratigny. The gas station next to the Winn Dixie-"

"Uhh-buh-thuh-uh-soo-as-uh-cuh-"

"What?"

"Uhh-buh-thuh-uh-soo-as-uh-cuh-"

I don't understand a word you just said, Trey. Did you say you're coming over to me?"

Stubblefield grunted once.

Across the parking lot in his car, Kenny looked at his phone, deciding that he had to make a call. It didn't matter to who. She answered off one ring and immediately he regretted calling her.

"Hey."

"Hi."

"What are you doin'?"

"I'm at work. I just stepped away for a minute, going to get a carrot juice."

"It's gonna make your mouth orange."

"I'll keep that in mind."

He imagined her smile and furrowing of her eyebrows then forced himself to think of something else.

"What are you doing?"

"Work stuff," he told her. He didn't want to lie, trying desperately then to rationalize the validity of his response by considering what he was doing did qualify as such, but then thought it no different than saying 'taking the old dog for a walk,' while omitting that the walk was to the back of the barn where the old dog would be shot. "Nothing. I just...wanted to say hi."

"I'm glad you did." Then a spell of silence. It sounded like someone had asked her a question that she was answering without words. *"So, am I going to see you later?"*

"Yeah, sure." This time the lie had no problem making its way into the phone.

"Okay. Call me later when you're done."

"Okay."

He disconnected and broke from his typical controlled discipline of keeping emotions in check, slamming his fist down on the steering wheel and letting go a short burst of expletives.

In Reed's car, he watched and assumed Kenny just heard something he didn't want to hear, guessing it was advice from his lawyer. For the first time since Kenny walked away from him a full ten minutes earlier, he thought that maybe not all was lost and replayed the words in his head that set him off.

To FBI Special Agents Walter Reed, Trey Stubblefield and their supervisor, it wasn't the foundation on which the criminal investigation into the *Mutual Fidelity Benefits and Trust* corporation was being framed upon, but what might be found within it that tantalized even the smallest of sensory receptors associated with the cravings of ambition, on a par with what the smell of frying bacon does to salivary glands. The possibilities they came across were as delicious and they were profuse, beginning with a nightclub doorman that became a hedge fund analyst overnight-

...Literally-

...And in the Mirriam-Webster definitive sense, not the outraged teenager usage of the word.

No one knew the name given to the doorman at birth. He was known simply as 'Lazz,' eponymous with nightclub extravagance in South Beach and well-known in the L.A., Vegas, the Hamptons and New York City scenes as well. The exact reasons for his success in the field was hard to pinpoint. He wasn't terribly bright nor good looking. He had hair plugs seemingly with different ideas as to what they were supposed to be doing, short legs and a low, egg shaped torso attached to disproportionately long arms. There was no magnetic ingredient in his personality, nothing radiant in his smile and no sparkle in his eyes. He was inherently skilled, however, at recognizing individuals of status and the members of their circles, effortlessly pushing the boundaries of patronizing them to points inches from absurd insincerity then inserting himself into their lives. He took great pride in the menagerie he'd assembled of professional athletes, stars of film, television and music as well as those famous for nothing, the personalities in the emerging world of this thing called social media influence, whom he considered close personal friends. When a Saudi Prince gifted him a new Maybach as a gesture of thanks for having accommodated him at the club, Lazz hired himself a driver instead of selling the car, adding to his legacy as being the only nightclub doorman with his own chauffeur.

On what was said to be a whim, the crazy-obscenely, obscenely-crazy wealthy Dale Marlin, founder of Inferno Capital, a hedge fund, offered him a job. Lazz certainly wasn't looking but didn't hesitate accepting the offer. In the face of his being at the top of his game professionally, he was still cognizant of the fact that everyone and everything had a shelf life, nightclub door men falling midway between those of fashion models and Drake's cakes. Dale Marlin was renowned in Miami for five things other than his extravagance: a penchant for thinking outside the box, dressing like a beach bum, facial twitch-ticks, mercurial mood swings and a gun collection that would be the envy of an Afghan warlord. Three wildly successful quarters had him considering one of two new acquisitions for the Inferno Capital office, an orangutan or a personal entertainment concierge. In that owning an orangutan was still illegal in the State of Florida, Dale Marlin chose to hire Lazz, pointing out that it was the closest he could get to enjoying the best of both worlds. Regardless of his being hired as an analyst, the role was titular. Lazz's job responsibilities were specific to his area of expertise. He was Inferno Capital's in-house director of vice, expected to utilize his vast network of gilded debauchery that extended from coast to coast. Dale Marlin had as much intention of letting Lazz analyze stock charts and execute trades as he did the orangutan had State law allowed him to onboard one. Lazz had different ideas, evidenced by a stealth campaign to shed the only name he was known as. His business card read, 'Guy Lasback - Analyst.'

Where Guy Lasback and Alan Copeland would have no reason to be acquainted, operating in two exclusively different upper-echelon South Florida social orbits, the same couldn't be said for two of Copeland's senior *Mutual Fidelity Benefits & Trust* executives. Howie Yglesias knew Lazz through Aléjandro Perez, who was familiar with the doorman enough so they called one another 'brother' at the velvet rope while doing the hand-slap-pull-into-the-chest-bump-hug, but not quite enough to be one hundred percent sure Lazz knew his last name. Perez and Yglesias were regulars, ordering bottle service and tipping the waitresses handsomely and whenever they happened to have a surplus of high-quality blow, made sure to remember the gatekeeper. Lazz returned their patronage by periodically asking for a favor, a habit as impossible to shake for nightclub door men as it is for out of work drummers. Ygelsias and Perez typically responded by tripping over one another to honor whatever request was made. So, when Lazz's Russian bottle rocket of a girlfriend at the time needed a job, the two assured him they could find a place for her. They didn't disappoint, getting her hired as a receptionist at their office, despite her seemingly indecipherable, lead-weight accent. The next favor of note was pitched to Ygelsias by Lazz, but under the persona of Guy Lasback, hedge fund analyst and less as a favor than an opportunity for them to do business together. It was at either a yacht party during the annual Miami Boat Show or a house party on Fisher Island during Fashion Week, late at night and with enough cocaine and ecstasy pills to fill a bathtub. Yglesias had casually let slip in Guy Lasback's presence the practice of procuring policies using clean-sheeting on terminally ill patients and including them in preferred bundles for sale. Guy Lasback's mind, already moving at red zone RPM's, ran through the possibility of acquiring some of these bundled policies for the Inferno Capital portfolio. A handful more inquiries regarding hypothetical rate of return scenarios, policy costs and time frames convinced him that Yglesias' willingness to sell him even a small amount of them would be the very thing to force Dale Marlin into seeing him in a light other than that of a glorified events coordinator. It would guarantee him a seat at the grown-ups table.

So he asked.

Immediately Yglesias regretted bringing it up.

Lazz pleaded.

Yglesias was uncomfortable.

Lazz put his hand on Ygelsia's shoulder.

It was explained to him that Alan Copeland usually had to give the okay on who got the preferred bundles and Yglesias knew he wouldn't warm to the idea of them being sold to a glorified vice concierge, even Dale Marlin's.

Lazz begged.

Yglesias suggested to Lasback having Dale Marlin call him and he'd see what they could do. Ygelsias missed the point. He wanted to be the one to bring the deal.

Guy Lasback implored him.

Just a handful, please. Yglesias probably felt both awkwardness and satisfaction listening to what sounded like groveling. *C'mon, bro. Please. I'll be indebted to you for like...ever, bro.* Ygelsias had begun to consider exit strategies, actually starting to feel embarrassed for the former nightclub doorman. *Bro. Bro. C'mon, bro. You wanna fuck Stacia?* Stacia was Guy Lasback's latest girlfriend. *Just say the word, she'll let you fuck her if you make this happen.*

Guy Lasback got the policies.

His girlfriend Stacia let Yglesias fuck her.

The small policy bundle procured for Inferno Capital consisted of five individual viaticals with a projected gross aggregate return of

4.9 million dollars on an investment of 1.95 million, expected to mature between six and nine months. After bringing his first deal to Inferno Capital, Guy Lasback hadn't become the hedge fund *wunderkind* analyst he might have hoped to be, nor did he fizzle out. He settled into a comfortable groove through understated but crafty, below the radar plays and formed alliances with actual producers, which Dale Marlin seemed okay with. All the while, he made sure his role as entertainment guy was diligently served. The five policy bundled acquired from *Mutual Fidelity Benefits & Trust* were long forgotten, seemingly lost in the deep end of the fund's portfolio pool-

...Until an audit report highlighted that in the eighteen months since the viatical policies were acquired by the firm, not one had matured to pay a dividend.

Not a single one.

All of the named insured, understood by Guy Lasback to be terminally ill, had still been alive. When he was presented with this inconvenient truth, Guy Lasback frantically reached out to Yglesias, thinking he'd been hustled. He cursed his ever trusting him, knowing that the moment he was off the nightclub door and in the business world, he had nothing to offer someone like him. His calls weren't being returned and when he raced to confront him face to face, he was told that Mr. Yglesias was out of the office. When Yglesias did call him back, he assured Lazz that this was an aberration, the insured had all been diagnosed as terminally ill and the fact that they were still alive was either a miracle or the equivalent of a statistical hundred year storm. Furious, Guy Lasback called bullshit, pointing out that one of the policies was on a perfectly healthy twenty-one year old male with no history of illness or malady, accusing him of switching it out with another at the last minute. Yglesias didn't know how to respond other than saying, *'that one must have been a mistake, I guess. But the other four should have paid off by now. I don't know what to say, bro.'* And with Yglesias hanging up, there was nothing to be done.

When Guy Lasback's phone rang and the caller ID displayed 'Dale Marlin - Mobile,' he began to hyperventilate. And when he walked into Dale Marlin's office not long thereafter, he was not given the opportunity to offer an explanation, let alone invited to sit down. Dale Marlin made a pointing gesture in the general vicinity where he thought Lazz's desk was. *'Your shit-'* then a motion with his head in the vicinity of where the office front door was, *'...the fuck outta here.'* He didn't give him the dignity of even using the word *'get.'*

He turned toward the door, head hanging in shame. As he did, he could have sworn he'd heard Dale Marlin mumble to himself, *'should have gone long on the real orangutan'* with no idea what he'd meant.

The financial hit wasn't expected to put any kind of consequential dent in Inferno's bottom line for the quarter, still Dale Marlin was infuriated by the prospect that someone representing him had been taken advantage of. He, too, smelled the rash of a hustling in the air.

He arrived at the offices of the *Mutual Fidelity Benefits & Trust* company for the meeting with Alan Copeland like he was off to a ball game. Flip-flops on his feet, loose fitting white cotton pants with a drawstring around the waist and a green vintage tee shirt that said *'Gettin' Lucky in Kentucky,'* an outline of the state around the words. He also had a sidearm noticeably strapped to his waist that the tee shirt rode slightly up on. It defied the laws of gravity being supported by such a loose fitting garment. The two men did the *nice to meet you* pleasantries as the left side of Dale's face involuntarily twitched. Copeland pretended not to notice. They adjourned into Copeland's office where Kenny was sitting with his back to them at a table against a far wall reviewing Copeland's personal phone bill for a discrepancy Copeland was sure had been there. He was completely ignored. A few more bullshit exchanges and Copeland had pointed out the not so concealed gun on Dale Marlin's hip and made a joke about it. Dale Marlin looked as if he himself had been surprised it was there, unaware of its presence like a shark is of the remora fish attached to its underbelly. *It was Elvis's,* Dale Marlin told him. His face twitched again, a quick cheek spasm, double winking of his left eye and the meeting diverted into a show and tell. *You want to see it?* He drew it from his holster then held out the small, K-frame revolver before Copeland could answer. The gun looked like it belonged in a treasure chest. It was a black, snub-nose .357 magnum with staghorn grips, inlaid leaf and scroll engraving with tiny gold depictions of big game animals, images more appropriately decorating a high-powered hunting rifle. Dale Marlin felt the need to explain. *Yeah, I know. All that on a .357 with a one-inch barrel. But that gun did belong to Elvis, Cope.* Despite the two never having met before, Dale Marlin still referred to him as if they were teammates. *And if the King wants little gold elks and elephants engraved on his snub-nose, the King gets it, right?* Copeland asked how he'd come to own it and Dale Marlin was more than glad to answer. *Some people collect art. I like guns. You ask me, collecting art's for fags, Cope.* Copeland laughed reflexively at hearing that despite often referring to himself as an art collector, then handed the gun back to Dale Marlin, who wasn't done qualifying his interests. *Yup. I like guns. Got one of Pablo Escobar's gold-plated .45's. The .9 mil Dennis Hopper used to put two rounds into his own Warhol. Fag. I had Omar Bradley's Colt 1908, his personal every-day-carry. A .380. Bought it at an auction. You know what I did with it?* Copeland shook his head. Of course he didn't know. *Took it to one of those dopey gun buy-backs in Sarasota, traded it for a pair of concert tickets. Vanilla Ice, I think.* Copeland was sitting back in his chair, anything but relaxed as Dale recounted the event. *For no other reason than it felt good to cast it off into obscurity. It felt good to completely render the sidearm of arguably the most effective field general in the World War II European theater into...poof...nothingness. Nothing against Omar Bradley. He was a brave man.* Another facial twitch, then he shrugged and told what was probably closer to the truth. *I didn't like the history buff I outbid for it. Knowing he'll never have that gun wasn't enough. When he found out it was destroyed by the Sarasota Police Department during a gun buyback drive? I heard he cried. Practically tickled my prostate.* Dale Marlin shrugged, unapologetic. *I do things that make me feel good, Cope. Even when it hurts people. Of course, only people who have it coming. I like things that make me feel good. To me, Marcus Aurileus? Dick. A sanctimonious, self-righteous, moralizing dickbag. You ever read his Meditations?* Copeland was beyond flummoxed, with absolutely no idea of what Dale Marlin was referring to, why he changed the topic and where he was being led. *Yup. Marcus Aurileus, dickbag. Could you imagine living in Rome in the Second Century and having a guy like him as a neighbor? My guess is he was probably a lot like John Glenn. The astronaut? Senator from Ohio, ran for the big seat in 1984? He was a dickbag too, you know. Popular, big on image, good at what he did but a complete moralizing dickbag*. Then Dale Marlin immediately and without hesitation went to the reason for his being there. *Anyway, the reason I'm here, Cope...one of your guys sold us a bundle of life insurance policies that were pretty much bupkis. Five policies. All bupkis. That's your language, right? Bupkis?* Copeland committed to only being familiar with the term and by then fully aware of where Dale Marlin was going. *You know it's not the money, Cope. It's the principle. And that becomes like an itch for me, an itch I need to scratch.* Another minor facial spasm and a silence followed, that unlike the twitch, had been completely controlled by Dale Marlin before he once again changed gears. *I knew a guy, right? In fact, he was in your old business. A trader from up in New York.* Hearing this had caught Copeland off guard. He was curious how Dale Marlin knew he had been an equities trader and assumed he was probably aware that he'd been barred for life from trading by the SEC, as well. Copeland sat up, leaned forward and with his elbows then on his desk, listened patiently as Dale Marlin continued. *This guy moved down here, massive dickbag. Well karma, if you believe in that kind of thing, manifests itself in the form of a personal trainer from the gym bangin' this guy's wife. Lucious Diaz, that was the guy's name. The trainer. Never met him, but it didn't matter. I took the Adopt-A-Highway on the stretch of 95 where this guy lives, the trader from New York. Had the sign put right by his exit. 'Lucious Diaz, Personal Trainer.' No idea if Lucious even had any idea about it.* Dale Marlin actually paused to ponder the possibility. *I'd imagine he eventually did. Regardless, I didn't do it for Lucious. I did it because it made me feel good knowing this equities trader has to drive by it every day on his way home and see the name of the guy who was knockin' the nickels out of his wife.* Dale Marlin smiled wide and Copeland shook his head and laughed along, but then it was a nervous, uneasy one. *Long story short, Cope, I do things that make me feel good. And one of them is fucking with people I think have it coming. I mean really fucking with them. And if it completely breaks them, fine. If they lose it all? Family, business, whatever? Fine. If it drives 'em over the edge, drives 'em to suck on an exhaust pipe or grab a razor blade, run a hot bath, blast Henryk Gorecki's Symphony #3, climb in and slit their wrists? Fine, fuck' em. I don't care. I don't feel bad because I don't feel bad. Ever. I'm about feelin' good. I'm all epicurean, not a stoic like that fag Marcus Aurileus. You know where I'm going with this, Cope?* Where Copeland understood very few of the references Dale Marlin made, there had been no mistaking why the eccentric hedge fund operator was sitting before him. And as quickly as he changed topical gears of conversation, Dale Marlin decided the visit was over. A good-bye and he saw himself out without so much as a request or even suggestion for how Copeland might make right what Dale Marlin perceived as wrong, let alone making anything that might be interpreted as a threat. Still, Copeland sat uneasily, turning to Kenny, who was still in the corner facing the wall, chameleon-like and going about the task he was assigned. Copeland asked him what he made of it all. Kenny turned around. He told Copeland that he didn't understand most of the references he made, but deemed Dale Marlin as someone who was obviously very smart and probably a little bit insane, comparing his mind to a pinball machine, his thoughts the silver ball ricocheting in unpredictable directions within it. Copeland digested Kenny's assessment then agreed with a head nod. It had been the first time Kenny had seen Copeland nervous.

Returning from an errard three weeks later down to the clinic with forms that needed to be signed by Dr. Elliot, Kenny entered the

Mutual Fidelity Benefits & Trust offices to see Copeland uncharacteristically upbeat, self-satisfied. Summoned into his office, he noticed Copeland had a gun in his hand. It was the small, black, snub-nose .357 magnum with staghorn grips, inlaid leaf and scroll with tiny gold engraved big game animals on it. Smiling, he held it out toward Kenny like a child showing off a new toy and asked him to guess who the gun had once belonged to. Kenny told him that it once belonged to Elvis Presley. Copeland had forgotten Kenny was in the room during his meeting with Dale Marlin. It had just arrived as a gift with an accompanying note telling Copeland that his having it made him feel good and he was grateful to learn that the five life insurance policies the company had sold to Inferno Capital had all matured since the time of his visit and he looked forward to their doing business again. Copeland then placed the Elvis gun on his desk, turned and walked out of the office.

Take a ride.

They stepped out of the building and got into Copeland's eight month old beige Aston-Martin parked outside the door. He sighed, trapped in a thought then seemed to move off it, considering the car, and with regret. He was unhappy with it, telling Kenny he planned on trading it in. *I think I want a Phantom. A Rolls. A white, Rolls Royce Phantom.* Kenny nodded, acknowledging he'd heard him without weighing in, a habit he had when not having anything to offer about the subject spoken. Nor did he play the role of amen corner troubadour, for which Copeland probably appreciated. They drove off toward Starbucks and Copeland mentioned the relief he'd felt knowing all of the five viatical policies Yglesias had sold to Dale Marlin's hedge fund, Inferno Capital, had paid out. His sigh was a bit theatric. *That was a headache we didn't need, right? That Dale Marlin? What a fuckin' wingnut. Even though it was sweet of him to send that gift.* Copeland spoke more for himself but obviously meant for Kenny to hear and when he did, he silently considered the reality of what Copeland was saying-

...They were dead.

All of them.

In the span of twenty-one days, which was six to twelve months beyond their respective windows of estimated mortality, all of the individual named insured on the viatical policies sold to Dale Marlin were suddenly dead-

...All of them.

Kenny again stayed quiet, letting Copeland casually reiterate the fact. To call this development convenient would be an understatement. While giving no indication, Kenny was rattled to his core, not wanting to consider the obvious next thought that was clamoring for his attention in blazing lights. That thought, that terribly odious thought. Had it a throat to clear, had it a newspaper to snap twice or hands to wave in his face, it would have. There was no ignoring it. Copeland then seemed to be shifting toward a superficial explanation for what to Kenny was still so unlikely, almost impossible. *That's the thing with statistics, right? You can have situations that push boundaries, give you results early or give you results late, spread out over time...or all at once...and then they get added into the statistics for the next time. But at the end of the day they pretty much predict results. Right? That's what statistics do. That's why you can count on them. They don't lie. Unlike strippers, they don't lie.* He laughed a laugh that Kenny thought was a nervous one. As they drove in silence, Kenny again played Copeland's explanation in his head, word for word and decided there was no way it made sense, more implausible than the child explaining to his mother the skid marks in his underwear coming from an imaginary bandit on a motorcycle coming out of his butt with a brown crayon in hand, marking them up and driving off, and certainly less imaginative. Copeland might have picked up on Kenny's muted uneasiness, looked over at him and smiled as if Kenny had a stake of ownership in the resolved predicament. *You know, one of those policies was the one you brought in.* Kenny had heard him but didn't respond, so again Copeland repeated himself. Kenny only nodded, giving no outward indication that he was overwhelmed by a wicked gut wrenching, or that his mouth was suddenly filled with the putrid, rank taste that comes after a kick to the balls. His mind had become frozen, then slipped into a drawn out time warp, a thought process assuming the consistency of a giant amorphous chunk of salt water taffy, a changing variety of flavors: stunned, confused, afraid, unsure and back to being afraid.

That policy. The one he brought in-

...He knew-

...He knew exactly what policy Copeland was referring to, as Kenny had brought in only one. And, as instructed. He was told not long after Yglesias took him out into the field to show him the ropes, to go out and find a life insurance policy that would have an inexpensive premium that they would pay. A policy on a young person in seemingly good physical health. A reckless young person. A person that Kenny thought might be prone to an accident or untimely death based on their lifestyle. Copeland was counting on Kenny's instinctive assessment through observation, the very thing that had so impressed him when they first met, the very thing that he seemed to have a preternatural gift for.

When they arrived at Starbucks Kenny didn't opt out of ordering a coffee or even go decaf. Doing so would have shown his nervousness so he asked for what he usually did when resigned to ordering something knowing he wouldn't touch it. And again the thought of what he'd just heard came back. Regardless of what any statistics might support, the possibility of five policies maturing in such a short period of time was more suspicious to him than it had been three minutes earlier.

They were killed.

They had to have been killed.

Someone had them killed.

The possibility burdened Kenny for days, keeping him from sleeping, from eating, fueling overwhelming preoccupation to the point that he was barely able to give any single task the attention it warranted. He'd even pretended for three days to be sick so he didn't have to go to work, so he didn't have to look at Copeland, so he didn't have to see anybody. He never mentioned his quandary nor lamented it to another breathing soul.

Not even Rosie-

...Rosie-

...Rosie-

...As he knew what she'd say.

For eleven days Kenny was mired in a web of distraction and on the twelfth it simply went away like a fever finally breaking.

The pangs were gone-

...Evaporated from his consciousness-

...Like ether.

They were gone.

After being unceremoniously dismissed by Inferno Capital, Guy Lasbeck endured a brief period of despondency to go along with his unemployment and worse yet, social irrelevancy. He holed up in his South Beach studio apartment condo, coming and going via the staircase so as to avoid the elevator on the chance he might have to share it with someone. At night he ordered in, played video games alone and drank beer before falling into a deeper concentric ring of hell, asleep on the couch where he was tormented by the kinds of night terrors that even the pills couldn't make go away. The incubus came in the imagery of a scene playing over and again as if on a loop, himself desperately working the floor at an auto supercenter near Miami Lakes trying to sell Mazdas to customers, all of whom had been denied entry by him at one of the nightclubs he was a doorman at. With each customer rebuking him and exiting, another would enter. He would never know that the one small bundle of viatical policies eventually did pay off, bringing Inferno Capital a handsome return. Nor would he profit from it. Then, in a brief Phoenix rising from the ashes moment, he knew even going back to the door would be better than his current situation and pulled himself off the couch. Despite having prodigal son expectations, Lazz 2.0 wasn't embraced, clothed in a fine robe and returned to his station at Miami's premiere velvet rope of the moment. He had to settle for a venue of lesser esteem where he had to work harder for what amounted to baksheesh, kowtowing and ass kissing to those he'd once looked through like window screens. Recruiting the coterie of A-list 'good friends' to support him by making showings yielded predictable results and the extent of Lazz's efforts to please through procurement for individuals he tried to win over saw him push boundaries into areas he might otherwise not tread. Unbeknownst to him, two of the three girls he brought to Puerto Rico for a weekend of revelry sponsored by the fat wallet of a New York real estate scion with an unsightly birthmark were only seventeen years old. He learned shortly thereafter how seriously the FBI took transporting a minor across state lines for the purpose of prostitution. Following his arrest he was given an opportunity for consideration of a lesser sentence, immediately offering up first hand information on Howie Yglesias and the *Mutual Fidelity Benefits and Trust Corporation* perpetrating insurance fraud through wet-ink and clean-sheeting policies. The United States Attorney's office deemed this information worthwhile. Alan Copeland had long been on their Christmas list. Instead of ten years, Guy Lasback would serve a minimum of eight. Before he was moved to a Federal Prison to begin his sentence, Heinz Lucic, Special Agent in Charge of the FBI's Miami office opened an investigation into the practices of the *Mutual Fidelity Benefits and Trust Corporation*, in which Special Agents Walter Reed and Trey Stubblefield were assigned to work on.

At the Quickie Mart gas station on North West Forty-Second and Gratigny next to the Winn Dixie, Kenny was still parked in the place he moved to when Trey Stubblefield turned into the lot in his predictable, generic sedan. Except for color, it matched Reed's. Stubblefield was big, evident even from behind the wheel. His seat was pushed back and he filled all of it both high and wide. Pulling alongside his partner, he lowered the driver's side window as Reed lowered the one on his passenger side. The conversation would be conducted with a half-effort toward discretion with neither getting out of their cars.

"What's up?," Reed asked.

"*Whuut's* up is *mah fuhkin' mouff* is killin' me." Projecting anger was not effortless to him. Even when he may have felt angry. Trey Stubblefield was a black man in his thirties and dressed with the exact conservative blandness as his fellow agent. He had a disposition that reeked of a middle class upbringing, one he was self-consciously aware of. His ornery disposition was probably a defense mechanism so that he was never perceived as the token ethic minority character in the light beer commercial where the guys in their perfectly pressed plaid flannel shirts and pearly tooth smiles are throwing a few back on a camping trip after a day of fly fishing.

Reed sized him up. "For what it's worth, you sound better than you did on the phone."

Stubblefield shrugged. "Novo-caine...*wear-uh* off." A pause, he looked around. "Where *eh huh?*"

Reed motioned with his head to the other side of the parking lot where Kenny sat idling in his car.

"At least he's still *he-uh.*"

"Yeah. He hasn't moved. He said he was calling the lawyer. He's probably waiting for him to get back to him." Then Reed looked at Stubblefield for suggestions on what they might do. "Probably better if I don't try to talk to him for now, right?"

"Yea-uh. No shi-uh."

Stubblefield looked like he was contemplating taking a shot at walking over to reason with Kenny but leaned against it, probably thinking his odds of making any progress with him were slim. His frustration was obvious.

"You know, Trey-" Stubblefield looked at Reed. "...In the spirit of full-disclosure, I mean, if it comes up...I kind of slipped up mentioning the-"

Stubblefield knew exactly what Reed was referring to. He closed his eyes and questioned why he should be shocked. It had been decided not to bring it up anymore, to not even touch upon the possibility of a homicide being connected to a life insurance policy paying out, as Kenny half-suggested to Walter Reed in the parking lot of the Lee YMCA. They had determined that the best course of action was to let it all play out and hope Kenny gave them what they wanted. Forcing him, or trying to force him was not the way to go. They all agreed-

...At least they said they did.

Reed went on the defensive and tried to explain himself. "I just kind of mentioned it in passing. How important this all was, how much we were counting on him and that he was in a position to do something really, really good-"

Stubblefield didn't say it but thought it loud and clear. *You dumb motherfucker.*

"I have a rapport with him, Trey. I speak his language. He actually thinks I like him." Then he paused, frustrated. "You know we wouldn't even be in this situation if you didn't tell me to tail him to make sure he gets to the meeting."

"*Me-uh?* Now it's on *me-uh? Fuh-you, Wahl.* That *cam-uh fruh* Looch.*"

Sensing his rationalization had failed, Reed tried another tactic in deflecting blame. "You know, sometimes I wonder if you forget he's not the one under investigation. He's not the perp."

"*Fuh him!* He's a one *uh-um, Wahl.* He's *Copelaah's-a* boy, been-uh work-uh *there two pluh* year-uh. He's *juh try-uh* to protect his own *asshh...*and he is *uh* perp. *He-uh got a record.*"

"You know what I mean. He doesn't have to be doing this. They're not even considering him a possible unindicted co-conspirator. He's an assistant, a gopher. He's doing this because I convinced him to."

"*Fuh-him.* He's cooperatin' just in *case-ah* any of the shit's gonna get *on-ah* his leg, *Wahl-*"

"I think you just don't like him. And that's fine, I don't like him either, but-"

"*Dam-ah* straight I don't like him! *Ah* said it *be-fuh,* I say it *aghun.* He wants to string us along, we *caaah* bury him. He got no *idea-ah* how *bad-ah* we *caaah fuh-kuh* bury him.

Let's not lose sight of his motivation for helping us. Yes, it's the expungement, but his being willing to walk away tells me he doesn't really give a shit about that. He's a swamp rat, a backwoods, redneck, swamp rat. I know the type. They're not rational."

The swelling in Stubblefield's mouth seemed to be subsiding with each word he spoke but his ire remained undaunted. "We can *fuh-kuh* bury him. He got no idea."

"I know what we can do to him, Trey. My point is you're going all in on the stick and I'm advocating the carrot as a much more effective approach. This hick thinks I like him. It's just a matter of time before he starts asking me about NASCAR and...fucking banjos."

"*We-uh decid-uh* not *tuh* bring up the-"

"I know what we decided." Reed was frustrated. "I just thought-"

The reverse lights on the tail of Kenny's car blinked, then the car gear slid into drive. He was moving, slowly gliding out of the parking lot into the street and diverting from the direction he'd been on. Stubblefield and Reed could only watch.

In his car, Kenny headed straight on Northwest Forty-Two, not sure where he was going to go. He didn't want to go home and couldn't go to the office. He regretted not talking about it all to Rosie from the onset, thinking he was protecting her, but at the same time protecting himself from her-

...And then the policy-

...The viatical policy that he brought in. He wasn't surprised Danté was dead, but upset nonetheless. There was no possible formula that could be constructed leading to Kenny being culpable in any way shape or form for that, yet he still felt partly responsible. Of course Danté wasn't going to live long. Kenny knew it the moment they met. He saw it as clear as he'd ever seen anything. And when he pitched him on the life insurance policy that he not only wouldn't have to pay

143

for, but get paid for signing over, Kenny hoped he was wrong. As wild, reckless and destined for an early demise, he liked him.

Kenny liked Danté.

Chapter Nine

Measured Risks

Please allow me to introduce myself-
I'm a man of wealth and taste-
I've been around for a long, long year-
Stole many a man's soul to waste-
Copeland engaged the washer pump and wipers.
Mistake.
The volume of fluid sprayed out onto the windshield only
tickled then diluted the massive blots of pelican shit.
...I was 'round when Jesus Christ-
Had his moment of doubt and pain-
Made damn sure that Pilate-
Washed his hands and sealed his fate-

The wipers quickly became a finger painting metronome
spreading out the mess further and rendering Copeland's vision more
obstructed than had he left it alone. In a near panic, he let loose
another blast of wiper fluid-

...Pleased to meet you-
Hope you guess my name-
But what's puzzling you-
Is the nature of my game-

"God damn it!" The only thing wiped away was the self-deprecating grin-chuckle that had been on his face seconds earlier.

So much for breathing.

...I stuck around St. Petersburg-
When I saw it was a time for a change-
Killed the Tzar and his ministers,
Anastasia screamed in vain-

He cut off the music as if it were to blame for the mess. Teeth clenched, he struggled to see the road in front of him, deciding then that his eyes weren't the same as they'd been even six months earlier. "Three hundred grand, this thing should come equipped with a water cannon! A fucking water cannon!" He turned on the hazard lights, looking for somewhere to pull over where he might be able to clean the windshield off. A gas station would have been ideal. Halfway up the block beyond the traffic signal was one step better.

A car wash.

Instead of feeling grateful for his luck he frowned, annoyed that it wasn't a hundred yards closer. He stopped for the red at the intersection and leaned over the wheel squinting through the slop that made the front of his car feel like the soaped out window of a vacant storefront and watched for the green. As he waited he must have felt the presence of another's eyes upon him because he looked to his left. The driver in the car next to him, an overweight and red faced middle-aged local, probably coming back from a round of golf at a public course, was laughing. "What are you laughing at, fat boy?" The comment was made without his looking in the other driver's direction but more significantly without irony. It wasn't as if Copeland could claim to have the Body Mass Index of a cheetah.

The light turned, he focused back on the road and *Mister Magoo'd* his way up to the car wash parking lot. He pulled off the road but stopped before getting into the cue of cars waiting to enter the narrow, dark shaft of the tunnel structure that gave off continuous, low, guttural sounds of a conveyor belt's gears grinding, water spraying and flogging soapy wet drapes, sounds that could be compared to a brutal bout of indigestion. He turned the engine off, opened the door and got out, stopping for a moment as he'd suddenly felt dizzy. He steadied himself, then again looked around. At three exterior side-by-side VIP detail stations past the row of coin operated vacuums and vending machines, what may as well have been a small swarm of bees in matching tee shirts worked around three high-end luxury cars. One of them was a black 750i and it made Copeland think of Haberman and what he might have been calling for. The team leader, a boyishly small Hispanic man in his twenties with seemingly boundless energy gave directives *en espa˜nol*, high-pitched and loud enough to compete with the overwhelming noise generated by the equipment being used. He saw Copeland, nodded to him and started walking in his direction. Copeland looked back at his car, the pelican shit covering nearly the entire driver's side of the windshield and part of the hood, far worse than his perspective from behind the wheel. As the car wash jockey approached, a shift change in the wind carried a large billow of mist from the power washers being used by the detail attendants directly into Copeland's path. He reacted as if he'd been poked in the eyes.

"How you doing, sir?"

Copeland waved a hand in front of his face, clearing the mist away.

"A pelican got you?" The car wash jockey smiled. "It looks like you got it from a...*comé se dicé...Velo-ci-raptór?*"

"A what?"

"You know? The dinosaur that flies-?", then motioned with his arms as if they were wings. "...Like in *You-rassic Park?*"

Copeland looked back at the windshield. "Yeah, you'd think I got shit on by a...what did you call it?"

"*Velo-ci-raptór.*"

"Yeah." He then took a deep breath and unconsciously pumped out his chest and folded his arms, making himself an inch taller than the man he already had seven on. "Listen, my friend. I'm running a little late. I don't have time for the whole-" then he uncrossed his arms so he could do the thing with his hand that he did when referring to a whole *she-bang*. "...And I don't like to put the car through that-" half-pointing his chin in the direction of the gurgling white mortar structure housing the conveyor belt, automated brushes and hoses. "Any chance you got like...a squeegee or something in the meantime? Just to clear the shit off for now so I can get where I gotta go?"

The car wash jockey shrugged and nodded, seeing the request as not unreasonable. He turned back to the crew at the detail ports and let go an ear piercing quick whistle then a rapid fire command *en espa~nol.* Without hesitation, two attendants stopped what they were doing and wheeled a power washer toward Copeland's Rolls Royce Phantom.

"Oh, you don't gotta do that," Copeland protested. "Just a squeegee'll be fine-"

The car wash jockey laughed at him and smiled again. "I see you never got it from a pelican before."

Copeland didn't get a chance to respond. From inside the Rolls, his phone rang. Without excusing himself, he spun on a heel and two stepped back to the car, getting in and shutting the door for privacy. The car wash jockey took no offense.

Copeland answered the phone. "Yeah?"

"Alan? I have Mr. Haberman."

"Thanks, Brenda."

She patched the call through. A sober, distinguished almost patrician voice came over the speaker. *"Alan, how are you?"* But before Copeland could answer, Haberman cut him off, as he'd just been unexpectedly interrupted. *"I'm sorry, Alan. I have to call you right back."* He then disconnected. Someone or something was more important and it frustrated him.

Without warning, one of the two attendants pointed the telescopic wand of the power washer at the windshield and let rip a five thousand pounds-per-square-inch torrent of water. The pelican shit was no match for it. Copeland sat in silence deciding if he should be offended by Haberman pushing him aside, then the phone rang again. Copeland immediately answered. "Put him through, Brenda. Thanks."

A pause.

"Alan! How you doin'?"

"Huh?"

It wasn't Brenda patching through Haberman. It was Yglesias. "It's me. Howie."

Copeland closed his eyes and sighed, annoyed.

"Alan? You there?," Yglesias asked.

"Yes, Howie. I'm here. What's up?"

"Yeah, um...that bundle of twenty-five A's and Double A's to Canary Group? Looks like it's a no-go. An unexpected cash flow issue or something on their end. I know Scooter would love to get his hands on them, but thought instead of pushing them over to retail, maybe we see if Dale Marlin might take them. I spoke with him and told him I know he doesn't like single A's, but maybe we can move them at a little bit of a cut rate and get them off the books for the end of the month, which is-"

Copeland stopped him. "Whoa! You spoke to Dale Marlin?"

A pregnant pause. "Yeah. I...spoke to him and-"

Copeland again cut Yglesias off, this time with a bitch slap of a rebuke. "You don't speak to him! YOU DON'T FUCKIN' SPEAK TO HIM! EVER! No one speaks to him except me!" He was incredulous.

"Jesus, Alan. I just thought-"

"Don't think! Don't fucking think, Howie! AND DON'T SPEAK TO DALE MARLIN! Do you understand?!"

"Yeah, Alan. I just-"

"DON'T FUCKING 'JUST', EITHER, HOWIE!"

The car wash attendants were drying off Copeland's windshield with orange microfiber rags, paying no attention to his screaming into the phone. Another deep breath and Copeland hit the auto dial for his office.

"Yes, Alan?"

"Brenda, get me Dale Marlin at Inferno."

"Right away."

"And then you can jump off the line, thanks."

"Understood."

The call was made, ringing now on the other end.

"Good afternoon, Inferno Capital."

"Hi, Alan Copeland for Dale."

"Please hold."

Dale Marlin's unmistakable voice was soon heard. *"Hey, Cope!"*

Copeland abandoned any and all suggestions of urgency or uneasiness in his tone, putting on his best sunny-side-of-the-street voice. "Dale, how you doin' my man?" It sounded like he was imitating a stoner.

"Crushing, Cope. Crushing, if you have to know."

"Good. Listen, one of my guys mentioned he reached out to you about takin' a bundle of policies, kind of low-grade, half-dog shit to tell you the truth-"

"Yeah. Sure. I know about it."

"I gotta apologize, Dale. They're not available even if you were interested. I already moved 'em out. And my guy?" Copeland wouldn't even say his name. "...Not for nothin', he was out of line reachin' out to you. He doesn't have the right to call you and I apologize for him assuming he did. I don't know what his fucking problem is. I think he might be back on heroin."

Dale Marlin could be heard laughing and Copeland was glad. *"No sweat, man. I don't care. Anyone can call me. Any time."*

Copeland quickly took advantage of the opening to change gears. "So all good on your end?"

"Crushing."

"Good." Then a thought. "How's your next week? Maybe we can get breakfast or something?"

"Sure, Cope. Any day. You tell me."

"Any day?" Copeland sounded like he thought he was being played.

"Yeah. Any day."

Copeland shook his head, amused and envious of how Dale Marlin could so effortlessly carry himself as if he had fewer responsibilities than a high school senior in spring with no plans on college for fall. "Okay, let's do Wednesday."

"Wednesday it is."

He told him Brenda would coordinate with his office and hung up, then immediately after one-touch dialed another number. Scooter Wrobel answered on the first ring. It sounded like he was in a bar.

"Hey, Alan. What's up?"

"Scooter, call Howie and tell him I want the twenty-five allocations that Canary was supposed to take moved to retail."

"Yeah, sure. How you doing?"

"How am I doin'?" Copeland paused to think for a second. "I'm crushing, Scooter. Crushing, if you gotta know. Listen, I gotta jump, okay?" He disconnected and looked ahead into a perfectly streak-free and crystalline windshield. Not so much as a scintilla of

Pelican bile remained and the two car wash attendants were walking back to their stations with the power washer in tow. The car wash jockey that made it happen was standing outside his door. Copeland lowered the window. "Wow. Great job. Thanks for that. What's the charge?"

"You're good. No charge, sir. Just look out for the *velo-ci-raptórs.*"

Copeland was surprised the cleaning was on the arm. He fumbled through his pockets for his billfold and freed a ten dollar bill. He folded it three times and slipped it in the car wash jockey's hand. The gesture was appreciated but not unexpected. Copeland began to drive off. He then regretted having not given him a fifty just for his positive energy and disposition but not enough to go back and actually do it.

Making his way back into the flow of traffic, he put the music back on, picking it up where it had been left off.

...Pleased to meet you-
Hope you guess my name-
But what's puzzling you-
Is the nature of my game-

Yglesias. He didn't feel bad for having blown up at him. It was the only language Howie understood. When it came to certain allowances, Copeland couldn't give Yglesias an inch. Dale Marlin was one of them. Yglesias could never have, would never have access to Dale Marlin.

...I rode a tank
Held a general's rank-

When the blitzkrieg raged-

And the bodies stank-

Copeland never lost sight of the unfortunate rule-versus-exception reality that the more essential an *MFB&T* employee was to the bottom line, the less trusted they could be. It was an inescapable fact, something he had to accept, understand and most importantly, manage. The character qualities needed to excel in their line of work were the very ones recognized in nearly every other social circumstance or interpersonal relationship as flaws, and when it came to ambition, craftiness, insensitivity and greed, Howie Yglesias stood head and shoulders above his even otherwise morally hollow colleagues. The possibility of Yglesias slitting the wrist of the very hand that fed him from radius to ulna was never in doubt. The only regulating factor to keep him from doing so was his aversion to taking risks. Copeland not only counted on this, but periodically fertilized it. And should the day come where he sensed Yglesias growing emboldened beyond comfort, he would immediately burn him down and cut loose whatever charred remains were left. Without hesitation. The risks taken with his associates, particularly Yglesias, were all carefully measured.

I watched with glee-

While your kings and queens-

Fought for ten decades-

For the gods they made-

He continued to drive along in steady traffic and got back to calm. He entertained several random unrelated thoughts, then decided he'd wished he were better at giving toasts.

Toasts.

To stand up before a gathered group, lift a glass and offer a few words before drinking to the health of, or in honoring another individual. The thought came out of nowhere, as serendipitous as a pelican shitting on his car windshield.

A fucking toast.

Not that he expected to be asked to make one at Lauren's wedding, which was fine. It would be digging for diamonds in a landfill to come up with something positive to say about her. He liked the idea of being good at making a toast at a small gathering of people he respected. Having them laugh and later overhear someone say what a great toast that was. According to Karen's mother, Haberman always declined when invited to offer one, redirecting in deferment to another he would humbly deem as more capable, if not worthy. And certainly less bland, Copeland figured. He thought of Charles Shack, whom he'd met one night at Haberman's home. A dinner party. There was a gentleman, in Copeland's eyes, of the highest order. A *mensch*. That was a man who could give a toast. Shack was in his seventies and radiated an impeccable manner matched by his dress, an effortless air of sophistication and baronial charm. There wasn't the narrowest fibril about him of the Chicago West Town Patch ghetto where he was born. The toast he gave that evening was perfect, effortless, smooth as the thirty-year old single malt they would later sip on. Copeland remembered the words flowing out of the man's mouth with the sincerity and gentle softness of a lullaby. Funny, heartwarming and thought stimulating all in what had to be more than twenty seconds but less than forty. Copeland wondered if he'd practiced in front of a mirror to prepare.

155

Charles Shack.

What a great dinner.

What a great night.

The nine hundred pounder in rooms Charles Shack occupied had obviously lost weight over the years so that it was now less than a feather, and that evening in Haberman's house assumably nonexistent. He had done too much good in the community for too long. And notwithstanding, he had never been convicted of a single felony or misdemeanor, let alone arrested for one. It was, though, almost universally known that Charles Shack was an original architect of international money laundering in the early 1960's, operating at the behest of Meyer Lansky, whom he was rumored to be both protegé and confidant of. He had many times publicly denied even having met the man. What a feat, Copeland remembered thinking, to be able to effectively scrub his past to be accepted and admired as a beloved, upstanding member of the community. The very fact that Haberman had an open friendship with Charles Shack spoke volumes, as Copeland had met very few people in his life as aware of public perceptions than Haberman. Over the course of dinner, Charles Shack effortlessly held court sharing anecdotes and stories that were nothing less than riveting. Informative. Entertaining. They were mined from his personal experiences or gleaned from books he'd read. The hint of so much as a half-boast nowhere to be found in any of them. He could segue from a story seamlessly into a joke that's identity as such stayed hidden until the punchline was delivered. And when others spoke he embraced the role of *audientia* with perfect sympathy and humility, his eyes on the dinner guest speaking as if they were the only ones in the room. Over the course of the evening, Haberman's guest were treated to hearing about the origins of a 'jam boy' custom as a way of controlling flies in colonial India, which apparently dated back to Ancient Egypt and how as recently as ten years earlier, Pepsi actually owned seventeen submarines as a result of a deal with the former Soviet Union in which they exchanged soda for military equipment and that one of the Wright brothers lived to see his life's great achievement be responsible for one of the most catastrophic single acts of destruction mankind had ever seen. The bombing of Hiroshima.

'Did you really know Meyer Lansky?'

Had a breadcrumb fallen from the table, it would have been heard whistling through the air then exploding onto the travertine floor, echoing through the rooms and hallways of Haberman's massive home like a canyon. Where Charles Shack may well have been caught off guard, he showed no sign of it. He let the question digest only momentarily before mentioning a largely unknown fact that one of Lansky's two sons had been a decorated Air Force Captain who had graduated from West Point. Then he answered the question by telling Copeland that he, Charles Shack, happened to be sitting across from Lansky playing chess when he took the call from his son, the Air Force Captain, telling his father that after ten years in the service he was leaving to take a job in the private sector as an engineer. Charles Shack paused for reflection, seemingly going in his mind back to that moment and place in time. 'There was never a more emotionally even-keeled man than Mr. Lansky.' And the conversation then continued, effortless and organically onto another subject. Where Charles Shack showed no sign of being offended by what was considered a *faux pas*, Haberman had been livid to the point of the incident becoming a near family crisis.

Oh, to be able to give a toast-

...Then his mind went back to Dale Marlin and the short conversation they'd had. He should have asked him more about what Yglesias asked him. Was there any small talk? Did he sniff around areas he shouldn't? Did he suggest the two meet for a drink? That could potentially be bad. That could potentially be very bad. Copeland considered what he should do...if anything, then decided to seek reassurance in knowing Dale Marlin was too smart to fall for any trickery Ygelsias was capable of serving up.

The phone rang. Copeland answered. "Yeah?"

"I have Mr. Haberman."

"Thanks, Brenda."

She patched the call through.

"Alan, sorry about that, before. I had to take it. How are you doing?"

"All good over here. You?"

"Good. Thank you for asking. Listen, a quick question. Karen mentioned a place a few weeks ago, a deli you said you got a platter from, Nova and scallion cream cheese? She said it was excellent."

Copeland was disappointed. "Yeah, I remember."

"Which place was it?"

"Mo's."

"Mo's?" Haberman was surprised.

"Yeah, Mo's."

"Oh." Now Haberman was the one who seemed disappointed.

A moment of silence. Copeland then told-asked, "Karen and I got roped into dinner at the Yosts later. Any chance we'll see you there?"

Haberman answered without hesitating. *"No. You said it was Mo's?"*

"Yes."

"Okay. Thanks for that. Talk soon." And he disconnected.

Haberman called to ask him about a deli platter. A fucking deli platter! He almost would have rather he'd been asking him to write a check to another charity or political campaign.

Tell me, sweetie, what's my name-

Ooo, who, who-

Ooo, who, who-

Ooo, who, who-

Chapter Ten

Danté

Special Agent in Charge Heinz Lucic had static bug eyes and a perpetual five o'clock shadow even when his face was smooth shaven. His skin was almost transparent with the consistency of rice paper. He took the call in his office with poor natural light and frustrating views. Facing north by northwest, it looked down on a dismal interstate to one side and on the other pockets of endless single story, south Florida signature stucco homes and the stagnant, brown-green ponds and reservoirs that lay between them. There was a snippet of the Atlantic visible in the distance but only seen with effort when pressed up against the glass that was never adequately cleaned. Lucic expected more when he was promoted out of the Detroit office a year earlier where from the Twenty-Sixth floor of the building on Michigan Avenue he enjoyed a spectacular panorama of Lakes Erie and St. Clair. Well, that was all changing. After the *People of the United States of America vs. Alan Copeland and the Mutual Fidelity Benefits and Trust* affair was over, with its bombshell revelation, he was going to ask...no demand, something to make his workspace more appropriate to fit the position. A bump in next year's budget to lease additional space or move to another floor would do it. The benefits of natural light, he preached incessantly, were too often overlooked when it came to mental acuity which in turn affected job performance. And this was Florida he was assigned to now, not a rock pile in Tora Bora. He was leaning back into the chair behind his perfectly organized desktop giving no indications to Walter Reed on the other end of the line of being angry. He was in agile personnel management mode, patiently listening as he was brought up to speed regarding the confidential informant Kenny Rehage's apparent change of heart. Reed was apologetic to his boss, acknowledging what he'd expected Lucic to say before he had the chance: his awareness of the costs the office had incurred on the investigation, specifically since they'd acquired Kenny as an asset and the excellent chance that it was about to become skyscraping high in profile, a career defining case for all involved. To his surprise, Lucic told him not to worry, words he may well have never uttered since learning to speak forty-four years earlier. He was taking a low gear pursuit of solution instead of spinning his tires in the mud puddle of problem. He had the phone wedged between his shoulder and side of his head that was slightly too big for his neck while fingering a baseball that might or might not have been autographed. "You do understand that Alan Copeland's going to go down, Walt. We're eighteen hours into a thirty day warrant with taps locked and loaded on targets most investigators can only dream of. Eighteen hours. You realize that? We're sitting pretty." He then adjusted the phone and held the baseball in one hand, squeezing it and silently

161

mouthing at the drop ceiling overhead, *Please God he didn't screw this up.*
Back into the phone, "...Is Stubblefield with you?" He listened, then
offered up a sentiment exactly matching Reed's previous one. "Great
day to pick to go to the dentist." He placed the baseball down on the
desk and with his free hand pinched the area between his thin upper lip
and nostrils. Then a double-tap sigh of vexation and he picked up the
baseball again, squeezing it as if he wanted to pop the stitches out of
the leather. A pause and he calmly launched into a homily about the
psychology behind what their asset, Kenny Rehage, might be
experiencing emotionally. He was after all, legally speaking, in a
position of control. He could walk away anytime without recourse.
That was what Reed was worried about. "I look at the psychology
behind it all, Walt. What are his motivations, this guy? He knows
people in his office are going to go to jail. That's a given. He's not
stupid. The party is about to come to a crashing halt. And he's afraid
of the possibility of being dragged down along with them, even if he's
done nothing wrong, which we have no reason to believe he has. Still,
it's fear. He's motivated by fear, Walt. Right? Even if he's got nothing
to be afraid of. You see, this guy...it's his nature, his temperament-"
Lucic considered himself an expert in the sciences of the mind, with
his undergraduate degree in psychology from Chapman College and
having been attached to a Bureau behavior analysis unit when he began
his career in the Sacramento office. "...His whole disposition,
everything he projects is right in line with a Myers/Briggs type...an
ENFJ." Lucic thought for a second, then spiced up his assessment.
"Maybe a little INFJ in there. I get this kid. I understand where he's
coming from." Then another pause for effect, giving the mostly one-

way conversation the hint of turning into a pep talk. "...I also know this, Walt. And you have to trust me. Those very qualities that are consistent with ENFJ? They'll also be the very things that bring him back. So give it a little room. We'll get him. The warrant's in place, the wires are dropped. Hard part's done. I know you're well aware that at this very moment everything Alan Copeland is saying we have ears on. And we have twenty-nine more days, twenty-nine more bites at the apple with this kid for the big prize, assuming he's the one who can get him to talk about-" He interrupted his thought with a pause. "He'll be back. We'll get it out of him. Just stay the course." Reed said something to which Lucic responded with a chuckle steeped in furniture salesman sincerity. "That's just you being a little bit of an ISTJ yourself, Walt. Right?" When Lucic hung up the phone, he squeezed the baseball in his hand again as tightly as he did his lips, then pointed his bug eyes toward the window with the underwhelming view and blurted out, "what a fucking idiot."

In the parking lot of the Quickie-Mart, Stubblefield watched as Reed disconnected, sighing a hint of relief.

"*Whah-a-he thay?*"

Reed shrugged. "I'm not sure."

"*Whaaah he pissed?*"

"Not like I thought. He's not worried about it. Says this kid isn't lost...he'll be back, something about his psychology type."

"We can *fuh-kuh* bury him."

Reed didn't acknowledge the statement this time. He looked back toward the empty place where Kenny's car had been moments earlier and Stubblefield turned away from him, not wanting to engage in discussion anymore. As far as he was concerned there was nothing else to be said. And his mouth was killing him as the effects of the novacaine increasingly subsided.

Kenny was around the corner parked curbside on a tree-lined residential street having brought his waiting game out of Reed and Stubblefield's view. He thought about how badly they wanted Copeland's fraud to be connected to a homicide. Had they been given a hypothetical choice between prosecuting a sensational crime prominently and it never having happened at all, in Kenny's estimation they would never be able to answer in earnest. They really were scumbags, he thought. Absolute scumbags.

After Alan Copeland had shared with Kenny the information that the bundle of policies sold to Inferno Capital had all conveniently matured and paid out in the three weeks following Dale Marlin's visit, he probably would have been better off never having had in the following days looked up the policy files in the insurance company databases they were affiliated with where he saw the particulars of the indemnifications. He did because he could. He had access to come and go into any part of the company database he wanted to. He had Copeland's passwords.

Three of the insured had cancer.

One suffered from Amyotrophic Lateral Sclerosis.

The other was Danté Billings, the named insured of the policy he brought in.

Danté.

Danté.

Dante-

...Whose only terminal affliction was behavioral.

The dates of death for the five named policyholders and subsequent payouts were listed as well as causes, which may as well have been afterthoughts. Kenny thought he couldn't find the smallest of dry spots upon the explanation when first hearing it from Copeland and in his estimation then had just gotten wetter. Of the five, he saw that only one succumbed to the perils anticipated for them.

The ALS patient had died in a house fire.

One of the cancer patients fell from the balcony of his fifteenth floor condominium in Aventura.

Another was killed by a hit and run driver while out walking at dusk-

...And Danté Billings died by what might as well have been listed as ghetto natural causes: a gunshot.

What he read in the files was to him as glaring as it was galling. Yet, the policies had been taken at their word, paid out and closed without contest or question asked. He couldn't help regurgitating in his mind listening to Copeland's periodic mafioso wannabe talk and Yglesias's boasts of connections to get or have almost anything imaginable, legal or otherwise 'taken care of.' It was amphetamine mainlined into an already hyperactive imagination. Twelve days spent suffering in silence, weighing out every imaginable scenario, the principle of the law of large numbers versus nothing more than his own visceral feelings, with the former unable to score a decisive, convincing point in his mind. And then the decision to suddenly deny the winner its prize, abrogating his instinct, the very quality that had so rarely let him down after he began paying attention to it.

Kenny gave in.

He turned heel one-hundred and eighty-degrees in a betrayal of his conscience, accepting the academic thesis of statistics as explanation instead of the conclusion which considered emotion. And he accepted the ratification of its accuracy with the enthusiasm that comes with discovery of something new.

Of course this could happen!

ALS patients suffer a deterioration of motor functions, they die in accidents they might otherwise have survived!

It was possible!

It isn't uncommon for terminally ill cancer patients to take their own lives!

Elderly individuals are periodically hit by automobiles! There was a good reason an entire industry used this concept as the foundation it operated upon!

Statistics don't lie!

Not like strippers!

And young, reckless, inner-city hustlers with impulse control issues do get murdered.

Every single day of the week!

Kenny Rehage had accepted the narrative, allowing what might be called his intuitive genius to be declawed.

Things got back to normal, Kenny's great rationalization and crisis of conscience had run its course, seemingly forgotten until several months later when FBI Special Agent Walter Reed exposed the true reason for his having inserted himself into Kenny's life by way of a pickup basketball game at the local Lee YMCA. Believing a friendly relationship between them had been already established, Reed had invited Kenny for a beer after they played. Four different times. He was turned down on each occasion. After the fifth overture which produced the same result, a frustrated Reed was forced to reveal himself in the parking lot as they talked small next to Kenny's car. Kenny learned that he'd come onto the FBI's radar during the initial pre-investigation into Alan Copeland and *MFB&T* for a variety of charges which included medicaid, wire and a variety of insurance frauds, money laundering and racketeering. While Kenny himself was not under investigation for any crimes personally, he had been established as someone close to Alan Copeland. The FBI was aware Kenny didn't hold the required licenses necessary to write policies or sell securities, by all estimations he was more of a personal assistant than an executive one. Kenny didn't dispute anything Reed said, nor did he cop to any. Reed then told him that while he was not a target of the probe, if he alerted Copeland or anyone else at *MFB&T* as to what he was being told, he could be considered a co-conspirator. Kenny showed no emotion, not the smallest hint of even having been surprised, outraged or rattled. He stayed silent, chowed down and digested what he was served. Reed suggested he might want to leave *MFB&T* as soon as he could and look for another job. Or he could stay on and help them out. He would be protected, made aware that there were laws to safeguard whistleblowers. The *People* might even be open to entering into a little *quid pro quo*, with the US Attorney's Office possibly considering an expungement of his past arrest record-

His past arrest record?

They knew about the swampers.

The bale of weed.

Of course they did.

167

...But most importantly, Reed stressed to Kenny, he would be doing the right thing. Alan Copeland and his associates hurt a lot of people. Kenny took some time to compose himself internally, as he had understandably been blindsided by Reed's overture. A chasm of silence grew between them as he sifted through his thoughts. He then told Reed he didn't know much about the law or regulations, but was aware of the business as pretty much being a shitty one and that he was never comfortable in it but it was a job that paid well for what he did. Kenny then spent a moment in reflection, and as if an alien element assumed his very corporeal being, trancelike, he stated in not much more than a murmur again what a shitty business the viatical one was, and that it had actually crossed his mind that some of the terminally ill policyholders not dying fast enough might have at times had a little help getting dead.

He said it.

The words were spoken.

Unable to be unheard.

And the fuse was lit.

Kenny snapped out of his reflective trance and told Reed he'd go get a beer with him, during which time he purposely didn't talk about anything other than basketball. Walter Reed listened but only with half of one ear, as he was contemplating his new found good fortune of the suggestion that a homicide might be connected to the fraud case against Alan Copeland. The possibility would get top story billing, page one coverage and reward those breaking the case with things like jumps in GS grade and fast track promotions to supervisor, something for which Reed had been long awaiting.

168

Later that night when Kenny saw Rosie he told her he'd found out that the FBI was investigating Copeland and the business practices of *MFB&T.* She broke down into a panic.

He had to quit his job immediately!

And if the FBI wants to talk to him, don't say anything without a lawyer!

Quit now, he had to quit now!

And when he said he didn't know what he was going to do, her hot-blooded Latina wrath was unleashed upon him. Like a knowing mother imploring her naive son not to go off to war, not to take his guns to town.

She yelled.

She cried.

She pulled him into a vise-like clutch, burying her face into the very chest she moments earlier was pounding upon with closed fists.

And then to the couch she went and sat, looking at the floor like it was a crystal ball.

He had to leave his job immediately.

He had to quit.

Call a lawyer. Her brother Jorgé could find one for them.

'Them,' she said-

...As this involved her.

Kenny shook the thoughts away and looked out his car window over the treeline. The top of the Quickie-Mart sign around the block was visible and he wondered if they were still there.

Yes.

He'd bet on it.

Then he thought again of Rosie and wondered if it was too late. He closed his eyes and sat back letting the head rest do its job. He thought then of nothing, leaving his mind a blank canvas. After a dozen or so controlled breaths, he considered something entirely unrelated. The fact that he hadn't gone fishing in years and how he'd like to remedy that. Even if it was a trip down to the pier. He opened his eyes, looked across the street and for the first time noticed a playground basketball court in a small park. Like it had just snuck up and planted itself there. The court was empty, probably the norm for this part of the city during a weekday. That wouldn't be the case over at Tropical, the massive park wedged between crime ridden Olympia and Glenvar Heights.

Where he met Danté.

Danté.

Danté.

Danté.

There was a run at Tropical every day from pretty much Eleven A.M. until midnight.

Seven days.

Three-sixty-five.

Some of which were chop and chucky and some of which were just plain slow, but during the peak hours, 6 PM 'till lights out, the pool of talent was first-rate, making the court a centerpiece of razzle-dazzle showtime events, especially on weekends when spectators would be lined up watching two and even three rows deep. Most came to watch the athleticism and skill of the players but the court had also established itself as a social event with all the trimmings. Part ghetto dance hall, part car show, part unsanctioned flea market and part tailgate party. The amount of boldness needed for an unassuming young, white male standing less than six feet tall and slight of stature to show up at the Tropical run alone during prime time had to have been immeasurable. Pulling up in a new black Cadillac playing Lynyrd Skynyrd either suicidally provocative or reflective of a painful lack of self-awareness. Kenny Rehage did just that and without a second thought. He made his way from the car and sat on the sidelines with the other waiting players, ignored and avoided as if he brought with him a virus.

And he waited.

He was passed over again and again, in defiance of pick-up hoop protocol. Then a few taunts and verbal jabs were lobbed either at him or in his general vicinity like horseshoes, supposed to garner laughs at his expense. Some of the jibes were actually funny, resulting in Kenny half-grinning without responding-

...And he waited.

Quietly he watched, periodically spinning the ball on his fingers one by one, the guitarist playing a progression to warm up for his set. And then he was asked to join-

...More like told.

Maybe it was thought of as an act of charity. Maybe out of curiosity or even as an experiment. Or to simply give them something to laugh at now and talk about later. Kenny stepped out onto the court softly, as if he might be second guessing his decision to come down to these parts to play-

...Until the ball was inbounded to the assumed point guard of the team he was playing with. In a Jeckyl and Hyde transformation, Kenny rotated around him in a half-trot and with his hands out, all but demanded the ball as if he were its deed holder. His confidence alone was the very thing to force the ball carrier to surrender possession and with it the display of holy shit proportions began. His signature game, but played with a vengeance. Not a wasted step taken, nor a hint of indecision on what he wanted to do. He immediately knew where each player on the court was going to go before they did themselves, both offensively and on defense. He had to have been studying them while waiting. He began to create openings like he had a video game joystick in hand, picking apart coverages and threading the smallest of openings with the ball as his needle. Each of the four other players on his side didn't have time to be stunned, immediately feasting on his playmaking largess. The gathered crowd grew and with each electric pass converted or seemingly impossible long shot drained, responded with exhalations of amazement, spasm-inducing outbursts that seemed more suited for spiritual revivals.

WAAAAAAAAAAHHHHH!

Of the spectator voices, the most enthusiastic hoot and hollering came from Danté Billings, whose thunderous voice overshadowed his diminutive five-foot-two stature.

WAAAAAAAAAAAHHHHH!

Danté was muscular and dark in complexion with a cherubic face, dimples appearing in his cheeks when he smiled, his teeth perfectly straight and bright white.

WAAAAAAAAAAAHHHHH!

He taunted the player Kenny had just turned around. *Nigga, he own-you! You his Kunta Kinte!*

While seemingly forever laughing, Danté was confrontational and fearless and had been for as long as anyone could remember. Where Kenny refrained from talking trash while playing, Danté assumed the part of doing it on his behalf.

White boy just shake-an' baked the black right off your ass, nigga!

And when Kenny feigned a lightning-quick ball-toss into a defender's face to freeze him then pulled back...a juke one way, then another, his defender's coverage betrayed by collapsing ankles and surrendering the lane, the entire court could hear Danté's play by play.

WAAAAAAAAAAAHHHHH!

Whitey just dizzy pilled you! Dizzy pilled you! You gon' wake up with a sore pussy, bitch!

And when Kenny chose to slow the pace of the game down, then catch defenders in a lull and let loose a rainmaker, Danté erupted, heckling the player whose confusion and broken coverage allowed the shot.

Smoked your momma's last cigarette with that shit! Wiped his ass on the bed sheets, too!

WAAAAAAAAAAAHHHHH!

The first game was closed out, twenty-one coming with a simple bunny from one of the players who never got as many touches as he did that night. The losers walked off the court, eyes on Kenny that might be interpreted as resentful, although could have been awe, with frustration and a touch of confusion, the kind that comes by way of card trick. A few hand slaps but still no one asked his name. The

173

next five stepped out and when the ball was inbounded there was no question whose hands it was going into. And then again, another show with Danté carnival barking on the sidelines, only taking a break long enough to engage in a not so indiscreet hand-to-hand transaction.

When the lights around the court were dimmed, the show was over. The park was closing. Kenny exchanged a few-half committed hand slaps and fist bumps with the other players, then made an unceremonious exit. He wouldn't have stopped had Danté not run over to him and begun tossing ten and twenty dollar bills at his feet like he were a street busker god, which Kenny refused to collect off the ground but thanked him all the same. No one else made for the money, either. No one would dare. While Danté Billings had established a reputation as a loudmouth, even at five foot two he was feared. And on account of his own merits not because of his half-brother Rahkeem, an original *Eight-Ball-Deucy-Deuce* out of Liberty City who was locked away in State Prison on a murder rap. Danté's resumé listed experiences on both sides of the barrel.

It was an unlikely acquaintance, Danté and Kenny, one that was limited only to the courts at Tropical before the run or after in the parking lot. Danté pursued him, as if auditioning to be his friend, even inviting him to his upcoming twenty-third birthday, which Kenny politely offered regrets making up an excuse that seemed plausible enough. Danté felt compelled to share his own hopes and dreams with Kenny, aspirations that were as ludicrous as they were heartfeltly honest. *I'm gonna rap, start a new brand of hip-hop mixin' diss comedy, like bacon chop shit and rap battles. Maybe get in movies and who-know what else. Build my base in SoFlo, go worldwide, then global. And then own a basketball team.* He loved basketball and wanted to know in detail how Kenny learned to play the way he did, how he kept his composure on the floor and specifically, why he never balled in college, as in Danté's estimation Kenny had mad D-1 skills. *Like what you do to my nigga, Jellybean. J-bean can ball, too! Like a m'fucka! Serious. And you made him your bitch out there. How you own him so bad? You D-up on him, he can't get a-inch. He usually blow by motherfuckers. It's like...I dunno...you read his mind.*

Kenny had feigned being flattered, then shared his secret. He told Danté that while Jellybean had good skills, he wasn't hard to defend because he had a tell. *A what?* Kenny had spelled out that when Jellybean wanted to make a move, it didn't matter from where around the perimeter he was, he would stick his tongue out in the direction he was going to go. *Like Mike stick his tongue out?* Kenny had explained it was nothing like when Michael Jordan did it. Michael Jordan didn't use his tongue like the blinker on his car. Danté was confused and Kenny had explained further that with Jellybean, his tongue was a tell. If he stuck it out of the left side of his mouth, he was going left. And on the right side, he would be going right. He didn't know he was doing it. And further, if he pressed his lips together, he would be trying to power through the lane on his strong side. *Damn. When I buy my NBA franchise, Imma put you on the bench with me. My right hand.*

It was no surprise that the life insurance policy pitch came organically, as when Danté matter of factly asked Kenny what he thought might be a good idea as a way to build hype for his impending media empire. His brand. *Y'know how rappers drive around in bulletproof cars and got-like entourages and body armour and shit? And then they rhyme about it? That's sellin' their brand.* Kenny considered the question way longer than he needed to and suggested Danté get a life insurance policy. *Huh?* It was explained to him what it was and that he could rhyme about how his record label or management team sweated him to get one because so many people were after him. *But I don't got a-* Danté stopped and smiled. *How much that shit cost?* Kenny told him he thought it would be around a hundred bucks a month for a million dollar policy, give or take.

And then there was silence.

I ain't got that kind of money. Kenny recalled Danté unconsciously touching the thick chain around his neck. *I mean...for that.* And so it went, Kenny told him that his boss bought insurance policies from people that didn't want them anymore. If Danté got one, he could probably get them to buy it from him. Probably even get him a couple of thousand for it. Danté didn't fully understand, nor did he need to. He was all in.

Later when they parted ways, Danté bounced across the street outside the park, already thinking of rhymes and counting his money while looking back at Kenny and grinning, the dimples on his face on full display. An oncoming passing car beeped hard and on reflex Danté immediately transformed to aggressor and barked at it. The car hit the brakes. Danté stepped up on it without hesitation, chest out and a string of threatening expletives behind it. The car slowly drove off. Kenny had witnessed all five-foot-two of him back down a car full of home boys with nothing more than bravado. Danté turned back to Kenny, smiled ear-to-ear and did the pow-pow thing with his fingers positioned like a gun held sideways. Danté Billings had to that point lived twenty-three springs. Kenny figured only a miracle would allow him that many falls. When his life policy was written and in turn sold to *MFB&T,* Danté got a check for two-thousand dollars. The next day he bought another chain.

Kenny started going to the run at the YMCA not long thereafter. He might have convinced himself it had players who were just as good and it was closer to where he lived or there was less arguing over fouls and fewer if not any periodic fights, or the style of play was more thought out and run in both directions with equal effort. Still, with all else being equal, the reason was Danté. If he was out of sight, he would remain out of mind. Which he did, until Kenny learned he'd met his fate in a salvo of bullets on a dark street not far from the Tropical Park courts, ending once and for all his dance with the devil across the razor's edge of an unforgiving ghetto. And with his death, the policy would pay out. Eighteen months into a five-year term at a cost of roughly thirty-six hundred dollars, it would yield a million in return.

Boy, could Kenny pick 'em.

Kenny looked from the car window over at the treeline again. His perspective of the top of the Quickie-Mart sign around the block only changed in that the palms were swaying about in a gentle breeze. He wondered if Reed and Stubblefield were still there and this time wasn't sure. Then he thought again about Copeland and wondered if it was too late. His phone rang, startling him. He looked down at it and his heart began to race.

Chapter Eleven

Loose Ends

Copeland wasn't going to dwell on Haberman for much longer. He'd decided to allow himself only a few moments more of wondering what he had to do to get the man to show him just the smallest bit of respect. He didn't want to get caught in an emotional riptide, the kind in which the longer he stayed in the more difficult it would be to get out.

The *Stones* were off, replaced by Rod Stewart, but just for one song. *Maggie Mae* was playing and he wondered why he was suddenly restless.

And hungry!

He wasn't supposed to be either. He'd just driven past another McDonald's and nearly turned into the parking lot on reflex. He resisted the temptation, rescued by the realization that he had to have Brenda get the breakfast meeting with Dale Marlin in the books before he forgot, not that there was a chance of that happening. He dialed his office.

"Hey, Alan." Upon answering she was unusually upbeat, picking up possibly straight off a laugh.

Copeland wanted to ask her what she'd just put in her coffee but didn't bother. "Brenda, set up a breakfast with Dale Marlin from Inferno Capital for next Wednesday. The Ritz Carlton, Bal Harbour at eight o'clock for two and call his office to give them details, no need to check times." He hesitated then, as he had a change of mind. "On second thought, make it at the Shore Club.

"No problem. Anything else?"

"Not now." He disconnected without thanking her.

The McDonald's was far enough behind him now not to be considered a viable threat. He then reflected on the Hispanic worker at the car wash who squared him away with the quick and thorough windshield powerwashing, figuring he should have gotten his card. Have him come out to the house, detail the car. All the cars. Then he mocked the very thought with a mumble that barely caused his lips to patter.

That fucking guy didn't have a green card, let alone a business one.

He shook his head and continued his thought in silence.

What kind of car wash worker would have a business card, anyway? Well, if any ever did it would be that guy.

He told himself to have Kenny track him down, get his name. Go back to the place and tell him that he had some work for him. Have him come out to the house, detail the car. All the cars.

What was the name of that place?

He looked in the rear view mirror as if the car wash could still be visible, knowing full well it was by now several miles back.

What fucking street am I even on?

He looked overhead to see as he passed through the next intersection and made a mental note.

"He'll find it. The kid'll find it."

The kid.

Copeland still was in the dark on what Kenny wanted to talk to him about, although after further consideration he discounted the possibility it was to ask his opinion on a personal matter, like getting married. That kind of ask would only come attached to something else, like a request for a raise or a loan. A buffer of sorts, a diversionary tactic to push forward the true agenda. But a move like that would be uncharacteristic of Kenny even though Copeland would welcome it. He was pretty straight forward and hadn't, in Copeland's memory, even asked for so much as an extra slice of cheese on his sandwich to that point. His raises came unprompted, as did the periodic bonuses, all which were generous as Copeland had come to count on him to do whatever was asked without question or hiccup and in complete confidence.

Maybe he's gonna warn me about something.

Maybe someone is trying to fuck me.

Yglesias.

Alé.

Scooter.

Maybe he's watching my back.

Then he switched gears.

Maybe he's moving on.

The idea of Kenny telling Copeland he was moving on suddenly became the odds on favorite and with that, he wondered why.

Who the fuck knows.

He spoke this time in more than a mumble and resigned, like he had a companion seated beside him he was venting to. Regardless of what Kenny's motivations were, Copeland couldn't let that happen.

He had to keep him.

He couldn't let him go.

Not now.

He needed him.

He knew too much.

And with that, his restlessness evolved into a strange sensation, a pins and needles tingling in his neck and shoulders that felt like a leg that had fallen asleep and he wondered if it might be related to nerves. He'd never experienced bouts of anxiety before but recently had been experiencing physical uneasiness when his imagination would get away from him, especially with negative connotations. He was thinking too much. The kid wasn't going anywhere. Even if he planned on it, Copeland propped himself up with the idea that he'd be able to convince him to stay. Even if it meant asking him to do so just for a little bit longer. That was the trick. Get them to give you just a little, then string it out. Cross the next bridge upon arriving at it. Not before. Copeland thought about the call he had later with Schwartz and his partners from the Triad Group. Schwartzy. The *Ponce de Leon* Project. Three-thirty. No need to call Brenda back and ask her. He knew. Right before the massage she was scheduling. The follow-up on their pitch and property tour that he was pretty sure he was a pass on.

Now, he was considering it as a way to keep Kenny. Maybe he should nix the massage appointment and spend a little more time on the call. Have the kid on it with him like he'd thought to himself earlier. Give him a piece of it. Just enough to whet his appetite to keep him from going anywhere, if that was what he had designs on doing. Yeah. That's a good idea. Bring it up to him before he even has a chance to broach whatever it was that was on his mind. The more he swished that idea around in his mouth, the more he liked the taste of it. And to think he only entertained the initial pitch because he'd felt bad, thinking he owed it to Schwartz to hear it out. Poor Schwartzy. He was a private equity manager he'd done a few small deals with who'd come to him eighteen months earlier to pitch him on doing a bridge loan that was short term, high-yield and collateralized but had to remain strictly confidential in that the borrower involved was a famous, household name of a celebrity whom the idea of needing a cash loan seemed ludicrous. Even more so in that famous, household name of a celebrity also happened to be married to another household name celebrity. The reason for the bridge loan being pursued privately was to keep banks or mortgage companies out of the equation for the sake of privacy. Copeland didn't trust what he was hearing, but needed to know who this famous, household name of a celebrity was. He suggested that he was willing to talk about it. And talk they did, with Copeland learning who this celebrity was and Schwartz feilding the obvious question: How could this be? This famous, household name of a celebrity made twenty million dollars a movie and for the past three years averaged three per. Not to mention the side deals, foreign endorsements, investments that had to include sycophantic Wall Street bankers serving up hot stock IPOs in exchange for the privilege of simply being associated with him. The sixty million dollars a year over the past three had to be a hell of a lot closer to one-hundred million. Copeland grilled Schwartz on how anyone with that amount of income could possibly need a short term loan and be willing to pay such a high interest rate. What about the wife? And with that, sworn to secrecy, Alan Copeland was given as juicy a tidbit of gossip which being privy to made him feel that he had arrived as much as anything else he'd experienced, more satisfying than looking down at the new Rolex Daytona latched onto his wrist or the steering wheel of the car he was driving. Firstly, he was told, the amount of money earned by the famous household name of a celebrity was unadjusted gross revenue. After factoring in commissions for agents, business managers, lawyers and publicists, it was whacked in half and that was before the taxman got his needle tapped into the vain. Still, Copeland wasn't buying. There were millions left over. Then it was explained the amount of houses this famous, household name of a celebrity owned, all over the world. And the island and private jet charters. And the obscenely overpriced macabré memorabilia, contemporary art and rare wine collections. Still, Copeland didn't see it. His wife's money was her money not to mention, they were getting divorced. His fourth. Copeland's skepticism wasn't quite satisfied. Then it was painted for him with an even more pellucid example. Schwartz recounted an incident that might sum it all up into one easily digestible portion. The famous, household name of a celebrity had not long earlier purchased a yacht for two million dollars. And on the maiden voyage of this two million dollar yacht, the famous, household name of a celebrity and his nearly as famous wife took a romantic cruise down into Mexico where he expressed his love for her with a gift of a two million dollar diamond ring he'd purchased from a Parisian jeweler. While making a port of call visit to a Mexican seaside town, the power couple decided to dine in a charming local restaurant where they would drink their faces off. At one point well into the evening, the wife of the famous, household name of a celebrity accused him of looking at the waitress's ass and he in turn told her she was crazy, using what was evidently a hairpin trigger of a word. The row was the glass throwing, table flipping, explosive sort and continued out the doors of the restaurant, back to the dock, on to the yacht and continued as they resumed sailing down the coast, climaxing with the wife of the famous, household name of a celebrity ripping the two million dollar diamond ring off her finger and with an emphatic 'fuck you' directed at her husband, threw it overboard into the depths of the deep, dark sea. The famous, household name of a celebrity ordered the captain to immediately drop anchor and called his handlers in a panic, who in turn retained for immediate dispatch a salvage dive team to comb the ocean floor in search of the jettisoned two million dollar diamond ring. At the cost of four hundred thousand dollars. After two days, the two million dollar diamond ring thrown off of the two million dollar yacht wasn't recovered and upon returning to port in Los Angeles where the couple made up, the famous, household name of a celebrity wasted no time calling the Parisian jeweler to buy his temperamental wife another diamond ring. For two million dollars. That, Schwartz explained, is how someone who earns upwards of sixty million dollars a year can put themselves into a situation of needing money. Copeland almost didn't believe him, his only comment being that he was sure one of the salvage divers had in fact recovered the ring from the ocean floor and probably shoved it up his ass for safekeeping until he got home. At least that's what Copeland said he would have done. Well, Alan Copeland had to meet this famous, household name of a celebrity for no other reason than to sit in the presence of what might have well been a Coney Island bearded lady or lobster boy, to which Schwartz said wasn't going to happen since the famous, household name of a celebrity insisted this business arrangement be handled without his being involved in anything more than signing the promissory notes from the privacy of his lawyer's office. That wasn't going to wash. If Copeland were to get involved as a loan financier, he insisted on first meeting the borrower personally. Shortly thereafter, a small, informal dinner for four was arranged by Schwartz. Alan Copeland sat next to him and across from the famous, household name of a celebrity, who in his estimation gave off the appearance of being no more interesting than a sock drawer. He was far smaller than the twenty foot tall celluloid hero Copeland had seen in the movies, devoid of any traces of charm, boring, timid and particularly nervous. He did, however, laugh at Copeland's jokes and feigned interest in the stories of grandeur he told but Copeland knew better. The man sitting across from him was, after all, an actor and one who wanted something from him. Schwartz had picked up the dinner tab and after the handshakes and *let's talk soon* pleasantries, Copeland drove home feeling superior to everyone he'd dined with that evening and couldn't wait to tell Karen all about it. The following morning when Schwartz called to get the process started, assuming Copeland had committed to finance the

185

bridge loan, he was turned down and told it wasn't going to happen. It didn't feel right. What Schwartz didn't know is that Copeland never had any intention of loaning the famous, household name of a celebrity the money. He only wanted to sit across from him as if he were a Roman emperor who with the simple *pollice verso* of an outstretched hand could save him. Again, a reminder that he had arrived. Surprisingly, Schwartz had circled back to Copeland a little over a year later with no hard feelings, as business was business. Whatever embarrassment he endured over the loan to the famous, household name of a celebrity was short-lived as he had not long thereafter found a partner to finance it. Schwartz was calling this time on behalf of a new venture which Copeland would at least listen to, promising himself he'd be more forthcoming with his intentions. The Triad Hospitality Group had big plans for the old *Ponce de Leon Hotel* across from the Olympia Theater in Downtown Miami. Designed in the popular Mediterranean revival style architecture of the early 1900's, it had deteriorated into a *purgatorio* for the downtrodden behind the grandiose but tired and worn façade. A third of the three hundred single room occupancy units had tenants living in them, mostly subsidized by the government as housing of last resort. A *de facto* human storage facility. Triad developed trendy boutique hotels, acquiring the *Ponce* intent on doing a massive remodel to launch a European-style *pensione*, incorporating a vibrant social atmosphere with two lobby bars and rooftop pool with a state of the art DJ booth. The current tenants were offered cash relocation incentives to move. Most did. Twenty-one didn't. They were those with nowhere to go or too unmotivated to leave. Or simply taking an opportunity to pass on a little bit of their own misery to another through recalcitrance. The construction team would do their eight million dollar renovation around them. As so often it goes, delays, unforeseen cost overruns and exhausted capital calls put the developers in a position where they needed another investor to infuse completion funds. The favorable terms offered reflected their desperation and Copeland, while only mildly interested, had agreed to tour the project site and hear the pitch, again thinking he owed it to Schwartz to do so-

...Who wasn't even at the property to walk him through it.

Maybe he was hedging off a second helping of embarrassment or maybe he really had been involved in a fender-bender down in Coconut Grove. Copeland was given the tour by two of the principals of the Triad Hospitality Group and the general contractor doing the build out. All were dressed business-casual and wearing hard hats that looked ridiculous on everyone except the contractor. They walked the dusty, unfinished hallways beneath exposed standpipe sprinkler feeds and work lights. Seeing the property and hearing Triad's vision impressed him far more than the simple perusal he gleaned off of the prospectus from Schwartz. He saw three completed model rooms that were immaculate. The furniture, fixtures and fittings were all well thought-out and in tune with the concept down to the smallest detail. Although not showing it, as Copeland made a point never to tilt his hand in that regard, he was very interested. When the subject of the remaining twenty-one downtrodden tenants was broached with Copeland asking if they'd be something of an eye sore and potentially scaring off guests, he was assured that it wasn't a concern. Those residents would be prohibited from using the main lobby, relegated to a service entrance on the side of the building to come and go and the common areas were to be off limits to them as well. Then there was the question of how long they would be expected to remain in residence. The principals of the Triad Group explained their strategy of tendering three more strategically timed buyout offers, incrementally increasing in amount with the last one right before opening to be hard and final. Their research showed that this formula typically resulted in moving most of them out, with an anticipated final resident count to be under ten units, or three percent of the total occupancy. The general contractor offered a concise summary by suggesting that it then becomes a matter of waiting around for them to die and made a lighthearted comment about high cholesterol diets and Do Not Resuscitate orders. One of the Triad principals added apologetically of that being the unvarnished truth, as horrible as it sounded. The looks on their faces suggested contrition and shame, even a tinge of embarrassment. While it made no sense at all, Copeland immediately felt that they were judging him and in the privacy of his thoughts grew uncomfortable and with it less interested in the venture.

He stopped at another red light and changed his music selection again. This time he wanted to hear *Journey*. Again to his non-existent companion in the empty seat beside him-

Fuck it.

If the kid wants to supervise the investment, I'll do it.

Give him an office on site.

He can come and go as he wants.

The Triad assholes can report to him.

And Copeland felt good about the possibility.

A horn blasted from behind him. It wasn't a polite *tap-tap* reminder honk or a *tap-tap-tap* to get the attention of another driver to convey a message or even a full blown honk to make their presence known, it was an elongated honk rooted in annoyance and frustration. He looked in his rear view and saw the car tight on his tail, then looked at his speedometer and realized how slow he was driving. He immediately sped up and for good measure changed lanes. The car behind him sped by, the driver looking over and cursing him as if he'd been dealt a personal insult. Continuing down the avenue, he continued to think about Kenny and regretted keeping him at such an arm's length distance personally, considering how much he counted on him, how trusted he was by him. He should have invited him into places he went instead of having him wait in the car. He should have had him over for dinner. The times he did invite him to events that were social, Kenny had still been "working." Copeland had wanted to get his take on something or someone or even hover around to eavesdrop on conversations, even use him as a seat filler. Copeland decided that was going to change. Even if he was leaving, Copeland would have Karen invite him and his girlfriend to Lauren's wedding. That would be nice for him. He probably hadn't been to too many formal events, if any at all. That would be nice for him. And a few dinners. At the house and out. Strictly social. And it was decided, Copeland was going to lead with pitching him on the *Ponce de Leon* development. He'd get him to stay. And from here on in, he'd be more welcoming on a personal level.

Definitely.

Copeland dialed up his office again.

189

"Hey, Alan." Brenda answered as if just coming off a laugh this time as well.

"What's so funny?"

"I'm sorry, what do you mean?-"

"You're laughing."

"Was I? Oh. I had no idea. What's up?"

"Can you set up a breakfast with Dale Marlin from Inferno Capital for next Wednesday at the Shore Club? Eight o'clock for two should be good."

"It's already done, Alan. His office confirmed."

Copeland was confused. "Already done?" Then he caught himself. "Shit, I didn't realize I already asked you to do that. Sorry, Brenda. My head's up my ass a little bit."

"No problem, Alan. Anything else?"

"No. Thanks. Talk to you later." He disconnected and sighed hard and with a head shake reprimanded himself. He had already turned into the parking lot of another McDonald's. He was still thirsty. And he'd just get some fries. Maybe some nuggets, the small one. He pulled around slowly to the drive thru and settled into the line. A deep breath and he turned off the music in anticipation of having to order through the intercom. Seconds later he felt the ground beneath the car begin to tremor and the reverberating head-splitting sounds of a bass-line. A low riding, metallic blue Nissan Altima hooptie with twenty-four inch rims and curb feelers affixed behind all the wheels, not just the right side, had just pulled in. Copeland looked over his shoulder as it slowly moved alongside the line of cars in the drive thru cue. The driver's heavily tinted window was up but the rear passenger one appeared to be lowering down to half-mast. It slowed down more, coming to a complete stop directly next to Copeland's Rolls Royce, then inched inward slowly forcing a wedge into the space between Copeland and the car in front of him, effectively blocking him from moving forward. Copeland quickly looked behind him in the line, as if looking for an escape.

There were three other cars behind him now.

Backing up was out of the question.

He was trapped.

Chapter Twelve

Rosie

Area Code 850. The following seven digits Kenny didn't recognize. It immediately created the kind of momentary fear and incapacitation that comes with turning a corner and finding yourself between the meat and a junkyard dog. The only people in Okaloosa County who Kenny might expect a call from were already listed in his phone. Mrs. Johnson, his next door neighbor from down near the swamp road turn was one. She called on his birthday and at Christmas or sometimes out of the blue to tell him, bless her soul, that she was thinking about him. Lee Chaulker, his former probation officer, was the other. He no longer had any official business with Kenny but called on several occasions to see if he was playing any hoops and ask for updates that amounted to trolling for thank you's.

It rang again.

Area Code 805.

Maybe it was one of his boys. The ones he'd been arrested with over the pot deal gone south. His power forward teammate from high school, Boss Hogg. Or Pete who he worked with for Bobby Flavor trimming trees. Or Benji or Calvin Milsap. Maybe they'd heard he'd found a good job and felt slighted, like they might be owed a cut of his gains. He could see Boss Hogg doing that. Maybe they wanted something else from him. Or had a perceived score to settle.

Swampers for life.

The phone rang a third time. Kenny knew one more and it would kick into the safe haven of voicemail, shielding him from what was unknown. He could then play it back with the comfort of knowing who it was and decide whether a response was merited. And with that, he thought of her again.

Rosie.

Confront it, she would tell him.

Pick it up.

Address it, get it over with.

She was an ardent believer that avoiding uncomfortable conversations only delayed what was inevitable and then it usually resulted in a higher cost than if it were addressed earlier. Emotionally, that is. She equated it to credit card interest on a purchase, in that ultimately you paid far more for something than you should. Rosie wasn't a disciple of any self-help betterment philosophies. She simply had a habit of advocating what she saw as common sense responses to everyday predicaments, which she would say most self-help betterment philosophies really were, just with the added component of one party handing over stacks of money to another to be told so.

He picked up. "Hello?"

"Hello, Mr. Rehage? Kenny Wayne Rehage?"

A hesitation, guarded. "This is he...uh, him. Yeah."

"Hi, Mr. Rehage-" The voice on the other end sounded sincere, in that it lacked any upbeat, feigned enthusiasm that came with sales calls. *"My name is Edward Wyeth, I'm an auditor working out of the Okaloosa County VA, the Veterans Administration in Crestview-"*

Kenny was disarmed but at the same time confused.

"You're listed as the beneficiary of the estate of Martin Rehage, Sergeant First Class, US Army, retired?"

Another hesitation, still guarded. Then he nodded to the affirmative even though the man on the other end couldn't see. "He was my father. Yeah."

"Reason I'm calling you is I was reviewing his file. One of many, unfortunately, to see whether he received the benefits that he had been entitled to as a veteran."

"Okay."

"There are several points I need to make you aware of. Some are minor, some might have a little more....significance." Then there was a pause, the kind that gives the listener a moment to set their feet. *"Your father, Sergeant Rehage, is deceased."* It wasn't so much a question as a cross reference.

Kenny again hesitated, but this time for different reasons. "Yes, sir. He is. He passed away."

A respectful pause followed. *"I'm sorry for your loss, Mr. Rehage."* Another moment of silence, more truncated. *"Just a few quick questions if you don't mind. Firstly, at the time of his passing, were you ever informed by anyone from the Veteran Affairs office that he qualified for a grave marker or headstone to be furnished at the cost of the Veterans Administration?"*

Kenny had to think about it. "No. I can't say that I was. But, uh...whether they did or didn't...that's...y'know, not really important now."

"Understood, sir. But I did have to ask as it's not indicated in his docket. Clearly an oversight." Kenny got the feeling something was being written down or noted on the other end. *"Would you know if at any time he sought out assistance for Mental Health related services through the VA? Anything that might be connected or related to any...Post Traumatic Stress Disorders?"*

Kenny took enough time to give the impression he was considering what was asked. "I'm not sure my dad had any issues like that, Mr. Wyeth. If he did, he didn't show them. I mean, his takin' his own life...I'm not sure it had anything to do with his time in the service, anything that happened during his time overseas and whatnot. Y'know?"

"Well, unfortunately that's not always so easy to determine, Mr. Rehage. My concern is whether he'd ever reached out to the VA in regard to that and didn't get the attention that was justifiably his to request."

"Well, he never said anything to me about it. Nothin' like that, no."

"Okay. I understand that's a pretty tough thing to be asked and I apologize, but I did have to check it off the list."

"I understand, sir. No reason to apologize."

"Has anyone from the VA ever reached out to you regarding benefits you, as the beneficiary, might be entitled to?"

"Not that I can think of. Maybe they mailed somethin' to the house, but I can't say, y'know...one way or the other. That whole time...is kind of a blur."

195

"I fully understand, and again I apologize for having to have to bring this up."

Kenny then took a pause, as if in search of a recollection. "He did once call the, uh...*Vee-Ayy* after he got ripped off in a...like an investment scam where it looked like pretty much veterans were targeted. I think he called, heck...I think he called a bunch of agencies, but nothin' never came of that."

The silence from the other end was the sort borne from disbelief. *"There's a special place in hell for anyone that would do that, scamming veterans."*

"Yeah. I agree, that." Kenny suddenly felt the need to move the call along. "But, uh...otherwise, Mr. Wyeth, I can't say I heard my father complain much 'bout anything, let alone the *Vee-Ayy*. Not sayin' he was happy with it, just...he wasn't the sort who did a whole bunch of complainin'."

"Understandable. Well, just know that you can reach out to the Administration at any time to see what benefits you're entitled to as his beneficiary. You can still do that."

"I'll keep that in mind. And thank you for, uh...callin'."

"It's my pleasure. And, one more thing. Please accept my sympathies on your father's passing and my gratitude for his service."

"Thank you, sir. I appreciate you sayin' that."

"I see here that he was attached to the 1st SFOD-Delta-" A pause. *"...He must have been quite a guy."*

"Yeah. That's where he finished up. Retired on top. Hoppin' and poppin' with the best."

"My father was a plank holder with the 10th SF Group. Served in Korea and Vietnam. A special breed of men, those guys. A real special breed."

"Yeah, you can say that again. Well, I appreciate you callin' me, Mr. Wyeth."

Kenny disconnected. He was rattled but still glad he'd taken the call, glad he'd heeded to what Rosie would have suggested he should do. He then decided he may as well call Special Agent Reed and tell him that he was okay, that he was ready to continue on and glad that he made the asshole sweat a little.

Then the vision in his mind of Rosie that had just appeared, her grin and precious, girlish half-shrug pushed everything else to the sidelines for a brief moment. Even though it didn't matter any more, he chided himself for placing value in what she would encourage being done in one area, taking a call from someone unknown, then having complete disregard for not only her opinion, but genuine conviction, in regard to another.

Rosie.

Excuse me, ma'am-

He smiled.

Those were the first words he'd said to her. The envelope with her receipt and work order had fallen from the purse slung over her shoulder as she left the tire center.

...You dropped somethin'.

She turned around as Kenny had taken another step out the door and toward her, leaning over to pick it off the hot asphalt parking lot.

He called me ma'am.

She wasn't sure if she should have been charmed by his politeness or taken aback by what she assumed was being thought to be far older than she was and by someone around her age. He handed it to her and smiled, but then looked away immediately, overwhelmed by the kind of shyness that really never goes away. She thanked him and meant it, tucked the envelope back into the purse that looked like it was expensive then walked over to her car that just had its tires rotated. He retreated back inside to the checkout area to finish waiting for his tires to be done without so much as a half-glance back at her. When he first took notice of her in the waiting room, he remembered thinking she was pretty, but nothing else. It was an observation and nothing more, no different than noticing the color of one's hair or a particular hat on their head. It came and went without even the briefest of fantasies, as any girl who had a handbag like that or drove a Lexus, even though it was the small one, would give a transplanted swamper like him the time of day. And that was fine, as they would probably have nothing to talk about. To Kenny, his instinct in addressing her was not incorrect. Rosie was definitely a 'ma'am.'

A little more than a week later but less than two, he'd gone out for an afternoon run beneath the shade of the giant Ficus trees that lined the loop at Hugh Taylor Birch State Park. Something about them reminded him of back home, despite the fact that Ficus trees didn't grow in those parts. He was running in one direction when he noticed a girl running toward him, not terribly fast but obviously working hard. It took a second to register where he recognized her from and as they passed, he recalled. He glanced once over his shoulder. It was her. The girl from the tire center who had dropped her work order-

And as soon as he turned back, she looked over hers. It was him, she thought.

He called me ma'am.

The two glances of recognition were mere seconds from clicking, with each unaware the other had looked back. There wasn't going to be another loop for them to pass again, as she was finishing her run and he was beginning his, making for the type of missed connections that gave birth to dopey metaphors. If there are mystical elements that control these sorts of things, fate and what not, they had to have been frustrated enough to allow for one more shot at interaction.

An overly lit *Smoothie Boss* in the strip mall with very little parking. She was ahead of him at the counter and would have paid for her medium *Papaya-Lime Dream* had she not forgotten her wallet.

Oh my God-

...My wallet-

...I'm so sorry, I'll be right back.

And from behind her she heard him speak. Kenny, waiting to order his *Pineapple-Mango Mash*, who hadn't yet recognized her, gave a directive to the cashier. *Um, you can just put that on mine, ma'am.*

Rosie turned, and had she been a smoothie herself would have been a *Bewilderment Swirl*. Collecting herself, she was having none of the generosity. No, she told the counter girl, she'd run home and come right back. The cashier told her it was no problem, she could come back later and he said again to put it on his, no sense making another trip. With the *Smoothie Boss* employee playing referee and siding with him, Rosie thanked Kenny and he waved it off, saying something about

199

it happening to the best of us before giving her the space a gentleman affords a lady. Both got their orders, she thanked him once, twice then a third time.

I'm Rosie...Rosie Ayala.

Kenny...Kenny Rehage.

Do you live around here?

Do you live around here?

She giggled.

He blushed.

Yes. Up on North Atlantic. By Northeast Twenty-Seventh.

I live on Ocean Boulevard. B'tween Seville and Granada.

You called me ma'am.

The volley had the innocence and curiosity of two children meeting in a sandbox-

...You want to be friends?

I'll ask my mom.

Okay.

I'll ask my mom.

All obvious or perceived external differences aside, there was a dynamic between them that suggested a confederated spirit, something shared that would take more than a scratching of the surface to uncover.

I can't believe you called me ma'am.

When it was time to part ways she thanked him again for the smoothie. He told her again that it was his pleasure. She offered to treat the next time they saw one another and he agreed to it. Phone numbers were awkwardly exchanged and to his surprise, the girl with the expensive handbag that drove a Lexus, even though it was the small one, was not only giving a transplanted swamper like him the time of day, she appeared to be enchanted by him. And the natural progression of Rosie and Kenny's interactions tracked forward in motion with a fluid ease, like they were resting upon ball bearings.

Rosie Ayala was raised in a homogenous and close knit Hialeah Gardens neighborhood on a vibrant street in an even more vibrantly painted house that was never not immaculately clean on both the inside and out. Her mother was a hotel housekeeping manager, her father a mechanic for United Airlines. Both were first generation immigrants from Medellin, Colombia, with steadfast work ethics. She had one older brother. When Rosie still lived at home they ate dinner together nearly every night and *always, always, always* on Sunday. Now, the gatherings were limited to holidays and then, still never quite the same as they once were. As the relationship with her new friend Kenny from Okaloosa County gently evolved, she volunteered small and sometimes vague, piecemeal morsels of information pertaining to a proud, religious family, not quite estranged from one another...just no longer as close as they once were. Kenny didn't push. And the sharing of his own family history was meted out to her in a similar time-release manner. They got along without effort, sharing established interests and finding new ones together. Rosie chased health, wellness and fitness trends, some of which Kenny adopted while refusing others and no one was offended. He, in turn, had ideas about current events that she didn't feel were worthy of expending any mental bandwidth on. He played basketball several times a week and she spent time with girlfriends from work, with neither expecting a monopoly on the other's time.

When Kenny told Rosie his presence was requested at his boss's home for a black tie charity fundraiser but with the proviso that it wasn't so much a social invitation as a work related mandate which he dreaded having to go to, and that he wouldn't put her in a position to feel like she had to accompany him, she said she would go with him anywhere. Even if they were parking cars out front. When he told her his purpose in being there was to observe and eavesdrop on a business associate of Copeland's, she *begged, begged, begged* to go along. They would be like spies! Kenny smiled, as he never thought of it like that, and realized right around then that he was sure he had fallen in love with her. At the event hosted by Karen Copeland at their home, Rosie blended in effortlessly. Despite being younger than most of the guests in attendance, she looked the part upon arriving, handling herself with the subtle poise and grace of a seasoned society veteran. When Kenny introduced her to Copeland as his girlfriend, she smiled politely and shook his offered hand. As discreet as Copeland might have thought he was being, she could feel his lecherous eyes moving ever so slightly up and down her body, in his mind doing who knows what to her. And the grin on his dull, bronze toned and leathery face, greeting her as if she were being presented to him as an oblation. She knew the type and detested it but never once let on. Karen Copeland, however, she found strangely likable even though her projected tireless benevolence routine was unconvincing. Kenny proceeded to casually set out to do what was asked of him, with Rosie doing just fine on her own, periodically drifting away to appear as if she were admiring the home, its artwork and furnishings. She smiled at others when eyes met, or nodded with familiarity upon passing others and engaged in small talk when it manifested naturally at the wine bar or buffet table. When asked by another guest what she did for a living, she told them and was prepared to share her opinion of local home decorators of distinction and the *en vogue* furniture designers of the moment. She listened attentively to tedious stories and anecdotes and managed not to burst out in laughter when one guest shared their misfortune of putting in an elaborate and expensive koi pond on the grounds of their oceanfront property home without considering the protected land adjacent had several active osprey nests on it. Kenny saw her interactions from across the room and was filled with pride. She carried herself perfectly. Periodically, as Copeland scanned the room, which he always had a habit of doing, his eye line would intersect with hers and he would seize onto it and make a quick approving facial expression to her that included what looked like a smirk. What he approved of was unclear, that she was Kenny's girlfriend or her appearance. He managed to catch her while she had stepped out into the garden where several small clusters of guests milled about on a veranda and quickly looked up and around momentarily as if to see if Kenny was nearby. He had just enough space for the brief interaction to be considered something of a private moment and beginning with an apology, started to ask her a question. *I'm sorry...I don't mean to be outta line or anything, but-* The way he loosely held the drink in his hand, a vodka on the rocks with a wedge of lemon, underscored the fact that he was feeling the effects of it and the shifting of his weight from foot to foot was obvious that he was posturing. Had there been a wall next to him he would have

203

leaned against it, thinking it suave. He seemed about to wave off the question, but forged ahead anyway. *You just look familiar-* And then a devilish grin, like she might have a dirty, little secret and he was the only one in the room who knew about it. *I feel like we might've met before. Did you ever work at-?* And he stopped himself from going any further. The implication can only be speculative, but Rosie sensed he was suggesting that she might have been a stripper at one point and now being cleaned up and clothed, free of glitter, fake eyelashes and stilettos made it difficult to conclusively identify her. He continued on, qualifying his assumption. *I never forget a face, especially a pretty one.* Her gag reflex was difficult to quell but she managed to maintain her composure and politely tell him she worked at a home furnishing boutique in Bal Harbour, suggesting he might have been in at one point. He shook his head implying that he hadn't and seemed disappointed. She complimented him on his lovely house and the job that their decorator did on it, as well as the delightful evening he and his wife hosted and politely excused herself.

She found Kenny in the parlour and sided up next to him. He smiled, leaned down and whispered in her ear. It was time, as the clock hand just made its way into the territory where guests might begin leaving without exits considered being premature. They did one pass through the house together, with Kenny making sure he was seen by Copeland and his wife, then made their way to the front door and disappeared the way steam does.

In the car on the way home, Rosie said nothing of Copeland's teetering on the cusp of impropriety, only pointing out what Kenny already knew.

And those hands!

...They're Mickey Mouse hands-

...His fingers!

...Like those little sausages that come in cans-

...Or sections of a balloon twisted and shaped into...a little puppy dachshund at a child's birthday party-

Kenny laughed. A little more small talk about the guests, the house and what he'd overheard said by the individuals he had been dispatched to eavesdrop on. She shimmied over a little closer so she could rest her head on his shoulder. The evening, in all of its absurdity, had been called back in reference by both of them without ever getting tired.

Kenny sat in his air conditioned car on the tree lined residential street side looking back at the empty playground basketball court, reflecting on it all. What he was doing. How he got there. His unexpected job with Copeland and his unexpected relationship with Rosie that was now coming to a close as well. And like Copeland, she didn't know he was leaving. He wondered if this was tied somehow into what she'd told him, the revelation she had shared with him and his not believing he could ever become fully reconciled with it. Her transparency in exposing it provided him a kill switch he could activate to end it all, what in effect he was doing right then. It didn't matter if she thought he was choosing his job or cooperating with the investigation into Copeland over her.

Rosie had been in a relationship until eleven months before meeting Kenny. It was with a married man. Like her, he was Latino and from a close family. He was well educated and successful, handsome and fit. Overlooking their twenty-two year age difference had been easy. The irredeemable aspect was not her falling for the lies and mistruths, as she was played perfectly, drawn into a seemingly inescapable tidal eddy with attention, a flattery that bordered on worship and a torrent of gifts. By the time she learned the truth, she was already in too deep, not able to imagine having to give up the feeling of security in his presence, the confidence that came with having him in her life. As far as Kenny was concerned, the irredeemable aspect that was chasing him away still was not in Rosie continuing to see her paramour after learning he was married. He understood how traps work. Even after hearing about the betrayed wife appearing in front of Rosie's family's house in Hialeah Gardens late at night with her three small children by her side, hysterically calling for Rosie to come out and face the wife of the man she was sleeping with.

> *¡Ella esta cogia con mi marido¡*
> *¡La puta escarlate!*
> *¡Puta barata, ¡Callejera!*
> *¡Sal aqui, puta!*
> *¡Venga aqui, puta!*

Rosie had not been home at the time, unlike her parents, brother and most of the neighbors but in the arms of the man married to the hysterical, scorned woman responsible for bringing the throngs of neighbors from their houses out into the street. The irredeemable component of her being, her fatal-flaw in Kenny's estimation, was still not her inability to break the relationship off. He understood people are weak. Rosie had fallen under a spell. She had forgiven this man for lying to her and told him if he was going to leave his wife as he'd promised, she would stand by his side. He could give his wife everything and walk away from what she was led to believe by him to be a toxic, loveless marriage and begin anew. She would stand by his side. And leave Rosie's lover did, after the wrecking ball had swung back and forth enough to have devastated two families. His departure though, did not include Rosie. He left both wife and mistress and relocated to Tampa, where Rosie had heard he was engaged to be married again. To Kenny, what was irredeemable was her answering a question asked by him. A simple inquiry to which she answered with complete, forthright honesty.

Do you still love him?

Silence.

If he called for you to come now, would you go?

Silence.

If he showed up at the door and asked you to leave with him, would you?

Tears welled in her eyes.

Would you?

Her wordless response was as honest as it was conclusive. She had simply hung her head and began to sob and Kenny wished he'd never asked.

Whether he was right or wrong in deciding to leave her, being rational or otherwise, he convinced himself that he'd never have the security of knowing he would be first in her heart. To him, there would always be the possibility that he would be abandoned. Even if the possibility remained remote, he reminded himself, it couldn't be more remote than his father abandoning him the way he did.

Kenny looked away from the basketball court and again turned his head across the street toward the tops of the palm trees and the sign of the Quickie-Mart around the block. He then looked for his phone to call Walter Reed, forgetting where he'd put it only to realize it was still in his hand.

Chapter Thirteen

Oh, Elliot

Copeland was stuck between the line of cars to his rear and the ones in front of him, the concrete, brick and metal ordering station of the drive thru on one side and now the metallic blue Nissan Altima with the blacked out windows on the other. Both flight and fight responses within him were disabled for different and glaringly obvious reasons. He could only hope a quick hope that was more like a prayer and avoided any immediate eye contact with whomever was behind the wheel of the Altima that had effectively boxed him in. But his flash panic only lasted a few seconds, as the car in front of him in line began to roll forward four or five feet toward the intercom where orders were placed and the metallic blue Nissan Altima forced its way further in between Copeland and it. He realized he wasn't being ambushed but simply cut in line. The occupants in the back seat of the Altima that were visible to Copeland through their open window were clucking and cackling, wagging their tongues and pointing at him with ridicule, even flipping him off and that was fine with Copeland. Just fine. Indulging them in their raucousness was a small, if not less than insignificant price to pay in the grand scheme of things. He was even okay with paying for their order had they asked. He took a deep breath and did a little examination of conscience, an inventory of sorts and realized if someone actually had wanted to attack him, it wouldn't be very hard. He then contemplated the possibility of being the victim of a random carjacking and quickly dismissed it with a childishly naive rationalization, as he'd never heard of a Rolls Royce being targeted. Still, there was a peace of mind factor he needed to consider. Maybe he should think about taking on a driver. An ex-cop who could provide security at the same time. Or maybe just start carrying a gun like Dale Marlin, which he liked the idea of more in theory than practice.

Now fully in front of him, the metallic blue Nissan Altima had lowered the volume of the hip-hop track that had been blasting out of its speakers, assumedly so they could place their order then immediately turned it back up once it was complete, so when Copeland pulled up to the intercom, he could hardly hear the voice of the attendant on the other end.

'WelcomeMcDonaldscanItakeyourorder.'

It dawned on Copeland that whatever craving he had was no longer with him so he decided on a large Diet Pepsi, but before he could place the order decided he didn't even want that. He leaned into the microphone. "Don't worry about it, okay?"

It went unheard.

'WelcomeMcDonaldscanItakeyourorder.'

He didn't wait around for another go at it. There was enough room on his right now for him to pull out of the line. On his way around the cue of waiting cars and out of the parking lot he rationalized it being just as well. He'd eaten only an hour earlier and would be having dinner at the Yosts around six, and if he knew himself, expected he'd probably have something when he met with the kid or got home. He then unconsciously tapped the inner tube around his waist that had him looking more and more like an overripe pear everyday.

A sigh.

Out into the street and continuing in traffic he found himself calm again, soon behind a car bespeckled with bumper stickers and wondered what was the point. Bumper stickers. They didn't accomplish anything.

Save The Manatees.

Who the fuck is out trying to get them?, he wondered. The manatees. Were they being clubbed like baby seals for their pelts? Rhinos poached for their tusks? No one was going out of their way to hurt them. Stupid bumpersticker.

Not All Those Who Wander Are Lost.

What's that supposed to mean? It's called killing time, stupid. Taking a walk.

My Child Is An Honor Roll Student at Lincoln Middle School. Big fucking deal. You gonna scrape the sticker off the car if the kid has a bad semester? Copeland was entertaining himself now. He looked up at the back windshield decal and crescendoed into his finale-

In Loving Memory of Sandy.

211

He questioned how he could be expected to have any memory of Sandy, let alone a loving one if he never met him. Or her. And with that, a few new questions arose. Was Sandy a man or woman? Could go either way, he thought. Sandy Koufax, Sandy Duncan, right? Should he pull up alongside at the next red light, lower the window and ask? Now he decided he was curious. Copeland managed a laugh and thought that would be a funny bit for a comedian to do, imagining for a second himself standing in a smoky Las Vegas casino lounge in a tuxedo with bowtie undone, drink in one hand, cigarette in the other and the audience bellowing with laughter. He loved stand up comedians and it brought him back to his envy of people gifted in giving toasts at dinner parties, imagining comics would be excellent at it. He considered the idea of hiring one to teach him how to tell a joke. Maybe give him a few to have on hand if he were ever asked to say a few words while lifting a glass, giving that memorable toast he dreamed about giving. Maybe he should have Karen tell Lauren that it would be the right thing to have him stand up and say a few words at her wedding after all.

Shit!

Perez!

He was supposed to talk to Perez about Gropinsky and his latest indiscretion or fixation or obsession or creep out. At this point it didn't make a difference how it was referred to.

Goddamnit!

Where there hadn't been, to Copeland's knowledge, any issues at the clinic, the same couldn't be said for the office. Dr. Elliot Lopinsky's unacceptable behavior was plainly of the off-campus variety, which included the *MFB&T* main offices where he did not technically work from. This time it was one of the bookkeepers. Valerie. Valerie Miller. And so unlikely in that she was truly a homely girl and constantly dour to boot. Completely devoid of personality. It had to have been her tits, Copeland guessed, as there was nothing else he could think of that would get his attention. They were gargantuan by nature's design as opposed to a plastic surgeon's. Where many men might find that feature attractive, Valerie Miller's lack of hips and short, spindly legs, cold persona and unfortunate face should have protected anything else about her from being objectified. Her head looked martian, shaped like an upside down teardrop with steely, large eyes perched over a small kestrel beak-like nose, her cheeks tapering down and inward below her small, pencil thin lips and tiny mouth, ending at a nearly invisible recessed chin. She was a far cry from the last one Elliot had obsessed over, the Russian receptionist who was a girlfriend of a local nightclub promoter, recommended for hiring by Howie Yglesias. At least that one could be seen as physically appealing, as she radiated nothing but sexuality. Elliot was so mesmerized upon seeing her for the first time, he fell into a salivating trance that bordered on catatonic stupor, nearly short-circuiting the entire ventral-tegmental province of his brain. He then retreated to the closest bathroom, locked the door and allegedly began having at himself furiously. He followed up his visits and assumedly repeated the routine, but with more discretion than the first time. As no one complained, it was responded to with benign neglect. Valerie Miller had no such appeal, yet still Elliot began dropping by the offices for no apparent reason other than to leer at her. She was aware of what he was doing, having pointed out to Perez,

213

who had become the *de facto* member of management for matters of personnel, that Elliot had been using the women's restroom. When confronted by him, Elliot feigned ignorance, claiming he didn't realize his oversight. This time, however, that excuse wouldn't suffice as it can only be used once. According to the bookkeeper, while using the ladies room last Friday, she heard the breathing of a man coming from the stall to her left. Having seen Dr. Lopinsky in the office moments early, she guessed it might be him. As she began to empty her bladder, the unmistakable din of her tinkling urine gently falling upon the still toilet water, an electronic chirping beep was emitted from down by her feet. When looking down to see where it came from, she saw a portion of a physician's dictaphone beneath the partition of the stall being held by someone unseen. Elliot, she suspected, was recording the sound of her relieving herself. She said nothing at the time but brought it to Perez's attention, who had remarked to Copeland later how cool she was about it, as most women would have had a reaction commensurate with their privacy being so egregiously violated. Perez assured her it would be immediately taken care of and never happen again and she was fine with that, not pursuing the matter further. Still, it had to be addressed, and from the very top. By Copeland himself, as Lopinsky was his guy.

Copeland found the number and connected. Perez answered off the first ring. *"Hey, Alan."*

"What are you doin', Alé?"

"At the office. Doing my act. How you doing?"

"Other than almost just gettin' carjacked by a bunch of *shvartzes*, I'm great."

Perez was alarmed. *"Get out of here? What happened?"*

"Ah, not really. I wasn't almost just carjacked. These kids were fucking around. But for a second I thought-" He let the statement peeter out on its own.

"Hey, you can't be too careful," Perez cautioned. *"...The 305 ain't kid's play."*

Copeland moved on. "I meant to circle back to you on the Elliot thing."

Perez let out an audible sigh, probably more for effect than out of frustration. *"Fucking Gropinsky. He's a real pain in the ass, Alan. How much more of this can we...you know...put up with?"*

"Yeah, obviously it's a problem. What about, uh...Knockers McBigtits? She bring it up again, or just the once?"

"No, no. Valerie's cool, Alan. Go figure. Like I told you before. Who knows? Maybe she was...call me crazy for saying this...flattered? I can't imagine she gets too many guys taking runs at her, you know? Even pervs like Elliot-"

"So that's it? What's the problem, then? Why do I have to address it with him?"

"Well, no. That's not really it. The problem is Elliot. He's the one that has the problem with her, apparently."

"Huh? You kinda lost me-"

"I don't know, Alan. He wants her fired. You have to talk to him."

"He wants *her* fired?" Copeland was astonished. "Is he fucking retarded? He's the one hidin' in the bathroom stall watchin' her take a shit and he wants *her* fired?"

"She wasn't taking a shit, Alan. She was peeing. And yes, obviously there is something wrong with him-"

215

"Yeah, no kidding!"

"Listen, Valerie's good, Alan. You know she's good. She does her job. Does what she's told. Doesn't question shit. And to have Elliot demand we fire her is insane."

"I know, I know, I know, I know. Where does he get off thinking he can-?" He stopped to ruminate on what he was hearing, then pointed out the obvious. "She could really nail him to a wall. He knows that?"

"Obviously."

"She could really nail us to the wall, too! He knows that, I assume."

"I would imagine he does." Now it was Perez's turn to consider the facts of the situation. *"I can tell you what I think his problem with her is."*

"Okay. I'm all ears."

There was a silence from Perez's end, the kind that comes when an opinion is about to be shared that might be rejected as ridiculous. *"I think she's been fucking with him, Alan. Playing head games with him."*

Copeland was confused. "Head games?"

"Yup. She's very smart, you know."

"Yeah, yeah. I know that. I mean I know that she's smart. But I don't know why she'd be playing head games with him."

"Well, that's why you have a conversation with him. Find out what that sick bastard is thinking. He's really twisted about this, Alan."

"Yeah." Then a moment of contemplative silence. "You know, Alé...I'm thinking, in fact I've been thinking for some time now...that maybe a change might be in order."

"With?"

"Elliot."

"Okay. You want to elaborate? Talk about exit strategies? While I agree a hundred percent that it should be on the table, it's obviously not that easy-"

"Well, first, a few considerations."

"Which are?"

He stopped. "I don't really want to talk over the phone. But the business, y'know...our business...recognizing that it's been...shifting...y'know...as we've grown-"

"I see where you're going. Sure. And I like it."

"My thinking is we start looking to find a job for him. Ask around. Find something for him, wash our hands of him. I'd kinda like to close down the clinic anyway."

"You've mentioned that possibility."

"And if we need to work with a doctor from time to time, you know...whatever, you and Howie can probably find someone to work freelance with."

"Yeah, sure. Between me, Howie and Scooter? We can find a few guys to have those kinds of conversations with. I can't see a problem there."

Copeland had another thought that he seemed concerned he might forget, so addressed it. "On that note, I also want to talk to you guys about doing more business in the inner city. You know, ghetto stuff. Maybe bring on a couple of sales guys that fit the demographic. I don't have the answer right this second, but I think that's an untapped market that doesn't need any of the stuff, y'know...Elliot stuff-"

"I get it. I get it. And I agree."

"Okay. Let me let you run. I'm gonna call Gropinsky and see what his fucking problem is. And make sure you let Valerie McBigtits know she's not going anywhere. In fact, let's give her a bump. Another hundred bucks a week for her trouble."

"You got it, Alan."

Copeland disconnected without offering any further goodbyes, and quickly. Like pulling a trigger. He liked to do that as it gave the impression he was busier than he really was. He shook his head reflecting on the tragedy that was Dr. Elliot Lopinsky, then scrolled through his phone and called him. The phone rang several times before Lopinsky answered.

"Hello?"

Hello?, Copeland thought. Like Elliot didn't have a caller ID on his phone? Like he didn't know who it was calling? Still, he assumed a childlike, disarming tone of voice in addressing him. "Hi, Elliot. It's Alan. How you doin', *bubala?*"

"I'm okay." His answer came like it was riding on the back of whine.

How's your day goin'?

"It's okay."

Copeland realized this conversation might be a little more involved than he expected and decided to pull off the road and into a Publix supermarket parking lot so as to give it his full attention. "Elliot, we need to have a talk. I'm told you have a problem with one of the bookkeepers at the office."

"--"

"What did she do to you?" He then turned the air conditioner up and adjusted the vent so it blew directly on him. Still, there was no response from the other end. "Elliot? What happened with the bookkeeper? Valerie? What did she do to you? Alé told me you want her fired."

Although he couldn't hear it, in his mind Copeland could see Elliot getting flustered and beginning to breathe hard. Then, he exploded.

"She's a bitch, Alan!!! She's a fucking bitch!!! An evil bitch!!!"

Copeland made a concerted effort at being even more calm than he already had been projecting. "Okay, can you tell me why?"

"No! You just have to get rid of her!"

"C'mon, Elliot. You know if I'm gonna fire her, I have to have a reason."

"No you don't!"

"Elliot, *bubala*. Talk to me, okay? You know I have to have a reason if we're gonna let her go."

"Make one up! Say she's stealing!"

"Okay. But that would be a problem if she wasn't stealing. We would have to have a valid reason. Or we could just fade her position out, but that would take time."

"That's fine. I don't care. But she has to go. I don't care what you tell her." He took a moment, not to calm down but to get further worked up. *"That evil fucking bitch!!!"*

"Elliot, I want you to try to relax. I'll figure something out, okay? Now, this is me and you talking right now. And you and me, we been through a lot. You're like a little brother to me. You know that. I shouldn't even have to remind you that you're like a little brother to me."

"_"

"Elliot?"

"Yes." He was still irate.

"You know that you're like a little brother to me?"

"--"

"You know that?"

"Yes." It didn't sound convincing.

"Let me hear you say it. 'You're like a little brother to me'."

"I'm like a little brother to you."

"Perfect. And you know I got your back. I'm always gonna take care of you. You know that. Let me hear you say that."

"You have my back and you're going to take care of me."

"Perfect."

Then he immediately exploded again. *"So fire that evil bitch!!!"*

Copeland matched the fury with a calmness equal in value. "Okay. But you have to tell me...between you and me...and I'm talking to you like an older brother. What happened?"

"--"

Copeland let his eyeballs roll to the very tops of his lids and took a deep breath. He waited, until he could no longer. "Elliot?"

"She calls me up. At home. The bitch calls me up. And she says things-"

"Valerie from the office calls you?"

"That's what I said, Alan!"

"Okay."

"And she says things."

"Like?"

"--"

"C'mon, Elliot. I don't have all day." Copeland wasn't feigning patience any longer.

"She calls me up and asks if I want her to come over-"

"Really?" Copeland's ears had pricked up.

"...And she says, she doesn't even ask...she says...she tells me that she's going to come over...and I can watch her pee. And things like that. She asks if I want her to pee on me because she will. She'll be glad to pee on me, she said. On my chest. And in my face. Even in my mouth-"

Copeland was flabbergasted, his mouth in full fly-catching mode. And he started to soundlessly laugh.

Elliot continued, getting more worked up as he further elaborated. *"...And...and...and she hears me, she hears on the phone that she's getting to me! She knows she's getting to me, Alan!"*

Copeland was glad he'd pulled over to do this call, as the words making their way into his ears could see him knocked over by the breath of a kitten.

And then silence.

"Are you still there, Alan?"

"I'm here, Elliot. Go on. I'm all ears."

"Well, then she changes her tune! She completely pivots into this nasty, evil bitch! She starts getting abusive, telling me I'm a 'sick fucking-fuck' and she's going to call my mother and ask what she did to me when I was a little boy that turned me into a depraved pervert. She said that to me, Alan! Can you believe that?"

"No, Elliot. I can't believe it."

"She called me a depraved pervert!"

Copeland's disbelief was in regard not to what Elliot was saying but the fact that Valerie Miller, the homely bookkeeper, had that club in her bag and with it just whacked the ball out of the rough and up onto the green within an inch of the hole. He was utterly astounded. In a good way.

"She asked if I liked watching my mother pee when I was a little boy. Then she asked if my mother ever peed on me!"

Copeland now had his clenched fist in his mouth, biting down on his knuckle to keep from saying anything he didn't fully think out. Or maybe he didn't trust that he wasn't going to explode in laughter.

"And she said she was going to call her! My mother! She said she was going to call her and ask. Then she recited my mother's phone number, Alan! She knew my mother's phone number! Where did she get my mother's phone number?!!!"

All Copeland could think of was his homely, quiet, martian looking bookkeeper with the surly demeanor and unnaturally large tits, and suddenly found something about her that was attractive.

"She said I should cut my dick off, Alan! She said she was going to tell my mother to talk to me about cutting my dick off. It was the only way that I could get better."

Copeland felt the need to weigh in. He tried to come across as serious as he possibly could. "Well, that's not right, Elliot. That's simply not right-"

Lopinsky trampled over Copeland's words. *"...Then, all of a sudden she changes her tone and gets nice and tells me she's only kidding. That she likes hearing me get me worked up, that it turns her on. Then again, saying she wants to pee on me in this real seductive voice-*

Again, Copeland leaned his head back, mouth wide open to take in as much oxygen as he possibly could. As much as he wanted to roar out to the heavens in an exaltation honoring this woman, he kept his internal mute button engaged, letting the veneration play out in his head.

Oh, my God!

She is outstanding!

A queen!

A killer!

A killer, queen!

Dynamite with a laser beam!

"She's playing with my head, Alan!"

Copeland brought himself back down to earth. "And that's not right, Elliot. She shouldn't be doing that." He managed to get the words out and in all earnestness. But still Valerie Miller, the bookkeeper, stood front and center in his mind. As soon as he hung up, he was going to call Perez and have him bump that extra hundred a week in her pay up to two-hundred and have him see if there are some things she might be able to handle for the company, things they never would have thought of. *Oh, my God! What a queen!*

"Alan?"

"I'm with you, Elliot. I'm right here. All ears."

"You have to fire her. She can't call me up in the middle of the night and say those things to me."

"You're right. It's completely unacceptable. And I'll address it immediately, okay? But first you gotta know, two wrongs don't make a right, okay? If you want to pursue this, file a harassment claim against her, she can file one on you being in the ladies room recording her...you know...doing her business-"

"--"

"That wasn't me." His answer was half committed and sounded like a child denying he plundered the cookie jar.

Copeland took a deep sigh.

Knowing his fib didn't stick, he tried another tactic. *"She didn't make a complaint, did she?"*

"Not yet. And the good news is I can probably make sure she doesn't. But you're gonna have to let go of the thing she did to you. That's usually the way it goes. You want her to give you a pass, you gotta give her a pass."

"--"

Lopinsky's silence suggested that he wasn't satisfied. He then changed tack. *"You know you can trust me, Alan. You know that."*

"Of course Elliot. I know that. You know that. You're like a little brother to me."

"Well, you know that can't be said for that evil bitch bookkeeper."

"I understand that, Elliot."

Lopinsky must not have been convinced of Copeland's sincerity. *"Or Perez! I know she said something to him!"*

"One's got nothing to do with the other, Elliot. If someone has a problem in the office, they're supposed to go to someone in management. It doesn't mean they're right, now, but-"

"You know Alan, I don't think you know who you can trust and who you can't. I think you're naive."

"I'm naive?"

"Yes. You can't trust her, you can't trust Perez. You can't trust the little mini-me protége you keep around, either."

"What's that?"

"The redneck kid from the trailer park who runs your errands."

Copeland was caught entirely off guard hearing this. He took a deep breath, cleared his throat and made an extra effort to maintain his composure. "Is there somethin' you want to tell me, Elliot? Somethin' that I don't know about?"

It sounded like Lopinsky wanted to backtrack and chose to stay silent.

"Elliot? Is there somethin' I should know about?"

"--"

"Okay, this conversation is over. Before I hang up, I want you to listen to me and listen to me good, real fucking good." Copeland had abandoned the reins of cool, calm and collective and unleashed furious tirade at him. "I will fucking bury you, Elliot. You want to start that kind of shit, I will fucking bury you. I will crush you so hard, you will curse your mother's cunt it'd ever spit you out. You hear me, motherfucker? You're afraid the bookkeeper will call your mother? Just imagine what I can tell her.

"--"

"...Don't you ever, ever, ever fucking tell me who I can and who I can't trust, you fucking piece of shit. You think I got where I am by not knowing who I can and who I can't trust? Copeland had to take a break, as he'd worked himself up more than he would have liked to. "And let me tell you this, Elliot. If it wasn't for me, you would have had your medical license revoked a long time ago. You'd be in jail if it wasn't for me and we all know how you'd do in jail."

"--"

"You hear me?"

Lopinsky had started weeping on the other end, barely managing to get his words out. *"I thought you said I was like a little brother to you?"*

Copeland took a deep breath, trying to calm himself down and was surprised he was succeeding. He found a modicum of compassion and was able to apply it to his words. "Pull it together, Elliot. Pull it together, okay?" They both had to have been exhausted. After another short spell of silence, Copeland continued. "...And never bring up what you just said about the bookkeeper again. Not to Alé Perez. Not to me, to no one. Ever. It's over. I'll call you later." Copeland didn't give him a chance to respond. He hung up no differently than he did when ending all his calls.

Another deep breath. He put his hand on the gear shift, but before putting it into reverse to pull from the parking spot he was in, had to reflect for a moment on what Elliot had said. About the redneck mini-me from the trailer park who ran his errands.

The kid.

Where did Elliot get off bringing Kenny into the conversation?

Chapter Fourteen

Probable Cause

Kenny found Walter Reed's number. It was not in the saved contacts but salted away in limbo, the recently-called list. He connected and took a deep breath as a practice run for the patience he knew he'd soon be relying on. Or at least give the impression that he was relying on it. The call was picked up before the first ring ended.

"Hello?"

"Walt. It's Kenny."

"Hey, man."

Silence.

Kenny again drew another breath right as he could sense Reed was about to say something, then spoke quickly over him. "Don't say it, okay? Don't apologize, don't bother. I'm goin' back over there, I'm goin' to go over and I'm gonna meet with Alan as scheduled-"

"Kenny, I can't say how much I appreciate it and-"

Kenny cut him off again. "Not interested in hearin' it, Walt. Serious. I'm goin' to do what I said I was gonna do and be done with it. You can believe me or not. You wanna follow me, follow me. You wanna watch me, listen in on my conversations, you can do whatever you gotta do, short of stickin' your finger up my-" He stopped and took a moment to let it sink in. "I'm gonna do what I said and then we'll all move on."

"Well, like I said, Kenny-"

"Are you not hearin' me, dude?"

Through the phone Reed's hard sigh was audible. *"I'll talk to you later, Kenny. And again, thanks. I mean it."* His sincerity was almost believable.

The agents were standing in the parking lot of a 7-11 were Stubblefield was working on a blue-colored Slurpee, probably more for therapeutic reasons than to quench a craving for something sweet and artificially colored. All the while, he was shaking his head in disapproval at what he'd just heard. Reed could feel his partner's displeasure and offered a commentary. "It's so much easier just dealing with guys pleading out, you know?

Stubblefield tried to respond with a dismissive *pffft* that usually sounded like air brakes but came out more like a geriatric's half-effort at blowing out candles on a birthday cake. Then another head shake. "So you *gohn* call Looch, or *whah?*"

Reed then looked like he'd just heard the alarm clock next to his bed go off and snapped his fingers. He looked down at his phone while Stubblefield took another pull off the blue Slurpee and turned away.

Reed's call was picked up by Lucic. "Hey, Heinz, it's Walt. Listen, we're good to go over here. I just spoke to our man, we're...all good. Just a little...miscommunication. He's a sensitive guy. You were right. Again." He looked over at Stubblefield who rolled his eyes at the blatant ass-kiss. Then speaking back into the phone, "Trey smoothed it all out. He gets all credit for the save, boss." Reed looked at Stubblefield again who'd turned back upon hearing his name mentioned.

As Reed listened to whatever it was Lucic was saying, he nodded a few times, slipping in several affirmative *yups* and *okays* then signed off feeling a hell of a lot better than he had moments earlier. He smiled at Stubblefield. "Gave you credit for it."

Stubblefield shook his head again, it being of no consolation to him. "It's all *fuh* shit if he *duh-uh* get Copeland to talk about the *oth-uh* thing-"

Reed considered what Stubblefield said, long enough to suggest he was taking it seriously. "I think there's a good chance he's going to step up and deliver. Gut feeling. I just think he's the kind that doesn't respond well to threats." It was said as a soft rebuke of Stubblefield. "...That's why I think you should have eased up from the get-go. You know?"

"I don't mean to *suh-ound* like a asshole, *Wahl*...but you *shoul-uhn't* think so much."

"What's that supposed to mean?"

"Some guy's *jus-uh should-uh* think so much."

He may as well have called him an idiot.

"That's a fucked up thing to say."

229

Stubblefield shrugged then pulled again on the blue Slurpee and swished it around in his swollen mouth to relieve the discomfort. "*Muh fuh-kuh* mouth is *kill-uh* me.*"

Reed had no interest in hearing it. He walked back to his car and got in.

The night he had revealed himself and his intentions to Kenny Rehage, Special Agent Walter Reed wasted no time calling his partner, Trey Stubblefield. Typically, he would have waited until the next day to report his...no their...good fortune but the prospect of there being more to it than they expected, the kind of jaw-dropping, career-defining development, justified interrupting Stubblefield's evening. First thing the following morning, they walked into Heinz Lucic's office with large coffees and a box of French pastries from *Lé Belle Figué*. After the supervisor's own *holy shit* then repeated in triplicate response, awkward high-fives were exchanged, the gracelessness a result of Lucic being mildly spastic. Several more *holy shits* then Lucic wanted to hear the editorialized, off the record, blow-by-blow account of how it went down in the dark parking lot behind the Lee YMCA, as if Reed had a date with the Homecoming Queen that wound up there. Lucic became so excited that he interrupted with a suggestion...no, insistence, they go for drinks after work to celebrate. Then, while brushing croissant flakes off his lap and shirt, Lucic got to the business of laying out a step-by-step strategy to bring what they had to the Assistant United States Attorney Jen Resnick.

Jen Resnick
Perfect.
Maybe she'll actually smile.

As Reed and Stubblefield pitched ideas and conjecture on procedure, Lucic tuned them out, scribbling a flowchart across the whiteboard of his mind. Naturally, he was at the center circle, from which all offshoots would run. On one side he drew a line to Alan Copeland, then continued on to Copeland's father-in-law, Louis Haberman the political kingmaker. From Haberman, the line went to the current administration in Tallahassee, the State Attorney General and the sitting Governor, all of whom had nothing to do with himself or anyone else in the room but represented a tremendous significance in the overall calculus of the opportunity before him. On the opposite side of the center circle, Lucic drew a line connecting himself to Assistant United States Attorney General for the Southern District, Jen Resnick. From her name, a line went to the United States Representative Kevin Breen of the 23rd Congressional District-

> *...Whom Lucic knew-*
> *...That Jen Resnick knew-*
> *...Well enough-*
> *...To not maybe-*
> *...But definitely lobby-*
> *...for something of her very own in exchange for something he might find*

priceless.

As sure as a dog with an itchy ear puts a hind leg to work, Heinz Lucic knew Jen Resnick would parlay the possibility of a delicious, headline making-arrest that would bring embarrassment to high level state political foes of the party affiliated handlers and patrons of the Congressman, she could and would-

> *...All but insist-*

...Clenched fisted-

...And foot stomping the floor-

...God damn it I earned this!

...Demand a nomination to a Federal judgeship in the Southern District of the great State of Florida.

Reed and Stubblefield were still batting back ideas in what looked like could soon become an argument when Lucic ended the meeting, excusing them so he could call her.

Jen Resnick

Perfect.

Maybe she'll actually smile.

Later that morning before walking into the building, Lucic turned to Reed and Stubblefield and firmly reminded them for a third time they were to stay quiet. He would handle her. He did so with a tomcat confidence that suggested she might have been to him one of many secret lovers.

At forty-three, Jen Resnick brought to the job a commitment not hindered by responsibilities to a husband or children. Despite the costume on her petite physique, there was very little that was feminine about her. Not in her choice of cigarettes or how she took her coffee, nor in the weighted stares and prolonged silences during interviews that intimidated even those who were not supposed to be. One old-time three martini prosecutor once summed her up as able to hold a stick of butter up her ass during a weeklong heatwave without it melting.

When Lucic, Reed and Stubblefield entered her office, she was standing in the middle of the room flanked by a paralegal and legal assistant, harridan-esque minion versions of herself in pursuit of the same brand of fuck you confidence she radiated. All wore designer neck scarves as an accessory, making them look like a trio of unhappy flight attendants holding lemon wedges in their mouths. The lack of casual banter exchanged suggested they were not much more than chess pieces, three a side with only two allowed to make moves. Lucic quickly moved through a recap of where his office was with the case into Alan Copeland and the *Mutual Fidelity, Benefits and Trust Company*, leading up to the crescendo of Kenny Rehange saying what he did to Agent Reed in the parking lot of the Lee YMCA. He did so with a masterful economy of language, to the point and hitting accents on the most salient details. Then he applied the hard-stop pause. Her arms dropped to her side and eyes widened at the perfect moment and Lucic knew he had her. It was flawlessly presented, wrapped in scented paper and tied in a bow, the perfect pitch to get everything he needed approved-

...Until Reed blurted out what they were all thinking but would never dare say aloud, a beer belch in an opera house gaffe-

"Oh, there's a homicide in this, Jen! I know it in my bones. And they're going to be lining up from here to Washington to shake our hands and punch our tickets when we blow this thing open."

The Assistant US Attorney turned to Reed, cutting him in half with her glare. Then Reed turned and let his eyes do the quartering.

After the meeting broke up, Reed and Stubblefield planned on how they would pay Kenny a friendly but unannounced visit under the guise of Reed wanting to introduce Kenny to his partner, Trey Stubblefield.

233

It was a midweek evening on his way home from the *MFB&T* offices. Kenny stopped into a convenience store a block and a half from his apartment. Unbeknownst to him, Reed and Stubblefield were following. Kenny pulled into the convenience store lot, parked and entered. He only needed a few items, enough for the check-out clerk to fit in one doubled-up plastic bag with a little room left over. On his way out he was caught off guard, surprised to see Reed and Stubblefield walking up to greet him, which Reed did with a familiar smile and an informally extended hand that was meant to slap then grip, as if they were at the YMCA playing hoops. Reed told Kenny he wanted him to meet his buddy and partner, Trey Stubblefield, who he was working on the case with. Stubblefield offered a big handshake and smile. *"Good to meet you, man. I heard you got mad hoop skills."* Kenny shrugged, feigning humility then asked more with curiosity than defensiveness if they were following him and was told that they couldn't exactly pop into his office. And Reed laughed at the absurdity. Kenny nodded, agreeing that made sense, even smiling as he did.

And then the small talk.

It was short lived. Kenny interrupted Reed and looked at the plastic bag he was holding and almost as if he were embarrassed, mentioned that he had a pint of butter pecan ice cream in it and wanted to get it home before it melted. He suggested the two agents follow him to his apartment. He'd run the bag up to his girlfriend who was waiting for him, then come down and they could chew the fat out in front of his building, no rush.

At home, Kenny parked the car in his assigned space. Reed and Stubblefield pulled to the curb across the street and waited. Heading into his building double-time, Kenny turned and held up a hand to Reed and Stubblefield with one finger aloft-

...Down in a minute.

In the kitchen of his apartment, he quickly put away the items purchased at the convenience store. There was no butter pecan ice cream among them. Nor was his girlfriend Rosie anywhere to be seen, as the immaculately clean apartment was empty. He disappeared into his bedroom, emerged seconds later with a face nothing less than dead serious and exited the front door.

On the sidewalk in front of his building, Kenny walked toward Reed's car. He thought to himself that if he had their jobs he'd never let his guard down like they were doing. Ever. As he got closer, the two FBI agents casually got out. Reed made a point of leaning against the car and Stubblefield's posture was an insouciant one. He wandered several paces, looking at the surroundings like he was considering moving to the block. Then a few paces back. Reed even went through the charade of undoing his necktie and pulling it off. Stubblefield made a half-hearted suggestion after what appeared to be a pretend epiphany. *What do you say we go for a beer?*
Kenny shot it down, as he said he had a bunch of things to do and with a chuckle of resignation, one beer always turns to five. A little more baloney-bending-small-talk and Reed again thanked Kenny, telling him his willingness to help out was appreciated more than he could imagine. But Kenny appeared to be showing little signs of hesitancy. Stubblefield sensed it then reassured him. *Serious, bro. You're doing the right thing. Serious. And I think you know it.* Reed had evidently not picked up on it, as he segued into what Kenny had mentioned then

walked back the night of their first conversation, his feeling that one or more of the insured *MFB&T* held viaticals on was possibly murdered for the purpose of the overdue policies paying out. And again Kenny walked the possibility back but this time with double the conviction. Stubblefield expressed the opinion that if Kenny thought it, it didn't mean that it definitely occurred but couldn't be ruled out. *Serious, man. Things like this do happen, hard as it is to believe. You're not being paranoid. You know? You probably had to have a good reason to think it.*

He floated the idea that if Kenny could encourage Copeland to talk about it, just get him to say something even close to alluding to the possibility, even if it were just hot air braggadocio, it would be enough for them to open an investigation. *And if there's nothing, a Grand Jury will shoot it down. No harm, no foul. It's real simple, bro.* Stubblefield came off with conviction but still, Kenny seemed reluctant to push the theory forward. He told the agents he could only offer them in good conscience what he knew as fact, the instances of suspected fraud and if any of those things were against the law, the agents could do with it what they needed to. *Think of the expungement, bro. Your youthful indiscretion? That could basically be guaranteed if you can connect Copeland to a homicide.* Kenny told them he didn't really care much about the expungement. What was in the past stayed in the past and he had no real need to have his record wiped clean.

It wasn't the response they were looking for.

The following morning Kenny began to shop for a lawyer. Dave Zuboff was second on Kenny's assembled list, chosen for no other reason than his name was in the middle. The theme of being in the middle, or the mean or average would run consistent in everything

Kenny would come to observe, or not be able to observe, about the man. His office was near the Federal Courts off East Broward Boulevard in a narrow, three-story building so average it was at times driven past with inadvertence by those who worked in it. It was just as ordinary on the inside. And to the naked eye, Dave Zuboff was average in every way imaginable. So much so that he probably fell into the fiftieth percentile in height, weight, waist circumference and percentage of hair loss for a thirty-seven year old American male of eastern European ancestry. Even his introduction upon meeting Kenny was delivered at average room temperature. The hollow, detached blandness Zuboff projected had Kenny wondering if he had been mistaken for someone that stole a parking spot from him earlier that morning.

The desk in his spartan office was large, made of fine hardwood and polished. The seat he sat in behind it was of an ergonomic design but not an art piece. There was nothing within the four walls that could be considered personal, with the exception of his framed diplomas from the University of Miami and Emory Law School and in the corner, an air purifying unit. No family photographs, no souvenirs or knick-knacks professing an allegiance to a cause, sports team or hobby. When considering it, Zuboff's aversion to small talk might have come across as rude, but appreciated by Kenny. He wasn't even asked who had referred him. It took less than twenty minutes for Kenny to paint a linear picture of why he wanted to retain his services, without excluding his prior brush with the law. Zuboff listened, expressionless. So much so that Kenny was unsure if a single muscle in his round face moved once in that time. With all the information disseminated, Zuboff offered his prognosis with a matter-of-fact confidence. Having Kenny's previous conviction expunged in exchange for his cooperation in the FBI's investigation into *MFB&T* and Alan Copeland was entirely reasonable, stopping short of guaranteeing it would happen. The reason, he explained, was that the federal government could not grant a decree on a state related matter. Kenny would have to file an Expungement Application with the county where the arrest took place, in his case back in Okaloosa. He could include with it a strong recommendation from the United States Attorney for the Southern District of Florida that would hold a silver bullet sway, which was as close to a guarantee as there was. Not absolute but to Dave Zuboff, this kind of request for a recommendation for expungement was not at all unusual and in his experience expected it would be granted. Kenny had a full understanding of the process and was comfortable with everything he had been told. With their bases covered, Zuboff ended the consultation instructing, then emphasizing, that Kenny was not to speak to the FBI agents again without him being present and recommended he find a new pickup basketball game so as to avoid running into Walter Reed. Any and all contact with the Bureau and US Attorney's office moving forward would go through himself. Upon parting ways, Zuboff didn't offer Kenny his hand to shake. Only a reminder. *"Remember, you can't lie to the FBI. It's a chargeable offense, punishable by up to five years in prison and a fine. Also remember that they can lie to you."* He took a pregnant pause so his words could take root. *"Again, you can't lie to them...but they can lie to you."*

When Kenny walked out of Dave Zuboff's office, he thought about the butter pecan ice cream in the plastic bag he told Reed and Stubblefield he was worried might melt and enjoyed a secret smile for himself. Then he experienced a slight feeling of vexation, as it dawned on him that he didn't know any more about the lawyer he'd just hired to represent his interests than he did before meeting him. Dave Zuboff had given him nothing, *nada*, *zippo*...not a hint in the clothes he wore, in the way he sat, in a passing comment of digression or from the surroundings of the ordinarily average place he worked from.

Zuboff made his preliminary call on Kenny's behalf to Walter Reed, whom he wasn't sure he'd met before. He did know Heinz Lucic, though, and briefly considered calling him first but deferred to protocol. He introduced himself to Reed, who sounded surprised Kenny had retained counsel. Zuboff, true to his personality, was not interested in the small talk. He asked, coming across almost abruptly, if his client Kenny Rehage was a suspect, a target or a witness in their probe. Reed assured him in no uncertain terms that they were interested in him as a witness and nothing else, but if for any reason that were to change, he would immediately notify everyone involved. Zuboff then suggested they schedule a meeting with the US Attorney's Office as soon as possible to ensure his client's rights were protected and they could iron out details of a recommendation for expungement of his previous conviction in exchange for cooperation. Reed agreed, adding that it was the obvious next step and more than a reasonable request to do it sooner than later. With the matter settled, Reed asked Zuboff if he was aware of how good a basketball player his client was. Zuboff's curt response to the negative made it clear he didn't care.

Following the call, Reed walked away from his desk, shaking his head. He made his way over to Stubblefield who was looking into the face of his laptop. *He lawyered up. Piece of shit.* Stubblefield asked who the lawyer was and Reed told him, then turned toward their supervisor's office.

I'm going to tell Looch. Stubblefield told him it didn't make a difference. He could hire ten lawyers, they were going to get it out of him-

...A connection to a homicide they could reasonably connect Alan Copeland to.

The meeting had all the ingredients of a proffer session without the active ingredient of an individual under indictment for a crime. Naturally, it gave the appearance of Kenny being in a position of leverage, boiling the possibility of cooperating down to what he wanted versus needed. Where he may have wanted his Okaloosa County conviction expunged, he did not need it to the same degree someone charged with a felony needed to cooperate with the authorities to avoid going to jail or for the extent of time faced upon sentencing, as was the case with short-legged, ovoid-bodied, nightclub doorman-turned hedge fund analyst Guy Lasback.

The parties involved sat in a conference room at the US Attorney's office in Fort Lauderdale, as opposed to Miami. Probably arranged that way by Dave Zuboff as a matter of convenience to not only his client but himself. The room had the feel of a parlor or private library. Rich wood-paneled walls and a grand mahogany table sat in the center. Present were Walter Reed and Trey Stubblefield, who sat next to one another at the narrow end of the table, far side. Lucic sat several chairs away, not at the table but against the wall as if he were a spectator, subliminally letting Jen Resnick know that he understood it was her baby now. At the long side of the table facing the windows Jen Resnick sat with her obedient underlings. Kenny sat next to Dave Zuboff along the other side of the table but there was a curious distance between the two, as if one or the other had done this deliberately.

Where it would be safe to assume that Jen Resnick might own the room during the proceedings, she didn't. At least not as long as Dave Zuboff was there. His stone-hard, devoid of emotion glares kept the others just off balance enough to keep them in check, like he was sending subliminal messages challenging them, daring them to try him. He had wasted no time in laying out the particulars of what his client, Kenny Rehage, would need in exchange for cooperating with the government's investigation. Firstly, the official letter from Jen Resnick's boss, the United States Attorney himself, to the State of Florida recommending the full expungement of his client's criminal record was not negotiable. Zuboff added that he reserved the right to approve the drafted letter before it was signed. He didn't wait for any objections, questions or qualifications. He also informed Jen Resnick and the FBI agents that his client would not wear any wires or listening devices that would need to be attached to his body, authorizing only his consent to be recorded by a listening device or devices, already planted by the FBI or other ancillary apparatus. His participation in the investigation as a witness would also require his being granted complete and unconditional clearance and future immunity from being charged in any related crimes beginning from the time of his commencement until the expiration of his tenure at *Mutual Fidelity, Benefits and Trust*, should anything arise in the probe that might point to his having been involved in any capacity, inadvertently or otherwise of something that might fall under a violation of the criminal code. Only then did Jen Resnick interrupt, stating that it was acceptable but within reason. Lucic watched, secretly satisfied, as Zuboff burned holes into her as he clarified his statement as limited to the scope of the charges being investigated and the assistant US Attorney replied that it was understood.

The conclusion was anticlimactic. Jen Resnick had nothing else. Everything being asked on behalf of Kenny was agreed to. She followed up with a few seemingly procedural questions to Reed and Stubblefield which were answered politely, then spoke directly to Kenny and not only thanked him for his willingness to cooperate, but smiled at him.

She smiled at him!

She smiled!

And so now did Lucic, as he knew what was playing out in her head, seeing herself in a black robe, gavel in hand.

When the time came for the parting, pleasantries were exchanged with Resnick addressing Zuboff as 'counsellor' and offering a nod of the head. Kenny noticed he didn't shake her hand or anyone else's.

Kenny and Zuboff walked out of the building in silence. When they got to the parking lot, Zuboff said he'd be in touch, and good-bye. Not "have a nice day." Just good-bye-

...And no offer of a handshake.

Driving back toward Miramar in Reed's car, Stubblefield rode shotgun. Lucic was not with them as he had made his own way to the meeting. Reed opined that he found it odd Zuboff didn't mention their prodding of Kenny to give them something they might be able to connect to a homicide. It wasn't lost on Stubblefield, either. Reed then made another observation. *"They're only agreeing to clearance on fraud related charges."* Stubblefield believed that was good for them.

The following Saturday morning, Kenny was down in Miami Beach having just played in a pickup game at a private residence. He was glad he accepted the invitation that was like so many he'd turned down before. He was driving north on Collins Avenue near where it split just south of West 63rd Street, stopping at a traffic signal. Out his window, he spotted Dave Zuboff on the sidewalk. He was relaxed and smiling, something Kenny hadn't seen him do to that point. He was walking with one, two, three, four, no...the woman pushing the stroller with the baby, that had to be his wife...five children. His family. His wife and the two girls were wearing long, modest dresses, the two boys had on dress slacks, shirts and ties but sneakers on their feet. How the baby was dressed, Kenny could only guess. They were either going to or coming from some kind of service as there were other families similarly dressed walking in the same direction. Kenny watched Zuboff interact with his children. He was holding one of their hands. Within seconds, it was as if Zuboff had felt someone looking. He lifted his head and turned toward the street. He and Kenny's eyes met but neither acknowledged the other. Zuboff was no longer smiling. Kenny felt awkward, as if he'd interrupted something sacred and turned away, looking down at the floorboard of his car. When the signal changed, he continued north on Collins, seeing his lawyer now not only in a different light but knowing all he needed to know about him.

What made him happy.

What he held dear.

And what he probably loathed.

Two mornings later he was at Rosie's apartment getting ready to head into the office. She had left for an early morning yoga class before work, the one she'd been jackhammering him to just try once...just once, swearing he'd love it. To that point he'd held firm in his position of not being interested. He touched his pants pockets for his car key, then did one last pass through the kitchen to make sure everything was in order. The counters were spotless and the stainless steel sink basin dry and streak-free. Out the door, he double-checked it was locked and walked over to the elevator.

In front of her building, he walked across the street to his parked car taking two steps at a time, even though he wasn't in a rush. It was a habit. Another look to his left, then to his right and a sudden shock at what he saw. Not one hundred feet away, sitting behind the wheel of his parked car.

Walter Reed.

Beside him, Trey Stubblefield.

Eight o'clock in the morning.

Kenny pretended not to see them as he headed toward his car. Thumb to key, one chirp, the door unlocked. He opened and climbed in, shutting the door but did not engage the ignition. Seconds later the door was thrown open the way one does when furious. Kenny stepped out and slammed it behind him. He began marching toward the FBI agent's car, blank faced. As he approached, Reed lowered the window and greeted him with a smile that might be reserved for the water cooler in an office. Kenny didn't let him speak. *What are you doin' here?* Reed told him that he and Stubblefield just wanted to catch up with him. Real quick. *My girlfriend lives here. This is my girlfriend's house.* He was incredulous, as if a line of decency had been crossed. Stubblefield looked over at him and smiled...smiled like he was enjoying Kenny's discomfort and asked him why he looked surprised they knew that. They were the FBI. *What do you want?* And Reed told him they just wanted to talk about what made him so suspicious about the deaths of the policyholders that were late in paying off.

You guys need to talk to Dave Zuboff. You guys are supposed to talk to the lawyer about any of this stuff. Not me! Stubblefield laughed again and it was rife with condescendence. Reed took the tact of petition, telling Kenny how important this was and what he already knew: Alan Copeland was a bad guy, what he was capable of doing was anyone's guess. They just wanted the names of the policyholders who Kenny thought might have died under questionable circumstances. That's all. Just the names. Even one name. Just one name. He wouldn't have to say anything else. They would do the rest. *Why would I do that? None of 'em died under questionable circumstances.* Almost in stereo, Stubblefield asked him what he had to hide and Reed asked why he changed his tune, asking him to come on, just tell them one name. *There were none.* Reed accused Kenny of lying, as he knew what he heard him say that night in the parking lot at the YMCA and Stubblefield told him he thought it once so just come out with it and think it again...just fucking say it. *I don't think it's true.* He was told that it didn't matter if he didn't think it was true.

You want me to lie? And there was silence. Stubblefield told him he could call it what he wanted to call it and Reed didn't object. *You want me to lie?* Reed told him they just wanted to make sure the fraud charges would stick-

> *You want me to lie?*
>
> Stubblefield told him then in no uncertain terms-
>
> *...Yes.*
>
> *They did!*
>
> *YES!*

Stubblefield didn't know what was so hard for him to understand. Especially being the former drug dealer that he was.

The silence between Kenny standing next to Reed's open window looking at the agents waiting for a response was not much longer than fifteen seconds but lasted an eternity. Kenny looked back at Rosie's apartment building, then back at Reed and Stubblefield. *I'm out. Y'all can piss off and pound rocks. I don't need the expungement that bad.* Reed tried to talk him off the ledge while Stubblefield released a fusillade of threats interspersed with the word "motherfucker." Regardless of how hard he tried to sound, his pronouncing every syllable underscored his glaring lack of authenticity. Kenny was not intimidated. *I don't give a shit. In fact, I got so few shits to give, y'all actually owe me a few. How 'bout that, big guy?* Hearing those words set Stubblefield off into a near tirade where he swore he would ruin Kenny's world. Don't fuck with the FBI. They would find something on him. Ruin his world and do so gladly. And with that, Kenny turned and walked back to his car, far calmer than most would have in the situation. He actually had a little bit of a smile on his face.

He drove to the office and got to the business of his day not thinking much more about the morning's confrontation. Not even enough to call Dave Zuboff and tell him what had happened. The day came and went no different than the others before it and that night, while relaxing at home alone, he waited for the buzzer to sound.

It did, as he expected.

Walter Reed was standing at the front door of his building.

Alone.

Instead of letting him in, Kenny went down. As he walked from the elevator through the lobby and out the door, he saw Reed standing five paces down the walkway looking like a drunken penitent. His tie was loosened, head hanging and hands buried in pants pockets. Kenny stepped outside, letting the door close behind him, standing just outside of the sphere of the lights. He didn't chase Reed away, let alone rip into him verbally. He simply presented himself and said nothing, poised to listen. Reed led with a string of heartfelt apologies, expressing his shame. *It wasn't supposed to be like this.* Kenny didn't respond. *I feel horrible. I feel like I put you in a terrible situation.* Still, Kenny said nothing. *I have to tell you, in all honesty? My partner? He's an idiot. And what makes it worse is...he thinks he's smart. He actually thinks he's smart.* Kenny gave him nothing, just an expressionless face and eye contact, indicating that he was hearing him. *You know what the problem is? With this job? The Bureau?* He didn't wait for Kenny to ask. *Guy's like Trey? They shouldn't have ever gotten hired. Between you and me? He's a quota hire, you know-* Reed had stopped so as to make sure Kenny was hearing him. ...*An Affirmative Action, quota hire. And he doesn't even deserve getting that leg up. He's not from the 'hood. He's not under-privileged. He just plays 'nigger.' He's from the suburbs! His father was in management at Coca-Cola corporate headquarters and his mother's a high school principal. If Trey wasn't black, he's working at the Post Office, best case scenario. And when you look at the Post Office, you know, that might as well be a car wash.* Reed stopped and smiled, hoping to have appealed to something in Kenny that didn't exist. For the first time, Kenny reacted, giving Reed a shrug, as if it didn't matter, then told him he didn't care about who deserved what or who was a moron or about the Post Office and who worked there. He even said he understood how their treating him the way they did wasn't personal, that he was aware of how badly they wanted to crush Alan Copeland and understood that because of Alan's money and influence he was hard to bring down on just a fraud case. *Exactly! Exactly! You understand!* Kenny nodded that he did. *It doesn't matter if he was involved in any of these deaths, or even if they were suspicious. Just the fact that someone brings it up, someone credible...it will level the playing field just a little bit more than it is...making it harder for him to defend himself against the things he's really guilty of. We've done it before and we'll do it again to nail who we have to nail. You get it! This isn't just me and Trey coming up with this, our Supervisors-*

And he stopped.

Kenny shrugged again, as if he wasn't surprised but still held firm in his posture of not wanting to be involved. *Look, what Trey said about you being involved in something? Something that he said we'd nail you on?* Reed shook his head. *No way. No way, no how. I told him that. We got into it. Oh, we got into it. After this morning. And you know what I told him? I told him if you were even remotely guilty of anything you would have been on the phone with your lawyer as soon as you got in your car and he would have been up our asses right after he hung up with you.* Kenny again didn't offer anything that could be interpreted as either an agreement or dissent. *And guess who we didn't hear from? All day? That's right. Your lawyer. You didn't call him, did you?* Kenny told him he thought doing so would be pointless. *See! That tells me everything!*

Again, Kenny shrugged and it was followed with silence. Long, but not as long as it seemed. He then told Reed that he was going back inside. As he turned his back to him he added that he'd see him around and Reed felt as if there was still hope. He might as well have salvaged him.

Once upstairs in his apartment, Kenny made his way over to the living room window that looked over the street. He saw Reed in his car, pulling away from the curb and wondered if he was already on his phone. He grinned and fished from his pocket a small dictaphone that was on and turned it off. It was the same kind of digital recorder that Dr. Elliot Lopinsky used. It might have even been lifted from his desk at the clinic. Kenny fiddled with it, playing back what Reed had said to him during his *mea culpa*. He played it through, beginning to end, stopping and repeating the entire section of unmistakable self-incrimination:

> *"...It doesn't matter if he was involved in any of these deaths*
> *that you thought were suspicious. Just the fact that someone*
> *brings it up, someone credible...it will level the playing field*
> *just a little bit more than it is...making it harder for him to*
> *defend himself against the things he's really guilty of. We've*

done it before and we'll do it again to nail who we have to nail.
This isn't just me and Trey coming up with this, our
Supervisors-"

Kenny had everything. From minute one of his interactions with Walter Reed and Trey Stubblefield.
He had everything.

Kenny dropped the phone on the car seat beside him. He looked in his rearview mirror and sucked his top teeth. He put the car in gear and pulled away from the curb, continuing on his way to meet Alan Copeland, whom he would knowingly engage in conversation that would be recorded by the FBI, with a very strong likelihood that something would be said to implicate him and result in his arrest and subsequent conviction. And while Alan Copeland might well be going down, so would the FBI agents who pursued him. Then, a sudden pause for reflection. Kenny contemplated for the first time if his recording the FBI agents without telling them was illegal.

Chapter Fifteen

One-Fifty Over Ninety

With his calls done, Copeland put his car in reverse to pull from the space in the supermarket parking lot when he realized he was once again overwhelmed by a sense of thirst and wished he didn't duck out of the McDonald's drive-thru line. He put the car back in park and got out. It was hotter than it had been earlier and he unconsciously waved a hand in front of his face, as if the motion might make a difference. After a couple of steps, he stopped and looked down at his feet, which felt as if they were now too big for his loafers. He lifted a pant leg to look at his ankle expecting it to be swollen.

It wasn't.

Just as orange and leathery as it usually was.

He continued on, squinting from stinging light reflections off of slow moving cars coming and going in the lot. He walked toward the entrance of the Publix pretty sure they had cold soda available. If not, he thought, the small bagel store next door would. Then, the realization that he might as well just go into the bagel store and in a mumble called himself a moron for not thinking of that from the get go.

Inside the bagel store, he took a sixteen ounce Diet Pepsi out of the case and walked over to the counter. He placed the bottle next to the register while the counter girl's back was still to him. A second thought and he turned back to the case, went and opened it and grabbed a bottle of spring water, bringing it back to the counter where the counter girl was now waiting for him, smiling.

Copeland was caught off-guard, startled. She had transformed her head into a road map lined with multiple metal piercings and unfortunately placed tattoos that would remain on her body long after her soul abandoned it. Why she would do that to herself was a mystery to him. So all-American and naturally...cute. Such a sunny disposition. And at one point she intentionally decided to vandalize herself. Motivated by what, he couldn't imagine.

She smiled at him again. Warm, welcoming. "Will that be all?"

He hesitated, as if wanting to say...or ask something but couldn't decide on what words to use. "No...I mean...yes. That's it."

She held a pause, as something about him caught her attention, like he was the one with the facial tattoos but instead of asking him what she might have been wondering, only smiled. "How are you doing today?"

Copeland nodded his head, trying to come off as natural as possible. "I'm okay." He felt like telling her how thirsty he was.

She told him the price, took his money, made change and asked if he needed a bag. He responded by shaking his head with a forced smile, he didn't. Still standing in front of her at the counter, he opened the bottle of spring water and took a long, hard pull from it, nothing that could be confused with a sip. He kept drinking the water until the coldness of it became too much for him to bear, then brought the plastic bottle down from his mouth and took a deep breath of relief.

"Are you okay, sir?"

He nodded that he was, then wiped his mouth with his forearm, then took another slug, half as long this time.

The counter girl watched him like a child might look at an animal taking water in a zoo enclosure. "I get it," she said. "It's kind of hot today. I have to remind my mom to drink plenty of water."

"Yeah. It's hot." He regrouped, took a deep breath then felt compelled to respond. "How you doin'? You okay?" He said it with a familiar smirk, as if he were playing with her.

She smiled a smile as bright as the midday sun on the other side of the door. "Yeah! I'm awesome! Thank you for asking."

Copeland nodded and grinned. Her enthusiasm was infectious. He took the two bottles and made his way to the bagel store exit, wondering why such a sweet, charming young girl would do that to her face.

Stepping out of the bagel store, he stopped, finished off the water then walked into the parking lot, tossing the empty plastic water bottle in the trash can less than three feet away. He missed, rimming it out, then continued walking to the car either not noticing or pretending not to so he didn't have to go back for it.

In the car, he opened the Diet Pepsi and took a long, hard swig off of it. The doing so caused him to place a hand on his tightened chest to contain the esophageal reflux caused by the carbonation.

253

Then a little burp and deep breath of relief. He started the ignition and grabbed hold of the phone, scrolling through it for Alé Perez and hit connect.

He picked up on one. *"Hey, Alan."*

One more burp. Smaller this time. "Alé, I got an idea. Elliot-"

"You spoke with him?" He sounded surprised.

Copeland paused, almost as if resenting the response. "I did. Listen, I want you to call Louis Haberman's office-"

"You're father-in-law?"

"Karen's stepfather. Yeah. Call his assistant and find out who's running the Haiti Children's Hope Charity he's involved in. I think he's on the board. I know he's on the board."

"Okay."

"See if they need a doctor on staff there."

"Where? At their offices?"

"In Haiti."

"Haiti?"

"Yes, Haiti. I want to see if they'll bring Elliot to Haiti. I'm sure they need doctors and Haiti is...well, not here."

"What makes you think Elliot will go?"

"Let me worry about that."

A pause.

"Alan, correct me if I'm wrong, but-" He stopped.

"What?"

"Nothing."

"What?!"

"Nothing. Haiti's a great idea."

"Not as good as the North fucking Pole, but good enough."

"What do you want me to ask them?"

"Are you kidding, Alé? What did I just say?"

"You want me to lead with that?"

"See if the foundation needs a doctor there. If not, see if they're open to carving out a position for him. If they're lukewarm to the idea, tell them the salary will be covered through our next year's donation and if I have to talk to Haberman about it, I will. If not, fine. It'll give me a reason to pass next time he puts the arm on me for a check." Then he felt the need to sell Perez on the merits of the suggestion. "And besides, Elliot's an excellent physician."

"Alan?"

"What?"

"It's...me you're talking to. Elliot's a pervert."

Copeland cut him off, impatient. "One has nothing to do with the other. Stop being so fucking narrow minded."

"So you talked to him, then? Elliot?"

"Yes. Yes." He sighed. "I talked to him."

"And?"

"He's got to go, Alé. He's got to go. Now call Haberman's office and call the foundation. Make it happen. I'll talk to you later." He disconnected before Perez could respond.

He took another sip from the Diet Pepsi bottle, this time smaller so as not to get the same reflux and wondered if he felt better. He leaned back on the head rest, shut his eyes for a moment. Yes, he felt better. But the momentary sense of calm he felt was short lived, as he had another thought and dialed the office.

255

"Hi, Alan."

"Brenda, listen...do me a favor. Call the kid Kenny. I'm on my way to meet him over at, um...um-" The thought momentarily escaped him. "...Well, it doesn't matter where. I'm runnin' a little late. Tell him I'm runnin' a little late."

"Okay. Do you want me to push your Triad Group call or your massage?"

He hesitated. "No. Just tell the kid I'm running fifteen minutes behind."

"Okay. Anything else?"

Again, he hesitated. "No, that's it for now."

He disconnected but didn't seem to be in a rush to get moving. He leaned his head back and closed his eyes making a conscious effort to think about nothing for thirty solid seconds but failed. Again, he was interrupted by a thought. He got out of the car and walked around to the trunk and opened it. He leaned over and poked around the contents, all neatly organized until he found a small, hand stitched leather satchel. He shut the trunk, walked back around to the car and got in. Opening the zipper, he took out an ambulatory blood pressure monitor. He studied the device with the kind familiarity, or lack thereof, suggesting it wasn't the first time he'd used it but well could have been the second. He pushed the baggy sleeve of his drab green olive cabana shirt up towards his shoulder and fit the monitor over his toneless, fleshy upper arm and tried to secure the adjustable fitting strap. It was becoming fast apparent that Copeland was doing something wrong. He removed the cuff and tried putting it on from the opposite end but that too, proved fruitless. Another once over at it, like there might be a tag sewn to it with a directional diagram but nothing new was gleaned. Back to fitting it the original way he had tried. Still, he couldn't figure it out. Almost resigned to defeat, he dropped it down into his lap and looked out the window of the car. As he did, he noticed a young man wearing medical scrubs and running sneakers heading in the direction of the Publix. He was Asian, slight of build and wore glasses. A lanyard hung around his neck, the card portion dropped into his chest pocket. Copeland hurried to open the door and stepped out.

"Excuse me!"

His call went unheard so he tried again, this time louder-

"Excuse me!"

The young Asian man in medical scrubs turned to see Copeland was addressing him and with a hand, waving him over. He did a double-take to see if someone behind him was being addressed, but there was no one there.

"No, you! Yeah, you! Can I trouble you for a second?"

The young Asian man in the medical scrubs shrugged and approached Copeland. As he got closer, he could see the blood pressure monitor in Copeland's hands.

"I'm sorry to bother you, this is kind of embarrassing, but I'm trying to-" he held up the monitor, putting on display what had him confused.

The young Asian man responded with a confident familiarity. "Trying to take your blood pressure?"

His response came without any accent, to Copleand's surprise.

"Yeah, and I'm having a little trouble, here-"

"In the front seat of your car? Are you...okay, sir? You don't need an ambulance, do you?"

"No, no, I'm fine." Copeland responded defensively. "I just felt a little funny and...I got this thing-" He motioned to the blood pressure monitor in his hands. "My doctor told me I have to watch it, you know...the blood pressure. He had me on Benazapril but took me off it when I leveled off and I try to check it once in a while. And I figured just now...I don't know what I figured."

"Sure. Let me see that."

The young man in medical scrubs took the device from him, looked at it and in little time had it connected and fitted on Copeland's unimpressive arm. Copeland watched him quickly and confidently look at the buttons, navigating through the settings then motioned for Copeland to sit down back in the car and relax. He engaged the device and shortly thereafter the sound of a chirp indicating the reading was complete. The young Asian man in the scrubs looked at the digital monitor.

"One-fifty over ninety. High side of normal. Nothing alarming."

Copeland tried to conceal his being relieved, but it was obvious and the young man began wrapping up the monitor so it could be put back into its satchel.

"Well, I'm glad you happen to be walking by. I'd have been here for a week trying to figure this thing out."

A smile and friendly laugh. "No problem, sir. Glad to help."

Copeland was curious. "You work around here?"

"Sure do." He turned and pointed in the direction opposite from where they were, but only generally.

"I gotta tell you. You look kinda young to be a doctor. Or maybe it's me, just getting older."

The young Asian man laughed while looking surprised. "A doctor? Me? No...no." Now he seemed embarrassed. "I work over at the veterinary hospital," accompanying the statement once again with a thumb pointed back over his shoulder.

Copeland laughed. "You're a vet?"

"No. No. I just work there."

Copeland was curious. "Doing what?"

"I work in the kennel, pretty much. Feed and walk the dogs that are in for treatment. Change the litter boxes for the cats."

"Get outta here! You clean up dog shit?" He couldn't believe the words came from his mouth.

"Yeah. Cat's too. A little more challenging. They don't always make it into the box. It's more stringy and slick. You know?"

Copeland nodded his head. "Actually, I don't know but I'll...take your word for it." He took a pause, as if formulating a question that simply had to be asked. "How did you know how to figure that thing out?" He was referring to the blood pressure monitor.

"My grandfather...he lives with us, he has hypertension and his eyes aren't great so I help him with it."

Copeland nodded his head. "You grow up around here?"

"Fort L. Born and bred."

"A-ha."

"Mom and dad have a dry cleaners on North Federal Highway."

"They do?" Copeland pretended to be surprised, then immediately regretted it, as it almost came off as sarcastic.

"Jim Dandy Cleaners. You know it?"

"No. But I'm gonna start going there. Say, I gotta ask you this and no offense but...you seem like a squared away young guy. I mean...not for nothin', I thought you were a doctor...you know, the scrubs? How is it that-"

"You want to know why I'm cleaning kennels for a vet?"

"Yes. Yes, I do! I do! Yes!" It was like Copeland wanted to know nothing else in the world.

"I failed out of Florida State. Last semester." He looked at Copeland and shrugged, one part contrite, one part apathetic. "I should be graduating next May. It wasn't like I got caught up in anything bad. I just...didn't care, I guess. It wasn't for me. To tell you the truth, I'm not sure what I want. And my parents...they kind of went nuts, because-" He shrugged again, this time suggesting he felt guilty. "Well, they gave me a choice. Go to work for my cousin the veterinarian, or-" He stopped.

"Or what?" Copeland asked, genuinely curious.

"They didn't say." And he smiled.

Copeland smiled too and nodded, slowly processing what he had just heard. "Are you gonna go back to school, or what?"

"I don't know. Like I said, I'm not sure I know what I want to do yet." It was said as if there was no pressure to make a decision any time soon.

Copeland reached into his pocket to grab a few bucks to show his appreciation for the help he'd been given. Sifting through his muddled bill fold, he freed a twenty and offered it to the young man, but the gratuity was politely declined with two waving hands, a step backwards and three short respectful quarter-bows that the young man probably didn't realize he was doing, the only hint of any cultural mannerism.

Copeland didn't press him and put the money back in his pocket. "Thanks again. And good luck."

"Thank you. And you, too."

Before turning away, Copeland had another thought he felt compelled to share. "You got great parents. You might not know that now, but-"

"Oh, I know it." It looked like the young man wanted to say something else but chose not to. He simply offered a wave and went about his business.

Copeland stowed the blood pressure monitor back in its place in the car's trunk. Before shutting it, he looked at the young man in the medical scrubs now walking into the Publix and was puzzled.

Back in his car, he started the ignition but again didn't immediately pull out. He thought about the girl in the bagel store with the tattoos and metal pierced in her face. She seemed so pleasant but must have somewhere along the line been pushed to a point where she chose to make a statement that screamed out to the world that she didn't give a shit. He understood the piercings could be removed and the holes left behind would probably heal, but the ink? Outside of a carnival sideshow, that was going to limit her options of what she was going to do for a living and with whom she might associate with in her personal life. And the Asian kid in the medical scrubs, he was obviously smart. Polite and pleasant but he may as well have been lost in the woods. His parents probably gave him every opportunity to make a life for himself and he didn't want any part of it. It all led him back to thinking about Kenny, who he was on his way to meet at the little bistro café in Bal Harbour. He was probably around the same age as both of them and wondered if he was that much different. Then, the reason for Kenny wanting to talk began to badger him.

I wonder what he wants.

He's leaving.

He's quitting.

He's moving on.

A deep sigh and Copeland pulled out of the space and slowly drove toward the exit, unable to get it off his mind.

He's leaving.

He's quitting.

He's moving on.

The possibility saddened him. He then played back Elliot's words saying the kid couldn't be trusted. Lumping him in the same heap as Perez. And the others. To Copeland, the suggestion was as ludicrous as it was offensive. Kenny was nothing like them, if measured only by their ambition and his lack thereof.

He's leaving.

He's quitting.

He's moving on.

The *Las Ventanas* project with the Triad Group.
That was a good idea. He would use it to keep him from leaving.
Even if he wasn't leaving, he was going to offer it to him. He wasn't

even going to let the kid speak. He was going to lead with that. The *Las Ventanas* project. Kenny didn't need this business of viaticals. He didn't need to do anything where he needed the bullshit insurance licenses. He didn't need to be acquiring policies and selling bundles. No. Kenny was better than that. Copeland wasn't going to take no for an answer. He wasn't going to let him leave. And fuck Elliot for saying he couldn't be trusted. How dare he! That sick, twisted, weak, degenerate bastard. The kid was a hundred times the person Gropinsky was. Copeland was experiencing a frustration that the parents of the young man in the medical scrubs and the girl in the bagel store probably felt with their children.

But Kenny was not his son.

He was not Kenny's father.

He made him wait in the car.

Copeland wondered if somewhere just below the surface of his consciousness he wished he was his son.

Maybe.

Probably.

He didn't know.

Copeland made his way through the parking lot. As he did, he took the bottle of Diet Pepsi from the console cup holder and had another long pull off of it. A few more breaths and he wondered what his blood pressure was now.

Looking to his left for oncoming traffic, then to his right for pedestrians, he proceeded to drive off-

...Off to see what it was that the kid wanted to talk to him about.

263

Chapter Sixteen

The Rub

In less than one hour-

Forty minutes to be exact-

Kenny would be sitting across from Copeland as the FBI recorded their conversation and using what he said as evidence in the case they were building against him. While he still had no idea how it would play out, Kenny was calm. All he had to do to keep feeling the way he did was to keep the thought of Rosie from sneaking into his consciousness. A look back at the clock on the dashboard and he wondered if he could take the slower coastal route that would let him see more of the ocean that continued to fascinate him with its mood swings. He liked the ocean. When he moved on from this place, he'd decided he wanted to go somewhere on the Atlantic side as opposed to the Gulf. Probably somewhere up the coast between Vero Beach and Jacksonville. South Florida was overrated. The people just tried too dang hard to be something no one ought to give a shit about.

The dictaphone.

He thought about the recordings he had of his conversations with Reed and Stubblefield and their pressuring him to lie so as to help stack their case against Copeland.

Gold!

They were nuggets of gold in Chip Corso's estimation.

Pure gold!

While not having Pulitzer delusions of grandeur, Corso did believe they had the makings of what would, at the very least, cement his credibility as a big game guy at the Miami office of the Associated Press, garnering him a full year's worth of back slaps, handshakes and maybe a break in gentle suggestions to cut his ponytail. Kenny had called the forty-three year old Corso out of a cloudless sky. While the two had previously met, Corso seemed to have only a sketchy recollection of the events they met under and still couldn't put a face to the name. Kenny found that amusing coming from someone who claimed to be a seasoned story hound for the AP. So much so, that he almost considered sharing how ridiculous he thought it was with Rosie. Obviously, he couldn't do that.

It was one week to the very day, hour and almost minute before Kenny first met Alan Copeland. Chip Corso's car had been flooded when it was parked in a low lying section, in fact the lowest lying section, of a parking lot next to a drainage grate that was already stopped up when the tropical storm dumped biblical volumes of water over the area in an unusually short period of time.

And to think he was happy when he found the spot open for him to take! To think he was lucky!

The interior of his three year old Acura TL sedan was submerged over the wheel wells and tires up to a few inches below the door handles resulting in the entire electrical system being waterlogged. When Kenny arrived at the Acura dealership maintenance department in Weston to adjust the claim, he was met by a distressed Chip Corso, who was so upset that Kenny wondered if his favorite hunting dog was left inside the car to drown, before noting that someone like Chip Corso would never have a hunting dog. Corso did not welcome Kenny as the person charged with making him whole, but treated him as if he were an adversary. It was not much different than the reception he received from Alan Copeland when his stepdaughter Lauren's claim was being adjusted. Corso was in the throes of a minor stress fit, one that was many things but most pointedly not age appropriate, like a refusal to eat anything that had been on the same plate as a piece of broccoli. He ranted about deductibles and rental car costs and premiums going up, all over something that was no fault of his own.

No fault of his own!

Kenny allowed him to vent, and while doing so thought of a phrase he remembered his father periodically using to describe certain men. As sure as the sun rose in the east, Chip Corso was the kind of guy who *ordered* barbecue, not the kind of guy who *did* barbecue. The comparative analogies were sometimes replaced with other things like changing flat tires and even occasionally of how a man wiped his ass, but the point was the same. After letting him calm down and assuring him that he was there to help, Kenny went over the damage report and the policy Corso had on the vehicle. The bad news was that yes, it was a total loss. Damaged beyond any reasonable hope of repair. But before Corso could have another meltdown, Kenny shared with him the silver lining. It appeared that he was covered under a Full Replacement Value Policy, meaning he would be given a settlement amount based on the lost property at the current day's price without factoring depreciation into the valuation. It took him a moment, but Corso realized that this was not only a good thing, but a great thing. He had assumed he was only insured for the current value and was about to absorb a blistering financial hit. Kenny told him that this was probably an example of an insurance salesman's upsell pitch being well-worth taking, one that Corso didn't fully recall and again Kenny privately found that hilarious, betting that this guy didn't remember what he had for breakfast the day before. As Kenny proceeded with the paperwork, Corso must have been doing some mental numbers crunching and actually became ebullient as he realized his own day, week and month just got better. As he waited, he began ruminating on a series of trivial subjects, one of which was the degrees of hoppiness in particular craft beers, none of which Kenny had ever heard of, and his vocational commitment as a reporter turning out whistleblowers on corrupt big business and government, with hero references made to Woodward and Bernstein that to Kenny may as well have been names of IPA's.

When Kenny reached out to him, Corso agreed to meet at a craft brewery near the downtown AP offices. There, Kenny got right to the point. He recalled him saying that he wanted to turn out whistleblowers. Against big business and government. Corso told him that was correct. Kenny proceeded, and in doing so was more open with Corso than he had been with Rosie and even his lawyer, Dave

Zuboff. He shared as much of his story as he felt he needed to, which was significant in that it included his motivation for wanting to expose the FBI agents that were pressuring him to lie about Copeland-

This, he had not yet told a single soul. He hated the agents, he told the reporter, and in doing so showed hints of revealing an intensity that was uncharacteristic of him to put on display. Bad as Alan Copeland was, Kenny swore to Corso, the FBI was worse. They were hypocrites and phonies who were never held accountable when bullying, threatening and pressuring law abiding citizens to advance their own self-serving agendas. Corso agreed, almost-

Sometimes!

Traffic was moving but Kenny stayed in the right lane. He was in no rush. His phone rang and he looked at the caller ID, then connected. "Hey, Bren. How ya doin'?" He was smiling.

"Hi, sweetie. How you doing?" Brenda's voice through the speaker sounded much different than when she spoke with Copeland. Much more relaxed.

"All good. Just doin' my act over here," Kenny said.

"Heading over to meet the boss?"

"Yeah. Yeah."

"Well, he wanted me to call you to tell you he was running fifteen minutes late."

"Of course, he is."

"Of course."

Kenny made an estimation. "So he'll be there in a half-hour?"

"Yes, but probably not any longer. He does have a dinner at six with his lovely wife and a conference call meeting...and he had me schedule him a massage, so I can't imagine he'll have you waiting much longer than that."

Kenny smiled. "Nice to know I got that goin' for me."

A short pause of silence, then Brenda seemed to shift into a little office gossip, as the tone in her voice treaded to near-whisper. *"Did you hear about the doctor?"*

Which doctor?

"Our doctor. Elliot. From the clinic-"

"Oh, yeah-" He was acknowledging that he knew who she was talking about, not about whatever it was that she was about to share. "...What now?"

"You know Valerie, the bookkeeper?"

"Sure. She's a kinda strange duck herself."

"She is. Well, apparently he's been harassing her. You know, like...sexually."

"Well, doesn't he pretty much creep out on every woman in the office?"

"Yeah, but I think he pushed it a little far with this one. And she said something."

"So, are they gonna blow him out, or what?"

"Hard to say. I guess if she makes enough noise, they'll have to. People get sued over that kind of stuff nowadays."

"Well, the second it costs Alan money, she'll be tossed overboard with a bag of bricks under each arm and a barn door for a hat."

Another telephone line could be heard ringing in the background on Brenda's end. *"Hold on a second, hon-"*

Kenny waited as Brenda fielded the other call. Crossing the intersection at South Dixie Highway, he looked over at the sidewalk in front of a strip mall where a fitness club was the primary tenant. In the parking lot, a group of weight lifter types in their late twenties, dressed in shorts and loose fitting tank tops were standing around bullshitting. They'd just finished training, or so it seemed. One of them was considerably shorter than the others. Well-built, muscular. And black. He was the center of attention, wildly gesturing as he spoke. He must have just made a comment, as the others responded with outbursts of laughter, all with the exception of the biggest of the group, who half-playfully reached out to grab him but missed. Then a few hand slaps and Kenny thought about Danté.

Danté.

Danté.

Danté.

What a funny little bastard, he thought. What a complicated, big-balled, funny little bastard who never stood a chance. The cops probably stopped looking for whoever pulled the trigger on him five minutes after he was pronounced dead. Poor Danté. That complicated, funny little bastard.

"Kenny, you still there, sweetie?"

He'd almost forgotten he was on hold. "Still here, Bren."

"So, what's up with your girl?"

The asking caught him off guard. "Rosie?"

"Unless you got another one?"

"No. No!" He laughed, defensive. "She's...she's cool." He then stopped, as if he might have been considering sharing something with her but decided against it. "Y'know...doin' her thing."

"You two make a great couple. A little unlikely, maybe...but sometimes those are the best kinds-"

Kenny cut her off, seeming to take exception. "What's that supposed to mean?"

"Don't be offended, sweetie! Just...you know...you seem like-"

He cut her off again but this time pretending to be offended. "It's 'cause I'm a redneck and she's a raft paddler?"

Brenda laughed. "I'm a raft paddler, too!"

"I know that, so what I think you're sayin' is you don't approve of your people goin' with rednecks. Rednecks is below you-"

"Oh, boy. Forget I asked."

"Nuh-uh, Bren. You brought it up. You ain't gettin' off so easy. You don't like rednecks, swamp people."

"Forget I asked!" She was laughing now.

And he was grinning now too, ear to ear, feeling like he won the point off the volley.

"So what are your plans for her?"

"Huh?" He pretended to not know what she was talking about.

"You heard me. What are your plans for her? You thinking maybe...y'know-?"

"C'mon, Bren! I ain't even goin' with her a full year...and a half-"

Brenda must have felt like she won the point back by his obvious defensiveness. *"You know me and Javier were dating only six months before we got engaged."*

"Awww, Jeez. That was like a hundred years ago. Times was different."

"Oh, my God!" Brenda feigned outrage.

Game, set, match.

Then again Kenny hesitated, again as if he wanted to share something with her...but didn't.

In the background the other telephone line could be heard ringing on Brenda's desk. *"Don't go anywhere, let me get this."* She put Kenny on hold but only momentarily, long enough to put whoever was calling on hold. *"You there?"*

"I'm here."

"Just a head's up. Alan sounded a little distracted when I spoke to him. And you know how that goes, especially if you're trying to get a straight answer out of him on anything-"

Kenny took a short moment of contemplation before responding. "Okay. Whatever." He chose those words instead of saying what he was thinking, which was more along the lines of "good to know."

"So, he said fifteen minutes late but I'd say it'll probably be thirty."

"Okay. Thanks, Bren."

And she disconnected. Kenny exhaled hard.

She'd be okay.

Working for Alan Copeland, constantly running cover, apologizing or even lying when necessary, taking blame for mistakes and blunders all while being underappreciated, built up within her the kinds of calluses that come from constant live fire exercises. Enduring his petulance and mood swings had conditioned her to be able to work for anyone and in any environment. Shit, when she hit the open market, they'd be tripping over themselves to give her a job, he thought.

She'll be okay.

She'll be okay.

When Kenny began working at *MFB&T*, Brenda understandably ignored him, as he had no defined job, even when Copeland pulled him into the office from babysitting the site where his new house was being built. To her, he was simply another one of her boss's whimsical ideas that would soon run its course, usually creating a mess that she would have to clean up. During the times he waited around the office when he wasn't at Copeland's heel he remained quiet, polite and stayed out of the way. He began to grow on her as she sensed he probably felt overwhelmed in the presence of the blustering tsunami that was Copeland, alone and maybe even a little confused. Brenda understood first hand how daunting working for Copeland could be, especially at the beginning. Soon Kenny sensed her innate maternal characteristics, her qualities of a protector and caregiver even though she was childless and approaching forty. Although he would never tell her, she reminded him of Mrs. Johnson, his elderly next door neighbor from the house by the swamp road-turn back in Okaloosa County.

Another hard sigh. He wished Brenda didn't bring up Rosie. Anyone else bringing her up would have been fine-

...Just not Brenda.

Brenda.

She'll be okay.

He just wished she didn't bring up Rosie.

Approaching a traffic signal, he made a left. He was going to take the coastal route and in doing so would hope that Copeland was running a little later than expected-

...Or maybe even call Brenda again but this time tell her he had to cancel.

"What?"

"You're *still-uh* mad *wha* I said?"

"It was a stupid thing to say, Trey. You can be a real asshole sometimes."

"Relax."

Reed was sitting behind the wheel of his car in the 7-11 parking lot, Stubblefield sitting now in the passenger seat despite the fact that his car was parked in the next spot.

"How's your mouth feel? Any better?"

Stubblefield shrugged. "Yeah. A *litt-uh.*"

The gulf between them was still there. Both looked out their respective windows, waiting with intermittent looks at their wrist watches and mobile phones for the time. Another car pulled into the parking lot, taking the spot next to them. It was another unmarked law enforcement vehicle. A sedan, bland. It made no attempts at complete concealment, as there was a row of lights on the dashboard and behind the rear seats. A man got out, wearing a dress shirt and tie, but the sleeves were rolled up toward his elbows making the unmistakable

USMC tattoo on his forearm visible. On his belt was his service 9mm Beretta and a small gold sunburst shield of a detective. Both Stubblefield and Reed looked over at him. He was in his forties and of average height and stature. He wore wire-rimmed eyeglasses and sported a hairstyle tightly close-cropped, exactly as it was when he served in the Corps. He looked over at Stubblefield and while not knowing who he or Reed was, recognized them as fellow Law Enforcement Officers. He gave them a friendly nod of the head. Stubblefield returned the nod with a little less enthusiasm and the two watched him enter the 7-11.

"*This-uh* guy." In full judgment mode, he scoffed. "They're so *predict-ab-uh*. Might as well walk around with a sign *tha-uh* says I *was-uh* in the Marines." Another head shake. "*Fu-ck-uh* clowns."

"What do you expect, Trey. It's Broward County."

"He was *Fort-uh-L*."

"How do you know?"

"*Saw-uh* his badge on his belt."

"Same difference."

Stubbefield looked at then shook the Slurpee cup in his hand. There was no more ice in it, just a thimble's worth of blue liquid which he wasn't going to drink but was too lackadaisical to get out of the car and throw it out.

Reed's phone rang. He looked at it, then answered with it on speaker.

"Walter Reed."

"*Hey, it's me...Kenny. I just heard from the office. Mr. Copeland is running fifteen minutes late.*"

"Okay, I appreciate you calling to let me know. Thanks."

Reed disconnected then turned to Stubblefield, grinning. Stubblefield wasn't impressed. "He *thinks-uh* we don't know that."

"Not the point, Trey. He called. The point is he called. And besides, why would he know Copeland's car was wired? You think I told him that?"

Stubblefield was unmoved.

Next to the passenger side door, the United States Marine turned Fort Lauderdale Police Department Detective was now standing, crouching down and looking at Stubblefield. In his hand was a small coffee. With the other he motioned for Stubblefield to lower his window.

"How you doing, brother?" The detective said, then held out a set of keys that he'd just picked up off the ground. "Any chance these belong to you guys?"

Reed cramped his neck over to see and Stubblefield tapped his pockets after recognizing them as his own. "Yeah. *They-uh* mine."

"Must've dropped them getting in the car."

"*Thanks-uh.*" The words came out of Stubblefield's mouth with difficulty, as if it were an apology he wasn't quite ready to make.

The Fort Lauderdale detective handed them over then gave the interior of their car a once over.

"You guys turn out of the Fort Lauderdale office or down in Miami?" He knew they were FBI agents.

"Miramar," Reed told him.

The detective nodded, smiled and turned to leave but not without wishing them well. "Stay safe, guys."

Stubblefield brought the window back up as if they'd just been insulted.

"Those your house keys?," Reed asked.

Stubblefield looked at him and instead of saying anything, sighed.

Chapter Seventeen

A Kind Of, Sort Of Reconciliation

Copeland continued driving in the monotonous South Florida surface street traffic.

At least it was flowing.

One-fifty over ninety.

Not bad.

He expected it would be higher, wondering then if the machine that he paid...he couldn't remember...at least a thousand bucks for...wasn't working correctly. No. It was working just fine and he embraced the results, a mini-victory.

One-fifty over ninety.

He didn't feel one-fifty over ninety. Looking at his eyes in the rearview mirror, he wondered if the bags under them had grown more pillow-like since the last time he took notice and pretended that he didn't care, then put a hand on his belly and gave himself a double-tap. He should probably drop twenty, he figured. Twenty there, yes. He didn't consider the twenty he could also drop in his ass and thighs.

Again, another look in the rearview, but this time at area beneath his chin, stroking between thumb and forefinger the fleshy submental space that was well into turkey neck territory and briefly entertained the idea of talking to the plastic surgeon who did Karen's tits and last lipo about having it tightened up. There was no point.

Bendel, the accountant. He needed to see him. He'd been meaning to move some money around and wanted to talk about a few new shelter scenarios he'd heard about.

Bendel.

That was overdue.

Bendel.

He was a good guy.

He almost dialed Brenda to ask her but figured it could wait until he was next on the phone with her. Sometimes hearing her voice grated on him and he didn't feel like hearing it unless it was necessary. It wasn't a nails on a chalkboard voice, by any means. It was sterile, monotone. Like listening to a robot. She never got excited or upset and he wished sometimes that she did.

Bendel.

He was a good guy.

He'd bring it up when he spoke to her next.

A traffic signal brought him to a stop. He looked to his left. Idling in the lane next to him was a tiny compact car with paint so faded that determining whether it had once been blue or was always gray was impossible. It was missing hubcaps, traveling on borrowed miles. Behind the wheel was a plump Hispanic woman. In the passenger seat beside her, an elderly version of herself. In the backseat was a young boy, no older than ten. His hands and face were pressed up against the glass, eyes looking in Copeland's direction. He was in awe, completely captivated. Without the smallest iota of guilt, Copeland reminded himself how much he loved his car, then figured that this kid seeing him was probably something of an inspiration. The man in the Rolls Royce was evidence that anything was possible in America, if you wanted it bad enough. Copeland almost considered lowering the window to tell him that, figuring the kid would probably remember the moment for his entire life. Satisfied, Copeland then turned in the other direction and did a double-take. A nine-foot-tall clown, obviously standing on stilts beneath its baggy, polka dotted pants, was standing on the street corner. Held in its hand was an assemblage of strings connected to a corsage of helium-filled balloons floating overhead. The clown on stilts was wearing a sandwich board over its torso advertising a sale at a mattress warehouse down the block. Copeland looked back at the boy, who he realized was mesmerized by the clown and not the car and for a moment resented him, whether he was fully aware of the fact or not. The light changed and he continued on.

The phone rang, Copeland saw it was Brenda and frowned. "Yeah, Brenda." He heard her mechanical in tone words in his head before she spoke them.

"Hey, Alan-"

Suddenly reminded of something, he barely let her finish. "Do we got Bendel in the books? Am I supposed to be seeing him this week?"

A short pause, as she was checking. It took less than three seconds. *"Not this week. You're seeing him a week from Monday at ten A.M."*

"Okay." That was settled. He got back to being annoyed with the interruption. "What's up?"

"I have Scott Stillwater, he says it's personal, you know who he is."

Copeland nearly drove off the road from surprise. "What? What...what do you mean you have Scott Stillwater?"

"On the line. Would you like me to put him through?"

Copeland's heart began to race. He was stuttering, bordering on speechless.

"Alan?"

He snapped back to. "Yes! Of course! Of course! That's my son, Brenda!"

Where it sounded like an admonishment, she didn't apologize for not knowing that. *"Putting him through now."*

Copeland's train of thought exploded out of the gates on a wave of adrenaline, wondering first how long it had been since he'd heard from his son.

A year?

No, longer than that.

Far longer.

Three years. Five years.

Maybe more.

Probably a hundred and fifty million dollars ago.

Then, the rush of euphoria gave way to worry.

Why is he calling now?

What did he want?

281

Was he in trouble?

He looked up into the rearview again, as if to see how he looked, as if Scott was about to walk in from an adjacent room.

Brenda's voice interrupted his moment of introspection. *"Alan, you're on with Mr. Stillwater-"*

"Scott?" Copeland sounded tentative.

"Hello, Alan."

For Copeland, hearing his voice was proof of life. "Scott, what a surprise. What a...nice surprise-" He wanted to ask if everything was alright but resisted doing so, instead going with something more rhetorical. "...How are you?"

Copeland could hear the sound of slow steady breathing, as if Scott was in the middle of a relaxation exercise. *"I suppose I'm well, Alan."* Another breath. *"I suppose I'm well."*

Another pause for a breath but before Scott could continue, the call dropped.

"Scott? Scott? Scott! Are you there?"

No response.

Copleand was fast moving into panic mode. "Brenda?"

No response.

"Brenda?! Get him back!"

Nothing.

"God damn it!"

Copeland dialed the office, Brenda picked up on a half-ring. *"Hey, Alan."*

He barked at her like the dropped call was her fault. "What happened?"

"I don't know, Alan. I don't stay on your personal calls."

"Well, it fucking dropped, Brenda! The call fucking dropped! Get him back!"

"Right away, Alan."

"Now!" Copeland could hear the phone ringing on the other end and Scott answering. *"Hello?"*

"Scott? The phone...I don't know what the hell happened-"

"It happens."

"Yeah, it happens." Copeland forced himself to settle into calmness, or at least convey the perception of calmness. "So, how are you?"

"Okay. I'm okay."

Another silence followed.

"It's nice to hear your voice."

Scott ignored the pleasantry and continued, as if he were following a script. *"A few things-"* he said. *"...And understand this was not an easy call for me to make."*

Copeland braced himself. "I understand that, Scott."

"My therapist believes that my reaching out to you is very important."

Copeland had an involuntary impulse to roll his eyes. "Well, that's...good. That's good."

"I'm not looking for any kind of reconciliation with you. I have no interest in that-"

Copeland processed what he was hearing without offering a response.

"...My calling you is about my being in the present moment. Acknowledging who I am and where I come from. I need to accept that before I can

move forward." Then there was a pause. *"I need to do this now, since-"* Another pause. *"I'm going to be a parent."*

"A father!"

"A parent."

"That's...fantastic. Fantastic, Scott!"

"Let me finish."

"Sure. Yes. Of course. Go ahead."

"One of my concerns is that I don't fail this child, this human. I'm terrified that I won't be able to break the chain of failures as a parent."

This silence was longer than the others. Copeland let his son's words sink in. "I understand that, Scott. You're probably entitled to feel that way. And I want you to know that I'm aware that in many ways I failed-"

Scott cut him off. *"You're not hearing me, Alan. I need you to hear me."*

"I'm sorry. Go on. Go on, Scott."

"My therapist told me that I need to air these things out. Not for you but for me. And for my partner and for this human-person we're choosing to bring into the world."

"Is your partner-" He stopped before finishing the question he was tiptoeing into.

"Meredith. My airing this out is for me, for Meredith and our baby. I need to air it, to hear myself say the words."

Copeland wanted to tell Scott he was pretty sure he'd aired it out the last time they spoke when Scott told him he was the biggest piece of shit who ever lived and was dead to him but decided not to bring it up.

"I just need to say to you in a way devoid of any emotion, that you failed, Alan. And I will not fail Meredith or this child."

Something overcame Alan Copeland. Another time he might have told his son to go fuck himself. In fact, he'd said those very words to him before. Now, however, he was pensive. A few silent but deep breaths. "I know," he said. "And not that anything I say can change that fact, but...for what it's worth, I'm sorry. I'm sorry and I'm-" He was looking for the right word. "...Ashamed. I'm fu-" He stopped. "...I'm ashamed."

Where Copeland's words were not what Scott Stillwater expected to hear, he still chose to continue as if they had not been said, reciting a litany of indictments against Copeland. *"Your disregard for everyone but yourself was the only consistency throughout my childhood. The abuse directed at me, emotionally and probably even physically has left scars that will never heal. Taking me to a prostitute for my fifteenth birthday did more damage than you could ever imagine-"*

Copeland closed his eyes and sighed as if agreeing that was not a good move, thinking he should have waited until his eighteenth birthday but dared not say a word.

"...Your verbal abuse and put downs, never asking how I felt or respected what I wanted to do...the psychological abuse you subjected my mother to."

It sounded like he was finished. At least Copeland hoped he was. "I failed, Scott. There's no denying those things and no explanation for them other than I didn't know what the...what I was doing. And I was probably a little bit scared. I don't expect you to accept my apology. But I do know...I do accept the fact that I failed. I was a terrible father...and a terrible husband to your mother."

"She's got MS."

"Oh, God." A short pause. "Is there anything...I can do?"

Scott sounded like he resented the question. *"No. She's in good hands. Larry has been very good to her. He's a rock."*

"Good."

"Good, what?"

"That your mother is in good hands."

"_"

"Scott?"

"_"

"Scott?"

"What?"

Is there anything I can do for you? Anything at all?"

"No. Nothing. I don't want anything from you."

"Would you take my good wishes, then? My good wishes for your baby and the baby's mother? Can you at least take my good wishes for you all to have a healthy and happy life together? Can you...at least take that from me? Please?" A lump began to form in Copeland's throat. "Because I mean it. I genuinely mean it. I'm sorry I failed you. I'm sorry I failed your mother. And I understand my behavior cost me my relationship with you. And I'm sorry. I'm sorry."

"_"

Copeland continued to drive. He thought he heard from the other end of the line a muffled sniffle. Scott was crying.

"Before you go Scott, I'm gonna ask only one thing of you. And that's...that's...don't hang up. Not yet. You don't have to say anything. Just don't hang up. I'm...I'm in the car and I wanna drive for a little bit with you being on the other end of the call. We don't gotta exchange another word. I just wanna take a minute...knowing you're on the other end of the call. I just wanna drive for a little bit and know you're there. You don't have to say a word."

And with that Copeland drove.

In silence.

Scott on the other end, but not speaking.

After more than a minute but less than two, Copeland spoke. His voice was softer. Lower in pitch. "Thank you, Scott. Thank you for indulging me."

"Okay."

"Good luck with your new life." Copeland didn't tell him to reach out if he ever needed anything. It was not out of a fear that his son would interpret it as a projection of Copeland asserting a position of power. He simply had no words left.

Scott disconnected.

Copeland stayed on the dead line and slowed for the next red light.

He was crying.

As he hung his head, without warning Copeland was unexpectedly catapulted forward as if he'd just been shot either from a cannon or by one, his seat belt keeping his inert body from being launched through the windshield, then whip-sawed limp back into the driver's seat.

Chapter Eighteen

A Man On A White Horse

Lives Are Defined By Opportunities...Even The Ones We Miss. Kenny found himself once again mired in the words on the sheet metal sign painted in school colors and riveted to the wall in the locker room back in Okaloosa County. There had been two others, one on each side of it, evidenced by symmetrical square sections brighter in tint than the rest of the room. They'd been pulled down for one reason or another. He had never once considered taking the message to heart in all the time he played there but recently they'd been making constant visits to him so vivid that the sounds of sneakers screeching on the hardwood floors and short chirps of a coach's whistle came along with them. He'd even begun to wonder what the other two signs had to offer.

Then Rosie showed up again.

He was visualizing how she had responded when she told him about his job, Copeland and *MFB&T* being under investigation by the FBI, desperately throwing her arms around him as if to keep both he and his soul from disappearing into a vortex. Her touch. Again, he was ashamed of himself for not considering that she might react that way, the way someone does when they truly care about both the physical and spiritual well being of another. His lack of consideration was just another example underscoring how he was not as good as Rosie and never would be.

I called her ma'am.

How thought again of how she would touch him, softly running her finger over his right inner forearm, along the scar, jagged, raised red and looking like a lighting bolt. The motion, soothing, as if she could somehow magically erase it along with anything other damage he might have suffered, physical or emotional.

I called her ma'am.

Watching how she carried herself, how she reacted to things, facing and accepting adversity with nothing less than grace. And her ability to see good in those who might ordinarily reveal little of it within them, it was an insight which rivaled his own preternatural ability to observe behavioral inclinations and proclivities of people upon meeting them. Kenny recalled the neighbor in her building, ever ornery who avoided eye contact at all times and could be heard behind closed doors saying the most horrible of things to the walls but in the lobby Rosie always gave him a smile never expecting it to be returned, only hoping to convey to him the subtle message that there was hope-

The grace!

The frail, elderly couple two buildings down. While she didn't know them...they'd never met, she saw them enough to know they cherished one another, evidenced by their little displays of affection. Without their being aware, she'd captured one of those moments in a photograph of them sitting on the bench by the bike path, hand in hand. She paired the photo then with a simple but elegant silver frame and left it gift wrapped at their door, anonymously-

The thoughtfulness!

Her cancelling concert plans so that she and Kenny might instead attend the birthday party of a looked-over stockroom employee from her job.

The compassion!

And the man who deceived her whom she continued to love, despite his transgressions and subsequent abandonment.

The capacity for forgiveness!

He was already through Oceanside and into Golden Beach, making his having chosen the coastal route meaningless, as he hadn't taken notice once of the ocean to his left for even a moment. From the point where he had been while talking to Brenda, he proceeded on autopilot. Only Sunny Isles now separated him from the place he would be meeting Copeland, so close to where Rosie was working at that very moment, so close that it wasn't out of the realm of possibility he might run into her after parking his car in the place Agents Reed and Stubblefield told him to.

I called her ma'am!

Traffic abruptly slowed as he approached the area where the landmass on both sides of the road began to narrow between ocean and bay before the bridge over the inlet. The traffic coming toward Kenny wasn't moving at full speed but gradually re-attaining it, as if they'd just gotten past the unseen logjam he was approaching. He noticed the flow of traffic veering right and onto the shoulder so as to give room to whatever the obstruction was, which Kenny assumed to be a disabled vehicle. The impediment, he soon realized, was not a stationary one but moving.

And very slowly.

A man, perched high upon a horse that straddled the center yellow divider line of the road. Kenny got closer and was able to see the horse was white...but not like a pearl, more like an old undershirt. It trotted along in an almost scoliotic gait, hindquarters slightly out of sync with its front thrusters. The man in its mount appeared to be old, given that his ample, shoulder length mane of hair was shockingly white, far whiter than the horse he rode upon. He had a Teddy Roosevelt Rough Riders hat on his head and wore a sleeveless red tee shirt that Kenny had no doubt while still behind him bore yellow lettering on its front that said *Hulk-A-Mania*. His exposed arms were unusually muscular for a man his age, skin deep copper-toned and naugahyde in texture. His pants were old Wrangler jeans, on his feet a pair of flip-flops resting in the stirrups. Where the majority of drivers inconvenienced by this man riding his horse along the middle of A1A were likely annoyed, Kenny was not. He was anything but. As he pulled alongside he looked over and up and saw on the rider a weathered face that probably spent most of its life looking into the wind. He had a thick, white walrus moustache, matching pork chop sideburns and slits for eyes with Quixotésque intentions. But as peculiar as the man was in appearance, it was the unremarkable horse beneath him that brought Kenny to another time and place and suddenly he was not seated behind the wheel of his car but on the top rail of a corral fence on a farm he'd visited as a child in Georgia, near the banks of the Withlacoochie River, not to be confused with the river in central Florida of the same name, the one that flowed south to north instead of north to south. They were visiting a friend of his family that he could vaguely picture at this point. He, his father, mother and older brother, Luke. He remembered the men in good spirits, laughing while drinking cans of what had to be beer, the women in the yard by the house setting the picnic table for lunch. Dirt bikes ridden by older boys that had ignored him and his brother, wildly cutting across the fields in defiance of every law of both physics and caution then disappearing from sight, only to circle back a short time later. The top rail of the corral fence he sat upon was higher than his eyeline. Luke was able to climb it, Kenny needed his father's lift and the boys sat perched looking at the horses penned inside. Of them, he'd chosen the one that walked differently than the others as his favorite. Its coat was white, but not like a pearl. And his father tousled his hair. The imagery triggered hearing the words of the VA representative who'd called him earlier.

Martin Rehage, Sergeant First Class, US Army, retired?

...He saw his mother on the patio smiling with the other wife, both wearing aprons and Luke, beside him. Times were good. Before Luke's blood turned bad and he died and his mother screamed, cursed and cried before one day leaving for Arizona then New Mexico or maybe it was New Mexico then Arizona and who knows if she's even dead or alive anymore...it didn't matter...and then it was just Kenny and his father.

Martin Rehage, Sergeant First Class, US Army, retired?

No more trips to places like that farm up in Georgia near the banks of the Withlacoochie River, not to be confused with the one in Central Florida where...and then it was just Kenny and his father. Going through the motions, doing the best they could in the house by the swamp road turn. Just Kenny and his father.

I see here that he was attached to the 1st SFOD-Delta-

Kenny slowly passed the man and horse walking along the centerline divider in a four-beat gait. The rider broke focus and looked down at him, offering a firm and hearty nod, as if he approved of Kenny and Kenny returned the acknowledgement with a half-hearted wave he wasn't sure the rider could see through the tinted glass window. Yes sir, he thought. You are a king. Of what realm, Kenny did not know but a king all the same.

Again traffic picked up and again he thought of his father. Trying to push the thought out of his mind only allowed Rosie to find her way into it. Where Kenny didn't believe himself as ever being worthy of her, he believed someone like his father was.

Please accept my sympathies on your father's passing and my gratitude for his service.

He was a man worthy of Rosie. And if anyone could have saved him it would have been someone like her.

Someone like Rosie.

Kenny wondered what he might say about all of this, what he was doing. His father. And the choices he was making. What would he say? The man who at one time was so capable, who suffered in silence, having had to have believed he'd been betrayed by both God and country but never saying it aloud.

Sweetie, what I'm gonna tell you is gonna hurt-

It was Mrs. Johnson's words now that he had heard.

Sweetie, what I'm gonna tell you is gonna hurt-

Just blow it off.

Blow off Copeland.

Blow off Walter Reed and Stubblefield and the rest of them.

Keep driving, right to where she was at that very moment and from there never leave her side.

Kenny imagined his father saying those words, telling him to keep driving right to where she was at that very moment and from there never leave her side.

...It's gonna hurt real bad, Sweetie.

He knew his father would not have approved of the choice he was making and with that Kenny became angry with himself for entertaining the possibility, slamming the thought down to the pavement of his mind. His father's approval meant nothing as Kenny certainly didn't approve of his father's choices...his father blowing his brains out in the front seat of the 71' Chevy pickup in the driveway of their house by the swamp road turn.

Rosie.

Rosie.

Rosie.

Someone like Rosie could have saved him.

Please accept my sympathies on your father's passing and my gratitude for his service.

Sweetie, what I'm gonna tell you is gonna hurt.

I can't believe I called her ma'am.

I can't believe I called her ma'am.

Kenny was over the bridge and now into Bal Harbour.

He was exhausted.

The phone rang.

He picked it up and recognized the number as Walter Reed's, then put it back down leaving it unanswered.

Chapter Nineteen

Same White Horse

One deep breath.

Two deep breaths.

A third.

All slow.

Copeland was stiff, eyes locked straight ahead knowing what had happened while at the same time not knowing. He slowly began to touch his legs, his chest then forehead. Another deep breath and he shifted ever so slightly in place, probing for a sign of pain that might jolt him back into immobility. He undid his seatbelt, opened the door, slowly stepped out of the car and looked behind it for whatever it was that had slammed into him. It was an American made four-door. A Ford or a Chevy. Copeland didn't make an effort to distinguish it. The front end had been compressed into a dropped accordion, the hood buckled up and radiator sibilant but understated as if it were trying to be polite given the circumstances.

The driver got out of the car.

"Oh, no-!"

He was in his thirties, maybe even forties, gawk-thin and wore a short sleeved collared shirt with a necktie. Had Copeland's mind not been elsewhere he probably would have wondered what public library the guy worked at.

"...That's a Rolls Royce!"

Copeland didn't seem to hear him.

The driver stayed locked onto the back of the Rolls, which appeared to have benefited from the law of tonnage. Only one of the tail lights was broken, part of the rear fender and downward portion of the trunk door slightly dented.

"Oh, shit-!"

"Are you okay?"

The man ignored Copeland's question.

"I...I just hit your car."

Copeland stated the obvious. "Yeah. You okay, though?"

"I...I hit-"

Copeland stopped him. "It's just a car." He then gave the driver a reassuring pat on the arm and turned around to go on his way.

He got back in his Rolls Royce with the freshly broken tail light and dented fender, started it and drove off as if nothing had happened. He looked at the time on the dashboard and was surprised to see he wasn't running as late as he thought he was. He then did a mental recap of what the rest of the day would look like regarding his obligations and appointments, speaking out loud in a simplified, pidgin-esque pattering-

...Dinner at the Yosts. There was no getting out of that. No, no way. Karen wouldn't hear of it. He'd much prefer just going to dinner with her, he thought. Just the two of them. Somewhere quiet. Easy. Maybe they could go to the Yosts just for a drink or two, then duck out. As long as he left a check they wouldn't be offended. Unlikely. Karen wouldn't hear of it. She liked Gracie Yost. He exhaled making a fluttering sound with his lips-

...Next was the phone call meeting with the guys from Triad. The *Las Ventanas* project. He wanted to do that from the office. That had a new life breathed into it. A priority, even. He then considered if it should be done in person. No, not yet. A conference call would be fine for now. They'd follow the call up with an in-person-

...Kenny, the kid. What does he need to talk to me about? He better not be saying he's leaving. No. No way-

...Kenny, the kid. He didn't know it yet, but if this *Las Ventanas* thing looked good, he was coming in as a partner on Copeland's end. There wasn't the slightest doubt about that now-

...Kenny, the kid. Copeland had plans for him. He was going to have him work on his son, Scott. Get him back in Copeland's life. Make things right between them. He had no idea how. Scott would never respond to money. The kid could probably figure something out. Yes, the kid could figure something out. The kid. He'd figure it out. He was a different kind of smart. Clever. He saw things three moves before anyone else did. Oh, he was clever, the kid. He better not be saying he's leaving. No. No way. No way Copeland was letting him go-

...Lauren. His stepdaughter who was getting married to Marcus Mendelsohn or Mendel Marcuson. Karen says she wants to have a wedding in Tuscany. Maybe that's not a bad idea-

...Kenny, the kid. He was going to invite him. Him and his hot little unit girlfriend. I bet he's never been to Italy. I'm inviting him.

Again, he looked at the time and decided that he was going to have Brenda cancel the massage appointment and wondered if he felt a little tight from getting rear ended-

...Bendel. The accountant. He's a good guy. We have him next week. Good. He's a good guy-

...Dale Marlin. Breakfast next week, too. That crazy bastard. Copeland smiled, thinking he couldn't wait to hear what batshit rant he was gonna launch into when he saw him.

Copeland was surprised that he was already on the Causeway at 112th heading into Miami Beach and he wondered, not for the first time, who this Julie Tuttle was that the portion of road had been named for and decided he really didn't care. He was slowed down by the perpetual congestion at Collins Avenue with no expectations that he'd get through this or the next green arrow. It might even take a third before he could make that left but it was okay.

The kid's not going anywhere. As Copeland waited, he felt something within his being, something visceral...and foreign. A feeling, an emotion that came with a lightness about it. He couldn't put his finger on what it was immediately and then realized it was gratitude.

He was grateful.

Not for any one thing in particular.

And nothing material.

He was grateful for not only how things turned out, but for how he decided what he imagined might be coming his way.

Something good.

A new kind of good.

He drove past the Fontainebleau and thought about a hooker, shook his head and grinned as if he were chastising himself for being a bad boy. Then he looked at the line of massive yachts moored in the canal on the other side of the street and it reminded him of once telling someone that instead of having one of those boats it was better to have a friend who had one of those boats. He still felt that way even though he could buy any one of them.

Traffic was moving nicely now. A deep breath and he decided that he was tired. But it was okay. Everything was going to be okay.

Further up Collins Avenue, he passed the Four Seasons where inside at the Surf Club they made the best damn hamburger he'd ever had. That well could be one of his favorite things in the whole world. The burger at the Surf Club and a bottle of red Bordeaux after an ice cold vodka martini straight up with a twist of lemon. A gin one for Karen. And the three piece jazz quartet on Monday nights. He nodded his head. He was going to tell Karen they should blow out of Yost's early and go to the Surf Club for a burger. And then he'd tell her they were gonna go home and he was gonna give her a throw and he smiled, picturing her reaction when he said that to her, the pretend shock she put forth as a veneer for her laughter.

96th Street was ahead in the distance and Copeland decided he was glad he'd taken 41st Street into Miami Beach but wasn't sure why as the cars on the bridge were moving. The thought hadn't fully evaporated when he came upon another sudden traffic build up on Collins Avenue. Ahead in the distance he could see something he wasn't sure was actually there, it was so out of place. A man was riding a horse in the middle of the road. As he moved closer he was able to see the horse was white...but not like a pearl, more like an old undershirt. The man riding it looked old. He had a helluva head of hair, though. White hair. Much whiter than the horse. He was wearing what Copeland figured was a cowboy hat and a sleeveless Hulk Hogan tee shirt, commenting to himself that this old bastard's arms were jacked, then wondered what the fuck he was doing on a horse in the middle of Collins Avenue. As he approached and slowly made his way around him, Copeland looked at the horse's face and decided it was miserable. The imagery brought him back to a December evening many years earlier in New York City. It was dark and windy and wet and cold, not quite freezing but more than enough to be awful. He was sitting in the carriage of a horse drawn Hansom cab, a six year old Scott snuggled tight between himself and the boy's mother. She was the one who wanted to do the carriage ride in the park. She pressed and pressed and kept pressing as Copeland protested, people from New York didn't do that. Even people from Long Island. That was for tourists. They weren't fucking tourists! Those rides were clip jobs, paid for in ten minute increments! Only tourists fell for that! And it started to rain harder and the sounds of the city that had been there all along became relentless assaults on his senses and Scott started to cry. The poor boy was miserable. His mother was miserable. Copeland was miserable. Even the poor horse whose coat was a dirty shade of white was miserable. The only one not miserable was the Hansom cab driver with the high-pitched fake Irish brogue pointing out obvious landmarks in a voice more suited for sending out warnings not to be *takin' me Lucky Charms*, and all the while stealthily banging Copeland for fifteen bucks every ten minutes spent in the carriage.

A hard sigh. With the traffic freed up once again, Copeland gave another thought to what he decided was Hulk Hogan's grandfather on the back of the poor horse that looked like the one from the horrible Central Park carriage ride of the past. He shook his head, a mix of melancholy and resigned acceptance that happiness didn't discriminate in its elusiveness. He made the next three traffic signals without interruption then turned left into the shopping center where the cafés were, where he would be meeting Kenny.

Pulling into the valet podium and stopping, he was greeted before the car was put in park. "How are you today, sir?"

Stepping out of the car, Copeland actually took a moment to consider the car valet's question as being more than rhetorical. "You know what? I'm good."

"That's nice to hear, sir."

Copeland nodded, then returned the question. "How you doin'?"

"Oh, very good, sir. Very good. Thank you. Thank you."

A ticket was exchanged for Copeland's keys. From one of the other valets standing by, a few words *en español* and the valet attending to Copeland pointed out to him in the manner one does when delivering bad news-

"...Sir, you know that your-?"

Copeland didn't let him finish, waving off the query. "Yeah, I know. Got rear ended on the way over here." He smiled and shrugged, a gesture that spoke volumes, suggesting that despite it all, everything was not only going to be okay, that better things were just around the corner.

Copeland walked into the bistro, casual and French in theme, white tiled walls to match the tablecloths. The kind of place that had its menu and wine offerings stylishly scripted on mirrors.

Only a third of the tables were occupied, as the lunch rush had ended. He walked past the young hostess wearing a skin-tight, red dress holding up a finger in acknowledgement but not looking at her. He was scanning the room, assuming Kenny had already arrived and was seated.

He didn't see him.

He looked around the dining room again. Still not seeing him, he turned to look over by the empty bar area...then out behind him in the parking lot.

The hostess followed him, politely interrupting. "Good afternoon, sir."

Again, he didn't give her eye contact. "I'm meeting someone here. A friend, I don't see him-" Then Copeland realized that he was thirsty. "Can you get me a glass of water? If you don't mind?"

"Of course," the hostess answered, well accustomed to unconscious brashness. "I'll get that for you right away."

She glided off and Copeland re-scanned the room in the same pattern as he had previously.

Where's the kid?, he wondered.

Where's the fucking kid?

He's supposed to be here.

Kenny was nowhere to be seen.

Chapter Twenty

Marty Rehage

At sixty-one years old, Kenny's father Marty Rehage maintained the embodiment of two things, an obvious hardiness and millpond-like calm. But over the past eleven months he'd slowly, and probably unconsciously, stopped keeping track of the days. Even the hours, to an extent. They came and went as things do when what resides within them, specifically plans and memories, aren't given much consideration.

Wearing old, familiar jeans and a threadbare black tee shirt that he wore the previous day, he emerged into the humidity from the back door of the small house by the swamp road turn, a scrunched and soiled rag resting upon the calluses between the palm and black grease stained fingers of his able hand. He'd forgotten it was still there and when he did notice would inevitably stuff it into his front pants pocket as he had a habit of doing. One firmly placed foot in front of the other, his pace was languid but not to be confused for a saunter. Out toward the garage, his old Danner boots trampled underfoot pecans in varying stages of decomposition that had fallen from the tree onto the hard dirt and patches of anemic grass. When he walked past the basketball half-court he'd constructed for his son many years earlier, which had since become nothing more than a rusting hollow metal post holding up a backboard and netless rim that looked down over a soot-covered concrete slab, he might have scowled and shook his head, like the whole damn thing had done him a wrong turn then stuck around to taunt him about it. He hadn't eaten all day but wasn't thinking about dinner. He was going to tinker around on the pickup he was restoring, doing exactly what he hadn't yet decided. His intention was nothing more than to burn an hour or two. He certainly had no expectations of doing anything that involved concentration.

Burn an hour or two-

...Tinkering-

...Mindless tinkering.

The '71 Chevy pickup was closer to the beginning of the restoration than the end. It was parked with its front bumper rolled tight up to the threshold of the open door of the garage that doubled as a mechanic's workspace. Marty wasn't sure why he'd pulled the truck up so far. He probably had a reason at the time. He entered into the dark and cool garage and looked around almost as if he didn't trust it was as it had been left...like something might have been moved, was missing or even added. It wasn't the sort of space that might ordinarily arouse suspicion upon entering, especially from the sole individual whose domain it was. This garage was very personal and reflected Marty's character in how it was set up. The sense of order was absolute, almost rigid and puritanical, exemplifying the old adage of a place for everything and everything in its place. Marty stood before the workbench. After a moment of pause, he looked up at the overhead light like he hoped it would turn itself on then tugged on the beaded pull-cord with reluctance. Again, he looked around as if he might have been unsure why he'd come out, then opened one of the drawers and took from it a small wire bristled hand brush with a wooden handle that was meant to clean things like rust off of metal. He noticed at that time he was still holding the scrunched up rag he'd inadvertently taken from the kitchen and stuffed it into his front pants pocket, then again looked at the small wire brush and for a moment seemed to forget what he had intended on doing with it. Something in his pause while looking at the small brush brought him back to the beginning of it all.

It was coming up on a year, a full year from when they picked him.

There were no coincidences.

They didn't care that they were destroying the life of a man who simply wanted to be left alone.

And they most certainly picked him.

It began with the old bush hog he'd restored for a farmer called McCutchen from nearby who he didn't know well, if at all, but thought he'd recognized seeing around from time to time. In fact, Marty had seen him drive by the swamp road turn not once but twice the week before he stopped and called on him. The interaction was organic enough, the transaction routine. The unannounced visit, which in those parts wasn't unusual, saw McCutchen the farmer finding Marty in the very place he stood holding the wire brush. He approached with an extended hand and smile, apologizing for the interruption and asking if he might be interested in doing a job he didn't have the hands nor time for and if he was open to bartering as payment for his services. Since Marty had the time and bartering was something he could get behind, he agreed. Fifty one-pound vacuum-sealed packs of frozen ground venison in exchange for the work on the bush hog was well worth it. Within a week services were rendered, payment made, along with some light conversation about things they seemed to share in common, opinions on the direction the country was going in and need for lower taxes and less government interference with things like small business. It was not the last Marty would be seeing of McCutchen the farmer.

He soon returned to inquire whether Marty did any gunsmithing work as he was interested in having the barrel of his daughter's Ruger 10-22 re-blued and the receiver on his own AR-15 modified from semi-automatic to full so that he might get a little bit more of a charge when he'd shoot the groundhogs on his property. While Marty was a capable gunsmith, he thought he'd accept the offer but pass the job to Norby Rice, who was even more capable and could certainly use a freezer full of ground venison. Barter was something Norby Rice could get behind, too.

Marty Rehage wasn't a terribly social man, typically keeping to himself. But for Norby, his occasional cup o'coffee and fishing buddy, he didn't have many friends. Almost as wide as he was tall and with one leg ever so slightly shorter than the other, Norby Rice looked like a shrub amongst bushes. He'd spent his career working the late shift at a food processing plant outside Milton. Unlike Marty, Norby had a vivaciousness about him, a perpetual itch for social interaction, which was limited as he was a man who tended to his responsibilities, particularly his invalid wife who had long been afflicted with Multiple Sclerosis. The camaraderie they shared was one that was almost by default, discovering a connection that had roots in a common experience. While both men were trying to navigate through domestic chores during difficult times in their lives, they'd each put a frozen turkey in a preheated oven on separate Thanksgivings. Norby liked to bring that up, like it made them related or members of an exclusive club. Norby had three children, and in his house the check out time was eighteen years for all of them. Upon coming of age, the boys enlisted in the Army and his daughter went to Millsaps College up in Jackson with designs on becoming a school teacher. During her first year, she was murdered by a stranger off campus. The loss of a child was the true shared experience between the men, the frozen turkey simply stood in as a surrogate. In the wake of his tragedy, Norby Rice was able to care for his ailing wife and still did. Marty often wondered if the reason she didn't break down and run away was because she couldn't.

Three weeks after farmer McCutchen visited him to pick up the re-blued Ruger 10-22 and modified receiver of his AR-15, Marty was driving back from his weekly run into Crestview. He was pulled over by not one, but two unmarked law enforcement cars just before he made his way to the on-ramp of I-10 at Ferdon Boulevard. Four agents, two from each car, approached Marty's vehicle taking positions but without guns drawn. Marty stayed calm. Calm enough to notice that aside from having identical haircuts, three of the four were wearing the exact same type of sunglasses.

One of the agents approached the driver's side door and instructed him to lower his window.

Marty complied.

The agent knew his name.

He identified himself as being with the Federal Bureau of Investigation and told Marty to step out of the vehicle. Again, Marty complied. They directed him to get in one of their cars then shuttled him to the Okaloosa County Sheriff's station over on James Lee Boulevard. There was an interview room waiting for them, seemingly set up for the occasion. One simple conference table and five chairs around it. A dozen small bottles of generic spring water served as a centerpiece.

The men entered and some informal dialogue was exchanged, initiated and supported by the agent who approached Marty's vehicle-

...All meant to set a tone.

Marty was then asked by the lead agent if he held a current and valid FFL-07 and SOT license allowing him to build, convert or modify a firearm classified as semi-automatic into full automatic. Marty needed to know nothing else as to why they'd come for him.

There were no coincidences.

He didn't need to hear the agent tell him that he had been recorded not only agreeing to illegally modify an AR-15 in exchange for payment but also what was coming next. He was facing some very serious federal jail time-

...But-

...If he agreed to help the government in their investigation into the Panhandle Patriots, a militia group they knew he attended meetings of, they might reconsider. Marty stayed silent, not denying he'd been to several meetings of the group, meetings that amounted to social gatherings of like-minded rural men. Where they drank coffee and talked about the direction the country was going in and the need for lower taxes and less government interference with things like small business. Where they also exchanged products and services as payment for products and services, bartering, something Marty Rehage could get behind. Still, his attendance was limited only to several instances. He was not a terribly social man.

...But if he agreed to help the government that he so faithfully served for an entire career in the United States Army-

...If he agreed to help the government in its fight against a clear and present danger to our democracy that they believed the Panhandle Patriots to be-

...That charge would never see the light of day.

Marty listened, but said nothing.

Fifteen years.

That was what they assured him he would be facing if the United States Attorney decided to charge him. Not to mention forthcoming IRS audits to see if whatever goods he appropriated through barter were declared on his tax return forms. Again, an appeal to his sense of duty and love of country, reiterating a third time the clear and present danger groups like the Panhandle Patriots posed to our democracy.

Fifteen years.

Or he could work with them, give the FBI information on what was going on at not only the meetings of the Panhandle Patriots, but other militia groups throughout the country that through his affiliations he might have access to, especially with his own accomplished military background. He was told that he wouldn't be the only one who was assisting them, which he knew was true...then told that there were plenty of other former Special Forces operators helping as well, which he knew was a lie.

He didn't have to answer right then.

He could think about it.

They'd be in touch.

He was released without being charged, excused from the room and told to stand by, one of them would drive him back to his car. After fifteen minutes of waiting, Marty chose to walk.

Fifteen years-

...For illegally modifying a semi-automatic rifle. Something he didn't do. Marty knew he could have given them Norby Rice and been done with it. Norby did the work on the gun. Norby actually went to the meetings regularly.

Marty never considered doing so for an instant.

Chasing the memory of that moment away, Marty looked up from the small, wire bristle brush he was holding, unconsciously tapped it three times on his open hand then returned it to the drawer he'd taken it from. He looked up at the overhead farmhouse dome light and squinted, seemingly curious, like he might be wondering how much life the bulb had left in it. Another contemplative moment then he thought he'd heard something outside the garage and turned to investigate, walking with an unchanged pulse rate toward the blinding light of the open door. Again, his gait was slow and deliberate. He stepped outside and looked around, the sun causing him to squint much like the overhead light had moments earlier.

Nothing-

...Only unseen birds chirping.

He returned back into the garage, back to his place in front of the workbench. Again he began to open and shut the small drawers looking for something, something that he didn't appear to be sure of.

It wasn't there.

He'd turned to look at nothing in particular on the wall to his left. A calendar was hung over by a sixty gallon tank of acetylene. He had the slow realization that it was coming on...three months behind. He did have a momentary impulse to step over and bring it up to date but like the last time he took notice, didn't bother. He went back to squirreling aimlessly through the workbench drawers. Exhausting his options, he went back to the drawer he'd put the wire brush back in and again took it out. He looked at it as if it might have had the answer to what he'd had planned for it a few moments earlier, but all it did was once again trigger the imagery of the four agents. He saw them in his mind when without warning, they came out to the house. Down by the swamp road turn. It had been ten weeks since the previous interaction which was in a grocery store parking lot. He knew that by coming here, it was an indication that the waiting game was coming to a close. Marty had been inside when they showed up in what had to be a brand new, showroom-fresh extended cab pickup truck that was probably a rental. Their efforts at being inconspicuous were anything but. The creases in their pants pockets where their badges were obvious, the unmissable bulges on their hips outlining holstered sidearms challenged the very definition of the word concealed, or at least its intention.

When he greeted them, it began with small talk, but they'd gotten to the rubber-meeting-the-road part a little more forcefully. He was told that the membership of the Panhandle Patriots had grown from eighteen members to twenty-seven and they needed him to make a choice on whether or not he was going to help them. They wanted him to start going to meetings wearing a wire. The agents didn't pause for questions from Marty, simply going into what his options were as far as working with them as an informant. If he declined to cooperate, he would be served with a warrant and arrested, facing fifteen years in federal prison. Marty ended that visit by telling them he'd be in touch and was told the matter was now time sensitive.

In the garage, Marty again looked down at the small wire brush in his hand and tapped it another three times against his palm. Thirty minutes earlier, the lead FBI agent had called him on the house phone, before he'd walked out of the back door of his house, unknowingly holding the rag that was now bunched up in his pocket. He was told to come meet them up in Crestview, at the North District Sheriff's Station to have another conversation. If he didn't, they would come to him. Marty had known full well by that point that they were chatted-out.

He again looked down at the wire brush, but this time as it might have an answer for him to a question greater than what he had planned on using it for. He turned toward the open garage door and again slowly wandered into the blinding sunlight that poured through it. Stepping out alongside the pickup truck, he looked over by the line of persimmon trees and toward the neighbor Mrs. Johnson's house. He figured her for being incorruptible, the way she looked after that girl and anyone else who might need it. The way she even looked after himself when he had been at his lowest and without ever bringing it up afterwards. He was reminded of what she'd done for him every time he saw the jagged, raised red lighting bolt shaped scar on his boy's inner forearm.

After Marty's eldest son Luke died and his devastated mother ran away, his spiral descended into an aquifer of liquor, preferably the unclear kind but vodka in a pinch, and subsequent periodic public outbursts of violence. During that time a hot afternoon saw young Kenny Wayne, all of twelve years old, tripping off a run through the glass pane of the house's front door. A broken shard opened up his arm, the bleeding was profuse. And when the boy cried out for his father, Marty, pie-eyed drunk, stumbled from out of the garage that doubled as a mechanic's work space, barely able to stand. Mrs. Johnson, in her yard at the time, witnessed what was playing out and knew that if an ambulance was called, the deputies were sure to follow and seeing Marty, all drunk'd up again, would have to by law alert the Child Protective Services. In her estimation, the boy would inevitably be taken away and then Marty would have nothing. Mrs. Johnson, the one time school nurse, chose to see Marty get another chance. She would stitch the boy up herself. While her efforts were effective, it was far from a work of art. But maybe, by the grace of the God whom she both feared and adored, the episode might see the boy's father mend his ways. From that point, Marty Rehage never took another drink.

He built a small basketball court in the yard and hoped doing so might help with co-parenting his son.

Marty looked up over the line of the persimmon trees and squinted, then turned again and began to walk toward the front of the garage door. He disappeared inside, but only shortly, stepping back out again into the sunlight. He was contemplating the inevitable and in doing so considered the moments leading up to particular high risk incursions he'd experienced during the war and the introspections that accompanied them. As he had done then, he replayed the words of the Shawnee Indian warrior, Tecumseh, who reminded the men following him into battle, *"when your time comes to die, be not like those whose hearts are filled with fear of death, so that when their time comes they weep and pray for a little more time to live their lives over again in a different way. Sing your death song and die like a hero going home."*

Marty looked down the road at the house with the flagpole used to tether the excitable pit bull. He then looked over at Mrs. Johnson's house, then toward his own, specifically at the window of the bedroom where his son Kenny Wayne was mindlessly playing some sort of video game. Maybe she would stitch him up again if ever he needed it.

Marty Rehage then walked over to the driver's side door of the '71 Chevy pickup he was restoring, opened it and got in. He was still holding the small wire brush in one hand. With the other, he reached under the front seat and took hold of the handgun beneath it.

Chapter Twenty-One

Gethsemane

Copeland stepped beyond the hostess area into the dining room looking from table to table as if he was the floor manager, except for the fact that he lacked an awareness of where exactly he was in proximity to the guests. The place he chose to stand had him positioned inches from an elderly man seated at a table late-lunching with his wife, creating enough of an encroachment that the man recoiled and looked up to silently beg pardon. Copeland was predictably unaware or uncaring. He took a few more steps and again swept the room with his eyes, still finding no sign of Kenny and with it felt a sense of annoyance. He didn't realize Kenny walked out of the rest room at the far end of the bar behind him.

As Kenny made his way toward the dining room along a row of empty stools, the young hostess in the tight fitting red dress was stepping from the service bar area holding the glass of water Copeland had requested. She yielded so that he could pass. Kenny stopped and held out his hand insisting she go first, then followed her toward Copeland. Reaching Copeland's side, she held up the glass like an offering. "Here's your water, sir."

"Thank you, hon." Copeland took the glass from her and began to bring it to his mouth but stopped as he saw Kenny behind her. Turning back to the hostess, he asked in what sounded like a rebuke, "why didn't you tell me he was here?" The hostess was startled by the barking, not to mention confused.

Copeland turned his attention to Kenny. "You just gettin' here now?" He then proceeded to drain the glass of water in two gulps.

"No. I been here about a half hour." He then motioned with his head toward a table against the wall on the far side of the dining room near the window.

Copeland nodded. There seemed to be something suggesting a discomfort settling in the space between them, not quite resentment but an uneasiness, palpable enough for him to pick up on. He made a conscious play to change the tone, putting his hand on Kenny's shoulder and looking straight down into his eyes. "How you doin', kid?"

Kenny grin-smirked and nodded. He knew the act. "I'm not bad, Alan. Not bad."

"So, where you sittin'? You got a table, right?"

Behind them the hostess still stood, looking like a small fish out of water gasping at the useless air trying to offer an apology for an oversight she hadn't actually been guilty of. Kenny again motioned to Copeland with his head in the direction of where he had been sitting before getting up to use the bathroom, then deferred to him to go ahead, but Copeland insisted on following him as he didn't pay attention to the exact table being referenced. The now ignored and subsequently relieved hostess took the opportunity to quietly retreat unscathed.

"So how you doin', kid?"

"I'm okay, thanks. Traffic was a little nuts, but I guess to be expected."

Copeland agreed. "You're not gonna believe what I saw out on Collins Avenue when I was pullin' up here. A guy on a horse. A fucking guy on an actual horse! Plodding down the middle of the street, not a care in the world...he may's well been whistling the theme to *Bonanza!*"

"I saw him too. Up north of the bridge. Long, white haired guy in a Hulk Hogan shirt."

Copeland didn't appear to be listening. They made their way to the table at the far end of the dining room.

"You know I'm glad you asked to meet with me," Copeland told him. "Because I got a few things I want to talk to you about. So we'll kill two birds with one stone."

"Okay."

Copeland did a quick perimeter check of the table. "That little cupcake got us over in Siberia."

"I asked her to sit us here."

"Never a bad play," Copeland said, approvingly.

They sat in their respective chairs and Copeland immediately picked up the menu, then looked down at his watch and back again at the menu. "You eat lunch?"

"I grabbed something earlier."

"Me, too. Let's order somethin' to pick on anyway. I'm still hungry." He then mumbled something under his breath about a tapeworm.

As Copeland reviewed the menu, the expression on his face suggested that he didn't see anything interesting. Still looking down, he closed his eyes for a moment.

"Everything okay, Alan?"

Copeland looked up, half-annoyed. "Yeah. Everything's fine. Why? You think something's wrong?"

"No, you just...for a second looked like something was...y'know-"

"I'm fine. Don't ask me that. You're not my mother." Copeland looked back at the menu, then quickly looked back up to catch an off guard reaction from Kenny, of which there was none. Copeland was smiling. "You know I'm just breaking your balls, kid."

The server shook leg toward them, falling short with her efforts at being convincingly perky upon arrival, as she probably thought her shift was over when told she had to take one more table. She was not young but well put together and presented well, having made the most of what she'd been given physically. "Good afternoon, gentlemen," she said. "How are we doing today?"

Where Kenny gave her the decency of eye contact and a welcoming nod, Copeland got right to the business of things. "Let's get some of these stuffed mushrooms, steak tidbits and a shrimp cocktail. Some fries, too, but tell the cook not to put any salt on them.

The parsley's okay, but no salt." He looked at Kenny. "You see anything else on there?"

"No. I'm not really hun-"

Copeland didn't let him finish. "You'll eat something." He then turned back to the waitress. "And a Diet Pepsi."

"Diet Coke okay?"

"Fine."

The server looked at Kenny. "Anything to drink for you, sir?"

Kenny thought for a second. "A bottle of spring water, please."

"Flat or sparkling?"

"Flat, thanks."

Copeland chimed in with a command. "Bring two. Big ones." The waitress smiled and thanked them before going on her way. Copeland took a deep breath, looked at his watch, then at Kenny with an undivided attention. "So, what do you got for me? What's on your mind? You and me have a 3:30 conference call to do back at the office."

Kenny half-shrugged and looked away. "I just wanted to talk to you about a few things."

"Well, I'm all ears, kid. Talk away."

Kenny shifted in his seat, looking for the words that might best express what he was about to say. He thought he had found his entry point and was in the midst of inhaling the way one does when they are about to speak when Copeland did it for him.

"You want more money-"

Kenny was ever so slightly taken aback.

"...A raise. You want a raise?"

Before Kenny could answer, Copeland expounded on a theory behind the request. "I know what happened. You might have gone home to your girlfriend after work one night...probably after a day when I was being more of a pain in the ass than I usually am, and she asked you what's wrong and you told her, 'you know what? My boss, Alan Copeland, is a massive douchebag. He's...he's...he's like a rash on my ass the size of a cheesecake that just won't go away-'"

Kenny laughed.

"'...And she said, fuck him! Quit!' And you said you weren't sure you wanted to quit, you might not have another job lined up and she said quit anyway and you said you don't wanna quit 'cause-" Copleand then pointed to himself, switching from third person to first person narration. "...As much as I'm an asshole, you love me...so she said-," back then to third person, "...Ask the douchebag for a raise."

Copeland was smiling, as was Kenny but in a way that suggested he might have been embarrassed if anyone in the room might have heard the exchange.

"She didn't say that, Alan. She wouldn't...she wouldn't...say that. C'mon."

Copeland was grinning ear to ear, as he'd gotten the desired effect he was looking for. "I get it, kid. I know. Working for me ain't easy. Ask Karen what it's like being married to me." He held up both hands like he was surrendering.

Kenny let his eyeline drift across the dining room floor to where the young hostess in the tight fitting red dress was wiping down menus at the podium.

Copeland continued. "I have to say I don't really know that girlfriend of yours. But when I met her she seemed...very lovely. And very pretty. Very pretty. Too pretty for you."

Kenny snapped back to being fully present in the moment. "Yeah, she is. She's pretty cool."

Copeland thought for a moment. "Was she ever up to the house with you?"

Kenny didn't have to think for long. "Yeah. The time your wife had a cocktail party and you wanted me to tag around Marc Driscoll and listen to what he was sayin' to those guys from-"

"Of course!" Copeland had cut him off again. Another moment of silence, ever so slightly bordering on awkward. "So what are your plans?"

"Plans...for what?," Kenny answered.

"Plans for what? What do you think, you schmuck? Plans for your girlfriend! What's her name? Caroline?"

"Rose."

Copeland snapped his fingers as if that was his second guess. "Rose. Of course. I knew that." Then a thought came to Copeland. "Did I tell the waitress no salt on the fries?"

"You did."

"Good. I gotta watch the salt. Too much salt, no good. So, what are your plans for her? What are you gonna do?"

"Plans, like what? I don't understand."

"Well, not for nothin' kid...I kind of had this feeling that you might've wanted to sit down 'cause you were thinking about maybe...y'know...maybe getting married or somethin'." He had another thought. "Did I tell you that Lauren, my step daughter's getting married?"

"You did."

"I guess every pot got a cover, right? Well, I want you at that wedding. For no other reason than to witness how pathetic these fucking people are. When I tell you what a drip this guy is? This guy she's marrying? Holy shit! Anyway, I thought you wanted to maybe talk to me 'cause you were thinking about getting married and wanted to run it by someone who'd...y'know...done that kinda thing once or twice."

Again, Kenny smiled. "No. I'm not thinking of getting married or anything like that, Alan. But it's funny you bring it up 'cause Brenda asked me the same thing before."

Now it was Copeland who was surprised. "My Brenda? She asked you that?"

"She asked me what my plans were. With Rose. Yeah. Just like you did. Are you guys in, like...cahoots or something?"

"Naaa. Brenda's a good girl. She obviously cares about you and wants to see you happy." A pause. "We both care about you. We both want to see you happy. You ever think of that?"

"No. No, to be honest...I didn't."

Copeland laughed.

The server reappeared at the table side with Copeland's Diet Coke and two large bottles of mineral water. The conversation paused as she placed the items before them. Copeland watched her as she walked away from the table, though it was only a move meant so he didn't have to look at Kenny while he was entertaining a thought.

When he turned back, Copeland asked Kenny, "are you happy?"

Kenny was surprised to have been asked with such directness. "Me?"

"No, the valet car parker outside. Of course you."

Kenny took a moment to consider the question. "More or less, I guess." He took a moment to decide if he wanted to expound on the question.

"What?" Copeland asked him.

Kenny shook his head. "I was just thinkin' of somethin'?"

"Well? Why don't you share it with the class?"

"It's really nothing."

"Come on. Out with it."

"My father...he knew this guy when he was in the service. The Army. This guy...he was an officer, but...he was okay." The qualification was entirely lost on Copeland. "And my dad said he used to say that it was okay to be happier than you thought you deserved to be."

"What's that supposed to mean? Was this guy like one of them self-help gurus?"

"No. He was just a guy my dad was in the Army with. My dad used to say that from time to time." Kenny stayed in the thought, then nodded to himself as if validating the assertion. "Is your father still alive, Alan?"

"My father?" Copeland didn't expect to be asked that. "No. He passed away a while ago. We were close, though. He was a great guy, my dad. Great guy. We were real close."

Kenny nodded, taking his word for it.

Two buildings south and across the street from the entrance of the bistro, Special Agents Walter Reed, Trey Subblefield, their supervisor, Heinz Lucic and two FBI surveillance technicians sat around a table of a nearly vacant office procured to monitor the transmissions of the conversation between Kenny Rehage and Alan Copeland. All were wearing earphones. On the table were several video monitors covering different camera angles of the dining room where Kenny and Copeland sat. Another monitor covered the men's restroom.

"This is getting kind of personal." Walter Reed's statement was offered nonchalantly, not directed at anyone in particular. Lucic didn't look away from the monitor, only acknowledging what Reed said by holding up a silencing hand. Reed then looked at Stubblefield, who too gave the impression he was hanging on every word coming from the surveillance, despite the conversation having nothing to do with the investigation.

"How's your mouth, Trey?," Reed asked.

"Fine." Stubblefield didn't look at him when answering.

Lucic shook his head, suggesting frustration. "I don't know what's going on here. I mean, I have no idea where he's going with this. Do they always talk like this?"

Stubblefield weighed in. "I think he's fuckin' with us, Looch."

Kenny and Copeland sat across from one another, idling. It wasn't particularly uncomfortable, probably not unlike the many moments they had between them when Copeland had Kenny take a ride with him to run an errand or had him sitting in his office doing a rudimentary task. It was hard to tell what either one was thinking.

Copeland began to say something but hesitated, something he ordinarily didn't do. "You know, we're gonna cut Elliot loose."

"The clinic doctor?" Kenny asked, despite knowing full well who Elliot was.

Copeland corrected him. "The degenerate pervert. And for me to call someone a degenerate pervert? *Pffft-*"

"Well, I gotta tell you Alan, the times I've been around him, I kind of felt bad for him. He struck me as a guy who's real uncomfortable with himself."

Copeland couldn't help but point out Kenny's innocence. "How could you feel bad for him? He's a creep."

"I dunno. A guy like Dr. Elliot? You can't tell me he doesn't have problems...issues...I feel bad for him."

"Yeah, well...Elliot created those problems for himself. No one to blame, it's a hundred percent on him."

"I guess, but still." Kenny then postured as if he had a thought. "You mean to tell me you didn't know he was a weirdo when you hired him?"

"Of course I knew. Him being a degenerate pervert made it possible to get him to do what I needed him to do. We made money with Elliot. But now, it's reassessment time." Another short moment of silence and Copeland confronted what he thought was the obvious. "You're leaving, aren't you?"

"What's that?," Kenny asked, pretending not to hear him.

"I said, you're leaving me. Leaving the company. You don't want a raise, you're moving on. That's what you wanted to talk to me about."

Kenny took a deep breath and looked at Copeland's face. He sensed a permeating sadness about him, a childlike vulnerability that even suggested innocence, something he'd never seen in him, let alone thought he was capable of. Instead of directly responding to the question, Kenny looked around the room uncomfortably, then pushed his chair back from the table. "Excuse me, Alan. I need to hit the men's room."

"The men's room? Weren't you just in the men's room?"

"To wash my hands. I gotta actually use it now. Back in a sec."

All three agents had their eyes locked upon the bank of monitors. Lucic was confused. "What is this guy doing?! He was just in the bathroom?!"

"He's fuckin' with us!," Stubblefield spit out.

And Reed stayed silent.

Stubblefield shook his head and mumbled. "He's up to somethin'. He's gonna try to tip this motherfucker off-"

On the middle monitor, Kenny could be seen walking across the dining room floor toward the back of the restaurant. The agents missed him taking a sideways glance at the young hostess in the tight fitting dress by the podium as he continued past the bar to the restroom.

The next monitor picked up Kenny's mens room entrance. He walked to the urinal with nothing in his doing so appearing out of the ordinary. He relieved himself then proceeded over to the sink, washed his hands and dried them but only to half-completion, then gave his palms a quick wipe on his trousers and exited.

The three agents traded looks to see if one of them saw something the other didn't.

Kenny settled back into his seat. "Sorry. I been drinkin' water all day and it's running through me like a damn waterfall."

"I been drinking water all day, too, and I haven't had so much as a tinkle since I took a shit this morning," Copeland rebutted. "But that's neither here nor there right now, I guess." Another pause. "So, you're leaving?"

"Well, to be a hundred percent honest, I'm thinkin' about it, Alan. And yes, that's what I wanted to talk to you about."

"Okay, can you give us the courtesy of letting us make you an offer to stay?"

"It's not about money. If I wanted a raise I wouldn't play games like sayin' I was quittin'. I'd straight up ask you for one."

Copeland nodded. "Maybe."

"I would. God's honest truth. Why play games, right?" Then Kenny seemed to be distracted by a thought. "You really thought I was gonna ask you advice about gettin' married?"

Copeland was defensive. "Yeah, why? What's the big deal?"

"No big deal. It's just kinda nice that you would think of me like that...that I would come to you about somethin' personal."

"Why wouldn't you? You think I was bullshittin' when I said that you were loved over here?"

"Well, 'loved' is a kinda heavy, Alan-"

Copeland cut him off as effortlessly as he had earlier, this time with a pointed finger. "You know what I mean."

Kenny nodded, conceding.

"You know, on that note," Copeland said. "The girl...your girl Rosemary-"

"Rose."

"Yeah. I'm just gonna...I'm just gonna leave this...this little thing-" He held out his hand pantomiming as if there was something between his stubby forefinger and thumb. "...I'm gonna leave this right here and you...you can do with it whatever you want, okay?"

Kenny nodded, agreeing.

Copeland then looked like he was shopping for the right script to best articulate what he had to say. He let his head oscillate from shoulder to shoulder and frowned. "...When it comes...to being selfish-" He stopped again to dig through his limited arsenal of words. "...When it comes to being selfish...which let's face it, all guys...most guys kind of are. At first it's a choice, being selfish. You know? But the longer and longer you go on like that? Being selfish? It starts to become part of who you are. You know what I mean? It's not a choice so much anymore. It becomes...part of who you are."

The genuine honesty in which Copeland delivered his words, his capacity for what had to have been a brief moment of self-awareness and maybe even regret, was not lost on Kenny.

"What I'm tellin' you," Copeland went on, "is wherever you go and whatever you wind up doing, whether you're with me or not...keep what I just said in mind."

"Well, Alan. With all due respect you're kind of way off. I mean, I understand that...and it makes sense but I'm not really in a place to think about gettin' married. And I'm not sure Rose is either."

"Forget I brought it up." Copeland was probably not as miffed as he pretended to be, waving the statement off with his hand as if he were swatting a cloud of gnats away from his face.

"No, no. I get what you said and I appreciate you sayin' it. I do. And you're probably right."

"Of course I'm right! You're leaving. Why?"

Silence.

"That's not what I said, Alan. I said, I'm thinkin' about it."

Copeland changed gears, sensing he was losing control of the dialogue. "How old you think that guy was riding the horse down Collins?"

Kenny entertained the question. "I dunno. Fifty?"

"No way. He was like seventy."

"I don't know. I didn't get that good a look at him."

"You think he was older than me?"

"Oh, yeah. That, for sure."

Kenny looked over Copeland's shoulder across the room and saw what he guessed was their order coming out of the kitchen. He looked back at Copeland and said in a matter of fact manner, "It's back down by the bar."

Copeland thought he'd missed the first part of what was said. "What's that?"

"The bathroom. It's down by the end of the bar"

"The bathroom?"

"Yeah. Didn't you just say you had to pee?"

Copeland looked at Kenny like he was speaking in tongues, not sure if he did or not.

"Sorry, I thought you just said-"

And with that, Copeland decided he had to do just that. "I know where the bathroom is." He pushed his chair back from the table, stood up and walked across the dining room toward the restrooms. Kenny watched him, only diverting his eyeline once toward the young hostess in the tight fitting dress still standing by the podium, but only for a little more than a second this time.

"Does this motherfucker think we're stupid? Seriously! Does this motherfucker think-"

Lucic silenced Stubblefield with a hand held aloft, then calmly gave instructions to the technicians. "Don't play it back now, but did we see anything on the last Kenny bathroom visit?"

"He's fuckin' with us, Looch."

Lucic ignored him, turning instead to Reed as if he might be able to offer some sort of hypothetical to explain what was happening. "Thoughts, Walt?

"No. Nothing coming to mind."

The surveillance camera in the bathroom picked up Copeland entering. He could be seen walking toward the urinal but stopping in front of the mirror above the sink first. He gave himself a look, lifting his chin and with the back of his hand tapped the turkey neck that seemed to be bothering him more than usual that day.

Lucic had a thought. "Turn the audio up."

Copeland continued on to the urinal, this time the movements could be heard louder than before. He undid his zipper and seemed to be having an unusually hard time urinating, shifting from side to side. He was mumbling.

"Louder," Lucic ordered.

Copeland made a few guttural grunting sounds then braced himself and let go a low and longer than ordinary fart and with it let out a sigh of relief. "Whew!" He then settled into what appeared to be a comfortable urination, exhaling a sigh not just once but twice, all while the technicians, Stubblefield and Lucic had their eyes riveted to the screen looking for the smallest of behavioral inconsistencies. Copeland finished his business, flushing the urinal with his elbow then making his way to the sink where he washed his hands thoroughly, dried them and gave himself one more look in the mirror before exiting.

As he walked out of the restroom, the agents all shared a look to see if they had missed something.

Copeland made his back to the table where the food was placed, but seemingly untouched. He looked at Kenny. "What? You're not eating?" He then grabbed a jumbo shrimp out of the iced martini glass, smothered it in cocktail sauce, shoved it in his mouth and asked again. "You eating or what?"

Kenny took one of the stuffed mushrooms simply to placate him.

While he was still chewing, Copeland assumed control of the direction he wanted the conversation to go. "You know," he said, "I want to run this thing by you that came up. Like I mentioned before, we're gonna do a conference call at 3:30 at the office-"

Kenny had to interrupt Copeland by holding up his hand. "Before you get into that, Alan, I have to talk to you about this."

Copeland complied, but showed frustration in doing so. "Okay. I'm all ears."

"Dale Marlin."

Copeland's eyes lit up on hearing the name. "Love that guy! What about him?"

"We sold him a bundle of policies. I think five. It was probably around-"

Copeland interrupted. "Don't remind me. That fucking Howie Yglesias. I can't tell you the ass-ache that caused me."

Kenny nodded. "Those policies. Five of them. They were all on people who were terminal-"

"That's what we do, Kenny."

"...Except for the one you had me go out and get. The kid from over by Olympia and Glenvar Heights-"

"I don't know who the fucking policies were on. All I know is that Howie sold 'em to Dale, who I didn't sign off on them being sold to. And it was a major ass-ache that thank God worked out. Thank God it worked out."

Kenny followed up. "If you remember, maybe you don't...but we sold Dale Marlin those policies and they didn't pay off for like...the longest time."

"Yeah, no shit. That's what I'm talking about-" Copeland shoved a steak tidbit in his mouth and immediately washed it down with a swig of Diet Coke as if he wanted to bypass his taste buds out of some misdirected spite. "...Where you goin' with this?"

"I thought someone had them killed. Or maybe one of them. Maybe more."

Copeland started laughing. "You think they got taken out? By who?"

"I don't know. It just didn't make sense to me. Maybe Dale Marlin. He's crazy enough. And his thing with the guns?"

"That's ridiculous."

"I don't know, Alan. It just seemed pretty convenient that they all died so close in time, and long after they were supposed to. And then when Dale Marlin came down and pretty much threatened you thinkin' he got ripped off-"

"Whoa, whoa, whoa. You think I had those people killed?"

"I didn't say that, Alan."

Copeland looked like he was going to laugh, but took a fast turn to being offended when he realized Kenny was serious. "You know, in all the time you been with me, never once did you say anything stupid. Not once. That's what I liked about you. But this?" He shook his head. "You think because we push some policies through that have a little wet ink on 'em...push a few clean sheets though...have a few doctors that can be worked with, that we're in the business of whacking people out?"

"That's not what I said."

"It's exactly what you said. I don't know what you think I am." Copeland seemed then more disappointed than he was angry.

"Sorry," Kenny told him.

Copeland shook his head, dismissive. He looked around the dining room. "Where's the fucking waitress?" Upon spotting her, he waved for her to come over then fished into his pocket for his bill fold.

"Everything okay, gentlemen?"

"Yeah, fine. Let me get a check."

"Right away, sir!"

Copeland dealt six twenty dollar bills onto the table and stood up. He looked down at Kenny, ever so slightly shaking his head suggesting he was disgusted. "Take care of that. I gotta go. And don't worry about that 3:30 conference call. I'm gonna punt on it."

He turned and exited, shaking his head and mumbling as he left Kenny alone at the table.

A pall hung over the agents. Lucic was pensively rubbing his chin. Stubblefield mumbled a string of expletives under his breath, clenching and unclenching his fist in repetition. Reed looked like he'd be deceived.

Stubblefield broke the silence. "There's gotta be something in that bathroom bullshit. There's gotta be. He tipped him off."

Lucic considered the possibility and didn't seem so sure. "I don't know about the bathroom. That looked pretty clean. We'll play it back, but...it looked pretty clean."

"He tipped him off," Stubblefield reiterated.

Still Lucic didn't see any evidence, but suggested what they got on tape had value. "He did walk him into talking about the fraud. That's not insignificant, you know...in relation to everything else."

Silence.

"Motherfucker."

This time it was Reed who muttered the words.

Chapter Twenty-Two

Check, Please

Kenny watched as Copeland made his way toward the exit. He passed the young hostess in the tight fitting dress standing now at the podium like a mannequin and didn't acknowledge her wish for him to have a good day or whatever it was that restaurant hostesses said to departing guests. His face was blank, lips compressed and pulled against his teeth. He was clearly stewing but not with anger. He looked like he might be about to weep, as hard as that was to fathom.

"Is everything okay?"

Kenny looked up to see the server at the table, pretending she was concerned.

"Yes. Yes, ma'am. Fine." While the inquiry was rhetorical, he considered the possibility she was referring to Copeland's abrupt exit. "We're all good, thank you. In fact, can I trouble you for a beer? Budweiser'd be great if you have it."

"Of course, I'll get that for you right away, sir."

"Thank you."

He smiled at her again, then reached for one of the shrimp, took a bite of it and thought to himself that there were few things as good as a mouthful of chilled jumbo shrimp fresh from the Gulf. Then, he turned and looked out the bistro's window. Although the angle was sharp, he could see Copeland through a line of planters standing alone at the valet stand to get his car and wondered what reaction he expected from him. He had assumed he'd simply dismiss what was said with a laugh then call him stupid, what he initially offered before seeing that Kenny was serious in his asking. Copeland being offended to the point of hurt was never considered. Kenny wondered if maybe that was because there was some truth to it.

No.

Copeland was probably offended that Kenny thought, if even for a fleeting moment, that he was capable of something so awful-

...Or ridiculously risky.

Another jumbo shrimp, this one he let kiss the cocktail sauce before eating and again Kenny considered the very idea of arranging the murders of a handful of already marginalized short timers so their policies could be collected on what was deemed to be schedule and how ridiculous it sounded in any other realm than a Hollywood movie that might have already been made. Even more ridiculous was the FBI agents entertaining the possibility Copeland would admit it to Kenny if there was any truth to his involvement in such a plot. Yet Walter Reed and Stubblefield bit and bit hard, ensuring that they not only would pursue Kenny's participation in the investigation but do so aggressively and without questioning even the smallest routine protections his lawyer might ask for in exchange. The full clearance and immunity from any possible fraud related charges he may have been party to, inadvertent or deliberate, during his time at *MFB&T* was for them, a meaningless throw away.

And again-

...Kenny smiled the kind of smile that looked like it was fast tracking into a laugh.

"Here you go." The server took a frosted pilsner glass from her tray and placed it before him, then put the longneck bottle next to it.

"Thank you, ma'am."

Kenny waited a moment then reached for the bottle of beer and ignoring the glass took a deep swig off of it, as swamper habits die hard. He considered Walter Reed, figuring he'd be hearing from him soon enough, and then the digital dictaphone that was in his pocket. He'd planned on giving it to Chip Corso, the pony-tailed AP reporter whose name, ironically, he was currently inches from forgetting. No, the digital dictaphone may as well be tossed from the bridge over the Biscayne Inlet on Collins Avenue before giving it to Corso. The idea of a reporter exposing illegal bureau misconduct and something actually being done about it was now as ridiculous to him as Copeland having insurance policyholders killed off so the person he'd sold them to might get paid out as promised. He trusted that the agents would bring themselves down, then got to thinking how he might help it along. He reached for the salt shaker, sprinkled the french fries with a heavy hand then took a generous handful.

He looked over at the podium and saw the hostess standing with one delicate hand resting upon the other as if she were being painted. She must have felt his eyes upon him and looked in his direction.

He smiled.

She smiled back.

Kenny turned away then took another pull off the beer and figured he might have one more after he finished it. He sat back in the chair, feeling almost satisfied.

Almost.

Almost.

Almost.

He continued to sit in contemplation and casually ate what was left of the food, leaving only a handful of the fries and the second Budweiser went the way of the first. He paid the check with the six twenty dollar bills left by Copeland, padding it by adding two of his own for good measure, then left to retrieve his car.

He drove north on Collins Avenue, the opposite direction Copeland had gone after leaving and figured on going back to his apartment and relaxing for a little while before going to Rosie's. After she got home from work. And with that settled in his mind, he began to second guess what he was going to do when getting there.

As he pulled into his parking spot in front of his apartment building, the phone rang. He looked down at the ID and although it was numerical, knew who it was.

"Hello."

"Kenny, Dave Zuboff."

"Hi, Dave."

He sounded like he was in a rush. *"Well? How'd it go?"*

"I just got home. Still in the car, in fact."

"Okay. How did it go?"

Kenny took a moment, although he wasn't sure why. "It went the way I kind of figured. I got there, went to the table they told me to sit at and waited for Alan. He was late, of course. We started talkin'. Pretty much natural, like usual. Touched on a couple of subjects and Alan kind of out of nowhere actually mentioned a few of the things that...as luck would have it are pretty illegal. You know? Like with the policy bundles, falsifyin' policies and what not-"

"He did?"

"Yeah. Kind of hand delivered what they were lookin' for with a bow on it, if you ask me."

"They should be very grateful to you."

"I dunno. Maybe."

"Okay. I'll reach out to the Assistant USA and get a sign off that we're done. You might have to testify if this goes to trial but given the nature of what I'm guessing they have on him, that will be unlikely. He'll probably be advised to enter a plea and that will be the end of it."

"So you think I'm done?"

"I'd be surprised if you weren't-," Zuboff told him. He paused before continuing. *"...You know now not to return to work and don't have any contact with anyone from there."*

"Yeah, I figured as much."

Then the line went silent.

"Kenny?"

"Yeah?"

"How are you doing?"

Kenny was caught off guard with the asking. As far as he could recall, this was the first question from the lawyer that waded even slightly into an area that might be considered personal.

"I'm good, I guess."

"You did the right thing. When they ask for cooperation, it's kind of hard to turn them down. Especially when they dig in. So you did the right thing by yourself and the right thing in exposing Alan Copeland. He's not a good man. In fact, he's a terrible man. So you did the right thing. And that expungement isn't meaningless."

"Yeah. Well thanks for your help, Dave. I'm glad I called you. This isn't the kind of thing I wanted to get into without someone advisin' me."

"You're a wise young man."

"I appreciate you sayin' that."

"I'll be in touch regarding any updates and the expungement process."

"Thanks."

With that, Zuboff disconnected.

Kenny had a thought, then put the car in reverse and backed out of his spot. He drove back down the street in the direction he'd come from. Five minutes later he pulled into the parking lot of a strip mall across the street from the hospital. He got out, looked around and figured he'd be back before any of the store owners might notice and complain that the lot was for customers only.

In the hospital lobby, he did a quick survey, then found his way to the telephone that was there as a courtesy to those waiting on patients. He picked it up and dialed a number.

The switchboard operator from the United States Department of Justice, Southern District picked up and asked how the call might be directed. Kenny asked for Assistant US Attorney Jen Resnick's voicemail. He endured the outgoing message and at the sound of the tone, brought his dictaphone to the mouthpiece and played a small portion of what he had recorded of his interaction with the agents. He then hung up, stuffed the dictaphone back in his pocket and left, confidently leaving the rest to Reed and Stubblefield.

When Kenny got home, he entered his apartment that was as spotless as he'd left it that morning. He looked around and wondered what he was going to take with him when he left, which he figured would be within the next day or two. Whatever could fit in the car. The rest he could come back for-

...Or not.

He kicked off his shoes, walked over to the couch, slouched into it and closed his eyes but didn't sleep.

And when the time came, he went.

He got in the car for the short ride to Rosie's. The evening air outside was perfect. The kind they tried to capture in advertisements. Maybe he didn't have to cut and run, he wondered. Maybe he could stay. Then he admonished himself for being so goddamn selfish and barked down the devil for telling him otherwise. He had to leave. He had to go because he loved her. And in his mind, a litany of assessments began to play, her virtues running against his failings in a slow moving scroll.

She's perfect.

She's truth, pure truth.

A battle-scarred angel-

I'll drag her down-

Down by her wings.

I'll hurt her.

I'll bring more pain.

I'm not honest.

She's perfect.

I'm not what she thinks.

I keep secrets.

She's perfect.

Not what she thinks.

I'm not like her.

I'm like him.

Like Alan.

Alan Copeland.

She's perfect.

I'm like him.

I can't have her.

Kenny parked in the place he usually did, got out of the car and walked across the street. He let himself into the main lobby with the key she'd given him. While pulling it from the lock as he opened the door for what was supposed to be the last time, he looked at it as if bidding a farewell to what had become a trusted friend. He'd be leaving it with her when he left.

The elevator door opened when he summoned it. He stepped in and hit the button for the third floor, then looked down at his shoes until he watched them step off and into the hallway where her apartment was.

He knocked on the door but didn't wait for an answer, letting himself in. Rosie was dressed as if she was about to go out for a run, sitting on the living room couch tying her second sneaker. She looked up and smiled. "Hey."

He returned the smile as best he could. "Hi."

"How was work?," she asked.

He responded with a sign. "It was work, I guess. How about you? How was your day?"

She stood up, smiled and walked over to him. She kissed him on the cheek and he felt his knees threatening to buckle from under him. His stomach pulled taut and made a go for his throat.

Rosie filled him in. "After I got off the phone with you I ran into Josephine Reinhardt. She told me-"

She then stopped.

"...Oh, she said to say hello. Anyway, she told me that her sister Michelle, the one who works for Marriott, is quitting her job and is...get a load of this, opening a pizza place in Coral Gables with the guy she's dating. The stock broker. Jay. We met him. Nice guy, kind of quiet. Both of them are quitting their jobs to open a pizza place! I think it's crazy, but hey...chase your dreams. Right?"

Kenny smiled, but didn't hear a word she said. He tried to smile. He looked at her and again noted what she was wearing. "Are you going to yoga?"

"No, I did that this morning. I figured I just go for a quick run. A quick, little shake out. Two or three miles. Want to come?"

He again forced a smile but looked away from her and shook his head indicating that he didn't.

"So work was good for you?," she asked.

Kenny shrugged. "It was work."

Rosie responded as she did the first time he gave that answer.

"I'm leaving," he said.

A deafening silence.

"I know," she told him, like it was the inevitable finally arriving and with it a shroud of sadness came over her. She knew what he was saying extended beyond his job.

She knew.

She knew.

She knew.

Kenny seemed at a loss for what to say next. The words coming from his mouth almost did so of their own accord. "It's not like there's someone else."

She took a deep breath. "I know." She then walked over to the couch, sat down and began to take off the sneakers she moments earlier had put on.

"I'm sorry," he said.

"—"

"...I'm sorry, I just-"

"—"

"...I'm not ready, Rosie."

A long pause.

She stood up, as if anything else might be perceived as succumbing to weakness.

"I understand," she told him. Even if she didn't. It was as if disappointment had been a lifelong affliction that went into, then out of remission for as long as she could remember and this was it reappearing, coming in from out of the cold that suddenly was south Florida.

Kenny looked at her face, her perfect face, eyes that held no secrets nor set screens for any lies and in them the hint now of a moistness forming but not yet enough to well up in its corners.

"I don't know what else to say, Rosie. I'm just tryin' to be honest-"

"There's nothing else to say, Kenny."

"I'm just not ready."

"I understand. I appreciate...I appreciate you being honest."

He hated that she chose those words and tried to say something else but failed.

"I understand," she said again.

Silence.

A terrible, mournful silence.

"Are you hungry?," she asked.

Kenny didn't immediately respond so she asked again. "Do you want to get something to eat?"

He felt like he was being tortured. "No. I'm not...I think I just need to go home right now."

"Okay."

She looked at him with sadness not only for the heartache she was feeling, but his as well. She stepped closer and gave him a hug but there was less torque in this one than so many of her others, the ones that seemed to be competing amongst themselves in intensity. She took a deep breath. "It's going to be okay for you, Kenny-"

"--"

"...I believe that. It's going to be okay for you."

At that moment he had been thinking the very same thing about her but didn't verbalize it.

"Do you want to talk in a couple of days?," she asked.

"Okay." He said it even though he didn't mean it.

She walked over to the kitchen sink and began putting away glassware from the drying board as if it were the first step in moving forward. He took her apartment keys from his pocket and softly placed them on the glass top of the console table so they made as little noise as possible. Rosie wasn't looking but heard it. For both of them it may as well have been a bowling ball.

Kenny walked away from her building. He searched for a numbness to take refuge within, then wished he was someone else. He got in the car, started it then looked up at her apartment. He could see her standing in the window looking down, arms crossed but with one hand held up and over her mouth. He felt an overwhelming sense of being blinded and without direction. Like for a moment in his life he'd stepped out of a dark room, then returned into it without the lantern he'd previously had.

He put the car in gear and drove off. The idea of him playing basketball that night, as previously planned, was now ridiculous.

Chapter Twenty-Three

The Collar

After leaving the bistro, Copeland handed his claim ticket to the car valet. His demeanor was schizophrenic by comparison to when he'd arrived. If the look on his face was any indicator, the jovial man who welcomed him had become his living room carpet that Karen's Pomeranian squirted diarrhea on the week earlier. His Rolls arrived shortly thereafter. Copeland's eyes fixed upon the back of it and the damage became his focus. He was furious with himself for his gesture of generosity absolving the man who hit him of blame. The valet stepped out of the car and stood by the open door. As Copeland climbed in and behind the wheel, he offered no eye contact nor gratuity.

Driving out of the lot, he made a right onto Collins Avenue.

He was going home.

Not back to the office.

Home.

Fuck Schwartz, he thought. And those assholes from the Triad Group. Fuck this red light. And fuck the kid, Kenny. He gave him way too much credit, he'd decided.

He was an idiot.

A fucking idiot.

Like the rest of them.

When he entered the house, Karen was casually pacing in the hall just off the main foyer by the landing of the cast iron and limestone grand circular staircase. A phone was to her ear. She looked over and immediately sensed his foul mood, noticing he'd pulled his ankle away from her Pomeranian that had run over to greet him. Holding the phone down, she asked him, *sotto voce*, so as not to interrupt what she was hearing from the other end, "What are you doing home so early?"

He didn't break stride walking past her. "It's my house. Am I not allowed to come home when I want? Holy shit."

"Oh, jeez. Someone's in a mood." With the accompanying eye roll, she went back to her call, not giving his reaction a moment's more thought.

Copeland continued into the kitchen and opened the stainless steel door of the Sub-Zero refrigerator, did an inspection then closed it as if it was someone else's fault that he couldn't make up his mind what he wanted. Then, across to the walk-in pantry where he entered and did a quick browse before grabbing from a shelf one of the matching translucent plastic containers filled with peanut M&M's. He opened the airtight lid, scooped out a handful and shoved the candies into his mouth, gnashing them like he were doling out a punishment, then stepped out of the pantry without securing the lid back on the container.

Karen strolled into the kitchen, still on her call but curious as to what was eating at him. She watched as he walked back to the refrigerator, opening it again as if something might be there that seconds earlier wasn't.

Again, he shut it.

She turned and retreated down the hallway that led to the maid's quarters and laundry room and from there, ended her call. She returned into the kitchen where she saw Copeland walking out toward the sitting room that overlooked the garden and swimming pool.

"What's wrong?," she called after him.

"Nothing." He didn't turn around to answer.

"Oh, don't give me 'nothing'. What's wrong?"

This time, he did turn around. "Nothing, Karen. Okay? Nothing."

She had no choice but to take his words as they'd been spoken. A deep breath and she exhaled, the overly dramatic kind that English actresses on Masterpiece Theater took when trying to convey patience before changing the subject. "So, we'll leave for the Yost's around six. Maybe, and just a thought, maybe we only stay for a few drinks then go eat somewhere else. Gracie's having that Sanjay guy from Shvertasvarta catering it. Or Shverta-something or other. Indian." And with that, she made a face. "I could have sworn she said she was having Ishiro from Takao do it and I'm really just not into Indian or whatever it is. Not right now, at least." Then she had a thought she'd decided to float. "Maybe we can go somewhere quiet, you and I? Like the Shore Club-"

He interrupted her. "I'm not going to the Yosts."

"What?" She was stunned.

"I'm not going to the Yosts."

"Oh my God, Alan. Why not? I told Gracie-"

Again, he stepped on her words. "Because I don't feel like it, Karen."

"Alan! She asked me three times! Are we coming? And all three times I told her, yes. Yes. We're coming. Is Alan coming? Yes, Alan is coming. You're sure? Yes. You're not going to cancel on me, last minute? No, we're not. And yes, I'm sure. We're coming. Alan is coming."

"We'll send them a fucking check, Karen! Whatever they want, okay? Ask her how much they want for whatever it is this time and tell her we'll give her double now and every time moving forward if she promises not to ask us to go through the motions of going over and pretending we like them just so we can give them money."

"Oh my God, Alan! What's gotten into you?!"

He ignored her.

"And for your information, I like going over there! I like Gracie! She's my very good friend!"

"Then go! Go over! Move in with them for all I care."

Karen shook her head, feigning disgust. Copeland turned and continued into the sitting room.

"I don't feel good." He sounded almost apologetic and conversational as opposed to argumentative.

Suddenly, Karen was concerned. "What do you mean you don't feel good?

"I don't feel good."

"Do you want me to call Doctor Issacson's office?"

"No. I just...I just want to be left alone. I want to shut my eyes."

"You're sure you don't want me to call Doctor Issacson?"

"I'm sure Karen. If you want to do something, you can get me a Diet Pepsi." He walked over to one of the couches nearer to her than far and sat back in it, suggesting he didn't want her to leave him alone completely. He shut his eyes and tilted his head up toward the ceiling.

Karen brought him a tall glass of Diet Pepsi with ice cubes. She put it on the side table next to him, purposely on a coaster. He picked it up, annoyed that he had to wait for the rising carbonation to settle, then took a sip not a gulp. He put the glass back on the side table next to the coaster. Not on it. She didn't say a word about that nor did she bring up going to the Yosts again.

Copeland spent the rest of the afternoon and evening in the house. He made a few phone calls, took a nap, made a few more phone calls, had a vodka, ordered dinner, had another vodka and made a few more calls. He then went in to watch TV and stayed where he was long after Karen had gone to bed.

At 5:25 AM the following morning, a thunderous series of booms came from the front door that coincided with the doorbell ringing several times in succession, echoing throughout the house. The Pomeranian began a non-stop and ear splitting yapping. Both Copeland and Karen were immediately jarred awake in the bed of the master bedroom. Soon motion sensor lights outside the house were illuminated, seen through the window treatments. Karen looked at Copeland, who was as confused, frantic and terrified as she was.

"*Alaaaan, Alaaaan*! Someone's outside! Someone's outside, *Alaaaan*!"

He didn't answer since her observation was unmissable. He got out of bed but was at a complete loss for what to do next.

"*Alaaaan, Alaaaan!* There are *people* outside!"

"Call 911." His words barely made it out of his mouth. He put on his robe but only after seeing Karen was already putting on hers. More banging on the front door and another series of doorbell rings all while the Pomeranian yapped at a torturous decibel level. Copeland made his way downstairs toward the front hall vestibule, a high-powered spotlight cutting through the windows, illuminating slivers of the first floor living room. More banging on the door, another series of doorbell rings and still, the fucking Pomeranian. Nonstop. This time, a loud and commanding voice called from the outside.

"*FBI!*"

"*FBI!*"

"*Open up!*"

"*FBI!*"

Copeland opened the front door with a trembling hand. In his confusion, he failed to disarm the alarm and upon doing so, a shrieking siren joined the cacophony. As the door opened, several agents in top to bottom tactical gear, helmets, goggles, gloves, flak vests and armed with Heckler & Koch MP-5's pointed outward and at the ready filed into the house and fanned out, all while the Pomeranian darted back and forth, barking shards of glass-

"*Alaaaan, Alaaaan!* What are they doing! What are they doing, *Alaaaan!*"

Another agent, unusually short and wearing khaki pants and a bulletproof vest outside his polo shirt with an FBI windbreaker over it, stepped in behind them holding a nine millimeter pistol in hand-

"*Alaaaan, Alaaaan!* Karen was nothing short of hysterical-

…And from somewhere in the darkness of the house, the Pomeranian.

Yap-yap-yap-yap.

Yap-yap-yap-yap.

Yap-yap-yap-yap.

The unusually short agent walked directly to Copeland, knowing full well who he was. "Alan Copeland, you're under arrest." He took Copeland's wrist and turned him around while reciting the federal statutes he was being charged with violating.

"*Alaaaan, Alaaaan!*"

Yap-yap-yap-yap.

Yap-yap-yap-yap-

Copeland ignored his wife's cries and referred to the alarm panel just inside the door. The arresting agent allowed him to punch in the code disengaging it, then continued handcuffing him. With the alarm silenced, it allowed for the ambient noise from outside to be heard through the open front door where Copeland could see at least a dozen and a half vehicles with siren lights that bounced off his neighbors' property walls. Then a sharp, piercing shriek from behind him, somewhere in the house. The Pomeranian had been inadvertently stepped on by one of the agents.

"Eloise! Eloise!" Karen immediately ran toward the sound of the dog's cry. *"Oh my God, what have you done to her?! Eloise!"*

Copeland closed his eyes, imagining that this was all a bad dream. Upon opening them, he was reassured that it wasn't.

"Karen?," he said.

She didn't respond.

"Karen?" This time a little louder.

"What?"

"Call Eric Platt. Right now. And your stepfather. Call your stepfather."

Heinz Lucic stepped in the house, dressed exactly like the lead agent but not holding a pistol. He was deliberate in his entrance and calm as he observed the arrest. Karen stood by the landing of the grand circular staircase swaddling the Pomeranian at her breast. She sensed, correctly, that Lucic had authority over the others and walked toward him. But as she did her words were directed at Copeland. "They stepped on Eloise, Alan! They stepped on Eloise!"

"Karen, forget the dog. Call Eric Platt. And call your stepfather."

Karen ignored him and directed her ire to Lucic. "You have no idea what you're doing! This is going to cost you your job! Mark my words! You have no fucking idea!"

"Karen."

Again ignoring him, she looked around as if making sure what she was witnessing was actually happening then inexplicably decided to direct her wrath toward another agent who was obviously not in charge. "What the hell is this? Do you think Osama Bin Laden lives here? You've got half the army in my living room! Trampling through my living room!"

"Karen, please shut up and call Eric. And call your stepfather."

"Where's my phone?! Oh my God, these people have no idea! They have no idea what they're doing. They have no idea who they're fucking with!"

She forced her way past another fully armed and tactically outfitted agent. "Get out of my way, you son of a bitch!" And with that, she scampered off to find her cell phone. As she disappeared down the hall she could be heard again referencing Osama Bin Laden and half the army trampling through her living room.

Later that morning, a significantly far less dramatic raid was made on the *MFB&T* offices as well as the Design District Health Clinic. Computer terminals and boxes of files were seized, then the doors padlocked. Copeland's arraignment was expedited by his overbearing and bombastic lawyer Eric Platt, whose efforts were buttressed by his equally abrasive associates Stephen K. Mitchell and Stephen R. Mitchell, no relation. Bail was set at five million dollars and immediately posted, his passport surrendered as a condition.

The following day, the Herald, Sun-Sentinel and local television news outlets simultaneously broke the story of the arrest. In doing so, none of them gave Copeland the due regard of referring to him as a businessman who built an empire in the viatical insurance industry. To them, he was a confidante and relative by marriage of Louis Haberman, the political donor closely tied to former Presidents of both party affiliations-

...Whom Copeland still had not heard from, despite Karen's multiple calls.

Before Assistant US Attorney Jen Resnick arrived at the FBI offices to meet with Lucic and Agent Walter Reed, Lucic gave his agent explicit directions to keep his mouth shut and let him handle everything. Lucic believed he could explain to her what she had heard on her voicemail and that it was taken entirely out of context.

She entered Lucic's office, who shut the door behind her and got to the matter at hand before he had returned to the seat behind his desk. "Something has been brought to our attention," she said. "Anonymously. A recording of what is, in all likelihood, Agent Reed's voice." She turned to look at Reed. "You'll be given the opportunity to listen to it and can confirm or deny if it is in fact, your voice." Back to Lucic, she continued as if Reed weren't in the room. "Now, speaking disparagingly about one of your colleagues, while being unprofessional and to be candid, beneath any member of the bureau, it's not against the law. Nor is it in itself a violation of any codes of conduct. However, the nature of how the grievances are stated, choosing to attach them to the colleague's race, religion or sexual preference, is a serious breach of the protections afforded to all employees under Equal Employment Opportunity mandates. This is very, very serious." She then played the recording that was unmistakably Reed's voice:

You know what the problem is?

With this job? The Bureau?

Guy's like Trey?

They shouldn't have ever gotten hired.

Between you and me?

He's a quota hire, you know-

An Affirmative Action, quota hire.

He doesn't even deserve getting that leg up.

He's not from the 'hood.

He's not under-privileged.

He just plays 'nigger.'

He's from the suburbs!

Jen Resnick stopped the tape and Reed went into full panic mode. He looked at Lucic for direction but got nothing.

"Is that you speaking, Agent Reed?," Resnick asked.

Again Reed looked at Lucic who must have been having second thoughts on how far he was going to go in defending his agent, judging by the seriousness projected by the Assistant US Attorney.

"Is that your voice, Agent Reed?," she asked again.

Reed was stuttering and again looked to Lucic for a life preserver that wasn't coming. With that, wallowing in frustration, he let loose a Hail Mary in desperation-

"Trey told him to lie-!"

With that, the trajectory of the meeting came to a screeching halt. Reed then took advantage to get as much information out before Lucic might silence him, like a child making a plea to an impatient mother. "...He told the witness to lie about viatical policies not paying off fast enough being connected to possible homicides! I was trying to save him! I was trying to save the witness by speaking his language! I was trying to salvage the witness!"

Jen Resnick had effectively employed a mute button in so far as what Reed was saying and stared expressionless at Lucic. He looked back at her as if he were hearing this for the first time-

...And it was convincing.

Reed went on with his appeal. "...You guys knew! C'mon! You knew about this! I was just trying to save the witness."

Jen Resnick took a deep breath and without taking her eyes off Lucic, directed her words to Reed. "Can you excuse us for a minute, Agent Reed?"

For Alan Copeland, eight months could have been eight hundred or eight thousand as he stopped paying attention to time. Mired in perpetual bouts of withdrawal and weighing fifty-five pounds less than he had the morning he was arrested, he sat in the passenger seat of Karen's car void of any energy, his new normal. He no longer drove. There was nowhere for him to drive to, at least not anywhere alone. They rode in silence, his sunken eyes looking out the window. They were returning home from the law offices of Eric Platt in Downtown Miami in a spectacular glass high rise. The regularity of his visits there were only outdone by doctor appointments, which he seemed to have six of for every one with his attorney. Other than that, he didn't leave the house. Any and all invitations had evaporated and no one visited them. On this day while meeting with his lawyers, Eric Platt reiterated the government's push for Copeland to give them something that might be considered during his sentencing. Not on someone random. They had a specific individual in mind, and what they wanted could be anything criminal in nature, financial or otherwise. They wanted something to pin on his stepfather-in-law. Something on Louis Haberman.

But Copeland had nothing to offer.

Nothing.

Not a thing.

Adding injury to this insult, Copeland asserted, Haberman had effectively cut off all contact with him since his arrest.

He turned his back on us!

Karen's own stepfather!

He turned his back on us!

Karen slowly drove over the bridge on Route 195 away from downtown as Copeland slumped in his seat, still gazing out across the perfect turquoise water of the bay that meant nothing.

"We have to go to the pharmacy," he said, seemingly from out of nowhere.

"I know, Alan. I'm driving right now."

"I know you're driving, Karen. I'm just saying-" His words trailed off.

At the time of his arrest, Copeland had been on three doctor prescribed medications, one for his blood pressure, another to address his high cholesterol and a third to treat erectile dysfunction, which he no longer took. Several had been added in its place, though. There were pain pills to relieve his forever ailing back, others to help with the migraines and ones to address his sleeping issues. He took anxiety medication and what seemed like an endless trial of combinations meant to stave off depression, none which seemed to work.

"I'm just saying," he repeated. "Just saying."

He looked out the window again, and again thought about Haberman. What they wanted was something to fuel a witch hunt against him, one in which the reticles of the scope weren't even necessarily on Haberman's back, but someone even more powerful with whom he was close. Probably a household name. Copeland lied to himself, thinking he wouldn't give the bastards a thing even if he had it.

No.

He had honor.

He wasn't like the others.

And with that he thought about all of those who, one by one, agreed to testify against him. The half-dozen insurance company executives he had come to expect, the ones he'd showered with kickbacks and gifts. They meant nothing to him, and were all making efforts to save their own asses. And of course he wasn't surprised to learn Howie Yglesias turned informant. Nor in hearing that Alé Perez and Scooter Wrobel flipped as well, as they were all facing felony fraud charges of their own. And although it made him furious, he understood Elliot Lopinsky, his clinic physician, cooperating. He too, was facing federal charges and imminent loss of his license to practice. His secretary Brenda Colon testifying for the prosecution was shrugged off, as he was already numb by the time he learned she was a prosecution asset. The one that stung was the kid.

The kid.

The kid.

The kid.

363

He had such high hopes for him. He thought he was different. Special. Regardless of what he'd thought after he'd asked the ridiculous question that day at the bistro. He had something. Special. He could have been great. He had something that put him in another league.

The kid.

Not the kid.

"Why the kid?" Copeland didn't realize he verbalized his last thought.

"What's that?" Karen half-squawked, without taking her eyes off the road in front of her.

Copeland turned to her from the window.

"Nothing," he said.

Looking back again at the water, he finished his mental inventory. They all went south on him. All of them. Then he looked back again at Karen, her eyes riveted to the road. He had another thought and it slowly manifested itself into the smallest of smiles on his face. A smile so slight that she wouldn't have seen it even if she'd been looking. Copeland turned back again to look out the window and the nothingness over the bay and wondered why. He wondered why she stayed.

She slowed down as they approached the exit ramp off the bridge and continued along it toward the intersection where the traffic light had just turned green in their favor. She prepared to make a right but suddenly stopped, the extra effort on the brake pedal causing them to slightly jolt forward in their seats. A pedestrian had jaywalked in front of them, paying no attention to oncoming traffic.

"What is this idiot doing?" she carped.

Copeland looked over, his mind still in another place. In the crosswalk he saw the man she was referring to. The jaywalker. He was black and could have been thirty-something, he could have been fifty-something. Dark complexion, not quite with the deepness of Haitian skin but more melanin rich than the typical African-American. His face was an expressionless rock, devoid of any emotion. Slits for eyes, the area around them appearing to be swollen, but matching. Like he'd had an allergic reaction or maybe just finished crying. His arms exposed beneath the short sleeves of his tee shirt stayed at his side. He could have been in those clothes for several days, but didn't come across as homeless. As he took his time making his way from one side of the street to the other, he stared directly at Copeland as if he was studying the deepest corners of his soul.

Karen was still shaking her head. "What is this guy's problem?

When the crosswalk was clear, she continued with her turn but noticed something in Copeland's face as she looked to her right.

"Alan?"

He didn't answer.

"Alan? Are you okay?"

"I'm...I'm not sure, Karen."

"Do you want me to call Dr. Issacson?"

Chapter Twenty-Four

A Funeral

From St. Augustine, it would take five and a half hours.

Maybe a little more.

Probably less.

Kenny made his way through the quiet residential streets with a familiarity that comes with living in a place for a year and a half. Long enough to know the shortcuts and where the speedbumps were but not quite enough to profess an unconditional love or commitment to.

He'd settled into a small house on Whitney Street located in a part of town that gave the impression of being secluded yet a bicycle could still take a barefoot peddler anywhere he might want to go. The homes were for the most part understated and set back off the long, narrow street that was lined with rows of Jacarandas facing each other, creating a magical tunnel effect when in bloom. Kenny's two bedroom, two bath was newly built, the interior wide and open and furnished with all the modern amenities a single guy might need to live comfortably. It had a long driveway of pulverized seashells and his front lawn was covered in the type of grass named for the city whose boundaries he lived within. A massive angel oak tree took up a huge swath of the back yard, which the window over his kitchen sink looked directly out on. It stood guard before what seemed like a canopy for flora that might have been endless. It felt just enough like the place he grew up in to remind him of the better times, yet not enough to rub in the bad.

It was just after six A.M. when he pulled into the lot of the place he liked to get coffee, which was out of the way but worth it. He'd again order *en español* and the woman would smile and exchange a few pleasantries in her native tongue which he was well-equipped by now to respond to.

Then, five and a half hours.

Maybe a little more.

Probably less.

Traffic was light. He bypassed Jax before seven, beating the local rush and from there expected nothing less than clear sailing. He drove in silence on purpose, not wanting to hear the radio, music or talk. Kenny was comfortable in silence, his appreciation for it one that was galvanizing more and more with each day. While they were ubiquitous in these parts, the billboards and road signs for the Waffle House started to poke their fingers into his chest about twenty minutes out onto I-10 West.

Yes.

He would have gone back to work there.

Absolutely.

If he had to.

Absolutely.

There was no shame in working at the Waffle House. In fact, he thought it to be a damn good company. He was grateful they took a chance on him when he needed it and proud that when his time came to leave they were sorry to see him go. He would have gone back to work there in a second. If he needed to.

Somewhere around Live Oak he passed another one and thought about Brenda. There was no connection to it and Alan Copeland's secretary, as the Waffle House signs had become nothing more than mile markers triggering memories of his evolution from Okaloosa County to down south and working at *Mutual Fidelity Benefits & Trust*.

Brenda.

He wished he'd kept in touch.

It was 7:55 A.M. He didn't know where she worked but guessed she was probably there or on her way in. With that, he picked up his phone and took intermittent peeks down as he thumbed through his contacts. He smiled when he saw he had her number, despite not knowing whether it was active.

She answered off one. *"Hellooo?"*

Kenny smiled. Her voice sounded exactly the same.

"Brenda?"

"Yesss?"

"This is Kenny Wayne Rehage-" He was about to further elaborate and maybe even apologize if he'd caught her at a bad time.

"Oh my God, Kenny! How on earth are you, sweetie?"

"I'm good, Brenda. I'm good. I'm just drivin' in the car and thought about you, figured I'd give you a call and see how you were doin'."

"Well, I am so glad you did! You made my day, sweetie and it's just started."

"I'm glad to hear that. And I'm glad this is still your number."

"You made my day already!"

"How are you doin'?"

"Well, pretty good. I'm working at a new job. Well, not that new. I got it as soon as they shut down the office, so going on a year and a half. I was very lucky for that. Very fortunate."

"Oh, I don't know about that. Whoever hired you is the one who got lucky."

"You're so sweet."

"Where are you workin'?," he asked.

"Still in Fort Lauderdale. I'm with a place called Seven Seas, they're a janitorial and maintenance company that serves mostly hotels, big hotels."

"Do you like it?"

She hesitated, as if she was making sure she answered accurately. *"Yes. Yes, I do."*

"They treat you better than Alan did?"

"Oh, my God, yes! I wouldn't call my boss nice, but he's fair. And he's a little crazy. Like OCD crazy. A real clean freak."

"Well it sounds like he's in the right business."

"Oh, you can say that again. What are you doing?"

"I'm up in St. Augustine. Taking classes to get my degree and I'm an assistant high school basketball coach."

"I am so happy to hear that."

Kenny smiled, a reaction she obviously couldn't see.

"You know, Kenny, that Alan passed away?"

He waited before responding. "Yes. I did. I knew that."

Another moment of silence followed but not one that might be mistaken for reverence.

"It was kind of sad when you think about it," she said.

"I guess."

"I mean for his wife. You know she stuck by him. She obviously loved him." Brenda's assessment sounded like the possibility was inexplicable.

"Well, on the bright side, she never had to see him go to jail," Kenny said.

"I guess that's one way of looking at it," she said.

"He wouldn't have lasted long in jail, anyway. Even without, whatever it was that he died from," Kenny opined.

"I think it was cancer."

"Yeah."

Another short moment of quiet, but not an uncomfortable one.

"You want to hear something crazy?" Brenda asked. Her voice sounded exactly as it did when she would share little nuggets of gossip when they worked together. *"Elliot? Dr. Elliot? And Valerie the bookkeeper?"*

"Yeah. He was sexually harrassin' her. Or she was him-"

"They're together."

"What do you mean?"

"They're together! Like a couple! They live together!"

370

Kenny's jaw dropped and he laughed. "Get outta here."

"*Kenny, honey. I couldn't even make that up.*"

"Well, I'll be damned."

"*You know they both were witnesses against Alan.*"

"Yeah, I knew that," he answered.

"*It was a much bigger thing than I ever would have guessed, you know. There was this whole Ponzi thing, Alan was paying premiums on policies with new investor's money. It was really complex. Howie and Scooter and Alé, they were really in this deep. They all made deals to go against Alan and I think they're all still going to go to jail. In fact Scooter might already be in jail.*"

"Yeah. I knew that, too."

"*I had to give a statement against Alan. I don't know if you heard that.*" She sounded like she was offering a confession.

"I did hear that."

"*I didn't feel good about it. I know he wasn't a good guy but I still didn't feel good about it.*"

"I understand."

"*I'm not sure you do. You know the FBI came to me and said if I didn't help them, they were going to deport my father-in-law. He's seventy-five years old. Been here for twenty years. They threatened to send him back to Ecuador if I didn't help them.*"

Kenny felt a surge of anger rip through his body. "Those-" He stopped himself from saying it.

"*Scumbags.*" Brenda finished the sentence for him. "*That's what you were going to say?*"

371

Kenny punctuated it. "Yeah. Those scumbags." He then changed the subject. "So, Dr. Gropinsky and Valerie. Who would have seen that comin'?"

"Yeah, unreal. Right?" She then took a pause in which she sounded like she had sighed. *"So, what about you?"*

"What about me, what?"

"What happened with your girl?"

"Rosie?"

"Yes. Rosie."

A paradoxical sensation came over him. He was upset she'd brought it up while at the same time was happy. He tried to come off as indifferent. "We broke up right before I left. That time, the whole Alan thing. I didn't know what was gonna happen. I wanted to move up here, get a fresh start, go back to school. The timin', I guess, it wasn't right."

"I understand, honey. Are you with anyone now?"

"No."

"Well, that's okay. You'll have it again."

Kenny managed a little smile, imagining her saying the words.

"I'm really glad you called, Kenny."

"Me, too. I'm glad this was still your number."

"I hope you're happy."

"I hope you are, too." He took a moment to reflect. "I appreciate you being nice to me, Brenda."

"Stop with that. You made it easy. You're a good person, Kenny."

Silence.

"Let's stay in touch, okay?," he said.

"Yes. Please. Let's. Take care of yourself, sweetie."

"You do the same."

"Bye for now."

He disconnected and looked to his right. He saw he was passing yet again another sign for the Waffle House and grinned.

Tallahassee made a quick appearance on his left and from there he was passing Crestview in less than two hours. Twenty minutes left before he expected to arrive, perfect timing for the 11:30 AM start. Not a second late and not too much time to have to hang around beforehand.

He pulled up to the small dirt parking lot of the First Baptist Church to see it had filled up. The turnout was obviously good. A few cars were parked on the grass over to the side by the neglected playground. Kenny slowly drove over and into a makeshift spot keeping the order that had been established. He sat in his car and looked at the small, red brick building with the modest white steeple. He felt an emptiness that he wished he hadn't. Several people were walking toward the entrance. They had parked on the grass that was on the other side of the lot. Kenny figured they were locals but didn't recognize them. They were dressed as best as they could have been. One of them, a man, removed his trucker's hat before entering and reverently held it in hand.

He waited a few more moments then got out of the car. He patted out his suit jacket and looked down at his shoes, then checked his look in the reflection of the car window, second guessing his choice to wear a necktie, thinking he didn't want to be confused with one of the pallbearers. He walked toward the church and entered. Inside was as he remembered it, simple in its bareness, maybe a little smaller now. He was relieved to see more of the men in attendance wearing jackets and ties than he'd expected and found a seat in a pew closer to the back than the front hoping to blend in. He picked up a hymnal and pretended to leaf through it, while sneaking sideways glances at the others in attendance, recognizing many of them as neighbors from down by the swamp road turn as well as others from in town. He spotted Mrs. Johnson's daughter Darlene in the front row standing with what Kenny figured were relatives. She was wearing a powder blue dress.

Shortly thereafter the organ began to play *Amazing Grace*, just slightly out of tune and the congregation sang. Mrs. Johnson's simple casket was escorted in and up to the front of the church where Reverend Elijah Beckett, wearing a black robe and holding the Good Book to his chest, stood waiting to receive her. He touched his nose and adjusted his glasses several times as Kenny remembered him having a habit of doing, then began the invocation.

Kenny drifted in and out of hearing the words of the prayers and scripture readings, surveying the pews of locals to see who he recognized and periodically looking back up to the front row where Darlene was seated, wondering how much of what was going on she understood. When Reverend Beckett began the eulogy, Kenny unexpectedly found himself listening with intent. Reverend Beckett was as dull as he'd remembered him to be, but the words he spoke resonated. Mrs. Johnson was a wonderful person who lived a wonderful life and Kenny considered if her being so good made the Reverend's job easy. Of course it did. A few parallels to Bible passages were referenced that he wasn't aware of and they made sense. Mrs. Johnson was a good person. A simple person who put others before herself and never wanted so much as a small, blue ribbon for it. Kenny looked over his shoulder to sneak another look at who he might see that he knew and did a quick, *holy-shit-forgive-me-for-thinkin'-that-in-a-house-of-worship* double-take. Standing in the back was his old high school teammate, buddy and co-defendant Boss Hogg. Standing with him was a girl he didn't recognize. Hogg was rail thin now but for the belly that was distended, looking like a rapidly developing tumor. His hair was long, oily and thinning. Neither he nor the girl he was with was dressed appropriately, even in a place where the standards were wildly relaxed. He had on a pair of camouflage pants and knee high rubber mud boots and a tee shirt that was barely holding on. Kenny considered what was impossible to believe now, that at one time and not long ago, Hogg could launch himself from the low post outside the paint and two hand slam dunk the ball with a force that would rattle the gym walls in the next town over. Hoping he wasn't seen by him, Kenny turned back directly into the words of Psalm 23 being recited by Reverend Beckett.

After the service, Kenny fell into the line of exiting mourners, a few muted nods exchanged with familiar faces as they funneled through the doors of the church. Out front, a handshake exchanged and then one of the neighbors from down by the swamp road turn asked Kenny if he was going by Mrs. Johnson's house after the cemetery where her extended family was receiving guests for coffee and cake. He saw Darlene in her powder blue dress being escorted to a car behind the hearse and thought he should.

As he made his way to his car, he was intercepted by Boss Hogg, whom he didn't see and wrongfully assumed made a hastened exit.

"My guy!"

Kenny did his best to look surprised and happy to see him, and although it was unnoticed, came up short of convincing on both counts.

"How y'doin', Hogg-man?"

A hand-slap-bro-hug then Boss Hogg looked Kenny up and down like he were inspecting a pedigree race horse. "Well, goddamn! You look like a million bucks, boy! Like you shittin' up in some way high cotton!"

"Nice to see you, Hogger."

Concerned that he wasn't being polite, Boss Hogg quickly turned to his companion and presented her. "Kenny Wayne, this is my lady, Leslie. Leslie, my oldest, bestest high school pal and teammate, Kenny Wayne Rehange, probably one a the best goddamn players in the state-"

Kenny smiled at Boss Hogg's girl, looking for traces of the lady she had been described as. She was gaunt, skeletal. The skin on her arms and hands looked irritated from excessive scratching, her facial complexion suffused with blemishes. She tried to smile back at Kenny but in a controlled manner, so as to conceal the story her decaying teeth were telling.

"Nice to meet you, Leslie." He then turned back to Boss Hogg.

"Goddamn, you lookin' good boy!," Hogg told him. This time it came with a forceful pat-slap on the arm.

Kenny shrugged off the compliment.

"Shame about Mrs. Johnson," Boss Hogg said.

"Yeah. Shame. She was a good woman." Kenny said. With that, he'd begun formulating his exit strategy. "You, uh, goin' over to the cemetery for the burial?" He couldn't imagine he was.

"Nah. We just wanted to pay our respects."

Kenny again nodded. He then made a motion with his head toward the hearse that was readying to drive off. "I'm gonna fall in with them. But it's good to see you, Hogg." He then turned to Leslie. "And nice to meet you."

"You gonna be around long?" Hogg asked, with an obvious urgency. He didn't want the opportunity before him to pass.

"Naa. Can't. I gotta get back home. I just wanted to-"

Boss Hogg cut him off. "You still down in Broward?"

Kenny thought about lying. "No. I'm up by Jax now. Outside of Jax. Saint Johns County." He took another obvious look at the hearse slowly moving. "I'm gonna-"

"You go do what you gotta do, bro. I'll see you before you leave. I wanna catch up."

Kenny was noncommittal to the possibility, then again nodded to Hogg's girl, turned and made his way toward his car. When he got in, he took his cell phone from the seat and saw that he had several messages. He thought about playing them but dropped the phone back where it was almost like he was repulsed. He turned and looked out his window to see Boss Hogg and his girlfriend still standing where he'd left them. While not speaking at that very instant, they were obviously engaged in a discussion, one in which discretion played a part in.

Their posture.

The direction they were both looking.

The looks on their faces and hanging of the head, then turning away.

Desperation.

It all rang of desperation-

...And hard not to surmise Kenny was the subject of conversation.

He started his car, pulled out of the spot he was parked in on the grass but instead of heading for the street, drove around to the top of the lot so he could pass where Boss Hogg and his girlfriend were standing. He brought the already slow moving car to a stop and lowered the window.

Boss Hogg looked at him and smiled. "Nice ride, bro."

"Car's a car, Hogg. Nothin' too fancy about a used Caddy. And cost a shit ton less than a Silverado 2500 HD."

"Still, pretty slick."

Kenny didn't waste time moving the exchange alone. "Listen, man. I'm gonna go over to the cemetery and I gotta get back home, but I'm gonna stop by Mrs. Johnson's house after. They're havin' coffee and cake and besides, I kinda wanted to do a drive by, by the ol' swamp road turn. See the old 'hood-"

Boss Hogg didn't let him finish. "We'll swing by."

Kenny looked like he was about to say something, but didn't. He simply nodded, put the window back up and drove off.

The graveside was more than ten minutes away but less than fifteen. Kenny was surprised to see how many from the church came. Reverend Elijah Beckett stood over the casket that rested next to a perfect rectangle open grave that Kenny figured to be far more than six feet deep. He hoped the actual internment would be after everyone had left, for fear of how poor Darlene might take it. To that point she showed no sign of distress or overt grief. A literal lowering of her mother's casket into the ground might be too much spectacle for her.

Thankfully, after Reverend Beckett's final prayer, the group dispersed and in small clusters comforted one another as they made their way to the parking lot.

"Hello, Kenny Wayne-"

Kenny turned to see his old neighbor who had the mobile auto glass repair service. Mr. Phillips was wearing a sports coat and necktie, probably for the first time in a while. Seeing the face of his former neighbor brought Kenny back to the time he stood at the front porch of his house on the swamp road turn, having just knocked on the door. It was after his father died. After he'd been arrested with his swamper buddies. Kenny remembered regretting opening the door. Mr. Phillips asked if he could come in. Kenny didn't want to let him, but did because he lacked the resolve to deny the request of an elder. He expected to be given a lecture, but instead had information shared with him about an uncomfortable subject. His father, Marty Rehage. Mr. Phillips told him that whatever he might think, his father didn't simply abandon him by doing what he did. There was more to it. He shared with him that Marty had been under investigation by the FBI, this confirmed by a friend at the Okaloosa County Sheriff's office. It was

Mr. Phillip's understanding that they were coming to arrest him when he took his life. Kenny was confused, as he couldn't imagine what his father would have done that would warrant his being arrested. Mr. Phillips told him what he believed the circumstances to be and wasn't far off from being exact, down to Marty's unwillingness to expose Norby Rice or anyone else to having their lives ruined by what amounted to fabricated plots. Kenny's father loved his country, Mr. Phillips told him. He loved his son. And where he might have been human, he was not a coward.

"...I'm glad to see you made it, son."

"I'm glad as well, Mr. Phillips." He smiled at him, but remained solemn. "She was a wonderful woman. Just wonderful."

"She was. She was." A moment of quiet between them. "You're gonna go by the house for coffee?"

"Yessir."

"Good." He then looked Kenny up and down, as if inspecting him. "You look good."

Kenny grinned, humble. "Tryin' to stay between the lines, sir."

"Good for you."

Kenny then had a thought. "Mr. Phillips, I'm not sure you got the answer to this or not, but I kinda had somethin' on my mind."

"Well, try me anyway."

"Darlene. Now that Mrs. Johnson's gone and all, what's gonna become of her? Who's gonna look after her and all?"

Mr. Phillips took a deep in and out breath and nodded, underscoring the relevance of his concern. "Well, my understandin' is that one of the relatives, Mrs. Johnson's cousin, down from Mobile, she's gonna stay in the house with her for a few weeks, slowly transition her into a group home."

"Where's that gonna be? The group home?"

"Not sure, quite yet. There's talk of back in Mobile. There's talk of one in Crestview."

Kenny nodded, contemplative.

Mr. Phillips continued. "I for one, trust in the Lord to keep her safe. Still, it's sad. I know Mrs. Johnson worried about this day comin'. But I also know she put a great trust in the Lord, too."

Kenny nodded. "Mr. Phillips, could I trouble you to maybe let me know when all that's final? Y'know? Where she's gonna be? I figured I'd like to maybe send her somethin' once in a while, a card, maybe even a visit. Mrs. Johnson was a wonderful woman, I figure it's the least I could do to honor her memory-"

Mr. Phillips smiled. "You're a good man, Kenny Wayne. Hearin' you say that makes me proud. Proud on behalf of your daddy. He'd have been real proud to see the man you become."

Kenny shrugged and looked away, self-conscious. He wasn't sure he completely agreed. "I appreciate you sayin' so, sir."

"I'll see you over at the house for coffee."

"Yessir."

Kenny watched him walk toward his van advertising his mobile auto glass repair services and climb in, then looked over at Darlene with her relatives, assuming one of them was the cousin from Mobile, then headed to his car.

The closer he got to Mrs. Johnson's house on his way from the cemetery, the more uneasy he became. As he came around the bend by the swamp road turn, he experienced an overwhelming sense of emotions. They ran chin to crown, ear to ear and from his fingers down through his toes, an amalgam of discernible sensations he knew well, none of which were soothing. The sadness was holed up in his eyes and throat, the inexplicable fear sat heavy in his chest and loneliness, the loneliness was riding bareback on his soul, wherever it was that his soul had set up shop for the time being. Kenny understood why they'd shown up, yet still couldn't negotiate them away. They were inevitable. They were expected. The ghosts and demons made sure of it.

There was nothing dramatically different about the street. Little had changed but for a few of the houses with different cars in their driveways. And when he looked at the house he grew up in, it was nearly identical as he'd left it, save for an American flag now flying from the pole on the front lawn, below it another one of a college football team. Cars of those visiting Mrs. Johnson's house lined both sides of the street, fifteen at least per side. Kenny decided to park at the far end, further away from his old house than closer, the choice unconscious. As he did, he was surprised to see Boss Hogg and his girl parked in the row, leaning against their car and sharing a single cigarette. He'd completely forgotten he'd told them he was going to be there. And with that, all his anxieties settled, a feeling of control came over him.

He parked.

He got out of the car.

He walked toward Hogg.

"Playa, you lookin' good! Steppin' outta that Caddy like you on TV and shit!"

"Naah. It ain't like that."

Boss Hogg stepped up to give him another hand- slap-bro-hug but this time the girl with him was ignored as if she were a shadow.

"So, you good?" Kenny asked.

"I'm good, son. All good. Waitin' for the new Jiffy Lube to open up over in Niceville. Stinky Franky Barnes is supposed to be Assistant Manager, he's all fixed to slide me in when they get goin'. All good once that's in place."

"Cool, Hogg. That's cool."

Hogg felt compelled to share, then hammer home, another point. "Sober now, too. Goin' on six months. Runnin' clean. Clean and mean like a machine."

Kenny politely nodded, pretending to believe him.

Boss Hogg shifted from side to side, giving a hint of being apprehensive. He again looked at Kenny's car, then back at Kenny. His shoes, his suit. The watch on his wrist. "You know, Kenny Wayne. I don't know how you's sittin' yourself an' all. Y'know, right now cash-wise and what not-"

"Well, not for nothin', Hogg, I'm only workin' part-time myself. I'm tryin' to get my degree. So I can teach at a high school. And coach hoops."

Hearing that knocked Hogg off the rails of his train of thought momentarily. "No shit!"

"Yeah, that's what I'm thinkin'."

"Well let me tell you this. You'd be as good with that as anybody, son! Coachin' ball? Goddamn! No one seen a floor like you. No one!"

Kenny nodded, pretending to graciously take the compliment. He then said, "So I feel you, Hogg. I feel what you're sayin', bein' tight on cash. You ain't alone there."

"Yeah. I'm just in a little pinch, temporary. Rent shit. Management company up where we live at, they real uptight. Real uptight." Boss Hogg shook his head then, abandoning his effort at elaborating further.

Kenny nodded, empathetically. The subsequent silence wasn't awkward for Kenny and Boss Hogg so much as it was for Boss Hogg's girlfriend, who sensed now that their efforts in getting any money from Kenny were futile.

Then it came out of nowhere, as if dropped out of the sky without warning. "Well, how much you need? For the rent and all?," Kenny asked.

Boss Hogg's head snapped up and to attention, a sudden sense of life breathed back into him. "For the rent?"

"Yeah. For the rent."

Boss Hogg quick-looked to his girlfriend, then back at Kenny before letting her answer for them. "It's nine hundred," she said.

Kenny appeared to be contemplating something. Both Boss Hogg and his girlfriend had their eyes riveted to his face, trying desperately to read his mind.

"Well like I said, Hogg. I'm really tight right now, myself. But let me run this by you."

"Sure, sure. Go on, son."

Kenny proceeded to explain that he knew someone that bought insurance policies from people that didn't want them anymore and put them in bundles to be resold, as they had value. It was hard to explain but he could fill out a little paperwork and there might be some money it in for him. Maybe even a thousand bucks. Boss Hogg obviously didn't understand what Kenny was talking about. He didn't need to. He was all in and beaming now over the possibility.

Kenny looked back at Mrs. Johnson's house, gesturing that he wanted to go in and pay his respects. "I gotta get goin', Hogger. What do you say we meet over at the Waffle House in Elgin in about an hour? I can walk you through how this is done."

Boss Hogg was elated. Even his girlfriend showed signs of hope. He threw his arms around Kenny. "I knew you was the man, Kenny! I knew you was the man! Swampers for life!"

Kenny ever so slightly pulled away, as Boss Hogg had a foul stench about him, one that was more than body odor.

They parted ways and Kenny went into Mrs. Johnson's house where he paid his respects to family and with old neighbors engaged in short conversation, doing so with all the poise of a gentleman. During his time in the house, he maintained a constant awareness of Darlene, who mostly sat on the couch with one of the relatives, still in her powder blue dress. He wondered what dreams her mother might have had for her at one time, dreams that were downgraded to simple hopes and then in all likelihood evolved into fears and anxieties, the kinds that can only be assuaged by something otherworldly. And when it was time for him to depart, he found Mr. Tom Phillips of the auto glass mobile repair van and reiterated his wish to be kept updated on any developments pertaining to Darlene and her living arrangements. No issue too small and none too big.

He got in his car, and saw his phone had another message waiting for him. He ignored it, then made a U turn and drove to the front of his old house where he stopped. He looked at the garage that once doubled as a mechanic's workspace. He didn't want to stay but strangely couldn't bring himself to drive off. He picked up the phone and played his messages.

"Hello, Mr. Rehage. This is George Alberts calling again. I've been trying to-"

Kenny stopped the message, evidence that he knew not only who it was from but what it was regarding. He hit the return call button and took a deep breath.

"This is George Alberts."

"Hi, Mr. Alberts. Kenny Wayne Rehage calling-"

"Well, my goodness. I've been trying to get hold of you for weeks now."

"I apologize, sir. I apologize."

"You understand sir, that we place a tremendous importance on making the indemnified whole as expeditiously as possible."

"I understand. I've been overwhelmed and just wasn't ready-"

"Okay. Well I would like to get the ball rolling on the three policies which you're named as beneficiary on. You're aware that the keyman policy itself is to be paid out at one million three hundred thousand dollars. And the two life insurance policies are for two million and three million respectively."

Kenny thought then about Copeland, who the life insurance policies had been taken out on, without his ever knowing about it.

They were policies Kenny had orchestrated and pushed along using the channels at the office he had access to, using Dr. Elliot to rubber stamp what needed rubber stamping while giving him as little information as possible.

The policies.

The policies.

The policies.

And not a soul had the slightest of clues. If they could see him now, they would think him a king. They would bow down, lay prostrate at his feet. Howie Yglesias, Scooter Wrobel and Alé Perez would kiss his swamper ass. Dale Marlin might even commission a portrait of his likeness to hang in his office.

Even Alan Copeland.

He would have been proud.

Humbled.

Then bragged to anyone who listened about what he'd done.

"Mr. Rehage?"

Kenny came in from out of his daydream. "Yes sir, I'm listenin'."

"So we just need you to sign a few forms and establish the wire routing you'd like for the payments."

"Yes, sir. I'll get right on that this week. And again, I apologize for not movin' on this sooner. It's just been, as you might imagine, a tough time and all. No reflection on y'all."

"I appreciate you saying that and understand. And I'm sorry for your loss."

"Yeah. Me too."

387

He disconnected then again looked over at his old house. He thought about his father, imagining him standing at his workbench, then turned away and drove off, driving away from the swamp road turn for what he imagined would be the last time.

He stopped for gas on Route 189 just outside of Elgin and as he self-served, he thought of her again.

I called her ma'am.

And he laughed at himself.

Rosie.

Rosie Ayala.

What a saint.

What a sinner.

What a saint.

He hoped she was happy.

He hoped she'd found someone worthy of her.

Someone who would never let her down.

He finished filling the tank and as he got back into his car caught something across the street on top of a building that looked like it was a warehouse.

A billboard.

Upon it was a quote.

"...Neither do I condemn you. Go and from now on sin no more."

He climbed into the car and pulled away from the gas station, continuing into Elgin. He looked down at the phone sitting on the passenger seat beside him and wondered if she still had the same number. He wondered what she might be doing at that very moment.

Before he realized it, he was approaching the Waffle House, where Boss Hogg and his girlfriend were presently waiting for him. He could see their car in the lot and then the two of them inside at a table in the window.

Kenny slowed down, put on his blinker and began to move over into the turning lane, but suddenly changed course, moving back into the lane he'd been driving in. He continued straight ahead, letting the Waffle House, Boss Hogg and his girlfriend slowly disappear behind him, wondering how much he really needed.

Five and a half hours, he figured.

Maybe a little more.

Probably less.

His mind then went back to where it had been seconds earlier.

Rosie Ayala.

What a saint.

And he picked up the phone and thumb-scrolled through his contacts.

Epilogue

Four Years Later

Outside it was dark and frigid. Livery cars and filthy second
shift yellow cabs were double parked unloading passengers and
luggage. Periodic clouds of black exhaust burped out of passing diesel
buses. Each time the sliding glass doors of the terminal retracted, a
stinging squall entered to remind those inside just how cold it was.
Bland and soulless secular Christmas music piped out of poorly wired
speakers. On the endless security checkpoint line, travelers sat on their
suitcases, others stood, zombies without expression.

The line had stopped even making caterpillar moves. On the
far side of the x-ray conveyor belt, a confrontation rife with every
imaginable expletive shouted had flared up. An obese woman in her
twenties was claiming that the equally obese female TSA agent had
sexually groped her during the pat down. The disruption was a cherry

on the cake of the never ending day that was Heinz Lucic's. He came directly from Bridgeport, where he'd stayed late at his office with a shitty view of a shitty city. Two and a half hours in traffic and now another hour on the line. He figured it would be at least another forty minutes before he would be within arm's reach of one of the gray plastic trays.

And now this.

The altercation between the obese passenger and obese TSA agent had escalated, the former loudly claiming the agent ran her hand through her butt crack like she was processing a credit card and again the TSA agents clapped back that she didn't.
The passenger got louder and the TSA agent decided to abandon any rules of professional conduct, threatening to bring physical harm upon her if she didn't shut up. Other TSA agents materialized and shortly thereafter a supervisor was on the scene.

Lucic's head whipsawed upon seeing him approaching the conflict in the blazer and tie with an ID hanging from the lanyard around his neck and a radio in hand. He remembered hearing Walter Reed had taken a job with the TSA after being forced to resign from the Bureau, but had no idea he was detailed to LaGuardia Airport in New York. Like he knew Trey Stubblefield worked for Coca-Cola in Atlanta, but didn't know in what capacity.

Lucic considered his good fortune.

He would try to get Reed's attention so he might spirit him out of the line and through the checkpoint. He slowly altered his posture, standing taller with head held high as he tracked each movement and turn Reed made while managing the conflict. He periodically looked

391

over, but hadn't yet seen his former boss. A few near misses, as when Reed did look over at the line of waiting passengers, it wasn't in Lucic's direction.

He thought about waving.

Reed continued to look around, but this time in the opposite direction. Then, again back toward Lucic, but not directly. Lucic thought about waving again, but this time with both hands. Again, Reed turned back to the combating TSA agent and passenger, and directed another agent to escort both out of the view of the public. He then looked back over the line toward Lucic.

The third time was a charm.

His eyes were pointed directly now at Heinz Lucic, standing not more than twenty-five feet away.

Lucic smiled and lifted a hand and half-waved.

Reed saw him and although it took a moment to process it.

He recognized him.

Lucic waved again, this time holding his hand higher and moving it back and forth a little more. Reed's eyes stayed on him, but his reaction didn't change. His face was static. Lucic was about to call out to him, but was rendered mute. Still, Reed held the eye to eye connection with him-

As Lucic was about to call out.

Before he could utter a word, Reed turned away from him. And Lucic became deflated as he looked down and cursed him.

About The Author

Billy Devlin has written for film, television and the theater. He is also the author of *Another Man's Woe*. He lives in New York City.